BOTTOMLAND

BOTTOMLAND

A Novel Based on the Murder
of Rosa Mary Dean

TREY HOLT

Thanks to Sally, Iris, and Henry. I am a lucky man.

Special thanks to Elizabeth Kemp Fellows, Kate Myers Cotton, Joel Rice, Sam Torode, Lynne McAlister, Allen Clark, and Ulrike Guthrie. Each of you moved this project forward in some way that would have been impossible without you. I am very grateful for your time, talents, passion, friendship, and support.

For Ellis

"We're all bastards
but God loves us anyway."
—WILL D. CAMPBELL

Franklin High School Gymnasium

CHAPTER ONE

I HAD BEEN MEETING Sharon behind Franklin High School, by the gym door, for the better part of the school year. Sitting in her old man's car in the early mornings from about 5:15 till a little after 6:00, I'd pull her body so tight to mine that it felt like we were one person. And then we'd talk … and then we'd do what we did some more.

"Tell me something you love about me," she'd say.

And I'd tell her that her hair was the prettiest, the blackest I'd ever seen.

"And what about my eyes?" she'd ask.

"They're still as pretty as I told you they were yesterday, baby," I'd answer.

"Do you think I'm pretty enough to be a model?" she'd ask. I bet she'd asked me that a thousand damn times.

"You are a model, aren't you, baby?"

"Well, yeah… but not really. I mean, I'm mostly just a department store counter girl. I just get to model sometimes."

"You're as pretty as any model I've ever seen," I'd tell her. I knew she wanted to be a model, had wanted to be ever since I'd met her.

She'd been in the front seat and I'd been in the back. Van had been with her; it was the same as always—most girls noticed him long before and after they ever paid any attention to me. I'd been with her sister, Sheila. When we left the restaurant, Sharon'd said she was hot, draped her coat over the seat and then put her hand under it, along the edge of the seat's back. Then I'd snuck my hand under her coat and we'd held hands. I thought she was probably doing it just to get back at Van, who could be a pretty big asshole.

I even felt surprised the next day as Sharon waved at me when I saw her uptown, right off the square just down from the bank. Her skirt was blowing a little in the breeze, showing off her legs, as she waved and tried to hold her hair in place with the other hand. She was pale and dark at the same time, if that makes any sense. I was sure that she must have been waving at somebody over my shoulder.

"What ya doin'?" she had asked after I realized she was waving at me.

"Goin' to get some stuff for L—my father," I said.

"Isn't he the Police Chief?" she asked.

"Yeah," I said. "He is."

"What're you getting?" she asked.

"Oh, just some stuff for the basement pipes," I answered. "He thinks we got water gettin' into the basement."

"You go to BGA with Van, don't you?" she asked.

"Yeah," I nodded.

"Don't you play football?"

I nodded again. BGA, or Battle Ground Academy, gave scholarships to four or five kids around town every year, kids who'd help their athletic programs and couldn't afford it or their parents wouldn't pay for them to go. I'd always figured I'd gotten the scholarship because of my old man, because some strings he'd pulled with somebody somewhere. He'd been appointed the Chief of Police when the one before him keeled over from a heart attack. He'd been the assistant before that. "Once a goddam assistant, always one," he liked to say around our house.

She licked her lips, honey red and flashed her pale green eyes at me. "Are you gonna go out with my sister again?"

I hadn't really thought about it. I figured if Sheila wanted to see me again then she'd let Van know and he'd let me know. That's the way it was with probably four out of five girls I went out with.

"Well, if you're not gonna go out with her … let me know and you can go to my prom with me," she said, smiling. "I don't think Sheila wants to go out with you anyway. She said you were too short. I think she likes Van."

And I thought I had gotten away with one on his ass. But that's the way it always was with him. You might think you had one on him, but he was two or three moves ahead of you already. Usually before I even knew what was happening in the present moment he was minutes or hours or days down the road, figuring what he would do in response to what somebody else did.

She popped her gum a few times. Looked at me, then over my shoulder at the forty-nine Ford parked on the curb. "So you think you will?"

"Will what?"

"Go out with Sheila again?"

"Hell no," I said. "Why would I wanna go out with her if she wants to go out with him?"

She laughed, then pulled a pen and piece of paper from her purse. Holding the paper tight to her thigh, she scrawled something on it. "Here," she said. "You can take me to the Franklin prom. Don't y'all have one of those at BGA?"

"Yeah," I said. "It's already gone."

"Who'd you take?" she asked.

"Um, um, Nancy. At least that's what I think her name was."

"You're more with it than you act, aren't you?"

I laughed because I didn't really have an answer. The truth was that Van had fixed me up with her, too. Another friend or sister of somebody. And the other thing on my mind was that this girl spoke the best English I had ever heard. You could tell she tried her hardest to be proper.

She reached and stuck the paper in my shirt pocket. "My work number's on there. Call me. It's in two weeks."

I don't know if I called her because of the look in her eyes or just to get at Van's ass.

ON THIS MORNING, December 13th, 1953, it didn't really matter anymore. As it seems any time we let go, take our brain out of its place of being in charge and let our heart start directing our actions, time had turned in on itself. I wasn't sure if the last seven or eight months now presented themselves in my memory as days or years. All I knew was that the current of this thing we call "love," I believe more powerful than all the rivers in the world, had taken me and was sweeping me into the rest of my days.

I waved at Jackson Mosby, the janitor at Franklin High School, who I saw every morning when I was behind the school, well really between the school building and the gym, waiting on Sharon to pull up. He waved back at me. In all the months I had been waiting out here for Sharon, there wasn't one morning I could recall when he and I hadn't waved at one another. I could even see him smile sometimes, what teeth he had left glistening white against his skin. Sometimes we'd even stand there apart, I bet you not more than seventy-five feet from each other, both of us smoking a cigarette, for five or ten minutes but we'd never say a word to each other. I often wondered what he thought, what it was like to be him in this town of Franklin, Tennessee. I often wanted to ask him about his family, his boy ... maybe even what it felt like to have to sit in the balcony of the gym during the basketball games even though he cleaned the damn place before and afterward. No matter, every once in awhile I would have sworn I could even hear him laughing a little when he smiled and waved, like maybe he remembered when he was my age or when he and his wife did something like this, maybe thirty years before. But we never spoke.

"How was the paper route?" she asked, as I was getting into her car after she finally pulled up and shut her lights off.

"Colder'n hell," I said.

"That's not too cold," she said back.

"Just turn the heat up," I said, knowing it didn't work too good or sometimes at all.

"Where's your motorcycle?" she asked.

"Where it always is," I told her.

"Why do you park it over there?"

"'Cause that's the easiest place to put it."

"Behind the dumpster?"

"It's an incinerator, number one. And yeah, that's the easiest place to put it where nobody thinks anything while I'm out here waitin'."

"Who's going to think anything?" she asked.

"Look," I told her, "most everybody in town knows that motorcycle. You say 1942 Indian and they think of Henry Hall, Lucky's son. They been watching me ride that thing around here for the last three years. Before that it was a bike. I been delivering papers all over this godforsaken town since I was nine years old. Since Lucky said, 'Boy, you're old enough to work. It's time to get a job!'"

She laughed the way somebody does when something's funny and not funny. I watched her face start to beam as she smiled. Every once in awhile, it would strike me like something thrown down from heaven: that she was the most beautiful human being I'd ever seen, from her black hair to her shining green eyes to her smell that was really no more than soap, hair spray and chewing gum. In the lack of light, it was still hard to make out her face. I focused on her silhouette, trying to remember what she had looked like the day before.

"What?" she said.

I didn't answer. Just kept staring.

"What?" '

I shook my head and smiled and she moved toward me in the passenger seat. As she leaned onto me and pressed her lips to mine she reminded me, like she had a thousand times in the last few months, that it would be worth Lucky beating my ass if he caught me. She scooted her butt from under the steering wheel and into the middle of the seat and swung her legs over mine. My breath hard to come by, I put one hand on her thigh and the other one over her shoulder and on her back and pulled her to me so hard that I thought our bodies might melt together. Over her shoulder, past Franklin High School, I could tell the sky was lightening with each passing moment. Two hundred yards south of us was the scourge of a place I went to school. BGA. Battle Ground Academy. The Academy. At this time of the morning I liked to pretend that I didn't have to go there in an hour or so. I liked to pretend that Sharon and I would just do what we were doing most of the day or that I would meet Van and Tully in the parking lot behind The Academy and we'd just stay out there and smoke cigarettes the majority of the morning. Or that there was some other way I was free of that godforsaken place where grown men tried to torture you into becoming like them. Discipline. Discipline makes the man.

"Hey, baby," I said.

"Yeah?" she answered. She was breathing hard, too. I tried to pretend she was breathing harder than me. That she was turned on more than me.

"What's say we skip school today. What's say we just skip the whole goddam thing. School. Work. Everything."

I could tell she was dreaming for a minute, like me. I swear I would have done it, though.

"Hunny, you know I can't skip school. You know I can't skip work either."

"Just a pipe dream," I said. And then we got back to doing what we'd been doing.

Between The Academy and Franklin High School lay the Carter House. I'd ride behind it every day after Sharon and I were through. Holes from bullets and cannon balls still littering its back, sides and front, when I slowed down and drew close enough to think about it, it reminded me why The Academy was so-named in the first place. Battle Ground Academy. A man falling to the ground every five or six seconds. "That crazy ass driving his troops over and over and over into Schofield's lines. Until there was nothing but goddam death," my uncle liked to say.

Sometimes I found myself still looking for him when I was riding my Indian around town throwing papers; I found myself looking over Sharon's shoulder while we sat in the car together, thinking maybe he might just appear on his way back from the river that seemed, as did many things, to speak with him in a language few others understood.

I often thought if the Harpeth River could talk, it could tell me why. Perhaps why Tully and I, against all natural odds, stopped short of it that night. Why, too, it seemed to lap up lives, rise and fall, at its discretion, unknown to logic or good sense. Why what my father told me about it all those years ago holds true even today. How he described it. Then and now, as I stand there on that land, the only sounds detectable are silence and the sound of the river passing. Or maybe they're one in the same.

SHARON AND I SAW the goddamned body, saw it as plain as day, as plain as anything I ever want to see again, there in the coming daylight of that morning, December 13, 1953. We saw her sprawled out on the pavement, one arm splayed above her head, the other bent grotesquely underneath her, flat of her back, one leg under the other, folded at the knee. And she had that quality that only dead bodies do, like death has its own face or something. Like no other. A body without life, without being prettied up at the funeral home, reminds you that it's just not made for death … ain't comfortable there. Like a fat man in a small chair, it's just not meant for that space.

I probably shouldn't have hollered and motioned for Sharon to pull back across the parking lot when I saw her there. If I'd had any consideration, I would have just let her go on. But there are just some things that you don't want to see alone. And God knows this was one of them.

The blood that had spilled from the four deep wounds at her neck had covered almost all of her, including her green-checked flannel shirt and these riding pants that not many women wore back then, looser at the hips and ass then tight below the knee and cropped. One of her shoes had come off and was laying by her foot. Her shoes were small, as she was not a big woman, and like slippers, a style that had been more popular a few years before. A heavy man's coat with fur at the collar lay more off her than on.

Sharon stood there as still as lake water after I'd called her over there, after I'd chased her to the edge of the parking lot and flagged her down and motioned frantically for her to come back. For a long time she didn't say a word. She just watched her like she was waiting for the body to start talking any minute and tell us what in god's name had happened to her. As calm as Sharon seemed, all things considered, I couldn't bear to admit to her that I had screamed at the top of my lungs when I'd stumbled over one of the dead woman's feet on my way to the Indian. That I had gasped so hard the breath had gotten lodged in my chest and nearly choked me. And that no more would come until I started to chase Sharon's car as she got to the edge of the parking lot.

The sky glowed and burned in the distance like somebody had mixed orange and purple and light blue and black together and flung it over the entirety of the horizon. Even though I'm sure there had to be some, I couldn't hear cars as they passed on Columbia Avenue. I couldn't hear the rustling of the wind that touched at my hands and face. I could hear only my own breathing.

I turned to Sharon, whose eyes hadn't left the woman since she had stepped from her car, walked over, and looked at what I pointed.

"My God," she finally said.

"My God's right," I said, and I could feel my words bubbling and bucking in my throat as I spoke them. Trying to turn themselves into more gasps, even tears.

"Oh my God," she said.

"Yeah," I said.

"We've got to go get somebody," she said. She made a step toward the woman.

"Who?" I said.

"The police," she said.

There was only one thing wrong with that. We'd be calling my father. Well, not really Lucky, but the city police and the dispatcher, Miss Helen Riley, would be in touch with Lucky in the time it took her to get him on the radio or at home. I looked at my watch. It was a Mickey Mouse watch I'd bought with the first paper money I'd ever made, one of the few things I still clung to from childhood. Other guys on the football team gave me shit because I still wore it. It was going on 6:30, which meant that Lucky had probably left home half an hour ago. About stuff like that he was the most responsible person I'd ever known. He got up at the same time every day, shaved at the same time, took a shit at the same time. Ate his breakfast that my mother fixed at the same time every morning. He had to walk out the backdoor within the same thirty-second period on any given day. All of which meant that Miss Helen could get him on his radio in the car in just a few seconds. And he'd be here in a matter of a couple of minutes.

"You mean goddam Lucky," I said. I turned my eyes on the woman again. The blood was dry on her shirt, around the huge gashes across her throat. Even dried on her hands where she'd obviously fought to keep the knife away, pawed at the wounds for the few seconds she probably lived after they were inflicted. There was none on the pavement. I knew this meant she'd probably been dumped there. I could hear Lucky's voice in my head, observing these facts.

"I mean get whoever, Henry," she said. Tears were at her eyes now. I could tell by the way her voice sounded.

"Whoever'll be Lucky," I said.

She turned her face to me and swallowed hard. "Then's it got to be Lucky."

I assured her as I had earlier that it wasn't that I was afraid of Lucky, but more that I just didn't want to get involved in something like this. That Lucky had no stake in where I was every morning. Again, I could hear him: "You been fuckin' that little girl behind the high school, haven't ya?"

And it wouldn't matter if I had or I hadn't. We'd still get to the same ending. His lack of temper would get the best of him.

"Do you mean that we should just leave her laying here?"

"No, I think we can just call from somewhere else. Like we can go to the Academy and use Coach Nedler's phone. He's down in the locker room. I can sneak in...." And then it occurred to me that Helen Riley would surely know my voice. She'd been hearing it since I was little. "I guess you could go and stop at a payphone and call, or we can just walk up to the payphone at the corner and you can call 'em. Tell 'em that we've found her layin' here."

By this point, both my stomach and my conscience kept me from turning my eyes to the body. The last look I had managed, from the vantage point I had, I had noticed that one of her eyes was slightly open, but cocked wrong, looking across her nose. I had noticed her hands again, bloodied, especially under her fingernails, like crimson dirt.

"Baby, we gotta go if we're goin'," I told her. "It won't be a coupl'a minutes till other kids start to show up. Hell, let's just let them call the the police."

By the time I talked her into us just leaving, the tears she'd initially held were making two thin but steady streams down her cheeks and then cascading down onto the collar of her blouse. Her makeup was starting to tatter, mascara following the tears down, cutting lines in the powder and the blush.

"It's the best thing," I told her. "Hell, some other kid'll find her and they can just call Lucky … or Miss Riley and then she can call Lucky."

"You really think it's best?" she had asked me as I was moving her toward her car.

And I had explained to her how I did. How she was right, if Lucky found out that we were meeting then not only would he be likely to beat my ass but he'd also be a hell of a lot more likely to ride by every morning or have one of his men do it. And neither of us wanted that. I knew that I didn't.

As I have done at some of the worse points in my life, I managed to sell her on choosing the easiest of ways. The path of least resistance that helps you avoid the pain in that moment but then gives it room to multiply later. Maybe exponentially. I think that's the word.

CHAPTER TWO

IT TOOK AWHILE for the smoke to clear. And I guess until it did, nobody had known just how bad it was. Maybe they'd seen the old man laying there at the bottom of the bridge, his head laid open and all the life having left him. Maybe some people even ran to him and tried to revive him or propped him up or something. But from what I know, he must not have ever said another word after the brunt of the impact, after he was thrown from the car. But Sheila was still alive and talking, is the way it's been told to me: sitting there, her head in her hands, crying because her daddy was dead over there on the pavement.

They'd been about twenty miles north of the Alabama line when it happened. Willy, Sharon's uncle, had been driving and, according to Sharon, drinking from early in the day when they left out from their house. They were originally from Alabama; I don't even know how they got from Alabama to Tennessee to begin with.

The heat and the humidity that day would choke you, she told me. In that part of the country in late May, June, July and August, even September, it feels like the air just sticks to your skin and drips off you at its own pleasure. Like it's more liquid than anything else.

Edward, Sharon and Sheila's daddy, was pushing seventy. I'm not saying that would make it any easier, but I believe it has to comfort people that somebody lived near a normal life span. But, Sheila … she was so young it still leaves me sick to my stomach to think about it. She was seventeen. Less than a year different from Sharon.

It was Sharon's half-brother Bobby who found her and told her. She always said she knew. "Somethin' bad happened, didn't it?" she asked him. She'd just been sitting in the car with a boy, talking.

"Get out of the car and walk over here with me," Bobby told her.

She says she was crying to beat the band before she even got all the way out of the car. Bobby took her in his arms, held her while she cried her heart out. Literally, perhaps. And I think it did her mother worse. She had already been through two marriages before that. Or at least one. Truth be told, I don't know if she was ever married to the first man. Bobby's father. Back at their little white-frame house, Ima sat down on the steps of the porch when they told her about Edward and let Bobby hold onto her just like he had done with Sharon.

It was my idea that Lucky avoided responsibility whenever possible and often asked me to do his shit-work. When he stopped his patrol car in the corner of the parking lot, he nodded at Van and Tully, then motioned for me to come over. He was always smoking a cigarette or lighting another one. He even smoked when he was on a goddam ventilator.

"Hey … hurry up. I got something I need you to do for me."

I looked at him as I made my way across the space between us. From the age and the whiskey and the years of cigarettes, his face was already starting to get flat, fat, and wrinkled. Like he was sinking into himself.

"They had 'em a bad wreck down south'a here today," he told me. He drew on his Lucky Strike and stared out the front windshield at the line standing at the order window. He cleared his throat hard, coughed a couple of times. "County called me, said that they'd got a call about a man that had died. Old man. But then they called again and said that they got another call about the same wreck and that the goddam car had rolled off the embankment half a' hour after the wreck and pinned a little girl underneath it."

He stared harder toward the Gilco Dairy Dip, at nothing in particular this time. Maybe just the white-washed cinder block wall. He bowed his back a little and pulled his handkerchief out of his back pocket and wiped his brow, covered with sweat. He folded it and used the other side to daub at the water in the corners of his eyes.

"Well, hell, I guess it didn't pin her under the car. It cut her head off. Or damn near. I don't know. I guess it don't matter … she's dead."

Rambling, he went on to tell me that it was Sheila Bishop and ask me, didn't I know her? Didn't Van and I go out with her and her sister? Hadn't she been the one I went out with? Weren't they them poor people who lived over in the mixed section? Wasn't there a bunch a' them that used to live in the same house? He didn't know why in the hell the county had called him in the first place; it was their responsibility. Basically, he talked every way in the world around the fact that a seventeen-year-old girl had died when a car rolled off an embankment almost an hour after a wreck and over her. But, would I go tell them? He didn't know 'em from Adam and they didn't know him. And shouldn't they at least have somebody who knew tell them that an hour after the father died the seventeen-year-old girl died too?

WHEN I GOT TO THEIR HOUSE, Bobby was still on the front steps of the house, a cigarette in one hand and a fruit jar in the other. I'd always heard about him that he ran whiskey from down in Alabama and a town a little south of us, a wide spot in the road called Peytonsville, up to Franklin. Was tied up with moonshiners down there, had been in and out of jail a couple of times already.

"Hey," he said, when I stepped from the Indian.

"Hey."

"Sharon's inside with Mama, but I ain't sure this is a good time to visit," he told me. I wondered for a moment if it registered in his head that he had seen me around for awhile and then I had disappeared.

"Yeah, I know," I said.

"You heard?"

"Yeah."

I started to search for what I'd say next. What you tell somebody who thinks they've had bad luck but it's worse than they knew. I didn't know whether to tell Bobby and then let him go in and tell them. Or go in myself and tell them. I figured the right way to go was to tell the mother, Ima. To let her tell Bobby.

"My daddy sent me down here to relay another message," I said. Bobby was still staring through me like he might get up and kick my ass just for being on the property. And even though I didn't have much respect for Lucky, I realized invoking his name would likely get me past Bobby Moonshiner. Truth be known, Lucky probably let him run through Franklin … probably bought some of the shine from him himself.

Bobby's last run-in with the law must have still been close in his memory. Without saying a word, he got up and climbed the three concrete stairs up to the porch and rattled the front door. A few seconds later I saw Sharon come to the door and open it then disappear back into the house. Bobby motioned me to go in.

When I made my way past Bobby and through the front door, Sharon was sitting in a chair to the left. She got up and hugged me hard. I could tell her eyes were red and tired from crying. Shadowed underneath from mascara that had run.

"Thank you for coming," she said.

I wanted to ask her if she didn't remember anything that had happened, but knew this wasn't the time.

"Yeah," I answered.

Next, I wanted with all of myself for her to believe that I was there like she thought, to comfort her in this terrible time. Not to make it worse. Goddam Lucky, I thought, over and over and over. He was probably out behind some building in Franklin smoking Lucky Strikes and sucking on that bottle he hid under the seat. Or out arresting somebody for doing the same thing. Or down at the filling station shooting craps.

Sharon's eyes about did me in anyway. Even from the first time I saw her, they were eyes that seemed in a strange way like they held everything. They were focused on you; and they weren't. They were jaded; they were innocent. They were full of joy. And sadness. On this day they had been set adrift in a river of grief. Full of shock. But knowing themselves that the shock would soon turn itself into emptiness. They were also eyes into which I couldn't bear to speak the words I had to.

"Where's your mama?" I asked her.

"In the bedroom," she answered. She motioned her arm toward a room off the main room of the house, one I had always assumed was her mother and father's bedroom. The doorway between the two rooms was covered with a sheet tacked to the wall above it.

I moved toward the doorway not because I was invited and not because I wanted to go, but simply because that's where Ima was, and I wanted to get this the hell over with. As I pushed back the sheet and crossed the wood floor toward the bed where Mrs. Bishop lay, I could feel her sadness overtake me … wrench itself in my own gut. She lay on her side, a wash rag covering the side of her face.

"Mrs. Bishop?" I said.

She made a sound that sounded like an acknowledgment I had spoken her name.

"Mrs. Bishop?" I said again.

"Yeah?" she mumbled.

"Mrs. Bishop?" I said.

"Don't tell me anything else bad," she said.

"Ma'am?" I asked.

"Don't tell me anything else bad," she said. And that was all.

She never looked at me.

"Goddam Lucky," I mumbled.

"What?" she said.

I heard noises behind me. Bobby and Sharon had come to the doorway, were holding the sheet back so they could see, could hear what was happening.

"It's Sheila," I told her. "She didn't make it."

She didn't say a word. She just lay as still as if I had told her about her own death.

"What'd you say, you son of a bitch?" I heard Bobby say from behind me.

I turned and looked him in the eyes. Normally I would have been scared of somebody like him but right now I wasn't scared of him at all. What I was scared of was part of the nature of life that I didn't understand then and not come to since. As Sharon and he looked me in the eye and their mother cried behind me, I spoke the words that told them that Sheila, seventeen, had been killed when a car, a car she was riding in at that, rolled off a south Tennessee hill after the old man had been killed himself by being thrown from the damn thing half an hour before. Willy, though, the one who had been drunk, was fine. Fine and damn dandy. Sitting on the side of the road after he sideswiped another car, hit a concrete pole and ran up the embankment. He sat there and watched the coroner pronounce Edward dead and then come back in thirty minutes to tell them that Sheila was not only pinned under the goddam car but was nearly decapitated. Or for all practical purposes, like a fine open casket funeral where everybody talks about how nice you look, she was decapitated.

In that moment, I was simply scared of the vacuum that sometimes pulls life into it, never again a trace to be seen. And I know this: what I'm talking about doesn't just happen to people who die. Sometimes it visits the living.

CHAPTER THREE

THE FIRST TWO HOURS I was at school I tried to talk about anything to keep that woman's face out of my head and erase the memory of what I had done. Like a lot of things, even though it had seemed as right as rain at the time, the reasons it was wrong now flew through my head at the speed of sound. As did reasons to justify it.

As I watched Sharon pull the old Ford from the parking lot a second time, I told myself that there was nothing wrong with it because the woman was already dead. As she took a right onto Columbia Avenue, I thought about the fact that I had convinced Sharon that there was really no other way out except the one we were taking. By the time I met Tully and Van in the parking lot behind BGA, daylight had come full enough that I was sure somebody would find her, laying there, waiting, like she had been for us.

A sophomore girl, Peggy Williams, stumbled on the body as she walked between the gym and the back of the school building because it was the easiest way from her house. Daylight had completely come by that time and I guess the sight was gruesome enough that she screamed loud enough that it caused several other kids to come running. At the same time, Tully and Van and I were in the parking lot at the Academy, shooting the shit.

"What the hell's wrong with you?" Van asked me when I grimaced.

Maybe I had been the only one to hear the scream. Perhaps I had been the only one listening. I wondered where Sharon was.

"Nothin', I just don't feel too good this morning," I told him.

"Shit, if I started my morning like you did every day, I'd feel pretty damn good all day." He elbowed me in the ribs in the backseat of Tully's granddaddy's car.

"Goddam, it's cold in here," Van said. "Roll that fuckin' window up."

"I don't wanna stink up Mr. Shafer's car with cigarette smoke," I said.

"I'm sure he wouldn't be too mad about that … compared to you all runnin' the thing off in the river."

Tully checked his hair in the rearview mirror then looked at Van. "It wasn't in the river," he said. "It was just in the bushes. And there was another car that ran us off the road. Don't you remember it that way, Henry? You remember that car, don't ya?"

For the second or two that I laughed I was able to forget what I had seen. What I had done. "Yeah, I remember." + + +

It took the news an hour or so to spread to BGA. It was between first and second period that Van came up behind me, rapping on my shoulder. I dropped all my books when he touched me. It was eight forty-five and the halls were full of assholes, seeing that it was mostly assholes I went to school with. It took four attempts and about fifteen feet before I was able to gather all my books after a few of them kicked them.

"Did I scare ya?" Van cackled.

Sometimes when he made this noise—and it's hard to describe, mostly like a laugh that said you're stupid, I'm not—I just wanted to bury my fist in his face, like I'd done once before.

"Why are your hands shakin'?" he asked before I could answer his first question.

"Let's get movin', gentleman," Mr. Nedler's voice called from up the stairs as he descended them. "This is no time for loiterin'. You've got another class to get to."

Mr. Nedler was your typical coach. Thick torso, tight butt over muscular legs. His britches hiked up to so high that I wondered how he walked. I hadn't looked him in the eye for going on three months. I didn't know what I'd say … what he'd say. It was simple, I guess: we were both stuck avoiding looking at each other, trying to keep from being reminded that the other still existed. There was a tone in his voice now that served to remind me that I wasn't his glory boy anymore. He'd have never said anything like that to me in September.

"Manor, Hall … get yourselves moving before I put some demerits on you that you won't serve off for a month," he said.

Demerits were the Academy teachers' way of keeping us straight. Or trying to. Every one they could pin on you meant an hour you had to spend at the godforsaken place on Saturday morning, doing yard work and maintenance and other stuff they were too cheap to pay more than one or two people to do. They had other ways of torture as well. Grabbing you by the hair. Kicking you in the ass. Pinching you on the shoulder or the gut so hard it would raise a half-dollar-size blood blister.

" Manor … Hall … I'm gonna give you boys one more chance and then—"

" We're moving, we're moving," Van kissed up. Something he was damn good at. He motioned me to start walking beside him, talking to me out of the side of his mouth.

" They found some woman up behind Franklin High School, have you heard?"

I forced my head to wag back and forth, squinted my eyes to look interested. Tried to avert the guilt banging at the back of them.

" They said her fucking head was nearly cut off. They said her throat was slashed like ten times. Laid open big enough that you could lay your fucking arm in the hole. They said blood was all over the place."

By this time, we had reached the top of the stairs and were getting ready to push ourselves into English History, a class taught by Mr. Langley, as grouchy a son of a bitch as I've ever seen. When he was mad—as he was as Van still talked to me as we entered the " sanctum of a classroom," describing what the woman had looked like—the veins in his head and neck looked like they were going to explode. His bald head and face turned as purple as any sunset. And he breathed like a mad bull: drawing air in through his nostrils that rattled like gravel in a can and then blowing it out, growling from his chest like a dog. We, for as long as I could recall, had called him Fester. Van had mentioned one time that he looked like a festered sore getting ready to burst. The name, fittingly, had stuck.

There was blood all over the fucking parking lot, Van told me. She was some woman who lived down there with the niggers. I knew her, the one who wore those funny damn britches. Looked like she might go ride a horse. But she was too poor to own a fucking horse. He laughed when he told me this, as did a couple of guys around us. Dickheads. The police were all over Franklin High School. Lucky, working his charmed magic, the great detective that he was. I knew how he'd be working the case; the same way he had told the Bishops about Edward and Sheila. He'd likely be sitting in the car while he had one of his lackeys do something about it, collect the evidence, do the dirty work.

" The police can't be all over the place," I told him.

" What?"

" The police—they can't be all over the place. There aren't but three of them. Well, four including Lucky."

I didn't look at him as I spoke. I couldn't. I knew that I might actually carry through the impulse of hitting him.

" Gentle-men, gentle-men," said Mr. Langley. " It's time to stop the chatter and engage some English History."

Van gave a " sshhh," his finger up to his mouth.

I stared at the desk, the kind that had the chair connected to it, made from wood off the ark. I looked at the scribbling, the marks left cut in it by all the ones who had come before me. All the poor sons of bitches that sat here before me, listened to Mr. Langley and other men like him tell them how to become men. Upstanding pillars of our society.

BY THE TIME LUCKY got home that evening it was past eight o'clock, his supper sitting on the table two hours by then. We had all heard the screen door on the back porch slam shut and Lucky's boots slide by us across the kitchen floor linoleum. No description. No words except, " What a goddam day." Then just right to his chair where he lowered himself into it and slid his boots off, each with the other foot. From my seat in the kitchen I heard him inhale a couple of times, breathe the breath out rough through his chest.

Normally he might offer us a word or two, tell Mama he was going to sit down a minute before he ate supper. But on this night, he said nothing besides his brief, profane description of the day. He just stared at the stucco wall on the south side of the house facing Cleburne Street. He looked like he might have worked a week's worth of hours in a day. I was sure that neither he nor Franklin had ever seen a day like this one.

By third period at the Academy, I could hear it echoing off the walls of every building I walked into, hear the whispers behind teachers' backs. Hear the jokes made. See the fear in the eyes under the jokes. But men didn't stop, in my imagination I could hear Dr. Bugg saying that. We wouldn't be able to just go home, because we had duties to fulfill, responsibilities. At the Academy were future lawyers and judges and politicians. All kinds of power brokers and shit like that.

Nevertheless, Dr. Bugg's voice had crept onto the intercom system with five minutes left in English class. " A special assembly," he called for. We had only had four or five of these in the time I had been there, since ninth grade. By the time everyone assembled in the auditorium, it was almost twenty minutes into fifth period. As they had in the hall earlier in the day, the words swarmed around me. There were even a couple of guys who asked me questions, like I might know something more about it than they did.

" Hall?" Allen Atheny called from three or four rows behind me.

" Yeah?" I hollered back at him. I was still trying to use my best, strongest voice. I could feel it shaking down deep in my throat, almost to my chest, every time I spoke.

" I heard we're gettin' our asses out of this place cause your old man's tellin' everybody in Franklin to go home and lock their doors." He wrapped his arms around himself and pretended to be shivering from fear.

Just as Mr. Hernando, a Cuban Spanish teacher who was famous for giving demerits, started making his way toward Atheny to slap a couple of demerits on him for his cuss word, Dr. Bugg called everybody's attention to the front. He always began every assembly with the same words.

" Now, boys," he said, his voice coming from the back of his throat and finding its way somehow up through his nose. " We have a very serious subject to talk about. So I need you to listen like your life depends on it. As you might have heard, we've had a terrible catastrophe in Franklin overnight. A local woman, Miss Mary Ivy, was found behind the high school this morning. Although they don't know yet because the coroner hasn't issued his ruling, they think she was—"

It was as hard for him to speak the word " murdered" as it was for him to acknowledge there was a lower social class.

I heard Van's voice behind me three rows. I don't know who he was telling. Maybe anybody that would listen. " Her fuckin' throat was cut ear to ear. That's what I heard."

Mr. Hernando cut him a warning eye. Van played kiss-ass again. Smiled at Mr. Hernando like he had been saying something sincere to one of his neighbors.

" ....They say two niggras followed her last night and did this terrible thing. Right now, they have one of those men in the custody of the law and they're trying to find out who the other one is."

Everything that happened in any proximity of the Academy was turned into a lesson of morality.

Dr. Bugg closed: " Of course we don't know what this woman had done … but Assistant Police Chief Dillard Hall, I mean Police Chief Hall, has told everyone to go home, stay home, lock their doors until they have more information on the situation. If one of the niggras that did this is still on the loose, then our town isn't safe for anyone. Go home, go straight home, lock your doors, and don't come out!"

THERE WERE TIRES SQUEALING and people shouting back and forth as the parking lot cleared.

" Hey?" Van yelled at me as I walked across the parking lot toward my Indian.

I turned but didn't speak.

" Chester and me are gonna go down to his daddy's store and get some beer and go to the Willow Plunge," he called. " Wanna come?"

" Nah," I said, seeing the note stuck to my motorcycle with just a little chewing gum. I knew that if I hadn't been where I was this morning, this would have been a holiday for me too. I would have felt like drinking beer and going to the Willow Plunge. But her face. Her fucking awful face.

" Suit yourself," Van said. " You wanna give me a ride? I don't see Tully. I figured he'd be here."

Starting to half-look at the note, I said, " He probably thought they'd keep us."

He walked up to me and tried to look at Sharon's note over my shoulder. I folded it and stuffed it in my pocket. I climbed on the Indian and Van climbed on behind me. Just because Tully wasn't there.

CHAPTER FOUR

E VEN THOUGH IT WAS just a ninety second ride from the Academy
to our house, it seemed like it took the remainder of the day. Maybe
that's what happens when we're pulled from our sense of normality, thrown
into the unusual. I could feel Van's hands pressing in on my sides, could feel
the brush of his legs against mine. My love and hate for him, both were
tremendous.

The HG Hill grocery store was closed, so was the Texaco Station. The
streets were as empty as I'd ever seen them. When Van and I pulled up at his
house, Tully was sitting in the front yard, his grandfather hollering at him.
" Nobody's s'posed to be in their yards. Some crazy nigger's on the loose."

" I ain't scared," Tully yelled back down the street.

His grandfather made a face like he was both sorry and glad that he
didn't have any control over Tully. We all lit cigarettes, trying to out-cool
each other.

" Shit, man," he said, " y'all should'a been at the high school this
mornin'. What a scene. Ain't often that you go to school and never get in
the door. They just kept us standin' out there in the schoolyard. Herded us
over to a corner and made us stand there like cows. Said the whole fuckin'
place was a crime scene."

" We didn't get anything at the Academy but a hard time," Van said, holding his cigarette down by his side so that his mother might not see how cool he was being. " Fuck the Academy."

" It was godawful," said Tully. " I just got a glimpse of her from a distance, but it was like it wasn't even real. Like somebody had planted her there play-actin'. I swear I could see the gash in her neck from seventy-five feet away."

The more he talked, the sicker my stomach got. Eventually I guess Van noticed that I looked like I might keel over.

" What's wrong with you?" he said.

I couldn't answer. I was too busy making my way toward the shrubs in the corner of his yard to throw my guts up. Maybe my body was trying to purge itself of the guilt. Maybe it was just that I hadn't eaten anything for lunch since the Academy had pushed us all out on the street with the dangerous " niggras."

Van laughed like he was watching Milton Berle with Lucky, which he often did because we were the first one on the block to have a television. Another of Lucky's deals, I assumed. He watched wrestling, boxing, Milton Berle and a few other things on it. When Van was there with us, he laughed loudest at the stuff he knew Lucky would think was the funniest.

" What a candy ass," he said. " He just hears Tully describin' it and he gets sick."

" Fuck you," I said from behind the shrubs.

" Candy ass," he hollered back.

I came from behind the shrubs, vomit still on my chin and my shirt and I shoved him. " I'm not a fucking candy ass," I told him. " We didn't eat lunch, asshole."

He shoved me back. Harder than I had pushed him. " Fuck you too!" he said.

If Tully hadn't stepped between us, I was going to do again what I had already done once a few months before.

" Look, assholes," he said, " if you all are gonna fight, then both of you are gonna have to whip my ass and neither of you can do that." He put one

hand in my chest and one in Van's and pushed us three or four feet apart. "
It almost made me sick to see it this morning. It probably would'a made
anybody sick."

For a few seconds, I wondered if Sharon had told about the sun rising
on us and the fresh corpse behind Franklin High School. It made me
wonder again what the note said. I wiped my mouth with the back of my
hand, brushed at my shirt with my palm. The taste of my stomach and its
contents still lay on my lips and tongue.

For thirty seconds or so, Van and I stood in the corner of his yard and
stared through each other with looks that could have left bruises. Tully still
between us, we looked around him, over his shoulders.

" Just let it go," he said to both of us. " It's a strange day. You fuckers just
need to get over yourselves. You been like this for months."

Van picked up the cigarette he had thrown down when our words
started. He drew on it, still staring me in the eye, unwilling to be the one to
look away first. I laughed his look off.

" Have you talked to Sharon?" Tully asked.

" Not since this mornin'," I said.

" You wouldn't have believed it," said Tully, his brown eyes shimmering
like wet beach sand as he spoke. " I guess the first kid got there and then she
started screamin'. And then you know it didn't take two or three minutes
until there were people all over the place, hollering their lungs out for the
teachers and Mr. Thompson to come. Pretty soon there were fifty people
standin' there and then your daddy came … and then his men came."

" I heard they arrested that nigger janitor," Van said.

" Yeah, that was the biggest part of the scene," Tully said. " They went in
the high school and got him and drug him out in handcuffs. The whole
time he was hollerin' that he didn't do it. That he didn't have nothin' to do
with it. He just kept yellin' that he didn't see the body because it was dark.
That he would'a called the police if he'd seen it."

Again, I felt like I was going to be sick.

" And that was when Sharon started. It was the oddest goddam thing.
She just started bawlin' her head off. She cried so hard that Principal Th-

ompson had to come help her to her car so she could go home."

" Was she all right?" Van asked. Like he really gave a shit. The impulse to lay him out came over me all over again.

" Yeah, she seemed all right after she sat in the car for a little while. She seemed to come back to her senses."

Tully watched Mr. Shafer come out two doors down and peer up at us to make sure we were still alive. He kept his eyes on him for only a moment then he turned back to us. Van lit another cigarette and smirked at me. It could have been a smile I saw as a smirk. Everything about him was arrogant to me. From his light green eyes to his skinny, lanky body to his peroxided blonde hair. His hair had been that way since early in the spring when we had all used a bottle of peroxide on the beach in Alabama one weekend. Tully had since let his grow out. Lucky had dragged me in the house no more than thirty minutes after we got back and held my head just a few inches over the commode water. Then he had thrown me in his cruiser and driven me down to Frank's on Main and told him to shave my head. Of course, Van's parents didn't do one goddam thing.

" Your mother's hollerin' for ya," Tully said.

" Huh?" I said back. I had been staring at him, of all things at the crease in his pants. He was immaculate. His khakis were pressed as smooth as a tabletop. His shirt the same. The tee shirt under it was snow-white.

" Your mama's callin' ya," he said. " She and your sister Jean just came out on the porch. She's motionin' for you to come over there."

" I don't give a shit," I said.

Van laughed. Tully said, " Man, you ought'a treat your mama better."

" Henry," she called. " Henry, come on home. Your father has said that shouldn't anybody be out on the street."

Jean bobbed her head up and down like a puppet. " That's what he said," she echoed.

" Come on," she said. " Just pull your motorcycle over here under the shed and come on in the house."

" You wanna go to the Willow Plunge with me and Chester?" Van asked Tully. " He was s'posed to go down to his old man's store and get us some beer then come by and pick me up."

" Nah," Tully said. " I guess I ought'a go down there and be with Mr. Shafer." That's what he always called him. Not Granddaddy, not Grandfather. But " Mr. Shafer."

" Suit yourself," said Van. " I'm goin'."

" When he picks you up?" I said.

" Yeah," he said.

" Times like this, I bet you wish you had a car."

LUCKY DIDN'T SPEAK to anyone for over an hour after he plopped in his chair. His dinner sat on the table, getting colder and colder until finally my mother had wrapped it in cellophane and put it in the icebox. When she finally told Jean and me we could eat, I shoveled a few bites of mashed potatoes and green beans into my mouth while I listened to Jean go on about what she had seen that day.

" It was Peggy Williams that came on the body," she said. " She said it was awful. Of course, I didn't ever actually see it. But they said it was like your worst nightmare. They couldn't stop people from gatherin' around to look at it. That's why they say Mr. Thompson closed the school. So he could just get the crowd to go."

Between bites of her roll and sips of ice tea, she told it like Lucky hadn't been there. She talked just to fucking talk. Like it was just in her nature for her mouth to run like a sewing machine.

" It was awful, Daddy..." she said. And Lucky listened like he hadn't been there, like he hadn't seen the whole thing for himself. Took the energy to turn his head toward the kitchen from his chair in the living room.

" And this one girl ... she just about lost her mind. She just cried and cried and cried. I felt so sorry for the poor thing."

Lucky sat and listened to every word she had to say. Or at least he bobbed his head up and down like he was. I grunted when spoken to and my mother said virtually nothing, like usual. Just cleaned up everybody's plate when they were done. And Lucky sat in his chair and smoked cigarette after cigarette, the same chair that reeked of his cigarette smoke when he wasn't there, over which there was a stain on the ceiling that grew darker with each passing month.

Finally, after Jean had shut her mouth and she and my mother had gone into my parents' bedroom to talk by themselves, Jean went on into her own room, the one with the window unit air conditioner that kept it frigid in the summer and the baseboard heater that kept it toasty in the winter. She had a four-piece bedroom set—cherry, that Lucky had bought at an auction in downtown Franklin—which included a chest of drawers, a bureau with a mirror so she could look at her ugly puss, a night stand, and a nice bed that had box springs. After the auction, when Jean got to move into what had been the " family room," my mother, always one to try to focus on the positive side of things (another way of lying to yourself, I thought), told me to look at it like I would then have a bigger room and my sister out of my hair.

As for me, my bedroom was up the stairs in the attic. Fifteen stairs that were akin to climbing the side of the damn house into a room that had to be hotter than August in hell. I had a mattress that sunk down in an old four-poster twin bed, its mate across the room, past where the stairs came up. Afraid that somebody was going to come up behind me and read over my shoulder, I climbed the stairs into hell itself.

Sweetie,

I thought maybe they'd let you all out of school. But after this last year, I guess I ought to know the 'fucking Academy,' as you call it, better than that. Anyway, I thought that I would stop by and see you ... or at least see your motorcycle. It smells like you, do you know that? Or maybe you smell like it, I'm not sure. Mr. Thompson let us out of school. It was crazy there. Peggy Williams came on that woman and pretty soon everybody was there. They didn't keep us long after that. Of course, your daddy came and all his men came. But I didn't utter a word. It was hard, but after I got to thinking about it, I decided that we really weren't doing anything wrong. She was there when we got there. At least I think she was. They think that that janitor did it. What's his name, Jackson somebody? Anyway, I guess they think he was going to try to get her into the incinerator and that girl stopped him. But, thinking about it more, how could that be? He was there when we were there. He always is. Do you think he had her in his car or something? Or does he even have a car? I don't think he does. Anyway, I thought I'd come by and see you before I left for Nashville. Call me at work if you have time. I'm hoping that we get to see each other tonight.

Love always and forever,
Sharon

And that's what I did for the next two hours—wait Lucky out so that he might go to sleep so that I could then go out my window in the attic, roll my motorcycle to the end of the driveway and then to the end of Cleburne Street and then ride to see Sharon after she got off work. But Lucky wouldn't sleep. Every time I came down the stairs and looked around the corner, he was still just sitting there in that chair like he was glued to it. Smoking. One after another. He hadn't turned on the television all night. Lucky did that like clockwork, the same way he shit, showered, and shaved. If he wasn't at the filling station shooting craps, he was in that chair staring at the television. Finally, I went in and sat down with him.

"Boy," he said.

"Hey Daddy."

He stared at the stucco wall, pulling his Lucky Strike to his mouth in rote.

"Bad day?" I said.

He nodded.

"That woman?"

"You heard?"

"How could I not?"

"I heard Bugg finally let you all out."

"Yeah, he let us out right before lunch."

"I haven't eat all day," he told me. "Is your mama in bed?"

31

I told him she was.

"Good," he said, "she was worried about everything."

"Yeah, so was Mr. Shafer. He tried to get Tully in the house when we were out front today."

Lucky pulled his bottle of Evan Williams out from the crack in his chair. It was the reason he had asked if Mama was in bed. She knew he nursed a bottle of whiskey most of the day; and he knew she knew. Nevertheless, it was never done in front of her. Denial of such things, I guess, is easier when you don't have to confront them with your eyes.

"I guess I ought'a try to go to bed," he told me. "I'm gonna have to get up before you throw your papers to go down to the jail. I got two deputies down there tonight." He lit another Lucky and pulled his bottle from the crack in the chair, took a swig then returned it there. "They think the woman was from over at the Burgess house," he said. "Ivy … something Ivy. Mary Ivy. Fuckin' Sammy Samuels came by today and told me he saw her out walkin' last night. Just out walkin' in those goddam riding pants she wore. Two niggers followin' her. Walkin' along behind her in the dark as pretty as you please."

It was like he was talking to himself. He stared out the window on the door that led to the porch.

"After I got that lead, I never got over to the Burgess house to even see if it was that woman. I spent my whole day at the high school trying to keep everybody in line there. Hell, I couldn't get some of the faculty to quit staring at the body. Couldn't get them to go home. Much less the damn kids. Never have understood that, like stopping on the highway to see something gruesome after a goddam wreck."

I thought about Sharon, the crying jag that she'd never mentioned in her note. I wondered if he was the one who put her in the car.

"I probably shouldn't have arrested that janitor," he said. "But what do you do? A white woman seen walking down the road last night, two niggers following her. She ends up dead this mornin' and the janitor who gets there before everybody else is a nigger. I guess he was going to try to get her into that incinerator before anybody got there. Who knows?"

He cupped his face in his thick, short hands and rubbed his eyes. "You got that money yet?"

"Not all of it," I told him. "I'll have it with next week's paycheck."

He didn't even acknowledge I had spoken. He snuffed out the last cigarette he had lighted and opened his bottle again. He didn't drink this time, though. He simply stared into the almost clear liquid, tinged barely brown.

"You really don't think Jackson Mosby did it?" I asked him.

He kept his eyes on the concoction in the bottle, that mixture that he loved so well. Smoke filtered around his face, the bottle. Covered him in a haze.

"I don't know," he said, drawing on the stub of a cigarette then chewing on the end of one of his fingers. He spat something out of his mouth I couldn't see. "I doubt it," he said. "I don't believe nobody would be so stupid as to drag a body to where they work to burn it. And if he was gonna do that, then why wouldn't he have done it earlier? When there wasn't anybody there?"

Maybe because I was there, I thought.

"I mean, he knows what time people get there. Hell, he's been cleanin' that buildin' every schoolday for years."

"Yeah," I agreed.

"And I tell ya this—I don't think the woman is from over at the Burgess house. Don't ask me why I think that but I do. Maybe she just don't look exactly like her or somethin'. I've run that Ivy woman in before for public drunk a coupl'a times. She'd just be runnin' down the street drunk, or wobblin', as pretty as you please. I'd pull up and ask her what she was doin' and she'd say she was ridin'. Crazyass. She come from a family that had horses or somethin' … I'll tell ya that. I'll get on it in the mornin'."

Lucky pulled a cigarette out of his pocket and turned his eyes to me only briefly. As my eyes ran away from his, he laughed to fill the silence. His chest rattled like loose tools in box.

"And I'll tell ya this:" he said, "if it's not that Ivy woman then that means it's somebody I ain't seen before. And if it's somebody I ain't seen before, then that means that she was from out'a town. And if she was from out'a town there's probably more to this than anybody believes right now or wants to believe."

THE FACT THAT LUCKY arrested Jackson Mosby was, I guess, partly my fault—a lack of courage, you might say—and because he was a nigger. I shouldn't use that word and don't now. But I'd be lying if I said we didn't use it then. Lucky used it. Jean, my sister, used it. I'd like to say I didn't. But the only one in my family who didn't use it was my mother. My saintly mother who used the term "colored." I didn't know if people in this world are ever really as good, as needless, as my mother acted, or whether it's just that—an act. Whether the bad in them has been so long denied that even they don't believe they have it anymore. Maybe people like her deny other people's bad so long that they convince themselves they don't have it in them either. I know, though, I have it in me.

Ten years before, I hadn't thought one thing about it being wrong to watch Lucky's friend Sammy Samuels beat the shit out of Arliss Mosby, Jackson's son. On this particular day, when I had been about ten, Lucky had gotten a call that there was some trouble at Frank's on Main, where Jackson Mosby had a shoeshine stand … where Arliss worked for him sometimes. Lucky was in the shop, me right behind him, in the time it took him to round the block and park.

The trouble had just started when we arrived. Evidently, Sammy Samuels had insisted that the shine he had gotten the day before hadn't lasted, had worn off before he got home to show it off to his wife and kids.

"Godammit, Frank," he yelled to the man who owned the barbershop, creatively named "Frank's Barbershop on Main." "That little nigger boy didn't do any kinda job on my shoes yesterday."

"We gave you a shine free, Sammy," Frank told him. Sammy was standing at the door, making sure everyone walking down Main Street and in the barber shop heard him.

"Look at my goddam shoes!" Sammy yelled. "Do these look like any shoes that have seen a shine?"

The shoeshine boy, Arliss, stretched his neck out to take a look at Sammy's shoes. "Sir, them ain't the shoes that I polish' yesterday."

Frank left the head he was working on and walked across the shop to Sammy and Arliss, and now my father and me. He was a small man with the only hair on the top of his head that which he swung over from the part just over his ear.

"As a matter a fact, sir them ain't the shoes that he wore in here awhile ago. Them ain't even the shoes that I shine then."

Arliss must have been thirteen, maybe fourteen at the time, and obviously still naive as hell when it came to black-white relations in this town.

"Sammy, don't you try to pull that shit on me," Frank said.

"If them is the same shoes," commented Arliss, "they so old that they won't hold no shine."

"What did that goddam nigger say about my shoes?" Sammy said, making sure to avoid the subject that he had already gotten one shoeshine free and now was going for another.

"He said that if he did shine those shoes yesterday or today that they're so old that they won't hold no shine," Frank laughed. As did his patron and the man in the next chair and the ones waiting. Lucky laughed, too.

"You just see if I get my shoes shined in here again," he said. "Or my damn hair cut, you bald son of a bitch. I don't know why I would'a ever thought a bald man could cut my hair anyway." A comment which drew about as much laughter as Frank's last one had. "I'll go up to the barbershop on Eleventh Avenue to get my haircut and my shoeshines from now on."

"Just don't take them shoes," said Frank, taking the apron off his customer and dusting his shoulders with a talcum brush. Another round of laughter spread through the room and made its way out the door to Lucky. Even Arliss and I laughed. I figure, though, that Arliss was a lot like me. He didn't know what the hell he was laughing at.

Thirty minutes later Lucky got another call, this time from a Main Street shop keeper that wanted to stay anonymous, that there was a fight taking place behind Frank's on Main. When we got there, it wasn't a fight as much as it was that Sammy, a pretty good-sized man, had caught Arliss alone and had knocked him down to the ground and was now systematically kicking the shit out of him with one of the shoes they had commented on. Arliss had been sitting out back drinking a Coca Cola because Frank didn't let him sit on the bench in the front of his shop when he wasn't working.

Lucky pulled up about seventy-five feet from the sight of Arliss scurrying around on the ground while Sammy Samuels' foot found its mark again and again. Arliss's stomach. His rib cage. His chest. His ass. His balls. Arliss crawled across the back parking lot, blood on his hands and knees from where he had hit the gravel, blood streaming from his nose and mouth where Sammy had hit him and kicked him, his little shoeshine kit scattered all over.

"What 'd you think about that, little pecker head? How them shoes now?"

I looked at Lucky, sure that he was now going to go handcuff Sammy and throw him in the back of the squad car. But he just sat there. Still seventy-five feet away. Still watching.

"He's awright. He'll get home," he said.

And I guess he did. But he never made it back to Frank's. By the next week, another man had taken Jackson's son's place and by the next year, Jackson Mosby had gone to work at the high school as their janitor. Shoeshining, I guess, had been too hard on him. And his son Arliss.

CHAPTER FIVE

WHEN VAN AND I had pulled up in front of the house the first night that we picked Sharon and Sheila up, in typical Van fashion he had told me: "Now when we get these people's house you're gonna realize that they're poor as shit. They ain't got a pot to piss in." He cackled. "Really, I guess they got a pot, but they don't have a bathroom." Van and I had always had indoor plumbing, didn't know what it was like to be without it. "But poor girls fuck like rabbits."

"I'm ready," I'd told him.

"That's the only reason I got us dates with these girls," he said. "Word is that their old man's been bangin' 'em for years." He laughed that laugh again. "Hell, girls like these, you buy 'em somethin' to eat, they'll be in the backseat with ya in a matter of minutes."

In a way I never liked to admit, if nothing else he was right about their house. It was little more than a shack. Mr. Bishop met us on the front porch. I got a glimpse of Sharon's mother when she passed by the doorway. Coal black hair like Sharon. Darker skin. She would later tell me her Grandmother was born on a reservation in Oklahoma.

"Hi ya doin'?" Mr. Bishop offered as he stuck out a calloused hand and I shook it.

"All right," I said. "Yessir. Allright."

"You boys from BGA, right?"

"Yessir."

"Play football, right?"

Van chimed in. "Yessir. I play tight end and corner back. Henry here, he plays half back and returns kicks. We're both s'posed to start this year. Henry … he's got college potential. Or at least that's what they say."

I nodded then wagged my head back and forth.

"Never had a chance to play that stuff myself. A' course, in my day it was just startin' to get big."

"When was your day, old man?" Van would laugh after we'd let the girls off that night. "When was your day?" and "Wonder why the hell they didn't do anything? Goddam, we took 'em to a nice restaurant. I bet they hadn't ever eat anywhere that nice before."

Sheila said she had never been to Dotson's. Sharon told her she had too. She reminded her it was right over the river when you came into town.

"Oh," Sheila had said. "The one with the fruit stand right there by it."

"Yeah, sweetie, that's the one," both Sharon and Van had said at the same time. Which brought a laugh.

Van's daddy, Scoot, had lent him the car for the night. For the most part, Scoot was a scared-faced, pale man who looked older than his years. I had been told that's why he got the name, always seeming like he might take off running from everything. Several times, I had witnessed with my own eyes Van driving his daddy's car with his daddy in the front seat, and intentionally speeding up to the four-way stop at the corner of Cleburne and Adams, and then throwing on the brakes at the last second. I had then seen Scoot there under those Oaks and Elms grabbing the dash like a maniac as Van locked the brakes and laughed.

It was easy for us to hold Scoot in disdain. He was only kin to us because my mother's sister had married him. His blood did not run in our veins. Nor ours in his.

AT FIRST GLANCE, it was hard for me to believe that my Uncle Percy was my father's brother. A thin, tall man, his hair hung around his face, often shading his eyes. He was well over six feet, the only member of my family who was so. My father, as I am, was five foot eight on a good day.

At first I acted like I didn't see him. I ignored him as my father had been doing for years. On the bench, it looked like his legs went on forever. His dirty boots, still wet from his walk along the river, were crossed at the ankles. He trimmed an apple with a pocket knife my father had given him.

Van grabbed my shoulder and pulled me to a stop. "Hey, look, it's your uncle. Hey, Percy. Hey, hi' ya doin'?"

My uncle threw up his hand at Van but didn't look at him. One of those early spring nights that the sky begins to last longer, it shone in colors evident no other time of the year. My uncle's movements were highlighted in the strange light, the sky mixed with the early glow of a light over the parking lot, as he shuffled toward us.

"How are y'all?"

"Pretty good," I told him.

"Is Dillard home tonight?" He seldom called my daddy Lucky.

"Far as I know," I told him.

He acknowledged Sheila and Sharon with a nod. Still didn't look at Van.

"Don't tell him you saw me–been studyin' the river," he said all in one breath.

"What you been studyin'?" Van asked. I was sure he just wanted something to talk about once we got back in the car with the girls. Both Sharon and Sheila had moved back a couple of steps from him. I guess I might have been frightened, too, if I hadn't known him.

"I been studyin' the goddam river," he told Van, "just like I always do. If you had any brains, you'd study it too."

Van leaned toward Sharon, took her hand playfully, and whispered loud enough for me to hear. "He means if I was crazy like him."

I wasn't sure if my uncle had failed to hear him or he was simply used to hearing things like that.

"What've you been studyin' about it?" Van said.

I had enough sense to know that I should route this conversation elsewhere. In times like this, though, my tongue was the last member of my body that knew what to do.

"I been studyin' how it goes in and out of town. I find it very odd that such a thing like that could affect the whole history of a state… A country. Not only that … but affect so many lives. And those men would have had children and their children would have had children and so on and so on. Do you get what I mean?"

"I think so," said Van. "I think I get it."

My uncle's eyes were cast toward the river again, its foliage leading to the edge.

Van looked at the girls and winked. "I'm not sure though."

Percy craned his neck, then stretched his shoulders, like his head might be hurting. "I'm talking about how something as simple as the direction that time cut a river might have in fact determined who was going to die in this battle and who wasn't."

"What battle?" I heard Sheila ask Sharon.

"Some things are preordained from the beginning of time. That's what I'm trying to say. I know there are people who will say that that's bullshit— 'scuse my language, fair ladies—but they simply haven't gone deep enough in the metaphysical nature of our existence."

"Percy, you're a smart son of a bitch," Van told him while he slapped him on the back.

Percy didn't crack a smile. Still never looked at him.

Van looked the sky over, beginning to become purple at its edges. "Need a ride?"

"No. I'm just gonna stay here awhile and study on this river some more. Don't tell Dillard you saw me."

"Yeah, fine. I won't," I reassured him.

He pulled at his britches until they were three inches over his ankles and pushed at the hair in his face only for it to fall there again.

"He's one crazy son of a bitch," Van said as Percy began to walk away.

There was nothing I could say. What he had said was true.

THE FIRST TIME I heard the knock at the door, I had opened my eyes and stared at the ceiling, watching the silver flecks dance there in the darkness. I thought it was probably Tully, who often climbed on the roof of the side porch of the house and rapped on my window. But momentarily I realized that the knock had in fact not been at the window but at the door at the top of the stairs that opened into the room where I slept.

"Boy," I heard the voice say. "Boy, are you in there?"

"Where the fuck else would I be?" I said under my breath.

"Can I come in there?" the voice said.

"Yeah, I guess," I said.

I heard the door come open and close. The radiator heater clanked a couple of times in the silence that came with Lucky's heavy breathing from climbing the stairs. Even though I didn't pray much, I prayed that I'd hear his footsteps move in the other direction as I heard his footsteps moving toward my side of the attic.

"Hey," he said.

"Hey," I answered him.

"I'm gonna sleep over there."

"All right," I told him.

I heard the friction between match and flint as he lit a cigarette, then watched its orange head glow as he sucked the fumes in. As my eyes adjusted to the darkness, I began to be able to see Lucky's silhouette as he stood there in the doorway. It looked to me like he had shrunk two or three inches in the last year. Or perhaps it was simply the fact that his shoulders were hunched now. He looked like a frog. Like a frog smoking a Lucky Strike in the darkness becoming gray from the moonlight filtering through the window across from him. A frog who had stripped down to his tee shirt and underwear.

"I figured there wasn't any reason to wake your mother up, seein' how I'm gonna have to get up in a couple of hours." He drew on his Lucky, hacked a little. "Started to go on down there now. But I decided against it. I thought if things weren't all right, I'd know it."

No, you thought that your goddam jailer would think you're drunk, which you are. You thought that everybody else would take up your slack … like they do. You thought you'd rather stay here and drink and hide yourself from the reality of what your life has become rather than go down to the jail and face the fact you might have arrested an innocent man.

"Yeah, they'd call," I said.

"He don't have a car," he said.

I could see that his outline had moved to the end of the bed on which I lay, feel that his weight had been deposited there.

"Sir?"

"That Jackson Mosby, he don't have a car."

"Yeah?"

"You know where he lives, don't ya?"

"Yessir. Down off Strahl Street." I almost winced as soon as I spoke the street name. One of the half dozen or so that was named after generals who died in the Battle of Franklin, as November turned to December, 1864.

"Could he have carried a woman that far? Or even if there was another nigger involved, could two of 'em, even if they was strong, carry a woman that far? Especially without being seen."

He was becoming more readily visible at the end of my bed. The shiny patches of skin showed through his hair where it was cut so short and he was losing the rest. His shoulders hunched where his chest was starting to bow outward from all the coughing. The orange head of his cigarette moved slowly to and away from his mouth. His tee shirt was becoming whiter as the darkness in my eyes dissipated, beginning to show the effort of my mother's regular bleaching.

"No sir," I said.

He moved his head up and down at my response.

"I'll never forget it," he said. "When I was a boy, my daddy thought I broke a window out of the old house I grew up in." Lucky stopped for a few seconds, turning to study me in what now had become a grayish light with a yellow tone from the moon. I think he was checking to see if I was listening. If anybody was.

"I knew when Daddy came home he was gonna believe that I done it. He'd know that his little boy, the one that's kinda strange, can't throw no rock through a window that high. And who the hell does that leave? Wanda Jean and Nelly wasn't home yet. They didn't throw no rocks no way. And Ine—anyway, an hour later Daddy was home rantin' and ravin' that there was all kinda glass in the floor upstairs. Course he tells me this when he's already on top of me in the yard and he's got a stick in his hand. He beat me with that stick all the way across the acre between where he found me and the house, and then all the way through the front door and up the stairs. He didn't never even ask Percy if he done it."

He looked into the darkness of the other side of the attic like he was looking back into time passed. From where I lay I could smell him. Sometimes it seemed like the bourbon was working its way out his pores, leaving its stink to waft across the room to remind me he was there. Bourbon mixed with the stale smell of smoked cigarettes.

CHAPTER SIX

ROM NINE YEARS OLD I had run that paper route, from Breezy Hill to the big curve on Lewisburg Pike, to Main Street as far east as the Harpeth River. Most of the houses had been built in the late thirties, early forties, had come on the heels of the economic rise after the Depression and the wartime economy. Further down Adams Street, left at the four-way stop after leaving our house was where the big, old houses started. The ones that had been built from the early eighteen hundreds to the eighteen-fifties, the "houses that had been there during that bloody, godforsaken battle," my Uncle Percy had told me many times.

I threw their papers, too. The rich people's. The Mayberrys' and the Croners' and the Renoirs' and the Gists', direct descendants—or at least they so-claimed—of General Gist, one of the generals laid out on December 1, 1864, on the porch of the Carnton Mansion after most of the fighting stopped. These were the houses where you had to have quite an arm to get those papers to the porch, most of them so far from the street that when I was nine and ten, I had to ride my bicycle into the yards and drop the papers on the porch. I had learned quick that you better get the paper where the customer expects it. Or else they complain. Nobody wants to go digging through their shrubs and bushes for one that went awry.

These houses backed up to the paper office, where I'd go in the morning to fill my bags. Over the years I had gotten good enough to fold most of them while I was on the road, on bicycle or motorcycle. Tri-fold and then tuck, that's the best way. They stay tight, sail like a kite on almost any wind, and the folds don't affect how the customer can read the paper. Of course, this can only be done with daily papers, the thinner ones—not the Sunday paper, a fat mother, which had to be wrapped with rubber bands.

When I'd first gotten my Indian, my mother had told me she was glad, that she could hear me wherever I went over the whole route. Made me feel both good and bad. It also made me wonder about the days before I had the Indian, when I was pedaling that son of a bitch of a bicycle up and down all those streets and hills, what she did then.

"I don't think he ought to have to work at eight," I remember her telling Lucky, when he had worked it out with Jack Charles down at the paper office for me to come to work for him. "I mean, I know Franklin is a good town, that nothing ever happens here. I mean, that good people live here. But he's just eight years old."

"He'll be nine," Lucky had responded. By the time he works, he'll be nine." And that was all he said. "And besides, a little work ain't gonna hurt 'im," Lucky told my mother, staring at the old tile on the kitchen floor that they would eventually replace with the linoleum. "Hell, my daddy put me to work in the fields when I was seven."

If there is hell when you're nine years old, it's having to learn how to fold and throw newspapers and where the five hundred people live you have to throw them to. Ronnie Langford, the guy who had trained me, a senior at Franklin High School at the time, had done more talking about his "girl" than he had trained. By the time I finished riding the two weeks of mornings I was supposed to ride with him, I knew little more than I had known to start with. I did know, though, his girlfriend's hair color, her height, her weight, and supposedly what she liked her to do to him. He described that in graphic detail as we knocked all around Franklin in a Chevrolet truck I was certain wouldn't go one more mile.

"I was gonna go to college," he told me, "but Barbara's done changed my mind. I got a full ride to go up to Knoxville and play for the Volunteers, but I'd rather stay here with her. She's got two years left in high school but man, she screws my brains out. Do you get what I mean?"

Of course, at eight almost nine, I didn't.

"I was the star fuckin' fullback at Franklin last year. Ran for more yards than anybody that ever went through the place. I guess I really ought to go to Knoxville. But she can't go. So, what do ya do? Do you think I'd leave that pussy that's better than anything in the world?"

Every so often, mixed with his words and their emphasis, he'd check his reflection in the mirror. He'd check his hair, check his eyebrows, see how good he'd shaved, all while he was driving down the road throwing papers.

"My father says I ought to go to college," he told me. "Says that goddam FDR'll be dragging my ass over to fight the Japs if I don't. He says the only chance I got to stay out'a the war is that it'll either end or I take my white ass to college. A'course I can't tell him what a piece a' ass Barbara is … so he just thinks that I'm stupid as shit."

Mostly I nodded at what he said.

"You gonna do this whole route on bicycle?" he asked me.

"I guess," I answered.

"It's gotta be ten miles."

"Daddy says it's only six or seven."

"You keep thinkin' that way, little fella'. That'll help ya when you're ridin' along in the morning, shivering your ass off, just hopin' that you get through. Hell, I don't know if I know of anybody that's done a route like this on a bicycle."

"Daddy says I can do it," I said. This is when I still called him that.

"Ain't your daddy that Assistant Police Chief?" he asked.

"Yeah, Lucky Hall," I said.

"Don't he run that craps game down at the fillin' station?"

"He plays in it," I said. "I never thought about him runnin' it."

"I've always heard that," Ronnie said. He pushed at his hair in the rearview mirror and lit a cigarette. "Damn things are supposed to be bad for ya. That's what they say—that they take your wind. But I guess if I ain't gonna play football no more then it don't matter much."

"You sure you're not goin' to Knoxville?" I asked him. I'd been telling Lucky about him the night before. He'd informed me what a "dumbass" he was for deciding something like that.

"Nah, it's too late now anyways. That's why I'm quittin' the paper route, 'cause I gotta get a full-time job. Daddy says if I'm not goin' to college then out'a the house it is for me. I figure I'm gonna ask Barbara if she wants to run off and get married. I figure if I gotta leave home and work at the goddam mill, then I might as well have her to go home to at night. That way, too, we'd have somewhere to screw besides the back of the car."

We were quiet for a few minutes, the only sounds when he pulled papers from the stack between us, did the tri-fold, and flung them out the window. Depending on the particular noises the old Chevy truck was making at the time, I could hear some of the papers hit the ground and slide to their final resting place.

"DADDY AND ME got in a big argument," Ronnie told me in front of the picture show on Main Street after he had stopped his truck when he saw me almost a week later. "He tried to make me go to Knoxville and play football. He told me he'd always been a fan of the big fuckin' orange and I didn't have a choice but to go there. I told him I did have a fuckin' choice and I didn't want to play football no more."

"What happened then?" I asked him. I had gotten better at the way we conversed. I knew he wanted me to ask questions so he could talk about himself.

He looked at himself admiringly in the picture window across the front of the theater. Puffed out his chest a little. "He took a swipe at me and I pinned his ass down to the ground. They had to send your daddy over there to pull me off him. I swear I would'a killed his ass if they hadn't pulled me off him."

Van, standing there with me, said, "You didn't hear about that? It was in the paper and everything. He almost beat his daddy to death. They said if Lucky hadn't got there when he did, he prob'ly would'a."

He looked at Van after he spoke, as if asking who the little shit was who knew so much about him.

Van watched him admire himself in the window again. "You're Ronnie Langford, ain't you?"

He broke his gaze on himself, nodded. Watched himself while he lit a cigarette.

"I told you he'd been teachin' me my route," I said. "Well, he was."

"You must be a better football player than paper-throwin' teacher," Van said.

I drew my finger across my throat, motioned for Van to shut up. Laughed like a I thought it was funny, too.

"Yeah, I saw ole Jack Charles," Ronnie said. "He told me you didn't have a' easy time with it the first few days. It takes a little while to learn it. I ain't missed it though. Been able to spend a lot more time with Barbara … you know."

I don't recall him ever looking at us between his inquiring stare at Van and when he told us that maybe Barbara was in the lobby of the picture show, not meeting him outside like he thought. He tousled my hair as he told us he was going to look inside. After his first two or three steps away, though, he stopped and stared at us from the edge of the street, where he'd stepped off the sidewalk.

"I'm leavin' in a few days," he said, in a voice loud enough to hear over the few cars that crept by. "I prob'ly won't see y'all again before I come back. I'll prob'ly be a hero by then."

"You goin' off to fight?" Van asked.

"Yessir," Ronnie told him, giving a mock salute just after he'd spotted Barbara a few paces down the street. "Goin' off to end the war. The boys in Washington need a little help."

After he'd crossed the street and held Barbara's hand in his, he turned and waved at us again, as if he knew we were still watching him. He held the door after she'd passed through and hollered back to us, why, I'll never know.

"Hey, Little Shit," which is what he had called me from time to time when, I suspected, he couldn't recall my name, "We're gonna go over on the tracks down below your house tonight, to have some fun ... celebrate goin' off. You ought'a come if you can get away with it."

I nodded, knowing I'd never go.

Van nodded and elbowed me in the ribs.

BY THE TIME that the first morning had come to throw the papers by myself, I had no idea where half of them went. The Nashville *Tennessean,* the paper I threw, was never a huge paper, just big enough to cover most of the national and local news, weather, and sports. The paper we got in Franklin itself, the *Review Appeal,* came only three times a week and covered really no more than local stuff. Ronnie had told me that this made it a whole other world of newspapers. On the last day he trained me, he was telling me as straight as he could, he said. "People don't fuck around with their news. They wanna know what's happenin' to 'em, when it happened and who did it. I guess maybe it gives 'em some kinda idea about what's goin' on around 'em. I think it's especially been that way since Pearl Harbor. Who might the goddam Japs bomb next? Hell, I forgot people's papers a coupl'a times and they called and raised holy hell at the paper office. Ole Jack Charles about put his foot up my ass."

The next night when Lucky got the phone call, I knew what it was about. "We'll take care of it in the mornin'," I heard him say as he hung up. I glanced into the kitchen, where the only phone was, and saw him looking at my mother dumfounded. I tried to get back around the corner before he saw me.

"Henry?" he half-hollered.

"Yessir," I said.

"Would you come outside with me a minute?"

"Yessir," I said again.

"That was Jack Charles," he told me when were outside underneath the oaks and elms in the backyard.

"Yessir?" I said.

He scuffed his feet at something in the grass and fished for his cigarettes in his pocket. They had yet to take their heavy toll on him, to leave a loose heaviness in his lungs. "He said that eighty-four people didn't get their paper this morning."

I figured playing dumb had to be better than anything else I could try. "Really?" I offered.

"Really," he said. "He said not only did eighty-four people not get their paper, but they found almost a hundred papers dumped out in the alley behind the paper office. Do you know anything about that?"

I wanted to blame it on Ronnie Langford, that he had wanted to talk about his girlfriend more than he wanted to teach me where the papers went. I wanted to blame it on Jack Charles because he had sent me out that morning not having any idea of whether I could do the job or not. I wanted to blame it on Lucky for making me try to do this when I was only eight turning nine.

"I got robbed," I told him. "A man stuck me up behind the paper office and told me if I didn't give him my papers then he'd shoot me.

"Why didn't you tell me that before?" he said. He wouldn't look at me, but cut his eyes to the floor.

Because I'm lying, I thought. "Because I was afraid," I told him.

The next morning found us throwing papers in Lucky's car. He drove and looked at a sheet Jack Charles had written the names and addresses on, and I threw the papers where he told me. Jack Charles had made quite an exhaustive list. I guess anything was better than having to hand-deliver eighty-four papers the day before. Lucky never mentioned the lie I had told him the evening before; just drove and read, drove and read.

THAT EVENING when he arrived home, he simply went straight to his chair in the living room, sat there like usual. Perhaps he was ashamed of what he had done or what people thought. Or maybe of what he was about to do.

"How was your day, Dillard?" my mother chirped as he passed her by at the stove.

He grunted, kept moving.

I moved into the living room and sat in the floor by him. In years to come I would pick up the cues I didn't then.

Lucky lit a Lucky and stared into the stucco wall. "We still missed two goddam papers. The Finchs' and the Birdsongs'. Jack Charles called me down at the station and told me that."

Truth be known, I suspected Jack Charles had told him at the craps game at the filling station while they bent over the dice. Truth be known, the other men there probably laughed at the situation, that his son was a dumbass.

"How'd we miss those two? Didn't we go over the list, name by name?"

"Yessir."

My mother called from the kitchen, told us that dinner would be ready in five or so minutes. Jean was at a friend's house. It was just us.

"You didn't see that robber again today, did ya?"

What robber? I thought. I remembered, then told him, "You know, this mornin' I saw somebody that kinda looked like him."

"Where'd you see 'im?" he said.

"Somewhere we were this mornin'," I said. "I think maybe it was near the same spot it was yesterday."

I could hear my mother banging and rattling around in the kitchen. I prayed that she would tell us dinner was ready now. This was his way. It was never direct.

He snuffed out a cigarette in the ashtray by his chair. "Do you know how we got ink on the upholstery in the car?"

I had to think what car he was talking about. I didn't answer quick enough.

"On the roof ... by the rearview mirror?"

"You told me that's where we ought'a put the rubber bands so we could run the paper through them," I said. He had told me that the papers would hold better if we rubber-banded them. Told me that Ronnie Langford was a dumbass again ... for not playing football, for getting his ass in trouble with his daddy, for thinking about marrying the whore he was. He was loud enough now that I knew Mama could hear him in the next room. I suspected that dinner was ready, but she would wait until he got through with me. Or it would be her, too. In the years previous, she had tried to stop it several times, only to get what I got.

"I didn't tell you that. Don't blame it on me," said Lucky.

"Look here—" he'd said, "this is the easiest way to do it. I don't care what dumbass said."

"He don't even use rubber bands," I'd told him. "He said that the tri-fold is the 'best damn way.'"

Lucky, for reasons unbeknownst to me, had been in a good mood that morning. His good moods normally had wide openings for cussing and laughing. At least when we weren't around my mother and sister.

"See –" he'd said, "just run 'em right through here. Roll 'em and then double the rubber band around 'em. They throw better this way, too. I've seen how most of 'em throw these things."

I didn't tell him what Ronnie said.

"Okay … yessir," I'd said.

"What I'm worried about is that goddam ink on the roof … the ceiling. That shit might not ever come off there."

He'd used our car, then a thirty-eight Ford, to carry me around that morning, because he hadn't wanted to his boss, Chief of Police Oscar Garrett, to see him using his police car while off duty. Or anyone around town to report having seen him doing it. Oscar Garrett, before he collapsed and died of that heart attack, had been like my father's second father. As a matter of fact, Lucky talked to him more than he talked to his own old man, who lived ten miles away.

"I didn't see anything on it this morning when I got out," I said. Which was true.

"Was the fuckin' sun shinin' when you got out of the car?" he said.

I should have known better. These kinds of questions weren't questions. Simply, bait.

"It was gettin' to be daylight, yessir," I answered.

"So you saw that there wasn't any goddam ink on the ceilin' of the car?" he said. His voice was starting to tremble.

"Dillard, you and Henry come on and eat," she said. She was a fucking professional at play-acting. Making like things weren't going on. "The potatoes are startin' to get cold."

From the living room, I could smell the mashed potatoes—they had been my favorite food as long as I could remember. I could smell the chicken my mother had finished frying ten minutes before. I knew there'd be biscuits. With Jean gone at her friend's and this meal—Lucky's favorite—I knew that my mother must have talked to him earlier in the day, after he had become convinced there was ink on his goddam ceiling. After his day had turned shitty and he had decided he was going to come home and take it out on me.

"We'll be there in a minute," he said. "Your son and I are havin' a little disagreement." He turned his eyes back to me. His speed of speech was more rapid now. "So you didn't see any goddamned ink on the roof? Are you sayin' I'm a fuckin' liar?"

"No sir," I offered. But an answer at this point made no difference. The content of what was said served only as fodder. The only fact that mattered now was that he was the powerful one, both in relationship and stature.

"I'm not a fucking liar," he said, coming out of his chair with one push. After the three steps that covered the distance between us, he peered down at me, still seated. I could feel myself grasping the arms of the chair, the roughness of the embroidered pattern under my squeezing fingers. I could feel my fingers, like leaves blowing loose from an autumn tree, releasing the chair I was sitting in as the force pulled me out and then toward him. In a moment quicker than I could even focus my eyes, I was neither on the chair nor the floor, as he had me by some combination of the shoulders and shirt. My neck snapped back hard from the one abrupt shake.

"I'm not a fucking liar! Do you understand me?"

"Dillard, put him down," I heard my mother's voice say from the other room. "You know it's not right to harm somebody smaller than you. To take out your anger about who knows what on him just because he's here. He's just a boy, Dillard. Just eight … or well, nine. Don't you understand that? He shouldn't have to work anyway! You've done this to me before!

You've done it to me for the last time! To him for the last time! This is where it stops! Do you hear me!?"

I could feel the skin on my shoulder ripping as I heard my mother's voice, still imagined, continue.

"The only one in this house you don't treat like this at your whim is Jean. She's your little angel. I know, though, that if you were married to her or she was a boy then you'd do her the same way."

I could hear the sounds as I moved from the chair to the couch, across the coffee table in my way. I could even hear the sound of the open-handed blows. Lucky had promised me that he would never hit me with his fist. The discipline would always be open handed, he had promised at one point.

THE FOLLOWING DAY my mother took a picture of me and my dog Pepper on the front stoop of our house. I'll never know why she took that goddamned picture. I had been in a fight, she said, when she was showing the picture to someone after a month or so had elapsed. I was like my daddy, I was a scrapper. Took things to heart that people said about me. And I really think she believed it. I really think she made herself believe that bruise that started above my eye and ran three quarters of the way down my cheek was from a fight I had been in at school. I really do.

CHAPTER SEVEN

By the time I was seventeen, the Indian was like a plane and the papers were like the fucking missiles launched from it. That route was almost as close to me as my own breathing. I felt like I could have thrown them in my sleep, which a lot of mornings I think I did. I'd had only a couple of complaints about me over the last couple of years—when I hit a door so hard with a paper that it knocked something off the shelf inside. According to Mrs. Barnes, this old widow that lived down Adams, I had knocked an antique "voz"—was how she said it—off the shelf and shattered it into a million pieces. Jack Charles about kicked me in the ass because the paper's insurance had to pay for the damn thing and according to him, it was likely to make the premium go up.

I could run the whole route in a little over an hour now. A half an hour at the paper office getting the stuff ready (tri-folding and putting them in separate bags that hung off the Indian) and then five minutes to get to the start of the route. I could have it all done in a little under two hours. The only problems I had now were when it was cold. "Cold as a well digger's ass" or "Cold as a witch's titty," which was one of Lucky's personal favorites. The hour and a half on the coldest mornings seemed like it took five or six hours.

Seeing my breath as I left my house and headed to the paper office to start my folding and bagging, I knew it had to be around twenty degrees. Every time I'd breathe out, the air in front of me would turn white and shroud my face for a moment and then disappear as I moved down Adams at thirty miles an hour. Lucky had warned me at least half a dozen times, the ethical son of a bitch he was, that he'd give me a ticket like anybody else; that he'd not spare me because I was his son. As I turned off Adams and onto Seventh Avenue, I tried to remember if he had said anything mean like that to me since Percy died. I couldn't.

When I got there in the mornings, it was always the same guys in the paper office. Raymond Collins, a fellow Academy student and asshole, Ralph Thompson, who went to Franklin High School and who I always thought might be a couple of bricks shy of a full load, and Chester Mott, a guy who was between thirty-five and forty and ran the rural route in the morning and delivered every *Nashville Banner* (the evening paper) in Franklin. All four routes.

"Good of ya to show up, Hall," Raymond Collins said as I walked in. "He thinks cause he's the sheriff's son that he can get away with fuckin' murder. Oops. That's a bad word to say around town this mornin'," he laughed.

"He's the Chief of Police, not the sheriff," I said. "And it *is* a bad word to say around town this mornin'."

Collins sat on the floor, rolling his papers as he always did. He was starting to get a little hunch-backed already. He had one of those bodies that was smooth all over. Not really fat but not a bit of muscle tone either. He had been a tight end on the football team ever since I had played.

"Your shoulder better, Hall?" he asked.

I sat on the floor and started tri-folding and bagging, ignoring him. The floor in the paper office was tile and looked as old as the building itself. Probably built around the turn of the century, when it seemed a lot of the stuff up and down Main Street had been built. Halfway between the Great Depression and the South's first great depression, the Civil War. Thoughts like this always brought to mind my uncle; I could hear his voice telling me.

"I don't know," I told Collins.

"Word is you might still play the last coupl'a games of the season," he said. He laughed a laugh that made me think of Van.

I didn't answer him. "Word is" was one of the worst ways I knew to start a sentence. Hell, I didn't even know if they'd have the games after what the last couple of days had brought around.

"What the fuck are you doin' over there, Thompson?" Collins hollered.

Ralph was about finished with his banding and bagging—he was a rubber-band man—and was starting to load his bags on his shoulders. He usually had about five bags like me.

"I'm gettin' ready to deliver my papers, that's what," he said. Ralph's voice always sounded like it might break at any moment. Into stuttering. Into crying. Into something, I just wasn't sure what.

"You got your Dodge out there in the parking lot?" Collins asked.

"Yeah," he said.

Ralph Thompson drove a Dodge just under the age of Methuselah.

"Is it still runnin'?"

"Why, yes," he said.

"You know," said Collins, Ralph now standing in the doorway listening to him, "somebody tells me that they saw that goddamned car leaving the high school early yesterday. Where'd you go after you threw your papers?"

"To school," said Ralph. Standing there in the doorway, tall and skinny, listening to Raymond the asshole Collins, I knew that he didn't know he could leave. That he could just give him the finger, a fine "fuck you," and turn around and walk out.

"Leave him alone," I told Collins.

"Maybe your car was there, too, Hall. Oh, I'm sorry, it wouldn't have been your car. I forget that you don't have one. You know, as a matter of fact, I'm sure that I saw that goddam Indian there before anybody else got there."

"You didn't see my bike there," I told him.

With Collins' attention off him, Ralph pulled his bags over his shoulder and made his way out the door while he could. Chester Mott sat in the far corner, all business, too old for Collins to bother.

"Oh, are you a badass now? Your ‚bike'?"

"Why don't you just shut your ass and do your job?" I said.

"Just jokin', Hall," he said. "No big deal. Just tryin' to make a bad situation a little better, that's all."

"It's nothin' to laugh about," I told him. If he only knew what she had looked like, had seen the slits in her throat, had known—and I mean, really known—that one human being could do this to another, he wouldn't be laughing about it.

"We all know who did it," he pronounced. "It was that fuckin' nigger at the high school. It don't take a scientist to figure that one out. Even your old man ought'a be able to get that one. Look right here, it even says that in the goddam *Tennessean*."

He held the paper up and pointed to an article on the lower right side of the front page. "WOMAN FOUND DEAD BEHIND HIGH SCHOOL IN FRANKLIN—NEGRO JAILED."

"They even got a coupl'a quotes from your old man in here. He's quite the wordsmith."

As Lucky did in most other areas of my life, and as he almost always did when he was quoted in the paper, I was certain what he said would probably embarrass me.

"Look here–" Collins said, holding up the article so I could see for myself, "'Dillard Hall says that he only arrested Jackson Mosby because he had suspicions of his guilt … that no one is guilty until they're proved that way by a court.' No shit?"

I looked at neither Collins nor the newspaper he held in front of him. I didn't want to see what Lucky had said. I didn't want to look at Raymond Collins, afraid I might try to break his fat, flabby jaw. Neither did I speak to him what Lucky had told me the night before. I was trying to get my shit together and get out of there as fast as I could.

"Hey—" Collins said as I was starting to make my way toward the door.

Jack Charles stuck his head out of his office and interrupted him. "A little less talking and more foldin' and baggin'. Don't want nobody callin' me and tellin' me their paperboy didn't throw their paper 'cause he got robbed in the alley." He'd never let me live that one down. Lucky had reported it to him about a week later, after he had cooled off, after my head had started to heal, the blood from the bruise dissipate.

I held my bags up and shook them at him. He cut his eyes out his office window at Collins like he knew he was a lazy ass. I turned my eyes to Collins for the first time that morning. A mistake.

"Hey, Manor and Chester and me are gonna get some beer and go to the Confederate Cemetery Friday night. Some smokes, too. You know, he's workin' at the store now, since his daddy has had that fuckin' back trouble and his uncle don't work there as much anymore. He can get all the shit we want. You wanna go? You wanna see if Tully wants to go?"

Tully was one of the few public schoolboys included in the crowd that could run with these guys. Somehow his personality helped him cross most lines.

"I'll ask him," I told him, the wind from the slightly opened door pushing at my back. Dreading walking out the door and climbing on that motorcycle. "But I can't go...."

"Oh yeah," he said. "I forgot that's the night you see your hunny on the weekend. Poke that little tight ass. Well, I'm not so sure it's so tight anymore," he laughed. That goddam Van laugh.

Before I knew what had come over me, I had dropped my bags and hit him at a dead run. Pinned him to the wall outside Jack Charles's office. Then we had fallen to the floor and I could feel the collar of his shirt ripping in my hands. I could also feel his hands as he struggled to get a hold of my short hair and then grabbed me by the ear. I could feel my knuckles as they began to move themselves into his forehead, once, twice, three times. He kneed me in the stomach and then the groin to get me off him. Then with a shove, he sent me three or four feet away from him. I could taste the blood in my mouth from biting my tongue when we hit the floor. Before he could get up, I was on him again. Mr. Charles grabbed me by the collar and pulled me off.

"Goddamnit, Hall," he said, "leave him alone! What the hell's wrong with you? He's almost twice your size. You ain't no bigger than your daddy was at your age." He had gotten his hands around my rib cage and was holding my feet off the floor. Blood dripped from one of Collins' nostrils.

"Come on, motherfucker," he told me. "I'll break your fucking neck. I'll tear that goddam shoulder out'a the socket again. Let his ass go, Jack. I want all hun'red and thirty pounds of him."

"I'll give you all hundred and thirty fuckin' pounds of me!" I hollered. Still trying to get loose of Jack Charles' grasp.

"Fuck you!" Collins said. "Mr. Charles, let him go."

But he didn't have the look in his eye that said he meant it. On this day, he didn't want to whip my ass. Didn't have the heart for it.

Mr. Charles still had my feet off the floor. "Goddamnit, Henry, stop kickin'. You've bruised my shin in two or three places."

I struggled harder to get free. Mr. Charles locked down harder. "Mott," he yelled to Chester, who, that I'd seen, hadn't moved, "get over there to the phone and call Lucky Hall and tell him to get his ass down here. Tell him his boy and another Academy boy are about to have at it ... already drawn blood from each other."

Chester Mott moved from the corner where he'd been, toward Mr. Charles' office.

"You gonna fight anymore?" Mr. Charles asked me.

"If he wants to," I said.

Like this thing I didn't understand had overtaken me, I felt myself pulling against Mr. Charles' grasp almost against my own will.

"Mott, get that phone and start dialin'," he yelled to Chester. Chester, who seemed to deem most all contact with other human beings bothersome or maybe even hurtful, sheepishly stepped into Mr. Charles' office and picked up the phone.

"Dial!" yelled Jack Charles. And I could feel my own body melting beneath his grasp. Softer...softer...softer.

Chester stuck his head out of the office. "I don't know the number," he said.

As MOST THINGS SEEM TO BE, throwing these papers had been the damnation and salvation of my shoulder. They were probably what wore it out in the first place, and probably what caused me to push through the pain to make it functional again. As well, they had been the thing that got me out of the house every morning, brought me two hours by myself no matter what. The thing I had to get up and do no matter what. The thing, also, that made my days twelve, thirteen hours long every day, as long as I could remember. On this day, though, the adrenaline pushed through me so hard that I couldn't feel a thing. Well, besides the grasp I had on the paper, tightening as I drew my arm back and cocked my hand over my shoulder, then beginning to loosen as my arm moved forward and then the final twist of my hand as my arm came to the place where my thumb and first two fingers released and the son of a bitch went flying. Right in front of me, taking every paper in the chest was Raymond Collins.

I had gotten used to riding the Indian with one arm. The only trick was that I had to stay in the same gear, and being right-handed, steer with my left hand—where the clutch is—while I let off the gas and fired each paper. Speed up, hand off the throttle, throw a paper, do the same again. Over and over and over. Down Lewisburg Pike and Adams Street after I left the paper office, then to the sporadic housing on the southside of town, then back down Main Street (or Columbia Avenue it was called there) through the "mixed" section of town, then to the west side of town, and then north. By the jail. Or at least two blocks from it.

I THREW THE INDIAN IN LOW GEAR and coasted, then I let completely off the throttle so there wouldn't be a sound that would give me away. Still pretty much pitch dark at 5 o'clock in the morning, the street, the town for the moment, had a quietness that almost anything would shatter like a rock through a storefront window. The jail backed up against the river just after it crossed what people outside of Franklin called Franklin Road, what we in Franklin called Nashville Pike. On the west side of the jail was the auction barn Sammy Samuels ran, Lucky's crap shooting buddy. The filling station where they shot craps was just up First Avenue, where it met Nashville Pike. Samuels' Auction Barn made a business of making money on dead people's things. Estate Sales, that kind of thing. A lot of times, I suspected that's why Lucky went to work so early, to smoke cigarettes and drink coffee with Sammy Samuels. But there hadn't been any smoking and drinking coffee on this morning, even any pouring a little whiskey in the coffee, which they might have needed today and which I had often seen them do. At least not for Lucky.

Sammy Samuels stood at the bottom of the four steps that led from the gravel parking lot to the front door of the jail. Behind him were several men, some of whom I recognized, some of whom I didn't. Paul Chester Sr., John Harvey, a foreman down at the stove pipe factory just out of town. The other five or six were further behind them, away from the light that illuminated the parking lot. From them stepped James Langford, Ronnie Langford's father. He was a large man, like Ronnie had been. Blocky more than tall. Big, barrel-chest, skinny hips compared to the rest of him. I bet I hadn't seen him a handful of times since Ronnie had left. Rather than eight years, he looked like he might have aged going on twenty. In the moment I saw him step out of the darkness and toward the yellow light hung on the side of the jail building, I remembered that Lucky had told me several times that he had been to his house to break up quarrels between his wife and him.

I shut the Indian down and rolled to a stop fifty or so feet away from the gathering. As far as I could tell Lucky was nowhere to be seen. It looked and sounded like the men were talking among themselves.

"How come he didn't come over and drink coffee with us this mornin'?" Paul Chester Sr. asked. He was red and ruddy like his son, the boy who got us the beer at the fucking Academy. The boy whose education was paid by the fact kids came from two and three counties away to buy beer underage. The boy of the father whose ass was kept safe by my father. It was one of Lucky's best, most endearing features.

"I don't know," Sammy said. "I'd thought he would'a. Who can remember the last time that Lucky hadn't been over to the barn to have a cup 'a coffee with us?"

"Yeah," said John Harvey. I guess John Harvey stopped by in the morning on his way to the stove pipe factory, which held at least half of Franklin's manual laborers.

James Langford had about made his way up the side of the small crowd now. He would normally not have been among the frontrunners of these men; he was just an electrician who worked for McFadden's Electric on the west edge of town. He normally wasn't a part of this good ole boy club. Perhaps, though, his son and what had happened to him, along with the fact that he had "lost his mind" since, had elevated his status.

"They still sayin' it was that woman that lived over in the Burgess house?" asked Sammy Samuels, smoke leaving his mouth and rising with the rhythm of his words.

"Yeah, that Mary Ivy woman," said James Langford as he finally made his way to the front of the men. He'd been fiddling with his britches, working his khaki pants out of his boot tops and down over the sides. "She was a little touched in the fuckin' head if you asked me," he said, straightening the hat on his head, tilted to one side from the work he had done on his boots.

Paul Chester Sr. and John Harvey laughed like people do when they realize something's funny and somebody else doesn't. Strong, hardy laughter trailing into shame when you figure out the butt of the laughter is laughing too.

By now, Sammy Samuels had made his way up the steps and was peering in the one window on the side door to the jailhouse. "I don't see his fat ass in there anywhere. He's probably back there talkin' to him. You know, he's always been kinda soft on coons. That's the reason that I always thought Chief Garrett should'a backed somebody else when it come to them appointin' somebody Police Chief."

I was sure that Lucky knew Sammy Samuels thought all of this—and I was equally as sure that Sammy would never say any of it to Lucky himself. Affection between these men was a lot like hospitality in Franklin, I suspected, just deep enough that you couldn't see what was underneath it. Never spoken.

Lucky opened the door just as Sammy Samuels had his face pressed against the small piece of glass at its center.

"Goddam, Lucky, you hit me right in the head with the damn door," he protested, rubbing his nose, his jaw, where the contact had been.

"What ya doin' lookin' in the door anyway?" asked Lucky.

"Lookin' for your ass," spoke Sammy. "You didn't come over and drink coffee with us this mornin'."

"I kinda had things to do," said Lucky. As with anytime he felt anxiety, or anything else for that matter, he lit a Lucky.

"You found that other nigger yet?" asked Sammy, who now lit a cigarette himself. A Chesterfield. He cupped his hand around his mouth and stuck the match to the cigarette, then fanned the match out like I'd seen him do a thousand times, it seemed.

"Nope, not yet," Lucky laughed. "I'm on the case though."

"You goin' to get him in a little while?" Sammy asked.

"Yeah, I'm gonna go out and check on several leads in a little while," Lucky said. He crimped his cigarette between his middle and forefingers like I *know* I had seen *him* do a thousand times. Blew out a grey cloud that dissipated from around his face as he began to speak.

"Who ya got with ya down there?"

Sammy turned and glared down at them, squinting like he couldn't tell … didn't know.

"Hey, Paul. Hey, John. Hey, James."

The other men were still standing far enough back and it was still dark enough that I assume they were unidentifiable from where he stood. That or he didn't want to know.

"Hey, Lucky," said Paul. John Harvey echoed him.

"How are things down at the plant?" Lucky asked John Harvey.

"Fine … fine," said John Harvey. "Can't complain a lick. Wouldn't do any good if I did."

"Everybody get home all right yesterd'y evenin'?" Lucky asked.

"Far as I know," said John.

"How 'bout with you, Paul?" Lucky said. "Everything all right down at the store?"

"Believe so," he said. "Didn't have any problems yesterd'y."

Yeah, I thought, I'm sure he didn't. His damn sales had probably been quadrupled because Franklin High School and the Academy had both been out. The kids had probably poured through there like water.

"Hell," said Lucky, "y'all must be the exception then. I think most'a the town rolled up the sidewalks long about two o'clock yesterd'y afternoon. You'd'a thought it was Wednesday."

Even though the mood was tense as hell, everybody there laughed. It was true, Franklin shut down as tight as a jug on Wednesday afternoon. The only things that stayed open were the groceries.

"Did you ever find out who she is?" Sammy asked.

"Ain't yet," said Lucky. "I'm plannin' on goin' over there this mornin'."

"Damn, Lucky! What you been doin'!?" exclaimed Sammy.

"I been workin' in there," said my father. "Makin' plans for the day. Since when did you become the fuckin' mayor? Ain't there nobody else dead in Franklin for you to worry about? Can't you go talk some old widow woman out'a her things while she's still alive? You've done that pretty well more than a few times."

"You tell me where they are and I'll go talk to 'em," said Sammy. He threw his Chesterfield to the ground and stomped it with his boot.

"I'll be on the lookout," said Lucky. "Hell, I'll do that in my spare time … when I ain't workin' on who slit that woman's throat yesterd'y."

A little laughter rumbled from the other men, then they fell silent. In the moments of emptiness of sound—no cars passing, the dark still trying desperately to hold away the light—was the sound of the river. And with it, every time I heard it, was always the sound of my uncle's voice. His words were never clear, never orderly enough to be made into a coherent sentence; but the sound of his voice was there just the same. I could hear it as clear as I could hear the water passing invisibly between the banks in that cut of earth behind the jail.

"Go in there and get that nigger, Hall," said James Langford.

Sammy turned to look at Mr. Langford. Flinched a little when he saw him. Eyes grew big as his mouth.

"Now wait just a goddam minute, Langford," said Sammy, "this ain't what we talked about. We was just gonna talk to Lucky, see if he'd let us speak to Mosby in person, see if we could get it out of him who helped him. Hell, I hadn't even had a chance to ask him yet. It ain't no need to act all crazy."

"Move out'a the way," said James Langford. Much like I could hear my Uncle Percy's voice in the passing of the river water, I could hear Ronnie Langford's voice—telling me about his "girl," about how to throw papers, about football, about all the things that happened the last time I saw him— in his father's voice.

"Ain't no need to act all crazy, hell!" James said. "There was a dead white woman fount behind Franklin High School yesterd'y mornin' and a nigger they put in jail just a little while thereafter because fuckin' Lucky here had a pretty good idea who done it. It's been said that two niggers was followin' that woman the night before. What else ya need to act crazy?"

It was when James Langford reached the second step that I noticed one of his hands was positioned strangely, like it held something. Sammy Samuels moved aside, so that Lucky was directly in Mr. Langford's line of progression.

"What you gonna do about this shit, Lucky?" he asked.

Lucky, as always, at least with people outside his own family, grew calmer as things grew more tense. His right hand now rested at his side while he propped the door open with his hip. His left hand had moved to Sammy Samuels, in a strange way, either protecting him or moving him out of the way.

"I's just tellin' Sammy here," said Lucky, "that the first thing I'm gonna do is go over to the Burgess house and see about that Ivy woman."

"Whether it was the Ivy woman or not," argued Mr. Langford, "there's still a fuckin' dead woman that they're gettin' ready to put on display like some kinda prime kill from a hunt and there was two niggers that followed her that night. And as far as I know only one a' them boys is in the jail-house."

"That man in the jailhouse ain't guilty until he's proved that way," said Lucky. "And the only reason that we talked about puttin' out the body is because we need to know who the woman is if it ain't Miss Ivy."

I hadn't heard yet of any "body" being out, but if it was out, I knew it would be at the same damn place they put Ronnie out when he came home, where Mr. Langford had insisted they put him at Franklin Memorial Chapel. His boy was a hero, he claimed, and he would be treated like one. Even George Preston, the only and therefore best undertaker around, couldn't make him look presentable. Yet Mr. Langford insisted anyway.

By this time, John Harvey had approached Mr. Langford from behind and begun to try to talk to him. "James," he said, "you know that Lucky here will do the job he's s'posed to do. You know we all want to know what the hell's goin' on."

For the first time I saw the gun clearly enough to know that's in fact what it was. As he waved what looked like a thirty-two caliber pistol over the men below, they flinched each time it passed back and forth. Mr. Langford took another step toward Lucky and Sammy Samuels, brandish-ing the pistol a little more plainly.

"This is still America, ain't it?" he said. "Where the guilty get what's comin' to 'em and the innocent are protected. That's still where we live, ain't it?"

"Far as I know," said Lucky.

"This is between you and Lucky," said Sammy. He slipped by down the stairs and didn't stop until he made his way to the base of the steps and the other men.

"What I want to know," said James Langford, "is how the hell they're gonna put enough makeup on that woman to cover the gash in her throat? Can you tell me that Lucky Dillard? Huh?"

Lucky acted as if Mr. Langford didn't have the small handgun he held in his right hand now, waving as he talked. His eyes were on Mr. Langford's eyes, his sorrow. And, I suspected, his own.

"First of all, Jimmy, I ain't decided that we're gonna put the body out ... 'cause I'm not even sure if we need to. I need to figure out if it's that other woman first, and then–"

"Why ain't you already done that, Hall?" he asked. Like he might have just remembered that Dillard wasn't my father's last name.

"'Cause I had all I could do yesterday dealin' with people like you," he said.

I could tell in the growing daylight that Lucky's patience was starting to grow as thin as the onion paper pages of my mother's Bible. His anger, although it was likely to come slower with the general public, was still as unpredictable as springtime storms. When things seemed their worst, his eyes would brighten and the cloud would often pass. When it all appeared clear, sometimes the thundering anger would come, rush in like pounding rain and hail, gale-force winds.

"Godammit, Jimmy," he said, "you been standin' on the side porch a' the jailhouse for goin' on five, ten minutes, waving a gun around as you spoke. Now, what I suggest is that you put that gun back in your pocket and go back down the steps. 'Cause if you don't, then I'm gonna have to take out my damn gun and—" " What the hell you gonna do with it?" Jimmy Langford now asked. "You gonna whip me with the butt of it like you did your brother? You gonna take me in the jailhouse and do it so's won't nobody see?"

Mr. Langford took a step back like he was surveying the situation, thinking about Lucky's words. Then he laid the gun on the railing, resting his hand on top of it. His voice began to break as he spoke. "Why don't you do that, Hall, Lucky Dillard ... whatever the hell your name is? 'Cause you know the truth, I ain't worth beatin' no more. The last coupl'a times that Ronnie whipped my ass before he left was the last good ass-whuppin's I got. Why don't you do that for me? Do that for me ... do it for him. Do it for his Mama. Do it for your brother. Do it for somebody."

James Langford then took three short, quick steps and was on top of Lucky at the railing. I heard the old wood rail whine as both men's weight rested against it. Heard it crack but not fall as Mr. Langford grabbed somewhere in the vicinity of Lucky's collar with one hand and raised the gun high above his head with the other. Lucky simply tried to protect himself, but didn't reach for his own weapon as Mr. Langford lowered the pistol once, then twice, then a third time on his head and shoulders. Perhaps he would have allowed Jimmy Langford to fire a bullet into him if he had so chosen. Only when John Harvey and Paul Chester Sr. grabbed him did Lucky take the gun out of his hand.

Mr. Langford, who had been screaming the whole time he hit my father, over and over and over, "The goddam guilty should be punished! The innocent ones should be protected!" said nothing, made not a sound, after the two men had wrestled him into their arms and Lucky had taken the pistol from his hand.

Lucky simply stood there and stared at Mr. Langford and shook his head, almost like he couldn't give voice to words that would wrestle the situation into any kind of understanding. As Mr. Chester held one of James Langford's arms and Mr. Harvey held the other, my father studied the men in front of him like they were a still picture, as if time or what would come in the next few days could neither alter nor detract from what was.

CHAPTER EIGHT

S HE HAD BEEN WAITING there in the dark and cold for me for half
an hour the next morning. But she wouldn't be mad, I knew that.
There was something about her, I realized for the first time in my life, that
took whatever I offered. My bike's light flashed quick across the windshield
of the old jalopy she drove and then to her face and then fell moot in the
merging trees and their mostly naked branches.

I pulled the Indian into a tree line that was as close to the river as I could
get. But as far away from the spot—or at least where I imagined it to be—
as I could. In my head, I imagined it to be just down the bank on the last
stand of this flat spot of ground, as the river bank was thick with brush and
mud as it made its way down into the almost black, muddy water of the
Harpeth.

My anticipation for her was so high I couldn't feel the cold on my hands
and face any longer. I forgot that my feet had long ago lost their feeling.
The pounding in my shoulder, ribs, and hands from my run-in with
Raymond Collins had left me. What I had seen with Lucky, Sammy Samuels,
and James Langford had gone from my memory. In my mind was just
Sharon, the vacuum she created. High, round cheek bones, skin that was
neither dark nor light, but mostly olive, almost iridescent. Teeth that were

a little separated in the front. Lips that were as deep red and perfectly shaped as I had ever seen. I could feel myself growing just thinking about what I imagined her face to be.

"Hi," she said when I opened the car door.

I could feel the wind trying to push it shut as I got in. I rested my hand on the inside door handle and didn't let the door slam. "Hey," I said. "How are you, baby?" I leaned across the seat and pressed my lips to hers. She smelled and tasted as good as she always did. Made me grow more. Made me glad I was sitting now.

"I'm okay," she said. She smiled the same way I'll remember if I live to be a hundred and fifty. "How about you?"

"I'm all right," I said. "Cold," I said in my best shivering tone, hoping she wouldn't notice my pants until it shrank.

"It is cold," she said, turning her eyes back out the front windshield, to the stand of trees, the almost darkness they created, directly in front of us. She pulled at the coat that covered her, pushed it up around her neck.

"Does the heat work in this thing?" I asked. Knowing full well it didn't at all, or at least very well.

"It does some," she said. "Aren't you warmer than you were on your motorcycle?"

"Yeah, I guess I am," I said.

"I was starting to worry about you," she said, laying her head on my shoulder.

"I went down to the jail and Lucky and Sammy Samuels and Jimmy Langford had ... they—" But then it seemed not to make one bit of sense in the world to go into it, to report what I had seen. Lucky would be all right, I suspected. As all right as people get, anyway. The same for Jimmy Langford.

I felt my eyes drifting to the spot where I suspected it had happened. I turned my eyes to the distant spot where Tully and I had almost gone in. Replaced, for a moment, the emptiness with quiet laughter to myself.

"Lucky took a gun away from a man and threw it in the river," I told Sharon.

"He what?" she asked. "When?" she said before I could answer.

"This mornin'," I said. "This man had a gun and Lucky took it away from him and walked two hundred feet and threw it in the river behind the jail." I could hear the same river moving past us now a hundred feet away, its water whispering its secrets as it traveled south.

"Is he all right?" she asked.

"Far as I know," I said. "He didn't know I was there."

"He doesn't know a lot about what you do, does he?" she said.

"Why would I tell him?" I asked. "It just gives his ass more ammunition to shell me with."

"How's he doing with all the stuff with the woman?"

"He's all right, I guess," I told her. "He sat up most of the night drunk. That's why I never got to your house."

"That's all right," she said. "I had to go home after I got off anyway. Mama went over next door and called me at work."

By "went over" I knew she meant to Edna Taylor's house and the nearest phone. Down the road, on the edge of the "mixed section," Edna's husband worked for the railroad, let Sharon's mother use the phone when she needed to.

"She said she needed me to come home," she told me. "She said her head was ,swimmin'" so bad that she couldn't take care of Suzy. When I got there, Suzy was sitting in the kitchen by herself in the dark. Mama was in the bedroom layin—I mean, lying on the bed with a washrag—wash cloth over her face."

I pulled myself close to her, across the ragged seat of the old car. I felt a spring poke me in the ass at about the same time my lips touched hers. I jumped and she laughed.

"You need a blanket to go over this seat," I told her. "If you don't get one, one mornin' you're gonna have to take me to the hospital with a spring stickin' out of my ass."

In the silence following her laughing, I thought of that asshole Collins again, of how I could have really been going to the hospital if Mr. Charles hadn't gotten in the middle. How anger fueled me into believing I could do anything. And then when it dissipated, how I knew that my judgment had been bad. But I just wanted to forget this morning, forget the stupidity, forget yesterday. Lose myself in the magic and the warmth of her arms, her....

"I just don't think I can this morning," she said. She put her hands on my chest and pushed me back a couple of inches.

I forced my flashing anger into a shrug of my shoulders. "Why?" I said, trying to sound sympathetic, no matter the cause—knowing as soon as I spoke that I sounded sarcastic.

"I just don't feel very good," she said. She wouldn't look at me now. Kept her eyes out the front window.

"What's wrong?" I said.

I felt good that I had forced my voice into a more even tone, knowing that being nice was probably my only chance. I noticed tears streaming down her cheeks as she spoke.

"All she talks about any more is Sheila," said Sharon. "She called me last night and told me that she'd been into town and seen her. Seen her outside the grocery. I told her that she must have been dreaming. But she swore to it. She's just like her mama that way. Granny was always sure she was seein'—seeing things she didn't actually see. Or at least she would have claimed that she saw them. You know what I mean."

Finally the bulge in my britches had mostly subsided, its tiny brain having given up hope. "I guess," I sighed.

I scanned the river bank, the open field of grass, turned brown from the winter cold. Looked how close Lewisburg Pike ran to the river itself.

"Did your daddy find out who the woman is yet?" she asked me.

I knocked out a cigarette, trading my thoughts of one pleasure for another.

"Naah," I told her. "All's he told me was that he thought it might be that woman from the boardin' house."

I started to tell her what I had heard Lucky and the other men talking about outside the jail. That they were going to put the body out if it wasn't her. Then I thought better of it. Remembered how I had seen her at her daddy and sister's funeral. Unlike Ronnie Langford at Jimmy's request, both the caskets closed, there side by side. Her mother too incapacitated to do much of anything. Suzy, nine years old, hanging onto her sister Sharon like she was her mother. For all practical purposes, I guess she was.

"I hope they find out who she is," she said.

In the silence that settled between us, she scooted toward me and laid her head on my shoulder. The impulse arose in me again, but this time I tried to fight it. I knew it would make me feel better, but probably make her feel worse. Like so many people, we had an unspoken trade. I was her emotional prop; she gave me what I needed … or at least wanted.

"Yeah, me too," I said.

I started to tell her in that same silence of how I had been in a fight with Raymond Collins that morning, how I had defended her honor. But I figured this would hurt her, too. It's my experience that it's the truest things that make us mad enough to fight, that hurt us the most.

I stroked her hair as her head rested on my shoulder. Her smell was the best thing I could ever imagine. Her softness. She nuzzled her shoulder into my chest.

"What'd you do last night?" I asked her.

"I told you while ago," she said. "I worked like I always do and then I went home as quick as I could because of Mama."

"So you did go home when she asked you to?"

I checked my cigarette, flicked some ashes in the dashboard ashtray.

"I got Teresa—you know, the girl who works over in sportswear—to close my register and I left right after they locked the doors."

"Was Mr. Smith mad at ya?" I asked.

"No, he's a really good boss. He tries to work with me. He knows we're going through a hard time right now."

She had tightened, raised her head up for a few moments. Lowered it again.

"Prob'ly ,cause he's got a hard-on for ya," I told her. "He prob'ly goes back in the stock room and strokes the thing while he's watching you out the door."

She sat up a little and smiled one of those smiles that's really not one.

"He's got a wife and three kids," she said.

"All the more reason he prob'ly does what I said," I told her. I reached over and cranked down the window a couple of inches and threw my mostly smoked cigarette out. Thought how Paul Chester was due to get us some more. How Van had got us hooked up in that situation to begin with. Son of a bitch. Heard Raymond Collins's big fucking mouth again. Saw those bulging eyes. Felt my fists wrapped up in his shirt collar.

"You don't ever go anywhere with him, do ya?"

"Mr. Smith?" she said.

"No!" she said. She returned her hand from my leg to her own lap.

"Don't answer like I'm stupid," I said. "It's not like you haven't before."

"I haven't since you got so mad that time. Since you threatened to go talk to him. It's like I told you when you got mad at me last night—I can't afford to lose my job. Mama just works at a school cafeteria and doesn't… Daddy didn't have any life insurance. We're about one check away from not being able to pay for that godforsaken house we live in. I know you and Van thought it was pretty funny. But it's a roof over our head."

It flashed through my head, what Van had said about it that had somehow gotten back to Sharon—that you could spit from one side of it to the other. Proved what an asshole he was. I pushed the thought away, focused on other discontent. Fear.

"So you haven't gone anywhere with him?"

"No, not since he asked me to a couple of months ago when he was having trouble with his wife."

Out the front window, the sun was starting to come up on the river, throw its strange light down its surface. Too many colors to say. Overall, one color I couldn't define or put a word on.

"You'll believe anything," I told her. "Trouble with a wife. Don't you know that's what men tell young girls when they want to reel ,em in?" Or at least that's what Lucky had told me.

"I just know he never bothered me," she said.

"And I guess Van didn't either, did he?"

She didn't answer. I assume she was smart enough by now to know it was one she would always lose. I knew all the details. Both he and she had told me. Him, bragging. Her, when I asked her. Over and over and over again.

"Huh?"

"I dated Van," she said.

"From what he said there wasn't much datin' to it."

In the beginning, she had told me the details. I had asked for them, wanting to know if what he had said was true. Why she had done it.

"I didn't know if you liked me. You wouldn't come out and say it."

"I held your hand over the seat, didn't I?"

"Yeah … and you went to my dance with me. Do you remember what a good time we had?"

Her hand moved up and down my inner thigh. I could feel myself coming alive again. And I didn't want to.

"It was all right," I said.

"It must have been more than all right," she said.

The truth be told, the feeling had been more intoxicating than anything I'd ever known. A dozen times as strong as a drunk at the Willow Plunge with Van and Tully and Chester and that asshole Collins. So captivating it felt like it might take my breath. That it took all my thoughts. Every thought carried with it an image of her face or the smell of her or what it felt like when she touched me. What it had felt like when she had taken my hand and led me to the floor to slow-dance, the band playing Perry Como's "No Other Love" while she laid her head on my shoulder and wrapped her arms around me. And even though I had never before felt the feeling that developed in me over those few hours, I quickly decided I could never again live without it. As I rolled up in front of their clapboard house on the edge of the "mixed" section of town in the car Lucky had let me borrow that night, I didn't want to let her out. Of the car or my sight.

"I had a really good time," she told me as she leaned toward me across the couch-like seat.

"I did, too," I had told her.

I was on my best behavior. Wore the only suit I had. No cussing. We had been together six hours by this point. Dinner at this restaurant in Nashville, the dance, sitting at a table with Tully and his date, Christine King. Me, faking—and probably not too well—like I could dance when she talked me into going out onto the gym floor turned dance floor for the night. A ride out through the springtime country after we left the dance. Making out in a church parking lot at the edge of a milky glow thrown by a light on the other side of the parking lot.

She pressed her lips to mine in the car in front of her house.

"Won't your daddy see us?" I had asked her.

"He goes to bed early."

I had begun to notice how she articulated her words so carefully. Tried so hard to speak proper. Before I could think much about it, I'd lost myself in kissing her again. Listening to her breathe as her head lay on my chest. Sitting with her until the night became so quiet and still around us that I felt like a part of it. Like a part of everything that ever was or would be. Even that night, if I could have pulled our bodies together as one, I would have. It was as if her broken edges fit my own.

PERCY WAS SO DIFFERENT from Lucky, both in size and temperament, his long frame stretched out to six foot three or four, most of it legs. Everybody else I knew anything of in the Hall family had long torsos, short legs. He walked with his hands in his pockets most of the time. His eyes, downcast. Watching the ground as it moved under him, his old boots as they moved across the earth of Franklin.

His clothes hung off him where in the last few years he had dropped twenty pounds he still needed. And though Lucky tried to get him to Frank's on Main at least once every two or three months, his hair always hung across his forehead into his face. At one point, though I couldn't remember exactly when, Lucky had thought it a good idea for him to live with us. But those days had quickly passed. Nevertheless, the pattern had mostly continued.

Jean had gotten her own goddam bedroom because they moved my crazy-ass uncle upstairs with me. In the first year he lived with us, he began to take me to the river with him, show me "how the water flowed," he said. "Most people don't want to know how the water flows," he told me.

"Everything comes from a combination of three things: randomness, a planned nature of things and human frailty. You take the ground on which we sit," he said, pointing to the earth beneath us, smoke rising from the stub of a cigarette in his pinched, yellow fingers. "It's covered with the blood of your relatives … my relatives. Of the men who came down here to try to straighten our asses out. Why?" he asked.

"Number one," he answered his own question, "because of the belief in this country that capitalism is *the way*, even almost a hundred years ago. The South's whole economy was based on work that slaves did. The money they could make from having people do your work for free after you bought them. Like we're all flawed people, it was a flawed philosophy. We're still sufferin' from it now; prob'ly still will be in a hundred years. Then you take Sherman's march. Human Frailty, too. Human behavior is always imperfect, done from a limited perspective. He had lived a long, bloody, tiresome war. By the time he made his way through the South, he was one angry son of a bitch, that General William Tecumseh Sherman. Of course, they were good battle plans, to cut off a great deal of the South from itself. Good enough plans that they made Lee rethink what he had to do."

He stared into the river for a few moments, its water bubbling quietly, its current moving undetected, silent.

"And Hood was a doped-up bastard. On that laudanum, they think. With a stub for a leg and a mangled, useless arm. Chickamauga had about finished him off anyway."

Uncle Percy reached to pull his cigarette to his mouth, but then realized he hadn't one. Hiking up one britches' leg, he pulled them out of his sock. He knocked one out of the pack with his long, thin fingers and raised it to his lips.

"So you had Sherman's anger, Lee's knowledge that he was at the edge of the bottomless chasm of defeat and Hood's basic frailty, fueled by the damn dope he was on. All of it caused by a flawed system to begin with. They all had their plans, too. Sherman's had been completed. Lee's was just a hope, peterin' out with every confederate that fell. And Hood's was just crazy as hell. I guess he was, too.

"Hood came up through Alabama, stopped only long enough to fight a skirmish. Then crossed the Tennessee River and the state line. Up through Pulaski to Columbia, he went. Tryin' to keep Thomas and Schofield's men from getting to Nashville. On the way through, they stopped to camp. Patrick Cleburne, the man the street you live on was named after, said as he looked at a church in the grove they camped by—'If I should happen to die in battle, I should like nothing better than to be buried here.' A week later, he was, along with Granberry and Strahl and so many others. Go look at that cemetery some time. Read the stones of the dead who still walk among us because they can't rest.

"And this very river played a part in it—the Harpeth! A river that was cut in this ground from the very beginnings of time. Franklin was built, facing south in the big bend in this river. Either army that made it through had to cross the river. When Hood had left Georgia and come up through Alabama, he was ahead of the Federals. For him to be able to pull off the plan that Lee and he had made, he had to get to Nashville before they did. But first he had to do the same at Franklin.

"But what did Hood do? So sure that he had everything perfect, he stopped outside of Franklin and bedded down. Now, it wasn't like his troops didn't need it. It was late November, cold…a lot of them didn't have shoes or coats. But they slept good because they had pushed so hard from Georgia. They laid down on that cold ground south of Franklin and huddled under their blankets and slept."

CHAPTER NINE

F ROM THE PARKING LOT to the shrubs to the scrubbed concrete
front porch, Franklin Memorial Chapel was pristine. The white paint
on the brick and clapboard of its facade was redone every spring. The black,
iron rails around the front porch re-blacked every season as well. Inside,
double front doors led to a floor that was finely carpeted and stretched itself
out as a kind of wide hall or lobby. Initially, off it was a room on each side—
both used by the families to find peace from visitation or to argue about
something that was or was not going to be put in the service. Behind these
rooms, on both sides of the hall, was seventy-five feet of white walls. The
doors to the visitation rooms these walls hid were a good hundred feet from
the front door. One on each side: "Celestial Gardens" and "The Zion
Room."

George Preston, the man who ran "The Chapel," as it was referred to by
most people around town, was dark-haired and pale man and lived alone
above the funeral home. Ever since I could remember, it had been rumored
that he was "queer as a three-dollar bill." His hands and handshake softer
than his quiet voice, he'd make eye-contact for only a few seconds before he
turned his gaze politely to the ground. His hand would then usually find its

way to your shoulder and comfort you. A well-respected Church of Christ deacon, and I reckon, a closet homosexual who had moved several "poor boys" in with him and out over the years, he just about had a corner on the market of death in Franklin. Franklin, Spring Hill, and part of Brentwood for that matter.

With both the Academy and Franklin out that day, I had gone with Lucky as he talked to Mr. Preston about what he needed him to do. I swear, it looked like he hadn't seen sunshine since 1949.

"Absolutely not," he told Lucky. "I cannot do that. It would make a mockery of death. A mockery of my place of business. This is not a show-room. It's a place where loved ones are laid to rest."

"I know that's what it says on your business cards and in the phone book, George, but that doesn't meet our particular need now. Evidently, this woman didn't have any 'loved ones.' Or if she did we don't know who in the hell they were. What we do know though, is that somebody slit her throat and was prob'ly gonna throw her in the incinerator, but didn't quite get her there. So, from that we can figure out that somebody, at least for a few seconds, hated her."

"It's so callous," he told Lucky. I noticed his milky white hands were shaking as he tried his best to find a cigarette. Lucky reached in his shirt pocket and knocked one out of the pack. He held it out then touched the end of it with a match when Mr. Preston took it.

"It's not callous," Lucky told him, lighting his own cigarette. "It's doin' somethin' nice for the woman. That's all."

"If I were to do this, how would you want her to look? Dressed nicely? The wound concealed as well as possible? New clothes? These services aren't cheap. And they're not easy. Especially since Michael moved away."

Michael had been Mr. Preston's last "roommate." The last poor boy he'd helped off the street. He'd been gone a couple of months and the next "case" had yet to come along.

"You know," he said, "that Michael moved back to Nashville where I found him. He's working in an antique store there. It's so hard to keep good help."

"I'll get ya good money to do it," Lucky told him. "You write me out an estimate and send it over and maybe we can get movin' on this. I'd like to have her out later today."

Mr. Preston had hedged a couple of more times, before Lucky had to indirectly remind him that he or one of his men had found him "loitering" several times on county roads that were on the outskirts of city property, with his helpers. How many times he had let his "helpers" slide on things he should have arrested them for, vagrancy, public drunk, DWI, and other things unmentionable. It was true; I knew Lucky hardly ever arrested anybody for anything.

Mr. Preston had agreed to a more than fair price, Lucky assured me as we pulled out of the Chapel's parking lot.

MY MOTHER WAS IN THE KITCHEN, stirring chili on the stove top. Turning over grilled cheese sandwiches in a pan on the next eye. Lucky had dropped me off after our distinguished conversation with Mr. Preston, told me I should go home and watch out for Mama and Jean until he came back, noon as usual, he guessed. As usual as well, when I had walked into the house, Jean had been whining about something.

"I feel safe with Daddy watching over the town," she told my mother, watching her work at the stove, not helping. "But he can't be a hundred places at once. He just can't. And I don't trust his men, not a one of them. You know how hard he always says it is to find good help."

Something George Preston and Lucky had in common, I thought. I watched her mouth rattle out sounds as she popped her gum in the infrequent pauses.

"I mean, I know that Daddy would come runnin' if he thought anything was going to happen to us, but what if he was all the way on the other side of town? I know he's going to be off hunting for that nigger boy. Not that I don't love being with you, Mama, but this is just before my last Christmas in high school."

If you hadn't failed the seventh grade, I thought, your ass would be out by now. Would have graduated the year before like you were supposed to.

"It'll be fine and don't say that word," my mother told her. "Your daddy will take care of everything. He always does."

As I sat at the kitchen table with Jean, I was reminded, when it came to Lucky, both she and my mother lived in the same world. An imaginary one. My mother, it seemed, had worked night and day trying to help her. But all she had wanted to do was talk about the people she was in class with. Finally, they thought it might be better to have her repeat the grade so technically she wouldn't flunk. I wondered if he'd take care of it like he had when I'd actually spoken the words about Jean I had thought a few moments before. That she had flunked the seventh grade ... was just *overwhelmed* by that tough seventh grade math. On the bad side of his whisky-drinking, he'd punched me in the face and knocked me over backward out a chair and then cursed me until I returned to the table to play my hand of Rook.

"What a goddam day," Lucky protested.

"Daddy!" said Jean. Fucking goody-goody.

Lucky shuffled to an ashtray on the kitchen counter, and knocked the ashes off the end of his butt of a cigarette. He took another deep draw, rattled out a couple of coughs and smothered the life out of the thing.

"What's wrong?" my mother asked.

He walked to the stove and pulled the top off a pot, smelled its innards. "Everybody in town's up in arms about this woman. Everywhere I go, it's all anybody wants to talk about. They keep asking me who it is. And I keep sayin' that I don't know."

"Is it the Ivy woman?" I asked him.

"Nope," he said. "It ain't the Ivy woman."

"How do you know?" my mother asked.

"I know because I talked to Miss Mary Ivy herself at the Burgess house. She was right there, pretty as you please, when Johnny Forrest and I walked in. Sittin' on the couch, smokin' a cigarette there in the main room of the place. Louis Woodson and Robert Smith was just sittin' there, too."

"Did Miss Ivy have her invisible horse in there with her?" Jean asked.

Lucky looked in the pot again and my mother started pulling bowls out of the cabinet.

"Nah," said Lucky. "She said he was tied out back."

Just as Lucky predicted the night before, after the moment or so it took for Miss Ivy's continued breathing to sink in, my mother and Jean came to the next conclusion.

Jean gasped. "Daddy," she said, "what does it mean?"

"It means, Jeannie, that we don't know who she is or why she was here. Or who the hell killed her, or why."

"Have you caught the other nigger yet?" Jean asked.

"Colored man," my mother reminded her.

"Then … colored man. Have you caught him?"

Lucky watched my mother begin to set the bowls of chili on the table in our kitchen—where we always ate breakfast and lunch unless it was a holiday—and propped himself against the counter. He took off his hat for the first time since he had been inside. I hadn't asked him and he hadn't volunteered the information.

"Daddy, what happened to your head?" Jean asked.

My mother, who no longer seemed excited about anything to do with Lucky, walked to him and examined the marks illuminated by the sunlight making its way in the kitchen window. One was the size of a half-dollar, raised and still crusty with blood just above his temple. The other two were smaller, one just below his hairline and the other an inch or so into his thinning hair.

"A goddam shelf fell over on me down at the office," he said. "We was back there, lookin' through some old evidence and the damn thing just come over. City won't give us enough money to do anything right."

"Did it hurt?" Jean asked.

No, dumbass, holes knocked in your head feel good. Oh, but I forgot, you've never been on the wrong end of somebody knocking the shit out of you.

"Oh, a little. But it's fine now."

After my mother set the food out and disappeared into the next room, she came back with a wash rag and some peroxide. She daubed at the marks, especially the larger one, until she had erased most of the dried blood from Lucky's head and scalp. Then she placed a light kiss on his head and sat down at the table with the rest of us.

As is often the case, the first few bites of everyone's lunch were taken in silence. Spoons rattling against the sides of bowls, the ruffle of shirt sleeves touching edges of bodies or the table. The almost silent parting of lips as they opened and food slipped through. Napkins rising from laps, wiping away what had not gone in. Returning to laps in the same civilized manner.

"She goes out at two," said Lucky. He spooned in another bite of chili, I guess, waiting on a response. "That's the earliest George Preston said he could put her out. He's charging the city double what he'd usually charge. He says the cost it'll be for him in—what'd he call it?—public relations, will ,far exceed what I bring in for doing this one thing.'" His nose remained upturned a little, his upper lip the same, trying to imitate the way George Preston spoke. "He says the next dozen or so people who have a funeral for a family member'll hesitate to bring them there … think about maybe goin' to Nashville or Columbia. He says the next four or five funerals ever'body goes to there, they'll just see her."

For a few seconds, my sister stopped the steady progression of shoveling into her mouth. Her face dropped in that same kind of pout I'd seen a thousand times more than I wanted to. Her eyes turned glassy. "Does she look terrible, Daddy?"

"She don't look like she's been to a party," Lucky answered. He spooned the last chili into his mouth, chased it with the last two small bites of his grilled cheese sandwich.

"You want some more?" my mother asked him.

"No thank you," he told her. He knocked around in his shirt pocket until he came out with his Luckys and a book of matches. "Do you know where my other cigarettes are, Mary?" he asked my mother. "God knows I don't wanna have to go see Paul Chester again today."

I heard the drawer shut on the bureau in their bedroom. Watched my mother as she walked back into the room, laid two packs next to Lucky's arm on the table.

I cut my eyes to Jean, who had been remarkably quiet for going on a record amount of time. Her eyes were far away, scared.

"What does she look like?" Jean asked.

Lucky drew what looked like half the cigarette in one breath and blew out a great bank of grey smoke. "You mean her physical appearance or what she looks like after what was done to her?"

Tears the size of small marbles hung in the corner of my sister's eyes. She tried to speak but her breath caught her words, slowed them in her throat. "I...don't...know."

Lucky picked one for her. "She's...I'd say ... early, mid-twenties. Dark hair. Average build. Pretty normal lookin', I guess."

Partly out of a desire to be mean to Jean and partly out of the suspicion that I, in fact, had information that would get everybody's undivided attention, I contemplated telling what I knew. Describing her as plainly as I could. Taking Lucky's wrath, my mother's disappointment, Jean's scorn for being behind the high school with Sharon.

Jean turned her eyes to the kitchen window, then out the back door and through the windows on the back porch.

Lucky stood, stretched himself out like an old dog. "I'm goin' to talk to Arliss Mosby in a few minutes. I talked to him this mornin'. Talked to his mama, too. He had a' alibi with his mother and his sister. Claimed his daddy was there, too. Neighbors on both sides claim they didn't see nobody leave or come. His mama says his daddy was there all night, didn't leave until when he had to go to school the next mornin'. I reckon' it'd be hard for either one of ,em to have slit a woman's throat and then take her to the high school if they was with the two women of the house."

I replayed in my head seeing Jackson Mosby appearing at the door the morning before, seeing the lights go on the same way, the same time they did every morning behind Franklin High School. Tried to imagine if he'd had time to dump a body by the incinerator.

Like Lucky could read my mind—which, sometimes, I was sure he could—he said, "Them first kids that found the body didn't call Miss Helen until around 7:00. Jackson Mosby, the best I can figure, comes to work between 5:30 and 6 every mornin'. Closer to 5:30. So, if it was him … or him and his boy, then it just don't make no sense that they would have brung her up there and dropped her by the damn incinerator at 5:30 in the mornin'. It would stand to reason that he either got there later … or somebody else dropped the body there. There ain't no other way around it."

I guess I had been around Lucky long enough now—had, I hate to admit, made his thinking enough my own—that I was able to conclude what he had not. Jackson Mosby could have been there when he usually was and saw someone so he dropped the body. But as soon as the thought passed through my feeble brain, I knew, too, that Jackson Mosby knew the time I…we…got there every morning. He was as accustomed to us, as I was him.

Lucky turned his thick wrist over, palm down, looked at the gold Bulova watch my mother had given him a few Christmases before. He rubbed his face with his hands, picked his hat up off the counter. I looked at the clock that hung on the kitchen wall over the table. It was one o'clock.

"Why you goin' to talk to that nigger again?" Jean said.

"Colored man," my mother reminded her again.

"I'm goin' to see that Arliss Mosby again ,cause I guess I'm gonna put him in jail," said Lucky. He lit another Lucky and made his way to the kitchen window. Looked at the mammoth oak in our neighbor's, the Smithsons, yard. He flicked his ashes in the sink, ran some tap water over them.

Watching his back, I thought of how odd it was that he had discussed this thing that had happened with us. In the long history of his work on the police force, I know I could have tallied the cases he had spoken about on both hands.

For a few moments, I played out all the possible options of the situation in my head. I'd tell him what I knew and he'd beat the shit out of me. For knowing and not saying anything. For my silence making me culpable in the crime, even making it appear like Sharon and I dumped the body. Him never letting me out of the house again except to work. Not getting to see Sharon again; telling him that I was going to see her, no matter what he said. Standing up to his ass. I was getting to the point where I thought I could take him, even though he had me by fifty pounds that middle age had dumped on him. The fact that if his son was the one to come forward and give information that acquitted this "colored man" in the court of popular opinion, how it could be construed as an inside job, Lucky getting me to say what he wanted. After all, Lucky was good at things like this, good at the deals under the table.

My mother was picking up the dishes, banging and clanging, washing, rinsing. Jean was off her ass, doing the only thing she was prone to do regularly: rinsing out the glasses for our tea and wiping the table down with a wet cloth. As I stared at Lucky's back, I wondered if he was thinking about what I figured he was … the only thing any of us thought of anymore when we looked into our neighbor's yard.

"Henry Boy?" Lucky said as he turned around.

"Yessir?" I said.

"Would you mind doin' me a favor?" he asked, turning back to the window after he spoke.

"What?" I said.

As he started to explain, I quickly remembered how I usually hated the things Lucky asked me to do. The things he himself avoided.

CHAPTER TEN

EATH DIDN'T LOOK near as much like itself by the time George Preston got through with it. It was part of the deal Lucky had made with him, I assume. I had heard Lucky on the phone after I myself had reticently agreed to what he had asked of me and George Preston had called. Much like the conversations had often been concerning my Uncle Percy, Lucky had said more "uh-huh's" than anything else. Between them, though, I had heard him utter that he thought George Preston could "work his magic" on the lady, use whatever he used to make her appear her most presentable. To put a smile on the face of death.

I knocked on the thick oak door after I had pushed through the double front doors and crossed the seventy-five feet of perfect paint and carpet before Celestial Gardens and the Zion Room. I had passed those doors without looking in them. I felt my eyes wanting to wander back, wondering where I would find her today. I knocked again louder, still waiting on the bastard. He usually gave me the creeps; but him on top of her in here somewhere, on top of being the only two in the building itself, made me feel like my head might explode. I forced the breath down into my chest. Told myself to quit being stupid.

What seemed like half an hour later, George Preston, in all his milky whiteness, appeared at his office door. Tears in his eyes, they spilled in two thin streams over his gaunt cheeks. His hands shook a little as he pulled a cigarette to his mouth with one and motioned me in with the other. I focused on a diamond set in yellow gold on his right hand as he lowered his cigarette.

"The solution we use back there often makes my eyes water," he told me as he wiped the streams away with an ironed handkerchief. "Although, I guess it's not really 'we' anymore. Have a seat, young Hall." He blew a cloud of smoke toward an opening in his office window and straightened some things on his desk. He asked me to sit again. A third time, I would remember later. I came back to consciousness with him looking me up and down, running his eyes from my face to my ankles, even craning his neck a little so he could see around the edge of his desk.

"Would you like to sit, Henry?" he said, once more.

No, I'd rather fucking stand here in this monkey suit my mother had talked me into wearing. Told me it was the right, the respectful thing to do. I thought about how Sharon and I had shown respect to her the day before, doing what we did not fifty feet from her body, then leaving her there on the cold slab of asphalt.

"Henry Hall?" Mr. Preston said. "Are you in there, Henry Hall?"

"Yessir," I told him. "Yessir, that'll be fine."

I moved the chair across from his desk until it screamed from being dragged across the floor.

"Careful," he told me, breaking his wrist back and holding his cigarette over his shoulder like women did. "That chair came from England. It's early nineteenth century."

"Okay...yessir," I told him.

"You look a little pale, Henry. Are you all right?"

 Not as fucking pale as you.

"Yessir. I'm fine. I mean, I'm just not looking forward to doing this."

It felt good to admit it. Like somebody pulled something off me. George Preston moved his head up and down like he understood.

"Yes, to be here is never pleasant for anybody."

His eyes were burning holes in me, made me flush with my own sweat, my heart pound in my ears. His voice was strangely rhythmic, though, soft enough to put me to sleep. The spell he's cast over his "helpers," I thought. His charity cases.

"When have you been here before?" he asked me.

"A few times," I told him.

"Who specif–" he said, but didn't finish when the phone on his desk rang.

"Franklin Memorial Chapel," he sang. "Two o'clock. Yes. That's correct. Thank you."

He put the phone back on its base and sighed deeply. "I'm afraid this is going to turn into a circus," he said. "I told your father that was my gravest fear."

And my gravest fear was realized five minutes later. George Preston, having told me that the phone call was about the twentieth one he had gotten—an exaggeration, I imagined—and that he had developed "a splitting headache," excused himself through one of the lounges and into the back work area. A place I couldn't even begin to imagine and knew I never, ever wanted to see, I decided as I stood at the entrance to Celestial Gardens, where he had left me.

THE SUIT I WORE had been too big to begin with, Lucky assuring me I'd grow into as Billy Biggs stood measuring me, trying to figure out how to cut down a suit that was three sizes too big. It had been the only clothes I could remember them buying for me since I had started throwing papers when I was nine. Lucky had held the same premise about clothes-buying that he did about working. The earlier you started doing it for yourself, the better off you were. The more likely you were to make it across the invisible line of "manhood." I stood there, still as a statue, looking at the stupid thing hanging off me in a distant mirror, remembering the places I had worn it. Sharon's prom. Edward. Sheila. Percy. How could that bastard Preston not remember? Maybe he was just nervous, too.

From a distance, she looked just like anybody else. Or at least anybody else I'd ever seen in a coffin. A body...something that carried a soul, if we have one. Empty now, void of the energy that had propelled it forward. She was dressed in a high-neck blouse that George had obviously picked out to be color-coordinated with the burgundy and tan pattern on the wall paper. I found myself making slow, quiet steps across the carpet, so not to disturb her or anybody else, I guess. At fifteen feet away, about the time she became other than just another person, I could move no further. Her hair, even though it was fixed now, her hands, the structure of her bloated face, they rushed back to me like the train's whistle cut through stillness of the south end of Franklin at night. I sat on the first row of chairs and put my elbows on my knees, my fists under my chin. I stared at the ugly-ass shoes Lucky had given me to go with my suit. Old scuffed wingtips that he hadn't worn in years. So scuffed up that all the polish in the world wouldn't have made them look new again. And I waited.

TWO WEEKS AFTER I had seen Sharon on Main Street and she had asked me to go to the dance with her, I did in fact go to the 1953 prom, at the gymnasium of Franklin High School. But on this night, troubles, both past and present, huddled together in a dark corner of that gym and hid themselves. Didn't make a sound. It was easy to pretend there was nothing else in the world but the night itself; no days that had come before it, none that would follow in its footsteps.

Somewhere between white and pink, the dress that she had bought at the department store where she worked was beautiful on her, dragging the floor just a little as we walked into the gym after we had parked. Her hair, black as coal, fell loose around her shoulders. When she smiled, her face lit like the sun rises in the eastern sky and throws light to a dark morning. Made me smile. For a while I tried to fight it, to keep up the perpetual frown I wore on my face. I was trying to abide by the advice Van had always given me: "Never let ,em know that you like ,em. Women always want something they can't have. If you always keep a little slack in the rope, then you can snap it any time you want to."

But his ass wasn't there on this night, at least not sitting at our table. He had opted to sit with Raymond Collins and some girl he was dating at Franklin High School. He only flitted by our table occasionally, to sip from the bottle Tully had tucked away in his coat pocket. He claimed it was moonshine he had come by it in a town six or seven miles south of Franklin, and that he could get some more if we needed it. Peytonsville, just a wide place in the road besides the bootlegging that went on there and the one beer joint, "The Rendezvous." We could be there in ten minutes.

"Goddam! This is good stuff," he said, wiping his mouth with the back of his coat sleeve and then taking another drink for good measure. "Fuckin' hundred proof," he said almost every time he took a swallow.

"I thought a hundred proof would kill ya, or make ya go blind … or somethin' like that," his date and part-time girlfriend Darlene would say.

"Nah," said Tully. "Nothin' kills ya unless it's supposed to. We all got our time and place. Ask Henry … he'll tell ya."

I nodded my head up and down in rote, still spinning from the couple of slugs I'd taken out of Tully's bottle. He pushed it at me again; I shook my head as he pulled it back and took another swig.

"I wish he wouldn't do that here," said Darlene, trying to bring a stern look to her round face.

"What're they gonna do?" said Tully. "Kick my ass out? Let ,em. Then I'll get to go back to Nashville or wherever he is to live with my Daddy and that'll last about two fucking weeks and then he'll be lookin' to send me somewhere else … and maybe my Mama'll finally take me back. I heard she's doin' better."

He had been telling me that, us that, anybody who would listen that, as long as I had known him. A month after he had moved in with his grandfather, according to him, his mother was better and he would be going back soon. Last thing I had heard Mr. Shafer had told Lucky that his mother had moved down in Georgia somewhere and nobody had heard from her in six months. According to Tully, it was Mr. Shafer, not his mother, who kept him from going back. Mr. Shafer liked having a yard boy and go-for, he often told me. I could only imagine Tully being a lot more trouble than he was help. A lot more worry than joy for an old man.

"Hey," Van said from behind us, like he hadn't seen us all night.

"Yeah?" said Tully.

"Are y'all gonna dance? These two girls we're with are wantin' to get out there. Y'all wanna go out there with us?"

The truth was, I didn't, and we had. We had been there when the doors opened. Thirty minutes before it started. I'd already made a fool out of myself before most everybody got there. When Sharon had mentioned that she was on the one of the committees that was working on the backdrop for the pictures and wanted to go a little early, I had seized the opportunity to get there, get a seat where you could go to and from the dance floor inconspicuously.

"We've already been out there awhile," I told him over the growing noise, chatter, and the band playing "Rags to Riches," the singer trying to imitate Tony Bennett's voice.

"When?" he said.

"Before your late ass got here," I told him. I swiped the bottle out of Tully's hand and turned up a drink.

Sometimes Van wouldn't swing back. Let you think you won. His stare was like a vacuum, drawing in everything about you. He'd let just enough time pass that you relaxed, breathed in and out a little. He'd smile just enough to ease you, and speak in a tone, its intent indiscernible.

"Nice suit," he told me. "Is that the one Lucky got for ya?"

He ran his hand down the lapel of his own suit, straightened his tie. Ran his hands over his wavy, blonde hair.

"Yeah," I answered.

His, I knew, was brand new. Scoot had bought it for him just a couple of weeks before. At the same store Lucky had bought mine, just not off the damn sale rack, marked down five times because it had been there three seasons already.

"Spare no expense," he said, averting his eyes, never letting them touch mine. "You got his shoes on, too?"

"None other," I said. I withdrew a foot from under the table and showed it to him.

"That's them," he said. "Still around from the Great Depression!"

"Fuckin' A," I told him.

Then it was like he saw Sharon for the first time, just noticed that she was sitting at the table with us. Keep a little slack in the rope. Women always want what they can't have.

"Hey," he said, showing all his hundred and two teeth to her. "How are you?" He made a couple of smooth steps toward her and patted her shoulder.

"Fine," she said. "How about you?"

"Fine as wine," he said, reaching to take the bottle from Tully again. Looking around before he took a secret swig. "Good dance, isn't it?"

"Yeah," she said. "Really good."

"Good fuckin' dance," echoed Tully. He held his bottle up, examined it. Shook it a little. I could see the flecks not filtered out dancing in the bottom in the strange light.

Darlene reached and patted his hand.

"Who'd you come with?" Sharon asked him.

His suit, the light made him look paler, his eyes bluer. "Marla Watkins. Collins is with her sister, Rose."

"She doesn't know who Collins is, asshole," I muttered under my breath.

He looked back at his table, I guess to check their welfare in his absence. The band set into "Where is Your Heart?" by Percy Faith. He waited till Collins looked back, threw up his hand. Marla Watkins and her sister Rose both waved and smiled. Marla made a dancing kind of gesture; he made the same gesture back.

"Good to see y'all," he said. Looked at Sharon. "Maybe we can dance after awhile."

"Yeah, come back. I'll dance with ya," said Tully. "We'll tear this place down."

He looked at me as he was walking away. A parting blow. "Get those wingtips on out on the floor now. Cut a rug. You know they still got the moves from when Lucky danced in ,em."

I hoped in the strange light still flickering, the redness of my face did not show. I manufactured another sound like a laugh and reached for Tully's bottle.

IT HAD BEEN LONG ENOUGH that the major part of the few mostly feigned drinks of Tully's moonshine had exited my body. My head had stopped spinning. Perhaps it had just been seeing Percy—stranger than that flashing light in the dance that made everybody's color a couple of shades different—that had sobered me up. I had rinsed my mouth out three, four times at the bathroom filling station, eaten the peppermints Sharon had given me. Then realized it was all for naught, because I could see Lucky through the window at Pruitt's, shooting craps on the floor, his car parked just around the edge of the building.

I had pulled Lucky's car in as careful as I could, because I figured he could probably tell you who's still it was just by smelling my breath. As I sat in the car, staring at the way the silver flecks danced on the garage wall in the darkness, I could still smell her on me. I could still feel the touch of her skin under my fingertips. See her green eyes as that light made them greener. I laughed, thinking about her telling me not to worry about kissing her in front of her house, because her father was old. She, Sheila, Suzy, they were his second set of children, she had explained to me. He'd had a truckload in his first marriage, she had laughed, before their mother had died. He didn't get too excited about anything anymore.

Of course, I had been only half-listening to her. The way you do when you have something else on your mind … when your body has taken over your brain.

"Sheila is a year older than me, I mean than I am … and Suzy is two years younger than I am. Bobby is four years older than I am and we don't have the same father. His father was my mother's first husband. Well, I guess it's really debatable whether or not she was married to him. She said she was. Other people tell me she wasn't. Anyway, Bobby's my half-brother. You know Bobby, don't you?"

I nodded my head. Didn't tell her I knew Bobby because Lucky had hauled him a couple of times, when the moral pressure from people around town won out, and Lucky would arrest a few guys who were hauling shine out of "Little Texas" or even North Alabama. Bobby had dropped out of Franklin High School a couple of years before and was usually just a couple of steps ahead of trouble. I knew he was Tully's connection for the moonshine he came by sometimes.

"Yeah, I know Bobby," I said. I kissed her again, the way we had done in the country church parking lot after we'd left the dance early. Pulled her to me tightly enough I was afraid I was going to hurt her. She moved her face away from mine, reached and stroked my cheek with her thin fingers then smiled. It was like I had known her forever. Been with her in another place and time … something.

"I really like your car," she told me. "It's real nice."

"It's fuc—Lucky's," I said, catching myself.

"Your father?"

I nodded.

"What'd you call him?"

"I started to call him fuckin' Lucky," I told her, "but I caught myself before I cussed in front of ya."

"You cussed in front of me at the gym," she said.

"Yeah, I probably shouldn't have," I said.

"It's all right," she assured me. "I'm used to it. Bobby curses like a sailor."

I brushed her hair back from her shoulders, started to rub her neck just behind and below her ear. Was an inch from the taste of her lips again.

"Your Uncle Percy that we saw—he's your daddy … Lucky's brother, right?"

"His one and only," I told her.

"They don't look anything alike," she said.

"Yeah, Lucky always tells me that. Says that they ain't nothin' alike in most ways. Looks, personality, brains … He tells me it's always been that way, since they were little. Sometimes I think Lucky hates him. Sometimes I think Lucky hates everybody."

Sometimes I think I hate everybody, I thought, but had the good sense not to say it.

"He seems nice enough," she said.

And *she* had been nice enough to leave it at that. The way people do when they don't know each other well. It was easier, I had learned, if I said it first. Gave people the freedom to think what they were thinking.

"Does he always talk about the kind of stuff he did when we saw him?"

"Yeah, usually," I said. "He's been talking about that kinda stuff ever since I've known him. He's lived with us off and on for years. He's filled me in on all of it. But I think it's worse now. Used to be he'd just talk about it and wander around. Now he's doin' some other strange shit—" I paused. She smiled.

We both laughed. It would have been funnier, I knew, if it weren't true.

"People call up here all the time, tell Lucky where he is … what he's doin'. Lucky then'll get in his car and go get him. In his regular car, though … this one. Not the squad car because he doesn't want Percy to ride in the front because how it might look, like he might worry about that, shootin' craps in the fillin' station at night with his car parked right outside. He doesn't want him ridin' in the back ,cause he doesn't want more people knowin' about the trouble than already do."

"What was he talking about, ‚Making things right'?" she asked.

"He thinks there was some terrible travesty done here," I told her. I hoped the word had made me seem smart. "In the Civil War. You know, in the Battle of Franklin."

She looked at me like she wasn't quite sure what I was talking about. I was often amazed at how few people really knew much of anything about the battle itself. Even though the people who lived right in the middle of the battlefield, like we did, where so many had fallen. I was different, I assumed, because I had heard it from Percy since I was old enough to hear anything.

As she did when I was delivering papers, Mama would be waiting up on me when I got home. Sitting there in the kitchen, the bottoms of her short legs sticking out of her cotton nightgown. Doing nothing except sitting. Nothing on the table to read, no magazine, no book. Not sneaking glances at the television two rooms away. Not knitting. Not smoking. Not drinking. Nothing. Just sitting there in the way that I will always remember her. Leaned slightly forward, her hands clasped together, fingers interlocked. Her legs crossed at the ankles, her sleepy face resting on her hands.

"Did you have a good time?" she asked me, the door shutting quiet behind me.

"Yes ma'am," I told her, trying not to say any more than I had to.

"Who did you go with?" she asked.

"Some girl from the high school."

"Does Jean know her?"

"Probably not," I said.

Although it was just Columbia Highway that separated the two sections, Jean lived here, Sharon lived in the "mixed" section, or the section for people that were at least a couple of rungs further down the ladder of poor than we were. Jean had friends that were "good" girls. Sharon didn't seem like one of those.

"Your daddy had to work late," she told me.

"Yeah, I saw him," I said. "Workin' late in the floor at the fillin' station," I mumbled under my breath.

"Hmm?"

"Yes ma'am, I saw his car around town," I said. I started to rifle through the refrigerator, looking for something to eat.

"You want me to make you somethin'?" my mother asked.

"No ma'am, I'm fine," I told her. I came out with a couple of pieces of white bread and a jug of milk. Poured some in a glass.

"You sure you don't want me to fix you something? I don't mind."

"No ma'am. I'm fine," I told her again.

As I shut the refrigerator and looked back at my mother, my eyes stopped on her face for the first time I could remember in a long time. Her poor, tired face. The face that had Lucky as a husband. Jean as a daughter … a best friend. And then me—no prize. No saint. I knew that. My mind wanted to make its usual turn toward running down Jean, cataloguing in my head how I was I was way better than her—because I didn't pretend to be something I wasn't. How that somehow made me different. A rung up the ladder of honesty. Strangely enough, though, all I could see was my mother's face. Her hands cupped under her chin, her eyes now cast to the same wall she usually stared at before Lucky made his grand entrance and immediate departure for bed.

"Three-thirty's going to come early in the morning," she said.

"Yes ma'am," I said, turning my eyes away from her when she looked at me. I reached for the counter with my free hand and propped myself up. Took half a piece of white bread in my mouth. A slug of milk.

"You just wake up now, don't you?"

"What do you mean?" I asked.

Now *she* studied me. Maybe like I had stared at her a few moments before. Looked into me like she was silently inquiring what I had become. This seventeen year-old boy...man...whatever the hell I was, who used to be her son.

"I mean, you used to use an alarm to get up when you do. I'd hear it everyday. You remember, Dillard got it for you."

Another bargain-basement purchase, I was sure. Or something he took out of some house he went in, I thought. He told me he had gotten it at the drugstore. Proud of me. Buy me a present. That was when I could still believe him. "Yes ma'am, I remember."

"You just wake up now," she said, like she was telling me.

"I've been doing it eight fucking years," I mumbled under my breath as I poured some more milk. "Yes ma'am," I said. "Time does that, I guess. We get used to almost anything."

"Do you think you need to set it for in the morning?" she asked. Standing by this point, she daubed at something on the table with her finger.

"No ma'am. I'll wake up," I told her.

"I don't mind getting you up," she assured me.

"I appreciate it," I told her, "but I'll be fine.

She stepped to me at the counter and put her arms around my rib cage. Laid her head on my shoulder, then kissed my cheek.

"I love you," she said. "Your daddy loves you."

"Goodnight," I told her.

CHAPTER ELEVEN

"WE'RE GETTIN' READY to make a run to get some more shine," Tully told me when I opened the window. He stood there on the roof above the side porch on our house, smiling. "Van says his ass won't go with me to pick up some more."

I stuck my head out the window a little, looked at Van across the way in his driveway, wagging his head back and forth.

"He says he ain't gettin' in no shit like we did the last time. I told him this was a whole different set a' people." He staggered a little, caught himself before he got near the edge of the roof. "You remember the last time, don't ya?" he said quietly, like he just realized he'd been talking too loud.

I leaned out the window enough to see if Lucky's car was under the carport, which it was. Then I recalled that he had looked in on me just a few minutes before, the best I could judge time coming in and out of sleep like I had. I looked back across the way at Van, who was no longer shaking his head, but now, even in the dim light of the street lamp, had that characteristic smirk on his face.

"I remember," I told him. "How the hell could I forget?"

Images of him trying to negotiate the deal at the back of the Rendezvous, then several men coming from the place, ready to whip our asses because of something he'd said. Van getting in the car with Raymond Collins and locking the doors. He swore he didn't. But he did. The only thing that saved us had been that Tully's trunk was open, where he was going to load the shine he picked up, so he reached in and came out with a tire iron. Scared the bigger of the four men into stopping, the others following suit. Van and Collins unlocked the doors when they believed the coast was clear.

"This is different," he told me, mimicking a dance step he'd done earlier. "The place I got, this was just some family's home. Well, I guess it's family. I mean people live there … you know. Anyway, they said that they'd have another bottle or two ready tonight if I wanted it. I would'a just got it earlier, but they were still cookin' it up. I should'a known that one bottle wouldn't do us."

The way he was using the term "us," I suspected he believed that Van and I had drunk as much as he had. Although I couldn't speak for Van, I suspected he was as I had been: feigning as much drinking as drinking himself.

"Come on," said Tully. "Are you gonna go or ain't ya? Don't be a pussy."

"He couldn't be anything he hadn't ever had," said Van from our driveway, where he'd slithered.

I gave him the finger out the window.

"Don't y'all start your shit," Tully said. "Y'all wouldn't know what to do without each other. Hell, you've lived across the street from each other your whole life." He stumbled again, this time coming perilously close to the edge of the roof.

I started to tell him that I knew what I'd do without him: the same thing I believed I'd do without Jean, without Lucky—have one less pain in my ass. But he didn't give me a chance.

"In just a minute," he said, "I'm gonna pull that car out'a that driveway and I'm goin' to Little Texas to pick up some more shine. All I want to know is who, if anybody, is goin' with me?"

Van threw up his arms like he'd been arguing with him about it for the last hour.

As Tully spun on his heels and began to make his way toward the edge of the roof, where I hoped he would slide down one of the porch columns unscathed, Van hollered from his own yard, "Get us some good stuff."

Tully gave him the "okay" signal as his feet hit the porch and he waited on me to descend the same column he had.

AND GET US SOME good stuff we did. So good that Tully couldn't resist opening one of the bottles before we got a mile from the shack he'd pulled up in front of, entered, and then returned from ten minutes later.

"I'm glad that the one thing Mr. Shafer does for me is give me money," he said. "Hell, that would'a cost you a week's work."

I started to offer him some money but then thought better of it. Thought Van could give him some of Scoot's money if need be. Van, who'd never worked more than two or three days in his life.

Within five minutes after we'd left the bootlegger's place, Tully pulled to the side of the road and was quiet as a graveyard. Taking drinks from the bottle, passing it to me and making sure I took my slug. Then, back on the road a mile or so, out of nowhere he had started.

"Hen, you know why they sent me to live with my grandaddy, don't ya?" he said. He was fumbling between his legs for one of the bottles, steering the car with his knee.

"Get your hand back on the steering wheel," I told him.

He got one hand on the bottle and let his knee drop back to the flat of the seat. He reached up and wiped under his eyes with the back of his sleeve, and I, of all things, felt bad because I had laughed. I didn't know yet that alcohol could be from God or the devil. Take you way up or way the hell down.

"'Cause my whore of a momma run off and left him and my daddy didn't think he could raise a kid by hisself."

All I knew was that Tully had come to live with Mr. Shafer, as we called him, when we were eight or nine years old, if I remembered right. He'd been the skinny little kid down the block with a burr cut that had to go in and change his clothes if he got dirty. Sometimes he'd change clothes four or five times a day. He went to Franklin High School because his family didn't have the money to send him to the Academy, or at least didn't want to spend it that way.

The tears were pouring down his face now. I couldn't see it in the dark, but I knew from the sounds he was making. Choking like, between his words. He rolled the window down and threw a cigarette out he'd been smoking and reached into his pocket for another one.

"Just watch the road … and give me another drink a' that stuff," I told him, my head feeling strangely lighter, heavier than it ever had from the two drinks he'd given me since we'd taken to the road.

"It just don't make no goddam sense," he said. "My mama and daddy can't raise a kid but some old man like my grandfather can. Does that make one bit 'a fuckin' sense to you?"

"Uh-uh," I said, shaking my head.

"Huh?" he said.

"No," I told him.

"I ain't seen neither one of 'em in two years."

There were a lot of days that this wouldn't have sounded like such a bad deal to me. As a matter of fact, a few weeks or months or maybe even a year without Lucky didn't seem too long.

Nevertheless, the tears that had come quieter before began to spill out of his chest in jolts, choking him again. "Goddam her!" he hollered.

I wanted to tell him he liked his grandaddy, that living with Mr. Shafer wasn't the worst thing in the world. But I knew what he'd say. He'd choked out stuff like this before when he was drunk.

I let a few more seconds go by, sure the car was more airborne than on the road. Sure we were coming off the ground on a few of the hills we topped coming back into Franklin down Lewisburg Pike. I was scared to look at the speedometer, but let my eyes inch to it. We were doing eighty-five.

"Godammit, Tully, slow your ass down," I said.

"My momma left me," he bawled.

"I don't give a shit," I hollered back.

"Neither did she," he said. I could tell he had mashed down harder on the gas. "And then they sent me to live with ole man Shafer."

"He's your grandaddy," I told him.

"Now I don't give a shit," he said.

Even though I couldn't see it in the darkness I knew that we were getting closer to Franklin, to the hairpin curve that I knew brought Lewisburg Pike around and then down a straightaway across the railroad tracks into town. He set both hands on the wheel and looked like he was trying to push his foot through the floor.

"Godammit, Tully, slow down! You're gonna kill us!"

"I might as well be dead!" he hollered.

"I don't wanna be dead!" I screamed back.

In the night I could only see the silhouettes of the trees as they moved in the grey blackness past the car. I could hear only the engine of Mr. Shafer's Buick and its tires whining on the road and the suspension of the car groaning and whining as it raised and lowered with the hills. Tully's muffled chokes had stopped now. I had quit begging. There was just a silence between us. An emptiness.

Even though the dark blinded me to the curve that would land us in the river, I could see it. I could see it as plain as if it were daytime under a noon sun. A quarter mile. An eighth. A football field away. Next, I could hear the tires screaming, Tully screaming as I knew we had to be right on top of the curve, and myself, screaming louder than either.

I felt the car as it rose to two wheels and it was almost like we were flying. Like the weight of this world had left us for a few moments. Maybe we were completely off the ground. I don't know. I only know that we missed the river and ended up with the car on its side in a thicket of brush and bushes, ten feet shy of the bank taking its last severe, downward turn.

"You all right?" he asked me, almost like nothing had happened.

After the flight, after the impact, then the final landing, I seriously doubted I was. But reality seemed to indicate otherwise. The coming back to earth had only proved to bump my head on the side window, then topple me into the roof before I landed almost perfectly in my seat again, my nose pressed strangely against the window like I was peering out at something along the roadside.

I wanted to curse my answer. Wanted to smack him in his mouth, which was now smiling kind of coyly. But I simply nodded and told him, "Yes."

"I think I am, too," he said. "By damn, would you a' believed that? I bet we flew through the air seventy-five feet."

Again, I had the same feelings as I had when he'd posed the last question. "Yeah," was all I was able to muster.

"Fuckin' A," he said. "That was the most amazin' thing I ever saw."

I drew in a long breath of air and let it run rough out over my tongue and lips, where he'd hear it. "Me, too," I said. "It's a wonder it didn't kill us."

"I guess it wasn't our time," he chirped, like a drunk bird singing its morning song.

I turned my eyes to him. Somehow, in the accident, catastrophe, circumstance, whatever you'd call it, he'd captured both bottles in flight. Had one nestled under one arm, the other gripped in the fist that he shook at me.

"Look what I got!"

"I see what you got," I told him.

"Here, take a drink," he said, "before we try to crawl out of this motherfucker." And then without provocation or reason, he began to laugh, as did I.

"You can't drink out'a the bottle without it runnin' out'a the side of your mouth," he said. "Ain't that funny?"

I assured him it was and experienced the same when he passed me the bottle.

"Gimme that bottle back," he said. "I think I'll need one more drink before we try to climb out and walk to the road."

I passed him back the bottle, the fact that I was sitting sideways, that I had a few minutes before flown seventy-five or so feet in a forty-nine Buick, exaggerating the experience of the world spinning, out of control. Pleasantly out of control.

ALCOHOL, BY ITS VERY NATURE is poison, Percy used to tell me. The body is the temple of the soul, it's true, he said, but also the temple of the mind. They're two different things—the soul and the mind—yet the same. Life is strange like that. While intellectual ideas are, by their very nature, strong, and language is what we use to describe those ideas, intellectualism and language are, also by their very nature, incomplete. Flawed, because they are part and parcel of, expressed by, flawed vessels. I am certain this is as true, he would say, as the fact that there are three prime ingredients to our existence and all the actions therein: Randomness, a Planned Nature of Things and Basic Human Frailty.

He's a fucking nut, Lucky would tell me by this point. The son of a bitch has never in his life had to do anything, because Mother and Daddy didn't make him do anything because they always needed to protect him. You know why I think they did that: I think it was because Mother had a brother who was the same way, crazy as a shithouse rat … and he didn't come to no good end. S'posedly he died in some crazyhouse somewhere because he couldn't live at home no more. If he wasn't already crazy, then one of them places would've done it to him. I didn't know the first thing about him till he died and we had to go to the funeral. Of course they didn't take Percy, because they tried to protect him from everything.

Some of us didn't have the luxury of sittin' up in a room in a farmhouse all day porin' through books that you spend all the day before searchin' for at the library. Did you know that they would make me take him to the library in Nashville when he couldn't find the kinda books he was lookin' for 'round here? Ain't that shit? Me, workin' by then for a goddam grocery store and helpin' them farm, and takin' him twenty miles in an ole farm truck so he could get some more inf'mation to help escape reality. If we could all be so lucky to be so fuckin' crazy!

Your daddy's too hard on Percy. He thinks that he can just be different. Be normal. He's the same way with hisself, I guess. He can't tolerate weakness in hisself. I know it's the same with you. He can't tolerate it in you either. I think that's why he pushed you so hard to play football and baseball. It shows you're strong. Little but strong. Just like him. He's a symbol of strength in our town, I guess, just like Mr. Oscar Garrett. You know, he tells me that one day, when Mr. Oscar retires, that he's likely to take his place. Wouldn't that be somethin'? Your daddy as the Police Chief? I guess in some ways things couldn't have turned out much better for us: you at the Academy, your Daddy the Chief of Police. We've got a nice brick house, a television, a nice car. You've got good friends, Jean seems happy. She doesn't seem to be havin' trouble in school anymore. You've got a motorcycle now and don't have to ride your bicycle anymore.

He kinda gives me the creeps sometimes. First of all, he's never been baptized, not even like the Methodists. No sprinkling or nothing. You know, he even says that he doesn't even believe in God. Bullshit, I tell her. Of all people, I can argue with her. Over anything. He does so say he doesn't believe in God. No, what he says, I tell her, is that he doesn't believe in God the same way they do at the Church of Christ. Then he's going to hell, she says. Stupid bitch. Fuck the Church of Christ, I tell her. Brother Brown says you go to hell for saying things like that. Yeah? He says you're goin' to hell for everything. He says you're goin' to hell if you wear shorts. You wear shorts, so I guess I'll see ya there. I hope my room's a long way away from yours. No, seriously, does he believe in God? she asks. He says he believes in a spirit that guides everything. I think that's in his "planned nature of things." His what? Never mind.

Well, I think we should ask Brother Brown to pray for him. Yeah? Well, I tell ya what, I wouldn't want to be your ass if Lucky finds out you're makin' our business public down at Fourth Avenue Church of Christ. Yeah, why don't you get him put on the prayer list on Easter or Christmas when Lucky gives in and goes to church with Mama. That way he won't even have to hear it second hand. He can just hear it and beat your ass right after church.

I wish sometimes you'd call him something besides Lucky. And I wish sometimes you'd just shut up. And by the way, Daddy has never laid a hand on me. No shit? I say. I wish I could say the same. You're the only one in the family who can say that. You know that, don't ya? What d'you mean? she asks. I mean, you're the only one he's never hit. He's never hit you, she says.

You live in make-believe, don't ya? I tell her. It must be nice to create your own world and live there. Make it just what you want. It must be twice as nice to be such an asshole, she says. The pout takes over her whole face, contorting it where it looks like her lips might fall off.

I'm still gonna ask Brother Brown to offer a prayer for Uncle Percy, she says, her heart now pierced.

You do that. You just do that.

And I'll have him say one for you.

I laugh. Don't even dignify the statement with a response.

Lucky pulls in and exist his own car, his face drooping in such a way that he looks like Jean when she pouts. Tired, I guess. Drunk. Some combination of the two. He doesn't even notice that I'm stretched out across the front seat of his car because I don't feel able to climb the porch post. I don't even understand the game, even after all the games I oversaw when he'd put me in the front door of the filling station to watch for Mr. Oscar Garrett to make sure that he didn't catch him playing. I laugh to myself, regardless of what has happened, somehow entertained with this different plane I've inhabited over the last couple of hours.

I'm not sure if I'm asleep and dreaming, or awake. If what happened really happened. If Tully and I really did run his grandfather's car off into the brush and bushes just west of the river and then walk home with two bottles of bootleg whiskey under our arm, or whether I've imagined it. Whether I left Van and Tully in the bushes at the edge of Van's yard to drink down what was left after Tully'd said he'd worry about the goddam car in the morning. I know my stomach feels like somebody's poured acid in it. That's probably why Lucky's told me not to drink shine. Says that's the only advantage to store-bought liquor. It's regulated. Coming out of Peytonsville or North Alabama, the only regulation's "don't let the wrong lawman catch ya." I figure the way my gut's feeling right now, that the last batch must have been bad, rotten … something. Lucky says this is why there won't ever be another prohibition.

Sweat breaks out on my forehead. My stomach feels like it might explode, tighten itself in a ball and throw itself from my body. It does. Or at least its contents do. I sit back in the car where I've found my rest, my temporary sanctuary. I pull breath into my chest, breathe out when my lungs get near full, and hope that the process does not repeat itself.

I LOVED SPRING MORNINGS on the Indian. The rumble of the pipe, the smell of the exhaust meeting the air, still cool but not cold. Only one out of every fifteen or twenty houses having somebody up. The world still asleep, still mine to make into what I wanted. An occasional dog or cat crossing the road, trolling for food. The sound blocked out everything. No one could reach me that I didn't want to.

Still feeling like my head might explode from the night before, my ride hadn't been quite as good as usual. I swore again that I'd never drink anymore of that stuff. I could just picture, had I drunk much more, them having to take me to Nashville General Hospital and pump my stomach. I wondered how Tully and Van felt this morning. If the one swig that Darlene had finally broken down and taken had made her sick. Maybe it was the just the second and third bottles that were the bad batch. To try to make myself feel better, I thought on the fact that school would be out in another month. Tully and Van and I would go to the Willow Plunge almost every day. We'd cruise Columbia, the next big town south of us, at night.

And then she was in my head. Her eyes. Her laugh. Still echoing in my memory, like the call of an angel across a canyon at sunrise. Like beauty had its own voice. Hers. I looked into her house as I passed it. One light in the back; she had told me that her father, Edward, got up early. He was a carpenter. Poor as dirt. I thought about what Van had told me about poor girls; how he had made fun of their house. How he had never worked a job in his life except for the time when he was twelve that he got jealous of me having a paper route and had Scoot get him on at the paper office, only to quit less than a week later. The bicycle was making his legs sore. His "studies" were suffering, is what Evelyn told my mother. I thought about how Scoot somehow wrangled him into the Academy after I'd gotten a scholarship. He had told me he was on one, but I knew enough about football to know that nobody would give him anything to play it.

Where Adams Street met South Margin was the last turn I'd make after the route was done. Having worked my way west, then back south, I'd swing through that intersection like I'd been shot out of a cannon. Lay the bike down. Feel the bottom of my boot go over the pavement like it was sliding on gray silk. Feel the back tire push as the engine began to toil and the front tire direct where the bike went over the next split second and then shoot across Adams toward the paper office to take any extra papers I had back.

At first, I didn't recognize the car pulled off on the shoulder of Adams Street, half on the sidewalk. Unless he had Percy in there with him, it was extremely uncommon to see him in the black Ford. It sat at home in the shed more than it was out. Jean drove it more than anybody besides Lucky himself. But there the son of a bitch was. Smoking a cigarette. His police uniform already on. That goddam hat sitting cock-eyed on his head like it most always did.

I had to force my eyes to meet his as I pulled the Indian to the curb and got off. Usually we at least had a feigned a smile for each other, one that hid his rage, my bitterness. As I approached him, he propped his arms on the top of the window of his car door, swung open. He raised his Lucky Strike to his mouth and took a draw. The displeasure on his face was evident, there in the half-light of the coming day and the street light still on a half a block away. Dillard Eugene Lucky Fucking Hall. When the liquor hit him just right and he'd had a good day, that's what he called himself sometimes. To Sammy Samuels, Paul Chester Sr., John Harvey.

"Is somethin' wrong?" I asked him.

"You tell me," he said.

"Sir?" I said. I stopped ten feet from him.

"You come here and tell me," he said.

It began to come back to me. Laying in the seat. My resting on the door … when I was afraid I was too drunk to go in.

I moved half the distance between him and myself. Stopped.

"You can't see nothin' from over there," he said. "You gotta come over here for me to show ya."

I took the three or four steps between us. Sucked my lungs full of air, breathed out real slow, deliberate. Now I stood on the other side of the door, so close to him that I could smell his breath, Luckys. The cheap aftershave he wore. Or maybe it was alcohol working its way out his pores from the night before. He moved to his left a foot or so and motioned for me to look on the far side of the car, where there were two footprints on the door from the worn-out wingtips.

"What is that?" he asked. "Bend down here … look. What is that?"

I tried to bend enough that I could see directly through the window, but because of the light and the glare and the darkness, I couldn't.

"No sir," he said, "come over here so you can get a good look … a good smell."

He took me by the collar and pulled me to his side of the door, forced my head into the middle of the front bench seat. I could smell the stench as soon as my nose entered the interior of the car. What had happened, what the alcohol had helped erase in the few moments of heaven it gave me, began to come back to me like the sky breaking open and pouring drops the size of marbles.

"It's footprints," I said, pulling at my collar, pulling for my breath.

He forced my head down closer to the seat, used his free hand to grab my chin and turn my head toward the floorboard.

"No, godammit. That!"

I felt his knee center itself right above my tailbone, pressing. He pulled me back with the hand in my collar. It felt like my abdomen might rip, my guts pop out. Like they had the night before, only not out my mouth this time.

"You know," he told me, like he was carrying on casual conversation, "when I got that call this mornin' about a car off in the weeds, it didn't even hit me that it had somethin' to with the fact that my car stunk so goddam bad."

I waited for him to break his hold on me, obviously one he'd learned in some of his police training. Tried to let the memories come as they did. Tried to remember what we'd done. How what he talked about had happened. I remembered seeing his car, the squad car, that is, knowing that I should stay outside awhile while the drunkenness ran out of me. Threw itself out of me. I recalled making my way into his car, believing in that impaired moment that was the safest place to be. Smelling her again, over his funky aftershave, when I lay down in the godforsaken seat.

"What is that in the floor?" he asked, like perhaps he was interrogating me. "What is it?"

Not able to come up with a lie quick enough, it seemed I had no other recourse but the truth. At least as I could remember it. "It's vomit," I told him.

"And how'd that get in here?"

Before I could answer, he's asked me if I knew anything about Tully's grandaddy's car. If that had anything to do with it.

The images hadn't settled, hadn't had enough time to simmer and come together to make sense of the whole of what had happened. "I'll clean it up," I said. "My back ... my back. It feels like you're breakin' it."

"It may feel like it ... but I ain't gonna break your back. I been doin' this when I had to for years."

He forced my head into the floorboard. "I ought'a make you eat it. I ought'a kick your ass all the way back home for what y'all did to Mr. Shafer's car."

I had closed my eyes and began to brace for the worst. Nobody was going to stop him, even if someone did see it, which was unlikely. Just somebody else Lucky was giving a hard time during an arrest. It's what kept Franklin safe.

"Get out'a the fuckin' car," he said, throwing me to the sidewalk.

Even though I didn't often pray, I prayed nobody from the paper office came. The embarrassment seemed to be so much worse than the physical pain.

"You better get home and get some shit to clean this up with."

"Can I take my papers back to the office first?" I asked him, picking myself up.

"You tell me," he said, his foot hitting me half in the hip, the rest on my ass. "Which would get it done quicker?"

"I'll take my papers to the office later," I told him.

"Goddam straight," he said. "After you've took yourself down to Mr. Shafer's and told him you're sorry. Lousy and sorry."

I started toward the Indian. Got maybe three steps.

"No ... hell no. You're gonna walk home." He drew back his foot, like he was going to kick me again. In the front if I didn't turn my ass to him. I turned. His foot landed just below my butt. "Go."

I began to walk ... watch my feet as they took step after step away from him, my boots kicking the sidewalk.

Another kick in the ass.

"Go!"

"I ain't gonna leave my motorcycle," I told him, stopping, still not looking at him.

"What?" he said.

"I'm not gonna leave the Indian," I said.

"Ain't nobody gonna bother your fuckin' motorcycle."

"I don't care," I told him. "I ain't leavin' it."

He studied me for a moment, the look on my face. He was breathing hard, his mouth open to draw in air. He turned and took a few steps toward my motorcycle. I figured he was going to kick it over, maybe push it down the hill on Adams Street. He kicked the ground.

"What'd you do that for?" he said. "I lent you the goddam car so you could have a good time."

My breathlessness was just coming to me, like I could let myself feel it only now that the crisis seemed to be passing. I pulled air in and pushed it out my open mouth, mirroring Lucky. I watched his eyes to see if the next wave would come. I reached and wiped at my knee, my blue jeans torn open over a bloody spot where I had hit the sidewalk.

"I've told ya that if you ever drank too much then I'd come get ya," he said, his hands on his knees. He wanted more air than he could get, I could tell.

I thought for a moment about landing my foot in his face. Pictured his teeth breaking, his lip splitting. But he couldn't breathe.

"Go—on," he said, "take—your—papers … to the—office. I'll take—the car—home … You can get—it—later … Just clean it—up—when you—get in—from school."

I nodded at him. " Yessir." Didn't have the heart to tell him that there was no school today.

" You better get them papers … back to the office," he said.

" Yessir, I prob'ly should," I told him.

He pulled a handkerchief out of his back pocket and wiped the sweat from his brow. He shook his head and looked around like he was trying to remember why exactly he was here on the sidewalk a mile from our house at six o'clock on a Saturday morning. His breath was coming to him again now. In and out easier, his chest rising and falling with less effort

" You ain't got—school today, do—ya?"

I had started back toward the Indian. I looked back at him. "No sir … I thought I might go…." I started not to finish, but it came out on its own, " … to Nashville, though."

"Hell," he said, "don't worry about it then. If you hadn't got to it later in the day, I can do it."

"I'll come home and do it after I go to the paper office," I said.

"It ain't nothin' if you don't," he said.

I nodded and started my motorcycle. I left Lucky standing there in the half-light of daybreak, hands still on his knees as he tried to get more air than he could, the darkness beginning to erode like the long rotting under-pinnings of our relationship.

CHAPTER TWELVE

W HAT IS DEATH but movement of our spirit into the next realm of existence? Percy once asked me. It was the summer that he first came to live with us part of the time, the summer that I turned nine and Jean got her own room. What is it but a kind of transition? Only someone who's foolish runs from something they cannot avoid.

It's true. We live our whole lives, almost everything in our culture geared toward our believing that we're immortal. And this television thing that's coming out: I'm afraid that it's only going to make it worse … take our capitalism to a whole new stratum. With these images so attractive to the eye, I'm afraid a certain few people will eventually be able to control what we desire … what we think we need.

Eight years later, his fingers were just starting to become stained yellow from the cigarettes he constantly pinched between them, which Lucky blamed on the first time he was in the insane asylum, even though he himself had the same frequency of the habit. He'd still pace to the window in the attic, open it a little more, shut it a little. Fidget with the lock. Move the fan around three or four times, just right, so it'd blow hot air in a different direction. He was quite a sight there by the window in just his tighty whities, almost as yellow as his fingers now because his mother had become too old to take care of him or his underwear when he was there. Lucky had bought him new ones earlier that summer, taken him to Biggs Men's Wear. Percy, though, wouldn't have any of them, saying he liked his old ones better. Two or three times since he had been there, our neighbor Ms. Smithson would call my mother, ask her to keep him from standing in the window in just his underwear. She had found her daughter, Christine, standing in their window, looking at the strangely thin man.

"Where was I?" he asked one night after my mother left the room.

"About death or capitalism?" I asked.

He offered me a cigarette, assured me that if Lucky knew he let me smoke then he'd beat his ass. I pushed a small chest at the end of my bed in front of the door in case my mother came back. I wished that Van could see me now, smoking with Percy. I made sure I was far away from the window so Lucky couldn't spot me when he came home from shooting craps at the filling station.

"Either," he said. "They're both very important subjects."

"We run from death. Capitalism is going to take us over," I said.

"And I think they're extremely interrelated," he said. "Do you understand why?"

I didn't understand half of what he said. I wasn't sure he was too concerned about that. I shook my head back and forth, acting interested.

He stood in front of the window only briefly, to jimmy the fan around. "How's that?"

"Still hot," I told him.

" It's because we want to believe two basic things," he said. " Number one: that we belong; and number two: that we go on forever. I think that these two desires may be the base psychic desires, or maybe even needs, of all humans. The ironic thing is that they're the things that we spend the most time on ... and they're what we already have. They can sell us anything, change the styles on us, tell us something is looking good when it's not and we have to have it. Do you know why? Because it makes us feel like we belong. From hairstyles to shoes to the kind of food we eat to the book we read, we are prone to do what's most popular because there's a strange kind of kinship, or at least feigned kinship, in it. Everything starts because it's practical. Clothes, cars … everything. Then these things are turned into something 'to have.' So somebody can look like they belong. What we don't realize is that we already belong. That we were born belonging. The spirit that runs the universe is the same spirit that drives us. You … me … everybody. Then there's the other part—the one that wants to believe that we won't die."

He made his way to the window again, studied the fan but didn't move it this time. The buzz from the cigarette was starting to make me shaky. Good shaky.

" Again, our basic desire comes from the reality that's already there. We don't die. Do we leave this world? Yes. Do we leave this plane of existence? Most certainly. Does what we are cease to exist? Hell, no!"

I held my finger up to my mouth, figuring he might draw my mother up the stairs at any minute. I didn't want to have to come up with a quick lie as to why the chest was in front of the door. Then explain it to Lucky when he got home.

" In a metaphysical way even I can't understand, the spirit which constitutes us returns to that from which it has come—the same as and separate from us. All truth, dear Henry, is dichotomous."

I was never certain if it was my eyes that would start to glaze over, or his brain.

" That's why it's so easy to go back to the three things that make up the transpiring of human events. Randomness, a planned nature of things, and basic human frailty. Many people would like to attribute most events to one of these things or another. Lessens our anxiety, I guess. Makes us feel like we're in control. But no event, even a natural disaster, rises or falls on just one of these. Perhaps two … but most times all three.

" Take Hood for example. John Bell Hood...."

Somehow we always got back to Hood. To what happened a square mile around where the house in which we sat was built. Sometimes, especially on a one-light bulb night in this attic, with the only sound the whirring of the window fan, Percy's voice and an occasional car passing down Cleburne Street, it gave me the creeps. Made the skin on my arms and shoulders feel like it was crawling all over me. I could hear the screams, the desperation, Percy, on his darker nights would describe. The bodies laying one atop another so that, he said, you could have walked a mile from our house and never touch the ground.

" Hood was a madman. His plans had come direct from General Lee. He liked to think of himself in the same vein as Lee. Kind of an aristocrat. High on the ladder in Southern social circles. They'd both gone to West Point, both ascribed to the theory that the 'leaders' had to acknowledge their superiority to their troops, because they were leaders and had great responsibility. 'A proposition that courage, discipline and will power of peculiar and exclusive sorts had to be possessed by officers leading troops into modern battle. The need to cultivate these qualities during a whole lifetime was the justification for maintaining an exclusive caste of professional officers.' Wintringham, *Weapons and Tactics*. So, basically, the son of a bitch thought he was better than everybody else."

He paced around the room a little, smothered his cigarette butt in the ashtray. Looked out the window into the darkness then checked for more cigarettes in his sock, the only other article of clothing he had on besides his yellow-white underwear. He knocked another one out of the pack and offered one to me. My head still spinning from the last one still smoking in my hand, I declined.

" He was mad, too. Mad the way any of us is when we don't really believe we measure up to what other people need us to be. Mad because Sherman had run him and his Army of Tennessee out of Georgia. Mad that he had failed to keep Sherman from takin' and destroyin' Atlanta. Mad that he'd lost a leg and use of an arm earlier in the war. Mad that he'd let them get by him at Spring Hill. Mad because he knew that if somethin' didn't change, the South was right on the verge of losin' the war. Hell, he was almost as mad as Lucky is that I always got treated better."

He laughed at his own joke, waited for me to follow suit. I did, wondering how Lucky's crapshoot was going, knowing that this more than anything affected how he'd be when he got home.

" And like I've told ya before—all hopped up on that laudanum … He had 'em here, though. With the help of Nathan Bedford Forrest, who knew the land between Columbia and Brentwood, he had them cut off. With the help of the Harpeth, there was no way they could get around him and to Nashville to join Thomas. But not only did Hood let Stewart's corps stay in the position they'd taken—the position that Stewart'd ridden back the two miles and asked him about—he let the rest of his troops bed down, satisfied that he'd positioned his troops where Schofield and his men couldn't pass through.

" And you know what happened next, don't ya?" he asked, the friction between match and flint sparking in the air.

I had drifted off. At least, almost. The kind of sleep that's not really, when you can still hear someone but their voice is serving more as a sedative than anything else. I opened my eyes, which, I am certain, he had never noticed were closed. He was standing full-fledged in front of the window now, underwear, socks and his arms tanned from the upper-arm down from where he walked around town in a tee shirt most days.

" You know, don't ya?"

I knew. He had told me a million times. But I never came far enough above the surface of sleep to speak it. I could feel my eye lids weakening as I drifted off to sleep, Percy still standing in the window, peering outward.

LUCKY, THE AVOIDANT BASTARD, tried to sneak back into the funeral home just after George Preston started to run everybody off at quarter till eight. At 7:30, when I had walked out of the room for the hundredth time, I saw his police cruiser pass and then disappear, only to reappear five minutes later, slow in front of Franklin Memorial Chapel, then disappear down West Main Street again. I wouldn't see Lucky actually materialize until he came from behind the building and tried to make his way through the manicured shrubs down its side and crawl over the railing on the front porch. Unaware that he was being watched or seen by anyone, he was cussing to himself, something he was better at than almost anyone I knew. At least fifty percent of the time I found him alone anywhere, he was accompanied by words of displeasure making their way out his mouth, almost like they had a mind of their own.

" Goddam George Preston ... queer motherfucker," he mumbled as he got one leg caught in a holly bush and the other suspended on the railing. He was blowing air through pursed lips, as he had become prone to do, trying to suck more in after he had expelled the stale from his lungs. He almost fell. Cussed about that, too. He pulled on his britches leg only to get his leg out of one bush into another, almost fall again. He found his balance, uttered a couple more curses toward George Preston and the world in general, and then secured his hands on the black railing that surrounded the concrete front porch. As he grabbed the bevel-edged iron and began to pull himself over, there was but a brief second that I saw his hands, the only thing about him that looked like Percy. Even though his hands were short, thick, and stubby and Percy's were long and thin, the nicotine stains notwithstanding they somehow looked much alike.

The previous time Lucky had returned, it had been clear out front, I assume. He had told me no different. He had just entered through the front door at a time when I had excused myself from the room and the crowd and stood in the hallway outside Celestial Gardens. As had been the case what seemed like every three or four minutes or so, George Preston had just made his way by the back entrance to the Gardens, lamenting in somewhat the same way Lucky would do crawling onto the porch later. Half to himself. Half aloud. To me when he saw I was standing there.

"Michael used to clean the carpets," he told me, the voices pushing out of the Gardens behind me, like a loud swarm of bees buzzing.

"Sir?"

"Michael ... my friend ... the boy who helped me here. He used to clean the carpets. He was so good at that. He had worked for a man who owned an antique store in Nashville before he moved in ... I mean, came to work here ... and the man had shown him how to clean oriental rugs. They had a big inventory of them. He showed him how to mix the solution ... everything."

I thought he was jobless, homeless ... a boy you were helping out.

"The least he could have done before he left was tell me how he did it." He glanced over my shoulder into Celestial Gardens like someone in there might be able to tell him how to make the concoction, but seemed to realize quickly that there would be no answers from that room. "But he just left. In the middle of the night of all things. Went back to the *antique store owner* ... I mean, back to work for him without even a thank you, notice, ... anything. He had worked for him, you know, before he got down on his luck and I helped him out. I didn't even get to say goodbye."

As it had seemed three or so hours before, it appeared that at any moment George Preston's heart might shatter like fine, fragile china dropped from table to hard floor. He pushed at the corners of his eyes with his thumb and forefinger, then pinched the bridge of his nose. Patted his hair, straightened his tie. Looked my tacky-ass suit over. His eyes stopped on my ugly shoes, then his carpet.

"It's really a shame," he said, "that this had to happen." Shook his head and sighed.

I wasn't sure if he was talking about Michael, himself ... or the woman in Celestial Gardens that I, with most of my heart, wanted to forget.

He felt for his cigarettes, well hidden in the pocket on the inside of his suit coat, almost broke down and smoked one in front of the line growing close enough that I could feel their warmth.

"Don't you think?" he asked me.

I, at the moment, had been wondering if anyone had any idea—that is, besides Sharon, who was at work—of what had happened to her, of the fact that I was behind Franklin High School almost every morning, of the fact we had seen her there, sprawled out by death ... by her killer in the parking lot. Concluding that our mornings would have to come to an end. That we would have to take up meeting somewhere else, maybe the river like we had on this morning. I wasn't sure I could do that. Even though I didn't know where the exact spot was, and I guessed nobody really did, I knew it was near. And I knew every morning I'd look for it, find my eyes wandering up and down through the brush, the weeds that raised themselves from the ground and stretched toward the blue of the sky showing through the leaves of the elm and oaks and birch on the bank. For just a moment, I was glad that this couldn't be blamed on Percy. Another scapegoat had been found.

"Young Hall!" said George Preston, turning several people's heads.

"Yessir?" I said.

"I would ask you if you, like I, think this is such a shame, but it's very obvious your mind is elsewhere."

"Yessir," I answered. "It is. And I do. The whole goddam thing," I said, my voice sounding much like Lucky's.

Mr. Preston's eyes, somewhat surprised, rose to my face for a moment, then averted to Mrs. Vickers, an older woman who had been in this place every time I had. She smiled, nodded, patted her stiff hair. He gave her a smile that ran the torment from his eyes for a moment. She took her place in the line and turned her attention to the lady in front of her, Mrs. McFadden, wife of Ed McFadden of McFadden Electric.

"I couldn't believe he just let James Langford hit him with that gun," said Mrs. McFadden. The line moved forward a few steps, Mrs. Vickers staying right behind her. "That's what Ed told me happened. He was down at the auction barn, you know, with Sammy Samuels."

"First of all," said Mrs. Vickers, widowed for many years now, "I can't believe that people are carrying guns around Franklin. Frank used to have two or three at home he hunted with … but to carry one in your pocket. Doesn't he work for you all?"

Mrs. McFadden frowned, nodded her head.

"And our sheriff didn't do one thing about it," said old lady Vickers.

It was the goddam right thing to do! I wanted to scream. For once, Lucky, the Police Chief, not the sheriff, ma'am, did the right thing. Old lady! Violence only begets more violence, Percy used to tell me. Rarely, it's a short-term solution in a world fraught with *Human Frailty*, a way to protect the innocent. But mostly it just makes people meaner … madder.

"I know," said Mrs. Mcfadden, now patting her own hair. "You have to wonder if he's going the way of his brother. You know sometimes it runs in families."

"I've heard that," said Mrs. Vickers.

"So does fuckin' stupidity," I heard myself utter under my breath. But as is often the case when anger goes unexpressed to the offending party, I felt more embarrassed than anything. I acted like I couldn't hear them, averted my eyes. Watched George Preston as his eyes moved to his carpet, noticeably dirtier, more worn than when I arrived a little before two. Finally giving in to a couple of impulses he seemed to have been having for hours, he dropped to his knees and began to inspect the carpet with close sight. His hand ran to his coat pocket, this time not stopping to feel for his cigarettes, but fingering one out of the pack and lighting it while on his hands and knees.

"My God in heaven," he mumbled, "This carpet will never be the same again."

"Are you all right?" Mrs. Vickers called to George Preston.

George was able to produce a smile again, nod his head. "Yes ma'am," he said to one of his most frequent patrons, "I've just dropped something. Young Hall here is going to help me look for it, aren't you?" He grabbed me by the britches leg just above the knee and pulled downward until I dropped to the floor alongside him and feigned the search as well.

THERE SEEMED TO BE a continual stream of people, some I knew, some I didn't, flowing in the front door of the Celestial Gardens and out the back, half of whom it seemed only to enter the line again, wait their turn once more to see this woman I was certain George Preston, by now, was wishing he had never seen. According to him, though, he had not had a choice but to do what my father asked.

"You put me in a bad position, Dillard," he told Lucky after he had made his way into the funeral home the first time, just after Mrs. McFadden and Mrs. Vickers were providing their commentary about him.

"George, what did you want me to do? Put her out in a pine box in the gymnasium we found her in front of?"

The tears that had been threatening to fall all the day, now finally started their steady treks down George's cheeks. He made no attempt to pinch them off or hide them this time.

"No. Nobody should be treated like that," he said.

For a moment, Lucky studied George like he might, in fact, be from the moon. Like they both might be so different, one from another, that someone was bound not to be human. He pulled off his hat, the marks on his head looking worse than they had earlier in the day, and laid it on the desk between George and himself. He scoured his face with his open hands, coughed a deep rattle a couple of times. Produced a Lucky. Leaned back in another of George Preston's fancy chairs and crossed one leg over the other, ankle to knee. Breathed the Lucky in deep and coughed again. George Preston reciprocated with his own cigarette, offered me one, to which Lucky cut a curious eye. I took it and George Preston touched it with his silver lighter.

"When'd you start this shit?" Lucky said, holding his cigarette out between us.

I wanted to tell him the truth. Oh, when I was nine and your brother used to give them to me. But it was just off and on for years. For kicks. For the hell of it. Still not too bad, though. It's only gotten worse in the last few months. After no more football; you know, you remember that, don't ya? Seein' me laid out on the field. It's the only time I can remember your ass cheering for me … when I was playing football, that is. You'd take your hat off and wave it around and scream at the top of your lungs. Almost dance in the stands. Embarrass Mama when she was there with you. Anyway, since then. Since all the shit hit the fan. You remember when that happened, don't ya? Right about the same time as Percy....

"I'm almost eighteen," I told him.

"What the hell difference does that make?" he asked.

George Preston watched the words pass back and forth like lobs in a tennis match.

"I guess it means I'll be out on my own pretty soon," I said.

"Yeah, I guess," he said. "You might have a hard time supportin' yourself, throwin' papers." He turned to George Preston, still watching. "You know, we thought he might have a chance to go to college. He had three or four schools lookin' at him last year. That would'a been two from here in the last ten years. Him and Ronnie Langford. But I guess neither worked out."

George Preston rolled his eyes toward the ceiling, tilted his head back. Appeared to be searching his memory. Made a sad face. One of the late casualties in World War II. He'd have done anything to get away from his father. Something we had in common. Now his father was crazy as hell—according to those old bags in line to see the dead woman for the umpteenth time, maybe another.

"Yeah, you didn't play after that injury, did you?" George Preston asked me.

I drew in deep on the cigarette, deliberately. Just to get at Lucky. "No sir," I said. "That was it."

"Didn't you want to play?" he asked me. "Was it that bad that you couldn't play again? Especially with it being your senior year."

His questions reminded me of the judge in my head that had sounded off over and over and over after it first happened. I could remember it starting even as I was laying there on the field, the pain of having my shoulder torn out of the socket and the crowd falling silent. It was like a part of me died and the pressure that went with it was lifted at the same moment.

"It was pretty bad," I said. "A couple of ligaments, the rotator cuff, cracked collarbone."

"He could'a played again," said Lucky. The same way he had said it back then until everything else happened. Until that part of him died, too. "Or at least that's what I thought at the time. In the end, though, it had to be up to him. I guess we all got to live with the decisions we make."

Outside George Preston's office window, under a light by West Main, I could see the cold rain that had been falling most of the day had almost stopped, a fine mist now floating downward on the slow wind. George Preston arose from his desk chair, a nineteenth-century Victorian, he'd told me earlier—whatever the hell that might have meant—and made his way to the door, barely cracked. He inched it open a little further and peered briefly out into the hallway.

"They're still coming," he said. "Either that or the ones that have come have never left."

"Yeah, the parkin' lot is spillin' over the edges," said Lucky. "There's a lot of people still parkin' all up and down West Main. I saw Frank and Jenny Bowman walkin' I know half a mile to get here."

Mr. Preston started back toward his desk chair, but then made his way back to the door and peered around its edge. I knew people like Eva Vickers would be here," he said. "The ones that come to the funeral home as some kind of odd hobby ... that are here every time the doors are opened know the people or not. But my God...."

"I ain't sure God's got much to do with this," said Lucky.

"Sometimes I wonder what God has to do with anything." George said, this time shutting the door completely and returning to his desk. "But then others it feels like everything that happens has got something to do with God. With some kind of guidance or something."

Planned Nature of Things. Randomness. Human Frailty.

"Death draws people to itself," said Lucky, sounding like Percy. "Rest from all the thoughts that swarm through your head, that drive ya day and night. Rest from wonderin' if what you're doin's right ... or knowin' what you done wasn't right."

George Preston, seeming a bit perturbed that Lucky had stepped on his philosophical property, quickly changed the subject to the more concrete.

"What time is it?" he asked.

Lucky looked at his Bulova, courtesy of my mother. The nicest thing she had ever given him. Would ever give him, besides herself. "Quarter till six. Almost dinner time."

"Maybe that'll keep people at home for awhile."

"I wouldn't count on it," said Lucky. "Y'all want me to bring you something when I run home? I'm sure Mary'd be happy to fix you somethin'."

"No thank you," said George Preston.

"I'm not too hungry either," I told him.

"You got your bottle with you?" asked George.

Does a bear shit in the woods? I thought.

Lucky reached into his jacket pocket and produced the thing, besides his Luckys, he was never without. He unscrewed the cap and wiped the top with his coat sleeve. Handed it to George, who took a drink like it was iced tea.

"Don't let Brother Brown down at Fourth Avenue know you're doin' that," said Lucky.

"We all have our secrets, don't we?" said George, arising, pushing his chair under his desk. Taking another drink, just as big. "That's one thing I never have understood."

"What's that?" asked Lucky, standing now.

I stood because they had.

"They say we're saved by grace. But then you have to live 'right' too. No living in sin or grace won't reach you. But they also say we're all sinners. I just really don't understand it. It seems like to me it has to be one or the other." He took another slug, shook his head.

Lucky wiped the spout when he got the bottle back, took his own swig. Shook his head along with George. George Preston turned his eyes to me, peered into mine the way somebody does when the alcohol first loosens them, or at least they expect it to.

"Young Hall," he said, "you make sure and don't speak word of this to anyone. Do you understand? One report that I was drinking whiskey in my office during this fiasco and I'm afraid people would be highly offended. Not everyone's as accepting as your father."

He took the bottle once more from Lucky and turned up another dose. Offered it to me. Lucky nodded his head when I looked at him. I took in half a mouthful, to show them I could. Almost choked, unsure if it was the whiskey or what George had said about Lucky.

"You've been a good friend to me the last six months," said my father. "I'm just returnin' what you've given me."

George nodded and searched through his top desk drawer. He placed a piece of gum in his mouth and offered Lucky and me one. Lucky declined, but I took mine. Thirty seconds later, George had spat his in the waste basket at the side of his desk and held it out for me to follow suit. You can't chew gum while you're dealing with bereaved people, he reminded me. Not only is it disrespectful but it gives an impression that you're flippant. I think that's the word he used. And no matter what reality is, he told me, people's perception of it is just as important.

CHAPTER THIRTEEN

THE HALL OF Franklin Memorial Chapel was still full of people when Lucky left George Preston's office, without looking at anything but the front door through which he would leave, and George Preston and I exited to return to Celestial Gardens. The reprieve George Preston had hoped the dinner hour would bring had in no way occurred. Conversely, more people seemed to have taken this time to make their way to the Chapel, see the woman who had been found dead behind the high school some thirty-six hours before. The circus sideshow.

Of the hundred and fifty chairs in the visitation room itself, a hundred and twenty-five of them were filled with Franklinite's asses. There were at least thirty or forty people standing near or around the casket (steel and aluminum, George Preston had assured me earlier, to keep the body from decomposing longer—a way to milk the city for more money, Lucky would tell me later). The line not only wound out into the hallway now, but around the casket itself, so the average person would have two looks as he or she passed.

The mud the rain had left looked as though it had begun to settle into the forming path on George Preston's carpet. Three or four feet wide, the swath was as apparent as it was that the woman was dead. I watched his eyes follow the trail of soil around the room until it exited along with the line going out the door of Celestial Gardens. Realizing he was outside his office now, where scowls and the like couldn't be shown and whiskey could not be drunk, he wiped the contemptuous look from his face and replaced it with a smile.

He moved close enough to me that I could smell the gum on his breath. "I'm sorry, but I have to go back into the office, Young Hall. I apologize for not helping you very much." He raised his brow and sniffed a couple of times, pinched at his eyes again. "But I feel like if I stay out here, I might have … have a nervous breakdown."

I nodded my head and turned my eyes to the floor, amazed that both "adults" in this situation had abandoned me. One for "dinner," one to keep from having a nervous breakdown. Not looking at anyone, I made my way into Celestial Gardens and grabbed one of the empty metal folding chairs. I folded it open quietly and walked to the door by which everyone was entering and exiting. Strange, I thought, how everyone was coming and going from the same door. Entering. Exiting. And equally as strange how no one looked at the other. People talked over one another's shoulders, or quietly cast words back over their own. Nevertheless, if their eyes were not on her, they were cast on the dirty carpet or the fancy French wallpaper. Until I found Lucky crawling over the railing on the front porch, I don't believe that my eyes made contact with the eyes of another human being in Franklin Memorial Chapel either.

"SONS-A-BITCHES," Lucky said to himself. "Goddam otherfuckin' sons-a-bitches. I try to do what's right and this is what I get in return?"

His eyes had yet to meet mine. And I had yet to look at the other end of the porch, from the iron railing on the west side all the way to the steps that led onto the porch itself. He glanced up at them then lowered his head and tried to make it in through the door. Three more steps and he would run chest to chest into me. He pursed his lips once more, continued his ongoing battle with the air, trying to draw breath from it. Placed his hands on his knees, opened his mouth wider.

Later I would tell him that I saw them, too. That it was the reason I had come outside, to warn him, to give him heads up. But he probably didn't believe it and I, too, knew it was a lie. I had come outside to have a cigarette to avoid the people, the situation, inside the building. George Preston had been right: it had turned into a spectacle, a circus. So much so that I found myself as ashamed I was a part of it as I had for having left her where we did the day before.

When my father was able to regain his steady breath, he reached down and picked up a plate of food he had slid under the wrought iron railing. One of my mother's white dishes, with wax paper over the top, covered what was our normal fare three or four nights a week. It was the same plate that would drop and splinter into a hundred pieces when the man spoke, scattering chicken and green beans and mashed potatoes across the concrete. Another stain for George Preston to worry about.

"Police Chief Hall?" one of them called. A medium-built, dark-haired man in his early thirties. "Any changes in the case? Anything new?"

Lucky finally noticed me as he almost ran into me, looked at the broken plate, the scattered food, but not at the man. Didn't say a word to him. Kept walking.

"Dillard Hall?" another man called. This one older, white hair topping his head.

Lucky took me by the arm, tried to make his way, while pulling me, through the double front doors of the Chapel, kicking the broken glass and, inadvertently, half the food through one door onto the carpet as he managed to get the door open.

"Chief Hall?" a third one called from behind the other two. "Any breaks in the case?"

The manner in which Lucky had me, my arm, the one door was not quite big enough for us to pass through quickly. My shoulder hit the door still closed. Lucky eyed the food spilled and now spread across the porch onto the carpet. He tried to reach and scoop most if it with one hand as he attempted to push me through with the other. Mrs. McFadden and Mrs. Vickers, along with three other women were slowly traipsing toward the door. Lucky raised himself right into Mrs. McFadden's ample bosom, pushed me there, too. From the impact, Lucky's hat flew backward and then his head and then his short legs, until he was resting on his ass there on the front porch of Franklin Memorial Chapel, the three reporters now circling him as Eva Vickers, Jeannie McFadden, and the other women cordially asked if he was okay then passed by and otherwise uneventfully out the double doors.

"Chief Hall?" the older reporter said, "we've heard you now have two men in custody. Is that true?"

Lucky looked up at him like if he could have gotten away with it, he would have, in fact, shot the bastard. He felt behind him, his stubby hands running over the concrete and through the mess of food, for his hat. The marks on his head, almost fully fermented by now, looked worse than they had even a couple of hours earlier. Or maybe it was the yellowish light. I remembered what George Preston said about reality and perception, wondering for a moment how bad his head was really hurt, if he needed to go see Dr. Guppy. With the hand free of holding the door open, I tried to reach Lucky and his outstretched hand after he had placed his hat, now decorated with green beans and some mashed potatoes, back on his head.

"Just let me sit here a minute," Lucky told me.

The three men converged around us, so close that Lucky couldn't have stood by himself if he had wanted to. Lucky took my hand and, with my help, pulled himself up, his shoulder hitting one of them in the chest as he stumbled a couple of steps and sat on one of the benches on each side of the front door.

"Did you take another negro man into custody, Chief Hall?" the older man asked, the one with a tuft of white hair. He had a pad in his hand, a pen ready for Lucky's response.

Lucky appeared, circled there on the bench on which he sat, to have resigned himself to the hard fact he was going to have to hold conversation with them. "Yessir," he told him.

"So, were they both involved?" the younger one asked, his pad and pencil poised, too.

"I ain't sure that either of them was involved," said Lucky.

It sounded like Lucky might have done more than go home for "supper." It sounded like—and I imagined—that he had been sitting out under the carport, nursing his bottle in the car. Probably the only place in town no one would bother him.

The other two scribbling, silence was opened for the third, Fred Creason, from our hometown paper, a three-time a week rag called the *Review Appeal*. "Why do you say that, Chief Hall?"

"Just a hunch I got," said Lucky.

Although I had no idea what they were writing, and would not until the day after when I sat in the floor of the paper office and read it, it seemed like they were noting ten words for his every one. As far as I could remember, reporters from the Nashville papers had never been to Franklin to interview him about anything.

"Then why'd you take them into custody?" the younger one asked. A tag on his shirt read, "Larry Beaman, *Nashville Banner*."

From the look on his face as each question was now hurled, one after another, I imagined the war in his brain waged between what-should-I-say? and what-shouldn't-I-say? somehow moderated or impeded by the alcohol it was swimming in. With each inquiry, he looked a little more deeply into the eyes above the mouth that had asked. He took out a cigarette, to calm his nerves, I imagined … for something to do with his hands, which had been picking and wiping at the beans and potatoes remaining on his hat.

"'Cause I thought it was the right thing to do," said Lucky.

"Why? If I might ask," the older one said. Herman Garrison, from the Nashville *Tennessean*.

I knew what Lucky didn't want to say. That some good citizen of Franklin—somebody he was probably friends with—would probably try to kill them, just because they could. Because not a jury in the county would convict a white man for killing a black man in Franklin, Tennessee in December of 1953.

"It's what we've got to go on right now. We're lookin' into every available lead," said Lucky. Having now fully recovered his breath and bearings and knocked most of the food from his hat, he arose from the bench and stepped between two of the reporters on his way to the front door once more.

"What other leads do you have?" Larry Beaman asked. He had positioned himself where Lucky could not pass through the doorway.

I looked in the door, to see George Preston peering out nervously onto the porch. I figured he was poised to attack the chicken and green beans the moment Lucky and the reporters cleared.

Lucky's feet weren't steady. On his second and third steps from the place where he had stood, they had moved laterally to help him steady himself. He raised his hand casually and propped himself on the wall.

"If you'll 'scuse me," he said to Larry Beaman, "I'll be passing through the door now."

Covertly rude but not obviously defiant, Mr. Beaman moved his feet enough to have appeared he moved, but still not enough where Lucky could pass easily.

"Have you been drinkin', Chief Hall?" he asked. His voice, its inflection, had a nagging quality, like fingernails sliding lightly across a chalkboard.

Lucky looked at him like he had been slapped. Nobody in Franklin would have ever asked such a question. With church and a beer joint every mile, a still in every stand of woods, it was as common for a lawman to drink as for his wife to attend church regularly. It was how he had gotten in with Oscar Garrett, his predecessor, to begin with. Drinking buddies. Crap-shooting buddies.

"I ain't sure that's any of your business," he said.

"Oh, everything's our business, Chief Hall," said Herman Garrison, the older one.

"Our business and the business of our readers," said Beaman, the little prick.

"How'd you get the marks on your head, Lucky?" asked Fred Creason. I was certain he already knew. If the busybody old women inside knew, then

I was sure it had made it back to the *Review Appeal* already. But they wouldn't run such a thing; they only ran the "good" things, or at least the civil ones.

Lucky there, propped up on the wall, appeared as if one strong breath might finish him. He eyed the men as if he were trying to decide what course of action to take. He drew from the Lucky in his free hand and started to drop it on the porch but seemed to suddenly realize where he was. He kept the cigarette in his hand, the fire growing ever closer to his thumb and forefinger. Finally, he exposed the bottom of his boot, and snuffed out the burning butt there. Then dropped it in his pants pocket.

"219 Russell Street," he said. "Ike Beatty."

Their pens went to scribbling again. "What's that?" Beaman asked.

"An address and a name," Lucky said sarcastically.

"Whose?" said Herman Garrison.

"Your guess is as good as mine," said Lucky. "It was the only thing we found with the body. In the pocket of them ridin' pants she had on. That's all it said. Just a name and number."

"And no idea who that is … or where?"

"No sir," said Lucky. "I've had a couple of men who've been checkin' but they ain't turned up anything yet."

Truth was there was more evidence than Lucky was letting on.

Now having given them the only piece of information I figured he'd been holding back for the better part of two days, Lucky must have thought them sated. He turned his bloodshot eyes from one to another, the little young man, our local man then to the older one, Garrison. His jaw locked, he turned his face to West Main Street, watched a couple of cars pass, people move down the concrete sidewalk glowing white in the darkness and toward their cars. He knocked some stray potatoes off his sleeve, a green bean off his pants. Then turned himself back to Beaman.

"Now, if you'll 'scuse me," he said, "I'll be goin' in. I've got some other things to take care of."

"Chief Hall?" he said.

"Yessir?" said Lucky.

"Why'd you take those negroes into custody if you don't think they did it?"

"'Cause the whole town thinks they did," he said. He grasped the door handle and passed through one of the double doors and motioned for me to follow him. He nodded at George Preston, still standing in the front foyer, now appearing none the worse for wear. Like he had set sail on the sea of contentment via another bottle somewhere. This time, he allowed his eyes to float toward the front, where the line seemed to have remained as long as it had been most of the afternoon and evening. He shook his head, I assumed, in amazement.

"What time do we cut it off?" George Preston asked him.

"What time is it now?" Lucky said.

George Preston said, "You have a watch, Dillard."

Lucky turned his wrist and peered at its face. "Son of bitch either quit or I forgot to wind it. I ain't sure."

I looked at my Mickey Mouse, sometimes the only vestige of childhood I had left. The reason I took shit from everybody about it. Seemed important for some reason. "It's seven-thirty," I said. "Or just a couple of minutes after."

"Quarter to eight," said Lucky. "I say that's when we stop lettin' people come in. How's that, George?"

George Preston turned and looked at the line, then turned his gaze to what had been a fine, deep burgundy, floral patterned carpet before this day. Now a soppy mess of embedded footprints and mud.

"Maybe I can find Michael in Nashville," he said. "Find out from him what his secret potion was."

Lucky raised his eyebrows, frowned, and nodded his head. I followed them as they both took refuge behind the closed door of the front office. Soon, Lucky and I would begin to turn people away at the front door, and George Preston would prepare to finish his job.

CHAPTER FOURTEEN

EVEN THOUGH IT'S THE MIDDLE of December, the attic is hotter than I imagine hell. My sweat has covered the sheet and I lay in it, that is, when I'm not rolling from side to side of that tiny bed. The bed on the other side is, of course, empty. Jean's fat ass is downstairs where she can hear my mother up tinkering around during the night, Lucky snoring like a damn freight train, when he isn't coughing and hacking, bringing up his lungs. Over the years, I guess, I remember Percy sleeping up here with me more than anybody else. Occasionally, Lucky makes his way up here like he did last night. When he's playing pretend with my mother. With me … that we really have a relationship. Every once in awhile, it seems like Percy's still here, still spouting all that bullshit he used to … moving around, arranging himself one way then the other because he's too long to sleep in the fucking bed.

For a minute I hit a position where it feels good. Throw the covers off, lay there in my own sweat, the air in the room cooling me as it merges with the water my body's produced. The ceiling as dark as pitch, the only light's the little coming in the window from a street light half way up the block. I try to imagine what Lucky and my mother are doing downstairs … what they're talking about. Probably Jean. If they do talk about me at all, I imagine that it's Lucky, lamenting what became of my football career. Saying that it makes him feel bad because I really don't have any other talents besides baseball and football. Not the smartest guy in the world—I mean after all, look what happened to him after his football career went down the drain. You know that was Paul Chester's fault, my mother would tell him. Hey, Lucky, I want to scream out in the attic, if I ain't too smart then I'm sure that I got it from you! But nobody screams much anymore. I've noticed that.

Turn over again. Sometimes, I think I can smell Percy, too. He had this strange scent, cigarettes combined with something. Kind of musty. Not stinky, though. Not particularly unpleasant. As a matter of fact, smelling it usually calms me. Makes me think in some odd way—maybe one of those ways he talked about—he's still around here. It's all about energy, he used to tell me. It's a fact of science: energy is neither created nor destroyed. The same energy that runs us will always be around, Henry. That's what he'd say.

A noise makes me come two feet off the bed. Something hitting the side of the house ... probably just a stray tree limb knocked loose in the rain earlier. Or it could be that person ... whoever he...they...she might be. I don't imagine it to be a woman. Women seldom can be as mean as men. Sometimes bigger pains in the ass, but not as mean.

I try to tell myself that there's nothing to worry about. That Lucky has arrested two people, although he believes it's the wrong two people. That whoever did this is not concerned with me, in the upstairs bedroom ... no, you can't really call it a bedroom ... in the fucking hotbox, I mean hotbox (no fucking; bad words might make them come, make something bad happen) of an attic of a little brick house on Cleburne Street. Maybe God will send whoever it was over here to strike my ass down. That's the way my mother and Jean and Brother Myron Brown talk about God. He's always waiting to catch somebody doing something wrong so he can kick them in the ass. Sounds a lot like Lucky to me.

Lucky and Percy used to fight about that. You gotta make somebody into what they become, Lucky would say. We don't have to be made into anything, Percy would say. We already are what we are ... what we're to become. But at the same time we're taught to run from that person because we're taught to avoid anything that's flawed. And I can guarantee you this, Henry Boy, that person is flawed. Human Frailty, my boy. If somebody is open to everything inside them, or even the majority of voices that fly through their heads, then they know how fucked we all are. But unless we live into that, then we never know. If we pretend we don't hear the voices, then we never know what they say. What they tell us about ourselves. It's easier to pretend we don't hear them.

He hears fuckin' voices all right, Lucky would tell me when I told him things like this. It took a while for me to realize it did no good, only made Lucky madder than he normally was, to tell him the kind of stuff Percy talked to me about. I was a captive audience, I guess. Somebody to whom he could spew his ideas like water coming from a spring in a feral field. The son of a bitch has always heard voices, he'd say. That's what happens to people when they don't have to do anything. By the time Mother and Daddy had him, they was too old to be hard on him. I guess he was a fucking surprise. In more ways than one. He wasn't right from the beginning … and I think it's just got worse with the years. I can still remember Mother and Daddy and Wanda Jean and Nelly and … me working out in the field and fuckin' Percy sittin' on the porch, readin' a book.

You know, that's what he always had thought, don't ya, Henry Boy? He's always thought that I got crazy 'cause Mama and Daddy were too easy on me. That they didn't hold me to the same standard they held the other ones to. He thinks they let me read too much. He belly laughs. It's a good sound. As good as I know. Like kindness dancing, holding itself out where you can hear it, know what it sounds like. He says that I use it to avoid reality. His eyes grow tired, the heaviest thing about him. And you know the funniest goddam thing? He thinks that I don't know I'm this way. He lights a cigarette, holds the pack out to me. I listen to see if I hear Mama moving around downstairs. Don't. I take the one he's shook out the furthest. He touches it with the match he's struck. Don't let your daddy find out that I'm givin' you cigarettes, okay? You know, he can be a violent man at times. The only ones I've never known him not to be violent toward is Mama and

Daddy. He's the same way as our daddy. It just comes over him, takes him like an evil spirit. As for me, I'm starting to enjoy the nicotine buzz, and even though Percy's a little crazy and the stuff he talks about doesn't always make sense, he keeps me from being lonesome. Lonesome in my own goddam house.

I tell you how I make myself feel better, though, Henry Boy. Do you wanna know that? I nod, so the silence won't close in around me, bring the voices, the evil spirits, the demons, whatever the hell you want to call it, along with it. I know that everybody's got it. Their own affliction. When *Randomness* meets *Human Frailty*. Gives us our own particular brand of frailty.

You know the trick, don't ya? he asks. The nicotine's taking its effect by now. My hands are shaking ever so slightly as I try to hold the thing to my mouth. I take its burn-off all the way to the bottom of my lungs and shake my head back and forth.

The trick's not letting the craziness in us turn into meanness. That's what happens when we convince ourselves it's not there. It bends all around itself, distorts itself into something that looks different. Something that swells beyond the person it's in and starts to hurt other people. Latches onto their life and starts to affect the energy coming through them. Takes their energy like a leech. Hood's a primary example of that, you know. I know, I know … you get tired of hearing about him. I can tell by the look on your face. I won't talk about him tonight. I shake my head back and forth, try to convince him with a feigned smile that I want him to keep talking, even if he tells me about General Hood.

He couldn't admit that his perception was primarily distorted, that his frailty was about to turn into randomness in the lives of so many of his men. He was more concerned with quieting the voices in his own head.

Percy paces to the window, like I've seen him do a thousand times, pulls his pack of cigarettes from his sock, the only one article of clothing he has on besides his skivvies. He touches the burning head of a match to the end of it, smoke wafting up, coloring his face hazy and gray for a moment. He checks out the window for Christine Smithson. He turns quick, like she might have been there, seen him. Takes to staring at his cigarette.

It *is* like John Bell Hood, he says, like he forgot he told me he wouldn't talk about him. He sacrificed so many men because he couldn't identify what were the crazy voices, what were the sane ones. Laudanum. Have I ever told you that?

I nod.

He's nervous now. Fidgety like he got both those times. The summer when I was nine and last summer. Pacing. Looking like his head might blow off if he doesn't find a way to get where he's trying to go with his words. He stops. Stares at me kind of insolently. Like maybe he's seeing Lucky, not me.

He'd been hurt at Chickamauga, he tells me anyway. He needs something to say, something else to focus on to help him avoid the voices in his head. He told me that just last summer. Got real sad and told me, like he was finally admitting he was crazy. Finally giving in to what everybody else already knew. Acknowledging that the voices in his head were worse than the average Joe. Or average Jane, he had laughed when he told me.

He had lost a leg and had a useless arm. Did you know that?

Yes, I tell him.

He gets up from the spot on the end of the bed he'd taken and paces to the window again. He stands there, his elbow cupped in the palm of his other hand at the bottom of his rib cage, puffing out the smoke he draws from the cigarette.

I believe in God enough to believe that what he, or hell, she made us to be is all right. It goes back to the whole energy idea, he tells me, knowing that God is spirit and in us is that spirit and in everybody is that spirit. The spirit … the energy … that's what drives us. But we live in a society of people that make themselves into something. What the hell does that mean? We all look alike, act alike, talk alike because there's a comfort there. It can't be wrong if everybody's doin' it. I tell ya this, Henry Boy, there's gonna come a day—not too long in the future, I might add—when people are gonna start knocking against this cookie-cutter mentality. Gonna see that there's more to life than a house in a subdivision, two kids, a sedan and decent job. We feel so good right now that the Germans and the Japs didn't take us over, we haven't thought about anything else in ten years.

He keeps his back to me as he speaks. Seems to have run out of words to keep away what he runs from. That feeling of not having control of one thing in the whole world, even your own mind.

Now, it seems forever ago when he told me how a huge pig with foot-long fangs had been following him for weeks, tracking him everywhere he went. Cussed at him when he wasn't paying enough attention to him. Snarled and called him ugly names. And the goddam pig was hungry, he added. It was all I could do to keep myself from laughing when he told me, until I saw his eyes, grievous and fixated on the place where he told me he sat waiting right now, to follow him again when he left and went somewhere else.

To know God is to participate in the ongoing process of disillusionment, he tells me. He sits at the base of the window, his head high enough that he can still see out the window. He smothers his cigarette in the ashtray he keeps up here. Shakes his head. And sighs as deep as a human can.

HE WAS HERE ONE MINUTE, gone the next, but I'm still here. Like a prisoner of this damned place. The doors are locked downstairs. Lucky's got his gun if he needed it. Probably too drunk to hit a bull in the ass with a bass fiddle, though. I can feel sleep coming finally, settling over me like a soft breeze. And God knows I need it after the last couple of days. My banging heart slowing down. There goes the stupid noise again. Nothing. Nothing.

I walk to the far window, on the west side of the house. I still don't look out the one on the east side. As a matter of fact, I took the ashtray he used and slid it under the bed, with his butts still in it. I knew if I had left it out, it would have just disappeared like him. It would have been just one more piece of playing pretend. With his cigarette butts under the bed, I can look and remind myself he was here. Really here. Not like tonight. There goes the damned noise again. It sounds like it's toward the front of the house, the south side. I wonder if it could be something on the inside. Without thinking, I open the closet within my reach as I stand near the window. She falls out on me. Takes me to the ground with her. Folds on top of me.

I can't get her off me. She weighs three hundred pounds, but it looks like she should only weigh a hundred and thirty. And she doesn't look like George Preston made her look. She's back the way she looked in the parking lot. But now she's got maggots eating at the wound. Oozing, working all down in it, spilling out down her chest into the collar of her shirt. And the goddam things are falling on me. In my hair, my eyes, my mouth, even though I've got my jaw locked trying to keep them out. She's dead but everywhere I move her, try to push her arms, her trunk, she falls right on me again. It's like I'm one pole of a magnet and she's the other. Now her wound's bleeding on me, all over me. At least the maggots are gone. No, there's one. I flick the motherfucker off. Just her blood mostly covering me now. Making her too slick to push off me. I begin to pry at her eye lids, thinking if I can get them open again, then everything will be all right. That I can turn back everything that's happened in the last year. For a moment I think they're open, but then I realize it's just been me holding one that way. When my finger moves, the lid drops shut again. I start to panic. I can't just leave her here. If I leave her on top of me, then I can't get up myself. I struggle again with all I'm worth. Can feel my shoulder grinding, pulling, acting like it might pop again.

Now there's no blood, just a dead body. As lifeless as an old tire fished from the bottom of the river. And now she's stiff as a goddam board. The way I imagined her to be when I let myself look at her in the coffin at Franklin Memorial Chapel. I roll her off me and she hits the floor hard, cracking so loud I'm afraid it's awakened Mama and Lucky.

And now I'm carrying her. She's lighter than I imagined. Her dark hair is falling around my face as I try to push it away from me as I run. She slips a few times, as I try to pull her up onto my shoulder higher. She's laying over my shoulder, her breasts just on the other side. Her arms dangle down my back. I can feel them bounce up and down as I run down West Main Street. In the distance, I see the Chapel, people pouring out of the Zion Room, stone-faced. I want to stop, to go back and see who's there this time.

But I can't stop running; even though she's become heavy as hell, I can't stop. My shoulder's the weariest thing about me. It burns like somebody's stuck a hot poker to it. I finally can go no more. I stop and lay her down on the sidewalk; they're a quarter mile down West Main. I think to myself that I have at least a minute, maybe ninety seconds, the way they're coming.

From the distance I am, I can see that Jimmy Langford is leading the pack. Paul Chester and John Harvey are behind him. Sammy Samuels behind them, with that characteristic smile on his face, one that Lucky calls "a shit-eatin' grin." They've all got bats or guns. They're grumbling among themselves.

"You know that little bastard had somethin' to do with it," Jimmy Langford tells them.

Now I can't pick her up. She weighs three hundred pounds again. I start to try to drag her down the sidewalk.

"I used to trust the little motherfucker," says goddam Sammy. "I trusted him when he was playing football. He could run with a fuckin' football, couldn't he? That was before he turned pussy, wasn't it? Hey, Jimmy?" he says.

Still coming, now an eighth of a mile away, Jimmy Langford says, "Yeah?"

"Ain't that a goddam shame, how your boy gave up his football playin' career to go defend his country ... and then you got this kid. I don't even know what to say or think about somebody like him."

"I tell ya what you can say," says John Harvey. "You can say that he's a fuckin' quitter ... and he's a murderer. He's been fuckin' that poor little ole white trash Bishop girl up there behind Franklin High School ever since Van Manor got through fuckin' her. Who the hell else would have dumped that damn body there? He's probably like his daddy ... not the sharpest knife in the drawer and given to fits of rage. Lose his head; not know ten minutes later what he did and what he didn't do."

As I'm still struggling to get her up, I begin to try to explain it to them, at the same time, surprised I'm an apologist for Lucky. "He didn't do that this mornin'. Didn't you bunch'a assholes see him? Jimmy Langford, you're lucky he didn't whip your ass. I've seen him whip the ass of bigger men than you. With one fuckin' punch from one of those short, ham hock arms.

"There he is!" yells Paul Chester. "He's been cheatin' for years. He and that goddam Manor. They're two of a kind. They both been cheatin' ever since the Academy let 'em in. Cheatin' and stealin' cigarettes out of my store. Somehow they talked my boy into gettin' 'em for 'em. Prob'ly just like they talked him into cheatin'."

"I don't reckon anybody had to talk little Pauley into doin' anything bad," says Sammy to John Harvey. Paul Chester and Jimmy Langford don't hear him. I do as I'm struggling to get her on my shoulders again and run.

But now she's gone. Into thin air. I turn and look behind me to see her rising into the early morning sky. The darkness has suddenly given itself over to daylight. She smiles and waves at me like she forgives me for all I've done to her. I'm relieved to see her without that fucking gash at her throat. Or really four gashes that George Preston was able to merge together with make-up to look more like one sewn shut. Her clothes are new now. No more riding pants. No cheap coat with fake fur around the collar. She has on a nice skirt, a sweater, hose, and high heels. I gasp for breath because she's dressed like Sharon. But before I can think more about it, I can hear them getting closer.

"There he is!" screams Sammy Samuels. "He's right there. We're right on top of him. He's waitin' on us. Get him!"

As they move their last hundred feet toward me, like I'm in a completely different time and circumstance, I turn to see where Arliss is, knowing now that they are chasing him. I can feel my heart jack-hammering so hard in my chest I think my ribs might break. When they're close enough that I can hear their feet moving across the pavement of the sidewalk, I extend my hands reflex-like to protect myself.

Both my hands are black. I pull at the collar on my shirt; my chest is black, the few hairs on it, dark, short and kinky. With Paul Chester a dozen feet away from me, I turn and begin to try to run. Knowing they'll surely kill me if they catch me, I imagine that they'll string me up from a tree out in the county somewhere, like's probably been done many times before. A bunch of proud white assholes posing for a picture like they've been hunting. I've seen things like that, I'm sorry to say, come from my state and the ones that surround it.

I'm trying to get up speed like when I used to return kickoffs, hit the best stride right before you fall in behind the wedge, so it takes more than slight contact to bring or slow you down. I try to push my legs harder, but I can't because I can't breathe. Can't suck in enough air to get my body to work right.

I feel Paul Chester's hand on my back then my shoulder as he takes a good grasp and then starts to bring me to the concrete. I feel the warmth of the other men as they converge on the prey Paul Chester has brought down.

CHAPTER FIFTEEN

"GODDAM!" I GASPED, trying to fight his hands away from me. I couldn't breathe, the air full of lumps as I tried to draw it past the profanity. Before I knew it I was swinging—flailing, I guess, is more like it—and my hands were striking his hands, his chest, his face. He was squinting, reaching for my hands as they tried to fight him off. Grimacing, each time one of my hands would make contact.

I looked into Lucky's face, for the first time in I couldn't tell you when. His eyes were green, and they were tired, pulled down at the corners. Sad maybe. His smell finally touched me. He reeked of cigarettes and whiskey and work. His tee shirt, like mine, was drenched with his own sweat. His chest still rose and fell hard from his ascension of the stairs to the attic. He stood and propped himself on a desk I sometimes did my homework on back when I did it, his hands on its top, holding his torso almost upright.

"I got Don Walton down at the jail, spending the night tonight. Him and Lucas Reasonover."

"Don Walton back in town?" I asked him.

"Yeah. He come back," he said. "I had to call him at his mama's in Paducah … get him to drive back. I need all the men I can get, I guess."

"Anybody say anything about knowing that woman?" I asked him.

"Not one goddam word," he told me. "You believe that? As many people as was there." He laughed. Sad and resolute.

"How many people you think came?"

He lit a Lucky. Surprisingly, offered me one. Lit it once I took it from his hand.

"From the looks of that register George Preston had out, quite a few hundred. And I'm damn sure a lot of them didn't sign it. A' course, everybody there was there for the good of the commun'ty."

"Sure," I told him.

He sat quietly for a few moments, staring off into the darkness out the same window Percy used to look. One eye mostly closed, contorting his face in a way he did when he was thinking hard about something.

"Had to fire a fuckin' warnin' shot at goddam Jimmy Langford tonight," he told me.

"Really?"

"Yeah, I fired it right into Sammy Samuels' grill."

"Of that new Ford?" I asked.

"Well, it's a coupl'a years old," he said. "But yeah, that's the one."

I nodded. Drew deep on the cigarette, like he was doing. "What'd he do?"

"He set there for a minute, I think, considerin' whether or not to pull that pistol I know he carries from under the seat while his headlights shined in my eyes. I couldn't see 'em good, but I knew who they were. Jimmy Langford was the only one crazy enough to stick his head out of the car. Crazy bastard. He hit me in the head with a pistol this mornin'." He reached up, patted his head with the flat of his hand. "He was yellin' out the winda' that this time he had a shotgun. He'd shoot me and the whole goddam Mosby family if he had to."

I was just coming back to the time and place in which we sat, rubbing sleep and confusion from my eyes. Just realizing that this, too, wasn't a part of that godforsaken dream I'd been having half the night.

"Just about the time the day started to turn gray, Miss Helen called me and said Mrs. Mosby had got out of her house and got to somebody's house with a phone and called. The fuckin' cowards was outside their house, hollerin'." For a brief moment, he stared into me like I might have the answer to some burning question he couldn't articulate. "I prob'ly shouldn't call 'em that. I guess they're just scared like everybody else. People want answers … want them answers to be the sure thing. If they're not, then I think alot'a times we do what it takes in our mind to make 'em that way. Like Percy and the goddam graveyard. Or Percy and them women. Some things just never come clear as a cloudless sky. Most things, I guess."

It was the first time I could remember Lucky, or anybody else in our house for that matter, mentioning Percy since the late days of summer had given way to early fall. It had not only been just like he disappeared—but like he had never been there in the first place. I started to acknowledge the fact that he had mentioned his own brother's name. But I was afraid it would cause him to never do it again. The mere mention of his name had been comforting, soothed something in me that stupid dream had only made more raw.

"So, did they want Arliss?"

"Yeah … and I guess they were gonna take him, too. I was hopin' at first that they was there just to scare him. But I think if I hadn't took him in myself, then they would'a hurt him. Prob'ly killed him. Anyway … I never give 'em a chance to get him. Miss Helen said when Mrs. Mosby called her she was cryin' and gaspin' for breath, sayin' that them men had been yellin' for that 'little murderin' nigger' to come on out or they was gonna come in there and get 'im."

I imagined Lucky holed up in his squad car under our carport, nursing one of the three or four bottles he kept different places. Getting the call from Miss Helen. Cussing a blue streak because he had to re-enter the world … do his job.

"When I first come out with him, they was yellin' all kinds a things at me. Nigger Lover. That George Preston and me was queer … had been suckin' each other's dick over at the funeral home. But there just stayed this strange calmness about me. Kinda like the situation with Jimmy Langford this mornin'. Doin' nothin' but lookin' at 'em like they was idiots seemed to be the best thing in the world to do. But then they got between me and my car as I took Arliss back up the side'a the road. That was a mistake, I guess, leavin' the car up the road. No matter … they said they wasn't gonna let me get to the car with him. That if I did, then I'd just take Arliss down there and store him like I had that other nigger, his daddy.

"Even though I couldn't see 'em, I asked every one of 'em by name to get out'a the way. But it didn't make no difference—they had made up their mind that they was gonna be the heroes a' the town. They was gonna keep workin' things up until somebody got a wild hair up his ass to fire a shot. After I'd tried five different ways to get around the goddam Ford, I finally just pulled out my pistol and let off a round into the grill."

"What'd they do?" I asked him.

"Jimmy Langford had that shotgun sighted on me, I could see that much. Me or Arliss. But the rest of 'em didn't do anythin' but sit there. Sit there and look like I did when I fell on my ass on the front porch a' the funeral home."

WHEN SHARON'S DADDY and sister died was one of the few times that I would go into that house. Or the shack, as Van the asshole called it. I'd usually make it only inside the door, or maybe halfway through the front room, which was the living room, when somebody would intercept me. Sharon's mother, Ima, or Bootlegger Bobby when he was there. Or one of Edward's kids from his first marriage, most of them as old as Ima herself, come to help her because she still hadn't recovered from the loss, the travesty fate had heaped on her. Goddam Randomness.

I always figured it was the house they were trying to keep me from seeing. I don't think Sharon ever got over what she came from, or what people like Van the Man, as he liked to call himself, said about it. That's why she dressed and talked like she did, I imagined, to prove to people she wasn't from exactly where she, in fact, was from. The "mixed" section of town. That's why she put on the nice clothes she'd bought on her employee discount from Castner Knott, drove to the nice area of Nashville to work every day.

No self-respecting white man or woman wanted to live there. The few square blocks that constituted this area were in fact for the poorest of the white people. White people, in essence, who had no more power than black people, except for the little that came from being white. Many people, including Sammy Samuels and Jimmy Langford (who they had called Little Nigger in school because of the dark color of his skin, and where he lived), had spent their younger days there, making it the goal of their lives to transcend the area. Rise from it like smoke and fade colorless into the sky. Fly away. In particular, their journeys had taken them only a few blocks, maybe four or five, to a section of town about that far away from where we lived. Far enough, though, that they could claim they no longer lived in the "mixed section."

After the Depression had flushed people from their farms and then the prosperity and spirit of World War II had built them brick homes in subdivisions, the section itself had become more and more black, except for the "White Trash," an expression I heard the first time from Jean. Only the white people who had no means to leave had stayed.

THE HOUSE NEXT DOOR to the Bishops had been empty since the white people who could had begun to flee the "mixed section," and the Samuels family had finally moved to the house where they lived after Sammy's idea of auctioning dead people's things took off. Pretty much just like the house that the Bishop's lived in, a little frame dwelling, small enough, as Van had said, that you could spit from the front door to the back door, John Harvey had refused to rent it to a black family and no white family wanted it. Believing that if somebody didn't take a stand then the "colored" people were going to take over the town, he had told Lucky he would refuse to rent the house at all. And it sat as empty as most of the neighbors' pockets.

It was useful at times, though. Bobby Bishop now sold bootleg whisky out of it. He'd just taken to doing this, Tully had told me, since he had turned eighteen, decided not to go back for his third trip through the tenth grade and left his mother's house. Running moonshine up from Peytonsville (better known as Little Texas) or even Alabama, and giving an alternative to Paul Chester and the four or five beer joints between Franklin and Brentwood and the one or two other people who sold it in town, was a lucrative thing to do, Tully had explained it to me. And nobody, including Lucky, really policed that part of town. Hell, that's where he should have gotten the shine rather than the stuff that nearly killed me. It should have been—from Bootlegger Bobby, he called him. He was thinking about setting a still up in the back of the house, Tully had gone on, because old man Harvey never checked on it. Was just gonna let the son of a bitch fall down before he'd rent it to a black family.

"Really, though," Sharon explained to me, "he's not a bootlegger. He just got mixed up with some of those guys down there in Little Texas. That's where his daddy was originally from and he's always gone down there since he was old enough to walk by himself. I'm not sure how much his daddy would ever have to do with him, but I guess he did make a lot of other friends down there. Older men who felt sorry for him. That's why Mama told him in the fall that she wasn't letting him live there anymore. I guess we're just as well off. He really didn't do anything anyway except give us a little money every now and then. He still stays at our house half the time, though."

She moved around a little. Tried to find a more comfortable position. Arranged the blanket under us some. The night was as dark as coal around us, the walls blending into the windows, even where light was supposed to come through. The old wall paper, a muted print, bled into the ceiling, having lost its whiteness over the years. The wood floor, cold under us as we lay there, felt almost icy to the touch. We had lain there long enough that I thought my eyes would have adjusted, my pupils dilated enough that I could make out one color from another. Everything, though, was colorless. The darkness bleeding color from itself, stripping it of its essence.

"Are you cold?" I asked her. I pulled the blanket high enough that only my nose and forehead were uncovered.

"Oh … a little," she told me. "But I bet you're colder. The girl's supposed to be colder."

"Well, in this case, it ain't true," I told her. I pulled her body as close to mine as I could get it. The place smelled of empty house, whatever that is. The smell of memory, of happenings with a voice no longer. She smelled like she always did. Somewhere between that perfume she bought at the department store and just clean.

"We haven't had heat all winter," she told me.

"Humh?" I said, trying to rescue my mind from the wandering it had undertaken.

"We haven't had any heat besides the stove and the fireplace all winter."

"Why?"

"The only money we have coming into the house is my check," she said. "That and what Bobby makes selling his whiskey. Mama hasn't gone to work in months."

"I thought she worked at the elementary school cafeteria."

"She did," she said, "but she left there a month into the school year. Well … I really don't know if she left or of she was fired. She's pretty much just walking around unconscious since Daddy and Sheila. She dreams at night, says Sheila calls her, tells her to come down to HG Hill and get her … that she's waiting outside. This morning, she told me that she had been to HG Hill in the middle of the night because Sheila had called her and asked her to come. She was inside looking for her when she saw that she was outside. Mama said she started screaming for her, hollering, running toward her. But all the lines were backed up and people were standing around in the aisles and she couldn't get to her. By the time she got to the door, Sheila was gone. She woke up screaming her name, woke me up … woke Bobby up. I didn't even know he was there. I found him standing in the door with daddy's shotgun."

I nodded, pulled her close. My other brain had started to think again. Previous to the present few moments, it had been quiet for half an hour … since its desires had been sated.

"Are you listening?" she asked me.

"You know I am," I told her, my hand starting its journey, under her blouse, down across her belly to the elastic on her underwear.

She took my wrist in her hand. Stopped my hand's descent. "Were you scared walking over here tonight?" she asked.

"Of what?" I asked, playing stupid.

"The killer, I guess," she said. "I mean, when I really get to thinking about it ... that somebody killed that woman ... did to her what we saw ... it makes me think it took somebody that was either really mad or with a special kind of meanness. Not just your run of the mill meanness."

"The guys who did it are in jail," I said sarcastically. I had already filled her in on what Lucky had told me. She didn't believe they did anything to that woman, any more than I did.

"I mean, just to leave her there ... laying ... I mean, lying there all sprawled out like that ... on that cold, hard December pavement. I just can't imagine what it would take in somebody's heart to do that."

"Yeah," I agreed. But I didn't believe myself. I knew I was lying. I also knew good and fucking well what it felt like to want in your heart to kill somebody. Or at least to hate them bad enough to want to do it. Van, Raymond Collins, Lucky. I had in me what Lucky had, I suspected. In me, it just didn't bubble to the surface so easily or quickly.

"So, you really don't have heat?" I asked her.

"No ... but I really don't think it's that big of deal. A lot of people lived without heat just a few years ago. I mean, except for what we have. We're going to get it turned back on. Are you forgetting we have an outhouse, too?"

I shook my head. I'd never used it, but I hadn't forgotten seeing it either. For the moment that we lay there quietly, I tried to imagine her using the thing. In her hose and heels, her dresses, skirts and blouses.

"We use the Sears and Roebuck catalogue," she said.

"Huh?"

"We use the Sears and Roebuck catalogue to wipe."

"To wipe your ass with?"

"Our asses ... and other things."

I shook my head again. "I'll have to try that some time."

"It's a lot of fun," she said.

We lay there, close enough to a window that we could see the December sky, hints of its stars littering the small section in view. My breath rose in front of me, hers as she breathed more slowly. I pulled her tightly to me once more.

"You never did answer my question," she said.

"What?" I said.

"Are you scared? Were you scared?"

"Uhuh," I said. "What's there to be scared of? When it's your time … it's your time."

I knew what I had said to be a lie. There was Randomness … The Planned Nature of Things … Human Frailty. Never knowing which was which. When one was going to raise its head, then the other, then the other. All of them biting you in the ass at one time or another. Leaving the scars of their teeth marks for you to forever contemplate.

"Why'd you walk?"

"I couldn't sleep," I told her. "Lucky came upstairs … was botherin' me again. The son of a bitch hasn't been upstairs in months … and now he can't stop himself. He's comin' up there every night."

"Maybe he just wants to talk to you," she said.

"He just wants to avoid my mother," I told her. "He's drinkin' more. 'Specially since … that woman. He's just been soused the last coupl'a nights. One of the reporters even noticed it. I don't think it's usually that obvious."

"Reporters?"

"Yeah. From the two Nashville papers and the *Review Appeal*."

"About that woman?"

"Yeah."

Sharon sat up and wrapped her arms around herself, like a chill had found its way to her. She patted and fluffed the back of her hair, trying to knock the flat spot out where we had been laying on the floor.

"So, did you go right home and go to bed after you left the funeral home?"

I sat up, too. Nodded. "Tried to. If Lucky had left me alone." Images of those damn dreams rattled through my head like a freight train. "Or if those dreams had left me alone."

"What'd you dream about?"

"Too much stuff to go into," I told her. I watched her as she stood, brushed herself off.

"Does your mother know you're over here?" I asked her.

"Yeah," she said. "If she doesn't know where I am, she goes into a panic. Thinks something bad's happened to me. Starts to fight to keep her breath." She made a couple of slow steps toward the door of the room we were in. What I guessed had been the living room. Stopped before she got to its edge. "Do you want to just come over here in the morning?"

I felt my eyes tighten around their rims. I tried to fight the feeling off, as I always did. Since I had it so much. I had only let myself come into this place a couple of times before; swore both times I wouldn't come back. The flashes of Percy in the front yard, proclaiming his message in his underwear, socks and shoes. The thought of what Van and Sharon had done in this house. He'd proudly told me that he'd fucked her in every room. "Wore her ass out," I think was how he put it. "And, man, she knows how to fuck. Somebody's, or maybe a lot of somebody's, been fuckin' her for a long time. She was all over me."

"Hunny, do you want to just go to the river? I don't think that we should go back to the high school yet, do you? I know we both go back to school tomorrow, but I don't figure it's safe, do you? I mean, we probably shouldn't be seen there, should we? I thought we could go to the river or come back over here."

Standing there in the dark, looking at her silhouette across the living room of this abandoned house, I wanted to cry. To grieve my life. Hers. That woman's who I was beginning to hate. Lucky's. My mother's. Percy's. Everybody's. Even her father and sister's, who I'd only met a couple of times. I wanted with all of me to give life to the feeling that pounded in my chest, that most often came out as anger. I wanted to scream at the top of my fucking lungs, to the heavens so maybe Percy could hear me, that he was at least partly right. That we all just want to be loved. What he was never able to escape his head and the pig long enough to tell me was this: the shit we put ourselves through to get it, or sometimes to keep from getting it, is absolutely amazing.

CHAPTER SIXTEEN

I'D BEGUN TO THINK that Percy was now like Lucky thought he was when he was alive. Always somewhere when you didn't want to see him. Like the wind, he seemed to be everywhere and nowhere, his presence known only when he wanted it to be, when his spirit somehow brushed across me. Untouchable, unpredictable. Or maybe I just wanted him back. Wanted to hear him tell another story, hear him laugh that strange, heartfelt laugh.

The house. The river. The attic. The Carter House. The Confederate Cemetery. I couldn't get him out of my head. The goddam fruit stand on the way out of town, where he'd held the only job he'd ever had ... one Lucky got him because it was across the road from where he shot craps so he could keep up with him. The one that he lost because he started "preaching" in the parking lot during one of his shifts. The jail cells that I'd only seen from the outside—knowing that whatever happened was likely to have happened in one of those three cells. The same ones that Arliss and Jackson now inhabited.

When he broke in 1953, it was only partially as it had been in 1945, the summer of Percy and Ronnie Langford. The summer when I started the paper route that I wouldn't stop until I got married. The summer that my

sister got her own room, a nicer bed that Lucky bought his favorite girl at
Sammy fucking Samuels' auction house.

I was never sure if his serious craziness only showed itself often enough
that you would know it was there. Or if in the blink of an eye he could
snap, like lightning strikes in a summer thunderstorm, scattering the black
sky with jagged light.

"THERE'S MORE TO IT than the main three components. *Randomness,
Human Frailty and The Planned Nature of Things.* If these things, although
they are fine ideas, wonderful concepts, were the final word in our existence, we indeed would be in deep shit. Although they are three components that are present in every human event, every human situation, there
is one concept—and I shouldn't even say 'concept' here, because this is just
a term, fallible, incomplete language representing a virtually unrepresentable
reality—that is greater than these things. And that concept is this:..."

He was poised on a car, in the parking lot behind the Fourth Avenue
Church of Christ, a lot that also ran behind most of the shops on Main
Street, where people parked to do their shopping on Saturday. The lot was
half-full, maybe fifty cars. When he had first taken to the top of the car,
there had been only one or two people, I imagined, but now there were
fifteen or twenty. Most of them knew him ... that he had acted like this
before. Perhaps it hadn't been noticed so much the first time, the Summer
of Ronnie Langford, the summer of the end of the war because in a strange
way it had been more discreet because Lucky had willed it so. Everybody
had been about to bust being happy the war was over. About to fold and
wither like an autumn flower with sadness. That the football star, the one
that could have played for the University of Tennessee, had gone, never to
return. Youth gone. War won. Innocence further tainted. Civilization saved.

And perhaps it is fair to say he had not been this bad either. The second
time the spirit overtook him—his words, not mine—he was worse, I guess.
Found himself so deeply in its possession that he could no longer wrest
himself free of it.

Just as I had arrived, he had turned his attention, his wrath on Hood again. Moved to the hood of the car as a symbolic gesture, he would later tell me. Hood, get it, Henry Boy? Get it? His mortal enemy that had lived almost a hundred years before him. He had been explaining how Schofield and his troops passed them as Hood and his men slept. I heard people in the growing crowd murmuring, gladly informing each other who he was.

He began to address Hood with just his shirt off. His britches didn't come off till he got to his theological principles.

"It's November 29th, 1864," he told them. "Right up here, not five miles down the road. Well, maybe nine or ten," he smiled. "The Yankees passed by Hood's men, sleeping within a few hundred yards of the road. Only when they got to Thompson's Station did Hood even attempt to bother them. And it wasn't Hood then; it was Forrest. Creaking wagons, thousands of marching men, they watched the Confederate campfires burn as they passed by in the night."

I had a feeling that most people in the crowd had heard this a thousand times, not listening the last nine hundred and ninety-eight or so. It was such common knowledge around Franklin, I imagined, that almost no one thought of its import anymore. He seemed undaunted, there on the hood of what I estimated a forty-eight Plymouth.

"There was a straggling soldier that evening. He found himself still coming up the Columbia Pike, well behind where most of his fellow troops were. Just before he made his way back to his own regiment, he saw Yankees passing by, heading north toward Franklin. Straight away, he went to Hood and told him. Hood woke up Pen Mason, his adjutant general, and told him to have Cheatham move his division—which, perhaps, he rethought from his earlier decision. Then the son of a bitch rolled over and went back to sleep. And Mason must have, too, because Cheatham said that he never got the order."

As I had seen Brother Myron Brown do at the Fourth Avenue Church of Christ many a Sunday, my uncle turned his head from side to side, surveying the attentiveness of his audience. His ribs were more evident than normal there in the springtime, morning sunshine, gleaming from the east off the windshield of the Plymouth. I imagined he had to be cold, the day yet failing to take on its full heat. He turned the intensity of his voice up a notch. Started gesturing with his hands as he spoke.

"Who, then, my friends, was responsible for this horrible blunder? Was it, in fact, Cheatham? Probably not … but he certainly could have been more painstaking in gathering information concerning the front. Was it Cleburne, another man on whom Hood tried to pin half-hearted blame? Especially after he had laid down his life on the battlefield just up Columbia Pike here. Bate perhaps? Who carried out the distorted orders Hood had given and left Franklin Pike wide open for Schofield and his men to pass through. Forrest? Bate? Brown? No!"

Uncle Percy bent and took his shoes off one at a time. He touched his socks but then seemed to remember he had a pack of cigarettes there. He produced one and lit it. Offered one to the people in the crowd who were close. No takers.

"Who, then?" he screamed in a voice so shrill it made the same people he had offered a cigarette jump. "In his book—and I will not mention the name here—Hood tells such a self-glorifying story that it shouldn't even be considered in a serious analysis of the events. He, my friends, John Bell Hood, the commanding general, was responsible. If it had been a great victory rather than an incredible travesty, then his would have been the credit!"

The crowd had grown to around fifty now. Shoulder to shoulder they stood, gathered around to watch this nut. To make sure this was really Lucky Hall's brother. The Assistant Police Chief's brother. I mean, Police Chief's. How did he get that job anyway? He and Mr. Oscar Garrett were drinking buddies, crap shootin' buddies, didn't you know that? Word was that they were both tied up with some moonshiners down in Alabama, runnin' whiskey up here through Peytonsville, or Little Texas as it's mostly called.

"Some people say Hood was drunk...." he proclaimed. He took the last couple of draws off the cigarette in his hand, picked up one of his shoes and put it out on the sole. Lit another after he had produced the pack once more from his sock. I imagined this would embarrass Lucky as much as him standing on a forty-eight Plymouth behind the Church of Christ, proclaiming his gospel.

"They infer that from the fact that there had been a raucous party at the Thompson House the night before. Celebrating, they were, the fact that they had Schofield cut off. That he would not reach Thomas and the rest of the troops in Nashville. That this was the turning point of the whole goddam war!"

He paused with his cigarette for a moment, almost like he was posing for a camera that someone in the growing audience—probably now around a hundred—might have. "Hood was a man in constant pain," he said. "The stump of his leg hadn't healed from Chicamauga. One of his arms was useless and hurt all the time. He'd had at least one fall from his horse that day. And, as a result, some believe that he was given laudanum and was euphoric—believed everything was going to turn out all right. Is it possible that this is what happened to Hood and his army?

"It's explained best, I think, by an old colored preacher who was a servant at the Thompson House the very night Hood stayed there before the travesty of a battle took place. He said, very simply, 'I tell ya why the Yankees passed by the Rebels in the night. God jus' didn't want that war to go on no longer.'"

Again, he paused, this time making his way to the windshield of the car and sitting on its roof. I suspected he loved having an audience. Almost like a playwright doing a one-man show, he was able to give his ideas birth outside his own soul and my ears. Tell himself that these people were listening to him, watching him, not because he was crazy, but because he was smart. Knowing, as I did about him, that if he was not smart, he was nothing. Knowing more and more each day that he, too, was crazy as hell.

Perhaps Lucky had seen it coming. When he had moved him back in with us. Told his sisters Wanda Jean and Nellie that he saw no other way but that he stay with us all the time. That their parents could no longer care for him. When he had traveled just a little past Thompson's Station and picked up him and few of his things up and took him back to our house. Because he didn't want him to go back to that place … that goddam place.

It about killed me to know I was the one who was responsible for what happened in '45, Lucky had told me. Keep him busy, is what Dr. Guppy told me. That's why I got him a job at the fruit stand down by the river. I knew Lucky would say if he was there. He don't change. He just gets older and does the same shit.

But in '45, it was the shit with the cemetery. A Confederate cemetery, at that. Where we are—not that I'd know about anywhere else—you've got two strikes against you if people think you messed with anything to do with the Confederacy (although, ill-fated and wrong, Percy would have said) or the military. Especially in 1945. That was the reason you wanted him to disappear, whether it be in a mental hospital or back to the country past Thompson's Station. You only felt bad when they started to fry his goddam brain. No, Lucky, he's changed. It's just you and I that haven't.

"THERE ARE THREE basic components to all human behavior and happenings in this world, that's where I began," proclaimed Percy, now standing on the hood of the Plymouth again. Not a soul had left. Across the way, I saw Van and Paul Chester. Down twenty feet from them, Lucky was laughing like he was certain the whole thing was a joke. My mother. Jean. Lucky motioned, sending them along to go ahead and do their shopping as Jean spat words of argument out her ugly puss. I'd just left them a few minutes before, after I'd finished cleaning out Lucky's Ford. Jean had seen the ripped place, my bloody knee, when I was going into and she was coming out of the only bathroom in the house.

"You all right?" she had asked. Her hair was still wet, curly in ringlets. A trail of steam followed the tail of her fuzzy robe.

"Did you use up all the hot water?" I said.

"I don't think so. Is your leg okay?"

"Yeah. I just went down on the bike. Took a corner a little sharp, wasn't payin' attention."

She took the towel from around her neck and wiped at the blood on my knee, long having dried as I had pulled into a vacant lot on the way home and sat by myself for near half an hour. Thinking about what had just happened. Wondering if the moonshine was still poisoning me. My brain now, not my stomach.

She wet it at the bathroom sink and wiped the blood away. Handed me the towel. Smiled.

"What're you gonna do?" she asked.

"Clean up myself … then clean up Lucky's car, I guess."

She frowned—a look I usually wanted to slap off her face—and nodded. In the small part of herself that didn't deny what he was, she knew what had happened.

"*Randomness, A Planned Nature of Things and Human Frailty,*" he declared once more. "I'd like to ask you if any of you conceive an answer for these things? Is there an answer for these things?"

Having turned away from his historical material to more philosophical subject matter, he lost a few of the crowd around its edges. Lucky, most likely unable to bear the embarrassment, had disappeared. Sensing he was losing their attention, Percy turned it up a notch. Took off his britches, threw them on the top of the Plymouth.

"Tell me!" he hollered. "Is there an answer for these things?"

A few people up front wagged their heads. Across the way, I saw that Tully had made it. He looked like shit, circles the size of quarters under his eyes. But he, as usual, was spit-shined. Pressed shirt … pants with a crease in them that would cut you. Not a hair out of place. He waved as he was talking to Paul Chester. I waved back.

"The answer is grace, my friends! That's the only answer for these three elements. No matter if it's our weakness that brings pain and suffering into our lives … or some strange happening that happened by chance … or the Plan—and by that term I mean where the energy that is moving through you, is directing you … directing everyone, trying to get everything in accordance. Move this existence somewhere that we can neither understand nor fathom, so we needn't try.

"And what do I mean by 'grace'?" he asked. "I'll tell you exactly what I mean: I mean the state in which we live. Like the air we breathe, it's there with us at every moment. Sustaining us the same way."

Percy now got a couple of amens from people a few back from the front. From the Pentecostal Church on the edge of town, I imagined. Most of the people who went there were considered as crazy as he was by the "normal" people around town. They were obviously able to overlook the fact that he was now on the top of the car with only his socks and underwear on. "Praise the Lord," one of them hollered. A couple of black people chimed in, one taking his shirt off, too, waving it over his head. "Hallelujah," another of the Pentecostals shouted.

"To live in grace is to live in the presence of the energy that flows through us. To be able to be what we are and act like no other. Because it is then, and only then, that we recognize the need for grace. Are able to come into contact with how imperfect we are ... with our *Human Frailty*! Only when we acknowledge these things are we able to stop 'acting good' and allow the spirit of the Universe to create in us something that is good! As long as you are involved in acting good ... acting like what you think other people want you to be ... acting like what you yourself think you need to be ... there is no room for the true spirit in you to come through. Falseness is the only thing birthed from fear. And nothing eternally good can ever come from falseness. Authenticity is birthed from strength ... openness ... grace."

He had begun to lose the Pentecostals now ... and the couple of black people a little away from the rest of the crowd. Ten or twenty other people had walked away in the last minute or so. Tully and Van and Paul Chester were talking to Marla and Rose Watkins and some other girls whom I couldn't make out because their backs were to me.

"Where's his brother?" I heard somebody murmur in the front.

"I thought I saw him a few minutes ago. Somebody ought to come end this stupid spectacle. It's a shame to see somebody do this to themself. Right down here on Saturday," said Jenny Bowmann, standing beside me, to nobody in particular.

Beside her, Jeannie McFadden said, "Somebody call Miss Helen Riley. Get her to get Lucky Hall down here. Lucky or Lucas Reasonver or Johnnie

Forrest. Even Don Walton … anybody."

"We're afraid … afraid to be what we really are, which at its base is what God made us to be, is it not? Afraid of what's going to happen to us after the day comes when we depart. After we leave this painful and beautiful place. Afraid of what might befall us while we're here. Afraid, mostly, I think, of *Randomness* and *Human Frailty*. Afraid to admit to ourselves that we're never static; that to live is fluid, to have the energy flowing through us that is behind the creation of this universe … this world… you … me … everything. That we are both separate from and joined with everything around us. That, indeed, God works in us every moment, no matter what we call him … call her! From the dark corners of the dirtiest beer joint in the county to the spic and span Sunday School Rooms of every church, God is there, working in lives that call him God … that call him nothing … that curse his name."

Seeming to have recovered his bearings for the time being, he scanned the audience that I imagined, from his vantage point, reflected everything from interest to disdain to apathy. He reached for his sock and produced one of the two packs of cigarettes there, a book of matches. He lit one and drew deeply on it, his eyes cast to the back of the now diminishing crowd as Lucas Reasonover made his way through the people toward him. He appeared as if he contemplated exactly what to do as Lucas grew closer. Whether to start speaking again or to somehow wind his last diatribe back to Hood … the battle that seemed to haunt him like the pig that followed him. The one with the huge tusk that might devour him at any moment.

"That woman needs her car," said Lucas.

Percy didn't speak. Only looked at him with slight contempt.

"Percy, that woman needs her car. She's been waitin' to leave for twenty minutes."

Percy turned his eyes to the woman of whom Lucas Reasonover spoke: Carolyn Nedler, young wife of Coach Nedler of the Academy. She had snagged him when he was near forty, she, in her early twenties, a cashier at the grocery store. Now she just kept house and wore low-cut blouses, short skirts, and high heels around town.

Percy looked at her and smiled, which it was hard not to. Then, like a chastised school boy, said he was sorry and began to climb down from the hood of the car. Put his britches and his shirt back on.

"That's all right," she told him. "I didn't have anything else to do. I kind of enjoyed hearing you."

Like the realization in the middle of a dream that you are, in fact, naked, the cognizance of what he had done just seemed to be coming to him. Tapping him on the shoulder like a silent friend, reminding him of its presence.

Percy opened her car door and shut it after she got in, then smiled at her and Lucas Reasonover, just as if he had seen the both of them on the street in the middle of a Saturday morning.

CHAPTER SEVENTEEN

A MILE AND A HALF off Lewisburg Pike, through fields relatively flat for middle Tennessee, and past a couple of old farmhouses lay the Carnton Mansion and the Confederate Cemetery. The flat piece of land itself, where so many bodies were laid after the Battle of Franklin, November 30, 1864. At Carnton, a mansion now empty and somewhat ramshackle, five generals, the most to die in any one battle in the war, had been laid on the porch, the faint blood stains still there eighty-one years later. Down Cleburne Street, through the stop sign at Adams, and then following the railroad track, it was maybe a mile the way a crow flies from our house. And, although he had not told me so, it was a journey I suspected Percy made often at night. When the darkness would protect his anonymity, his strangeness. Keep people from calling and complaining to Lucky about what they saw. Anybody else that was out at this time of night, I suspected, as I imagine did he, was up to their own brand of no-good.

"Probably a bunch of goddam bootleggers is all we'll see out at this time a' night," said Van. He kicked down the tracks in front of us, swinging his cigarette at his side like a badge of honor. The night was hot, the air thick around us.

"What'd you know about bootleggers?" I asked him.

"As much as you," he said. He took a drag off his cigarette like he knew what the hell he was doing.

"What'd either one of you know about bootleggers?" Ronnie said.

"He thinks he knows everything," Van said. "He knows everything because his father is a *police man*. Fucking everything."

We were just dawning as cussers. Just away from our parents long enough to start to experiment with new words. Their meanings. I knew Van was trying to impress Ronnie, too. Convince him he was older than he was. Maybe ten or eleven. After all, this was Ronnie Langford. I glanced back at him, just over my shoulder, an imposing presence next to my skinny body. Six foot tall, two hundred and twenty pounds if an ounce. His arms hung to his sides, swung like hams as he walked.

"You know, every once in awhile I see this strange fellah walkin' around back here. I used to see him pretty regular when I ran the mornin' paper. Then I didn't see him for awhile. Now I've started seein' him again. Not as much … just every once in awhile."

Listening to his voice, it seemed his calm demeanor, the confidence that permeated every part of him, seemed to have vanished. Perhaps had dissipated with his football days or was covered by the fear of what he was getting ready to do.

"Fred's supposed to meet us back here," he said. "S'posed to have stopped by Chester's Store earlier … picked up some beer. I don't care if you boys wanna split a bottle," he told me. Or, I guess, us.

Van responded like he'd been talking to him. "Yeah. Great. I like beer."

"When have you ever had beer?" I asked him.

"You don't know everything I do."

"No—but I do know your parents are stricter than mine and if Scoot or your mama catches you, either one of 'em'll whip your ass."

"I think Lucky likes the ass-whippin's more than my parents," said Van.

I nodded, knowing he was right. Took the air down deep into my lungs a couple of times, to forget what he'd said.

"My daddy was always big on them, too," said Ronnie. "Sometimes I think he liked to whip my ass more than he liked to eat. But he don't do it no more. He still gets a wildass hair and tries ever' once in awhile, but he just ain't big enough no more. He don't have a hold on me at all no more."

I remembered what Lucky had told me. What Ronnie had said on this morning when we'd seen him in front of the theatre. Having to go pry Ronnie off his daddy a couple of times. His daddy trying to get him to take the University of Tennessee scholarship. Then telling him he could get married if he wanted. Anything to try to keep him from his desire to be a hero.

"I turn eighteen day after tomorra'—hey, ain't that Burkitt up there in the dark? Silly son of a bitch. Hey Burkitt! That you? Anyway—that is him, ain't it?"

I told him yes. Him or somebody.

"Hey, Burkitt, we're here! Anyway, I turn eighteen then, then the next day I leave. Paris Island, boys! Here I come!"

Like he was storming a beach somewhere, he ran, arms over head with what I guessed was an imaginary rifle, the moonlight strangely making him appear as if he were moving in slow motion. I watched him as he faded into the milky darkness toward Fred Burkitt.

"He's one bad ass," said Van.

"I guess," I told him.

"Ain't you glad we came?"

"I don't know. I guess."

What I did know, though, good and damn well, was that I wouldn't be there if it weren't for him. Whatever he gave off, even at ten, suggested that he was older than he was. Knew more than he actually did. What I also didn't tell him was the fact of how much I feared seeing Percy. Lucky had taught me at an early age to be ashamed of him. To hide him whenever possible. Because people think things like that run in families. Because there's never any telling what he'll say. If I could find some way to keep his ass out there in Thompson's Station, I'd sure as hell do it. Lucky's voice usually rang in my ears like somebody had just fired a loud gunshot near me.

"Burkitt, come here, man! Come 'ere," Ronnie motioned when he was close enough to make out that was in fact who it was. Burkitt waved until we got close then took a seat on a rail again, shining white-silver in the night. By him sat two cases of beer. Pabst Blue Ribbon.

"Goddam Burkitt, you went all out this time, didn't ya?"

Burkitt nodded, raised a bottle at us, then finished it. He clanked it down beside him with three or four more. "Get the Japs," he said, raising another bottle to us. "We finished off the Germans, now go get the Japs!"

"Me and Truman," said Ronnie. "We're gonna finish 'em off."

"Coward bastards … slant-eyed bastards," said Burkitt.

"I'm goin'," said Ronnie. "Got the papers signed a couple of weeks ago … everything."

I assumed since Ronnie Langford had quit school and decided to go into the armed services, he probably hadn't seen Fred Burkitt. He had told me he didn't see a reason to finish. If he was going to be a hero and everything.

Ronnie took a beer out of the box and sat on the railroad track beside Fred Burkitt. Clinked it against his when he raised it.

"I got two questions for ya," said Burkitt.

Ronnie nodded.

"How's your girl? And, who are these little shits?"

"She's fine … still fuckin' me like a mad woman. And these two little shits are Henry and …."

"Van!" Van chimed in.

"Van," nodded Ronnie. "I taught Henry everything I know about throwin' papers." He turned to me. "He's your cousin, right? Lives across the street from ya. He's the one that we pissed on his daddy's paper a couple 'a times when it was rainin', ain't he? You said they wouldn't know the difference."

"Yeah, I knew the difference," said Van the man, "and I switched it with his daddy's before he took it in."

"Lucky don't take the paper in," I told him. "He reads it in his car when he leaves. Has his coffee and reads the paper while he watches down Columbia Highway to see if anybody's speedin'."

"And smokes thirty or forty cigarettes."

"At least he knows how to smoke one," I said, motioning at the strange way he was holding the one he had. "He don't smoke it like a queer. Like that queer fucker down at the funeral home." Or at least that's what Lucky had told me. Showed me how a regular man held one, how a queer did.

"Girls … girls," said Ronnie Langford. "If y'all keep arguin' like that, then I'm gonna send ya packin' back home."

Van positioned his cigarette different, his wrist bent more forward than backward, and shut up. Didn't say another word like I knew he wanted to.

"Here," said Burkitt. He held a beer out to Van then gave him an opener to pry the top off with. Van tried to look smooth as he fought it. Burkitt followed suit with me. I handed mine to Van after he had popped the top on his own; he opened it without comment. Propped himself against the rail on the same side as Ronnie.

"So … did y'all see the picture show today?" Ronnie asked after he took half of his beer in one slug.

Van sipped at his, trying not to making slurping noises. I turned my bottle up and down quick like I had seen Lucky do since I could remember with his whisky. Let the sweet-bitter taste run into my mouth, sit there long enough to burn my tongue and gums a little. Do the same to my throat when I swallowed.

"Yeah," said Van. "That girl … what's her name? She was hotter than hell … than a July afternoon."

"You mean Elizabeth Taylor," said Burkitt. "She is a damn pretty girl. Stupid movie, though. A little bit sappy."

"Yeah, Burkitt likes them war movies," said Ronnie. He don't like ,em where the guy ends up with the girl. ,At's ,cause he ain't ever had one. He's too big. They're all scared he'd crush ,em."

Burkitt coughed out this deep sound I assumed was a laugh. As low and nasal as a cow. For the first time after my eyes had made the adjustment to the darkness I looked at him. He was a huge man. Made Ronnie, who was a big man himself, look small. They clinked their beer bottles together again, I guess, for old time's sake.

"What Burkitt don't realize is that you can be a war hero and get the

girl, too. I'm gonna go over there, finish off the Germans and the Japs …
and then come back to my wife Barbara."

"I heard Truman might not fuck around like FDR did," Burkitt said.
"At least that's what my daddy said."

A little over a week before, FDR had died. Harry S. Truman, his vice-
president, had taken over for him.

"I just hope he gives me enough time to get over there and get me a few
of ,em," said Ronnie.

"I'd go if I could," Van interjected, his voice sounding like the three
drinks of beer he'd had had already gone to his head. He pulled on another
cigarette, mindful of his wrist position. Offered me one.

I shook my head. Knew that he'd probably stole them from Lucky the
last time he'd been at our house, probably to watch our TV in the few days
after FDR had passed away. Or Lucky had left them out for him, pretended
not to see when he took them. As my eyes left Burkitt and moved through
the black, empty space between us, the thought went through my head for
the first time—at least the first time that I had ever recognized it—that
Lucky had probably rather have him as a son. The silver-tongued devil!
He'd talked all week with Lucky about FDR, the war, Truman, like he
really knew something about the siti-ation, as Lucky said it. With pearly
white teeth and a smile that would make you believe he would always be on
your side. Blue eyes … blonde hair. Built taller than we were. Yeah, Lucky
would rather have him because he was not like himself. Lucky was more
like me—when he was nervous, his words tangled in his throat like vines
around his feet in a thicket. When he ran out of things to say that would
convince you he was right, he knew nothing else but to hit you. Make you
scared to believe he was wrong. Give himself space one more day to believe
he was all right, because he knew he really wasn't.

"Me and Barbara's goin' to get married tomorra' night," said Ronnie
Langford.

"Get the fuck out'a here," Burkitt spat, pawing the box to find another
bottle. He threw the empty in his hand at the rail close to Van, shattering
the bottle and the stillness. Van jumped and screamed like he'd pissed on an

electric fence.

"Goddam, boy!" said Burkitt. "You almost made me piss my pants."

"Sorry," said Van. "I was just excited."

"Excited, my ass," I said, the few swigs I had having started my brain on its journey toward peace. Lack of inhibition. "You screamed like a woman ,cause you were scared. Excited like my ass's excited. Humff."

Like times when I had heard bobcats scream after the darkness and silence had wrapped themselves like a blanket around a summer night, this blood-curdling sound made its way out of Burkitt's mouth. Caused me to scream out like Van had. Thankfully, though, he produced another one with me. Truth be known it was probably the first time that either of us had ever been out this late. I'd gone out the window for the first time. Down the huge oak that lay its limbs on the roof of the side porch by the driveway. Van had come out through the cellar door, which he had unlocked from the outside earlier after he had decided we were going to sneak out to meet Ronnie Langford and Fred Burkitt.

The way Fred Burkitt began to dance around, run down one sliver of train track fifty feet or so, then turn and run back toward us, he looked like a grizzly bear on a tricycle. His hulking body swallowed the silver train rail as he came back toward us. His arms to his sides, he glided like a delicate ballerina down one way, then would scream that sound again and make his way back the other. The only thing I'd ever seen like it was when I'd gone on a call with Lucky after a black woman had been killed. Several others had decided that God had come to claim her during the service itself. Had done their best to welcome him, entertain him. Something. Lucky had described it to me as they were "slain in the goddam spirit. Niggers and Pentecostals … they're both like that. Hell, I've heard sometimes at funerals they get the body out of the casket and dance around with it. They have a goddam good time at anything. I tell ya that."

But whether Fred Burkitt was slain in the spirit, in that moment I did not know. As far as I knew, there were no holy rollers nor colored people in his family. Nevertheless, he'd been overtaken by something.

"Shit goddamnit to hell!" he hollered, loud enough you could have heard him in town. His voice split the virtual silence like a midnight rock through a plate glass window.

"Kill the Japs!" yelled Ronnie.

"Kill the fuckin' Japs!" Burkitt echoed. Grabbed another bottle out of the box, popped the top with his teeth and took off running again. Hollering indecipherable sounds as he made his way seventy-five, a hundred feet down the track, hopping on one leg, somehow keeping his balance on the rail.

"Kill the Germans!" Ronnie Langford yelled once more.

"I'm gonna kill me some Germans and some Japs!" Burkitt yelled from what looked to be a quarter mile away.

"Y'all better be a little quieter," said Van to Ronnie. "Mr. Oscar Garrett'll be down here."

"Shit, he's drunk as a skunk right now. Prob'ly down at the fillin' station shootin' goddam craps with Henry's daddy."

I'd been so glad to finally get to the ground and out of the oak tree, I'd failed to even look to see if his car was there. After I'd met Van, he'd pointed out that the police cruiser wasn't under the carport, so we'd have to go from yard to yard, tree to tree, making sure we hid ourselves well till we got close to the railroad tracks.

"I'm gonna go with ya!" Burkitt yelled from his stopping point. Threw the beer bottle he'd opened with his teeth then drained into the woods, the foliage notifying us of its descent and landing.

"You can't go with me," yelled Ronnie. "You ain't got but a little over a month left in high school … and I don't think Franklin needs but one hero. And plus, you ain't even got a woman to come home to after you kill your share a' Germans and Japs."

Ronnie's voice had grown slower with the beer and now quieter as Fred made his way back close to us, the spirit of what had overtaken him either gone or, at least, resting.

Burkitt's was the same. "I got just as much right as you to go."

"Yeah, but you hadn't already dropped out'a school. You might as well graduate. Don't you think that would be a grand fuckin' idea?"

For a matter of seconds, it appeared that what few cogs there might have been were turning in Fred Burkitt's brain. Hero? Finish high school? No girl to come home to. Maybe I'll have one if I'm a hero like Ronnie. Hell, he's always been the hero. He was the star fullback; I was a linebacker. Everybody knew who he was; the only time my name was ever spoke was when I made a tackle … or even missed one. No, godammit, I wanna be a hero too!

"My country needs me," he said. "I don't think I'd really ever thought about it before the last few minutes. Hell, with everything that's happened in the last coupl'a weeks, I'm sure they could use me for somethin'. They're in Germany now. They're on that island now, too—what's it called?"

"Okinawa," Van told him.

"Yeah … yeah … that's it. It's like God's callin' me to help. Like God said to me, ‚Fred Burkitt, you can go help, too.'"

"I think the beer's callin' him," Van leaned over and said to me.

I nodded, careful not be seen, since either of them could have swatted me like a fly.

It was when Ronnie Langford was explaining to him how he had enlisted almost two weeks before in the Marines—the day after they raided Okinawa and lost five thousand men—and that they were highly unlikely to be in the same unit or even battalion that I thought I saw him for the first time. A little further down the track than Fred Burkitt had made it in his journey with the spirit, I saw the silhouette I immediately suspected to be him. As Ronnie Langford explained to him that if he enlisted on the spur of the moment it was unlikely he'd even get to pick the branch of the service he'd be in, I knew I'd recognize his posture anywhere. His gait. The oddness that seemed to surround him like an aura. Follow him like a pet dog. The oddness I seemed only to recognize when I was with someone else I knew would see him that way also. The love I had for him was choked by the shame of what others thought of him. Another way I was like Lucky, I suspect.

After all was said and done, especially done, I wondered just short of a million times if I had done something different in that moment, if it would have set the wheels of fate to turning in a different direction. Steered its eventual course even a degree or two different, taking life as we all knew it into another future. If I had acknowledged his presence in that moment, rather than trying, as I most often did, to pretend that I had in fact not seen him, would Ronnie and Fred Burkitt have acted different? Would their acting different have steered their lives another way? His? Mine? Van's? Lucky's? Who the hell knows. I only know the questions themselves can make you crazy sometimes.

"Five thousand lost when they raided Oki…Oklahoma!" Fred Burkitt screamed. To which I saw the figure down the track respond by jumping, startled. I imagined it was the first sound he'd heard besides the year's earliest bullfrogs singing their songs to one another. His figure disappeared as quickly as I had seen it. Down the hill on the Lewisburg Pike side of the railroad tracks.

"What's next, Texas?" said Van.

"It ain't funny," said Ronnie. "The damn fool's likely to go over there and get hisself killed."

Again, Fred Burkitt, now a beer in each hand, took himself—or was transported by the spirit—down the railroad track to the south. He screamed the whole way, his voice now close to indecipherable. Something about Oklahoma again. The Japs. The Germans. The Russians. The Jews. Benjamin Muscleddy. Hitler. He turned up one of the beers, downed it and threw the bottle into the woods once more. Somewhere close to where I'd seen him enter them. And then he, too, disappeared.

In the sense of strange immanence, it was I who began to run after him first. I imagined that Ronnie and Van behind me were moving slower, that they hadn't the same urgency in their heart I did. By the time we reached the clearing, I found Fred Burkitt standing there, his hands on his knees, breathing like Lucky would come to do years later.

"There was some … crazy ass …runnin' in front of me," he pushed out. "I saw him when we … were up there on the tracks and chased his Jap ass … all the way through the woods. I lost him though. All I could see was his cigarette as he moved further and further away. I couldn't get through all the goddam vines and brush. Thick as fuckin' molasses. Done tore my britches all to pieces."

I looked at his legs. In the given light, the holes and the blood were just visible, like shadows. He pawed at them with a mammoth hand, took the last swig of his beer and hurled the bottle, I assumed, toward where he had seen the figure disappear. He looked around himself, examined his surroundings like he might have just been realizing where he was.

"Ain't that the Confederate Cemetery over there?" he said, throwing his hand in the general direction.

"Yeah, I think so," I told him. I heard Van and Ronnie coming up behind us. The bottles of beer rattled in the box under Ronnie's arm, clinked as he set the box on the ground.

"Goddam Yankees," said Fred Burkitt. "No better than the goddam Japs."

Burkitt's voice was like one I had never heard previous to this moment. As he stood there, conversing with Ronnie Langford after he and Van had arrived, it was not the first time I saw alcohol change someone, but the most significant. Even though I had seen Lucky drink whisky, he was only likely to become sullen and angry if the alcohol affected him badly, not like another person.

"Burkitt don't say much when he's sober," Ronnie explained to us after Fred had left to go piss in the woods. "He'll be all right. Just put up with him. I ain't seen him like this but a coupl'a times. He gets pretty crazy. I should'a thought about that before I told him to get that beer at Chester's … before I told you boys you could come. Wonder why in the hell I did that to begin with?"

Ronnie opened another beer while he watched Fred Burkitt as he looked through the next patch of woods into the clearing that led to the cemetery. Like a dog who smelled something of which he couldn't extinguish the memory, neither his head nor his attention wavered. For a brief moment, he appeared almost sober again.

"Goddam the Japs!" he screamed. "Goddam the Germans! Goddam the goddam Yankees!" And, having mostly regained his breath, he was gone again.

As I chased Fred Burkitt through the last thicket of trees and then the hundred or so yard clearing before the gate that led into the cemetery, I was only worried about him confronting the shadowy figure I had seen make his way down and across the track just after Fred Burkitt had been slain in the first place. Halfway to the graveyard, Ronnie Langford passed me, his legs pumping like pistons. As I imagined had been reversed a thousand times in practice, Ronnie Langford was going for a tackle. Thinking he was intending to stop something, rather than incite it more severely, I stopped as he passed me. Van stopped beside me.

"He sure can move," he said. "Your daddy said he was the fastest fullback he'd ever seen. A fullback that ran like a halfback."

Lucky, never one to miss a Franklin High School football game, had seen every home game of Ronnie Langford's career, as well his two-year ascension to state-wide notoriety.

Van and I squinted through the milky darkness as Ronnie reached Fred Burkitt and, still running, took hold of his shirt collar. And then as the shirt pulled and tore and made itself limp in Ronnie's hand. Fred Burkitt, shirtless, ascended and descended the four steps on each side that led over the rock fence.

Perhaps again in this moment, something could have happened differently. If Ronnie Langford had tackled him, if his shirt had not ripped. If Ronnie had not fallen when the shirt ripped and gone headfirst into the second and third rock steps of the gated opening, perhaps he, too, wouldn't have been pissed off. Maybe, as he was making a second attempt to tackle him, if his weight had not been behind the first blow when Fred Burkitt, the blitzing linebacker, made his initial hit, like he was tackling a quarterback. Like he was taking down Benjamin Muscleddy. Like he was raiding Oklahoma.

CHAPTER EIGHTEEN

L UCKY LIT A LUCKY and leaned back at the table, surveying what he had done to the next room. It was what made him a good cop: at his best, he had this strange sixth sense about things, like he could read what was happening before it was all the way there. The day before, he had been to the newly opened Sammy Samuels Auction barn, bought the bedroom set and hauled it into the room that had been the family room. This had come about, he said, because we would soon start spending our evenings in the bigger of the two available rooms: the living room. It would be better, he told us, to watch the television he would be bringing home in a few days.

Dillard "Lucky" Hall never told any of us where he came by the thing. Just brought it in three or four days later—with Percy's help, reluctantly— and set it under the bay window that looked out of the living room. Its blue glow at night was a status symbol only one other family—the Pitts, almost all the way to the other end of Cleburne—on the street had, and something, I would guess, about which our neighbors concluded fairly quickly that someone had supplied my father with it as a reward for an ongoing overlooking of something.

During the first two weeks we had the thing, the shades open and the sheers thrown back, everyone on the street except the Smithsons and the Pitts came to our house to watch it. Perhaps it was the ten days or so of

Lucky's life, besides football games, that I had seen him the happiest. Like a tour guide, he would usher people in, have them sit around the living room like they were at the picture show, and then turn the lights down and bring up the blue glow with a flip of the switch. The only one I'd ever personally seen before was one in the front window of McFadden's Electric. The one Percy would not look at as we walked by it.

"They're trying to take over our minds," he had told me not a month earlier, as we made our way half a block down from Main Street. When I slowed to look at it, to try to catch a glimpse of it around the four or five other people who were looking, he had not stopped, but simply kept his feet moving toward where he said he was headed in the first place.

"That's amazin'," the kid standing in front of us turned and said to me. I recognized the man he was with as Mr. Shafer, our neighbor just past the stop sign below our house. The kid himself was runt of a child. Made me feel big, which was unusual.

I puffed out my chest, nodded and told him I agreed. Behind me, Percy nervously paced up and down the sidewalk, a strange, rhythmic twitch coming over him every once in awhile like a phantom surge of electricity. Deep blue circles under his eyes, he had told me just before we stopped in front of McFadden's that he'd been walking back and forth between Thompson's Station and Franklin every day.

"My daddy's got one of those," the little boy told Mr. Shafer.

Mr. Shafer nodded his head politely. Patted the little boy on the back.

"When's Mama comin' back to get me?" he asked.

Mr. Shafer told him, "She said she'd be back by next weekend."

"Where'd she say she was goin'?" he asked.

"Off down in Alabama somewhere."

"To do what?"

"To go see some fella'," Mr. Shafer told him.

"She told me she was goin' for work."

"Maybe she was. Maybe it had somethin' to do with her job."

I would later find out that the boy's mother's job was men. Not in a literal sense, but it was all she thought about. Would do anything, move anywhere to be with one. Leave her child behind.

Behind me, a horn blared that turned all our heads. Percy had started to cross the street in front of a work truck. The city workers smiled, laughed and roared away.

Perhaps this early in 1945, few people actually knew that he was Lucky's brother.

"Come on," Percy said, pulling on my shoulder from behind. "We got to go. That was one of them."

"One of who?" I asked as he pulled me twenty feet down the block.

"One of them," he said. "I don't need to say more!" Abruptly, he stopped and spun toward me, took me by the shoulders and peered into my eyes. "They and that goddam pig follow me. They know I have the insight into world affairs. From the civil war to this tragic thing we're involved in now, they know I have the answers. The pig knows it. Those guys while ago … they may have looked like dirty city workers, but that's just a brilliant disguise! Don't you understand?!"

I turned down the block to see if they were still in view.

He grabbed me by the shoulders and snapped my head back toward him. "Don't let them see you looking! They know you're my nephew."

At this particular moment, I wanted to deny it for all I was worth. His eyes were wild, and seldom blinked. Above blue saucers, tiny bloody rivers cut jagged lines to the irises.

"Percy, that was just Elmer Murphy and Jack Hooper," I told him. "Road men … trash men. They know Lucky … know you."

"That's what you think," he said.

"I gotta go," I told him.

"Suit yourself … watch for that pig though. He's big. Big tusks, the size of baseball bats. Red eyes. He was there when the goddam Germans massacred almost every living soul in Oradour-sur-Glane in Haute-Vienne last summer. Do you know what that was?"

I shook my head.

"It doesn't matter. What does matter is the son of a bitch is mean. I mean mean."

As I watched Percy saunter off toward the river, just a few buildings down, I saw Mr. Shafer arguing with that boy about something. Mr. Shafer finally nodded his head, reached into his pocket and gave the little boy what appeared to be a couple of dollars. As Percy passed them, he spoke something to them also. Probably about the pig or the trash men or whatever the hell else he was talking about, I assumed.

"WHAT'S THE GODDAM PIG Percy's talkin' about all the time?" Lucky asked me.

I looked at my mother and Jean's backs as they washed dishes. Watched a gray bank of smoke leave Lucky's mouth and hover over his head before it started its rise and dissipation.

"Sir?" I said, trying to turn off the projector flashing images from the night before in my head like I was at the Saturday afternoon picture show.

"I saw Percy this mornin' walkin' back toward the homeplace ... and besides the fact he looked like shit, he said that he'd been at the woods all night hidin' from some goddam pig. He said the damn thing chased him down the railroad tracks and then into the woods. I don't know ... I couldn't make any sense out of it. It's really kinda embarrassin'. I'm glad Mother and Daddy are too far out in the country and too old to know much about it. I think the best thing I can do for him is get him a job."

Lucky's solution for everything. Work the piss out of you.

It hadn't done much for me yet except get me mixed up with Ronnie Langford and Fred Burkitt. The one check I had gotten, Lucky had taken me straight to Franklin National Bank with it, made me open a savings account.

"You look tired today, too. Hell, you look almost worse than Percy," he said. "You know, he almost looked like he'd been in a fight. He had a big skinned place over his eye ... a couple of cuts on his arms ... a bruise on his head. He told me that shit again about the pig with the big teeth chasing him through the woods. Finally catching him over in the graveyard. I hope he hadn't got hisself into any shit I can't get him out of. Mr. Oscar wouldn't appreciate that."

Lucky was in his last couple of years of being Mr. Oscar Garrett's lackey. He never wanted to go back to working at the mill just out of town, where he'd met Mr. Oscar to begin with, when he came in to get feed for his cows and chickens.

He wouldn't appreciate what had occurred the night before either, I thought. I wondered if the word was out yet. Who knew? Who was telling who at this exact moment? If Ronnie or Fred Burkitt even remembered it? If they'd really cut Van's and my dicks off like they'd told us they'd do if we ever told?

"Spit on that grave!" Fred Burkitt had yelled as he took me by the shoulders and raised me four feet off the ground. Shook me till it felt like my brain rattled. "Do you hear me? Spit on that goddam Yankee nigger's grave!"

Van tried to tell him that there weren't Yankees or colored people in this cemetery. It was a Confederate Cemetery, for the dead Confederates from the Battle of Franklin. November 30, 1864. Hood's troops. Right over there at Carnton.

He started to squeeze me. I could smell his breath and his body odor as he tightened his bearhug, both foul. He squeezed hard enough that he began to grunt. Ronnie Langford laughed, said it sounded like he was taking a shit. Van started to kick at Burkitt's shins. He was so drunk he probably wouldn't have felt if you'd set him on fire.

"Spit on it, you little dickhead or you're gonna knock the next one down! With your fuckin' head. Do you hear me, little bastard? Huh?"

"Just do it!" Van screamed. "He's gonna kill ya!"

I would've screamed long before if I'd had the breath to do it. At the same time I spat, Van hit Burkitt in the leg with a nearby rock he'd found.

"Goddam little fucker ... broke my leg!" hollered Burkitt as he took the first two steps after he'd dropped me on my shoulder and arm. On the third step, he went down. By the time he arose, Van had another rock, chambered above his shoulder. His voice was trembling as he spoke.

" If you come toward him again, I'll knock you in the head with this goddam rock! Do you understand me?"

Fred Burkitt stared at Van like only a drunk can do. He stumbled a little, staggered, then turned his eyes to Ronnie, then back to me and Van. I had moved far enough away I was certain I'd have four or five steps on him if he started after me again.

" He spit on the thing, didn't he? That was all I wanted. He spit on the Yankee nigger's grave."

" I told him there ain't no Yankee niggers in here," said Van.

" Would you shut up!" I said. As is often the case in such situations, the shakes had overtaken me only after the crisis had passed. My hands and my legs trembled so hard that I was certain all three of them could see the movement in the moon light.

" He did it," said Van. " Now leave him alone."

I am not certain why, at that moment, we did not hightail it… go through the couple of thickets of woods, across the railroad tracks, through the field and back to our houses.

" I'll do it, too," said Fred Burkitt. He cleared his throat and sent a hocker flying at the same grave I'd spat on. Laughed that same strange sound again.

" Stupid ass," Ronnie commented.

" That's easy for you to say," said Fred Burkitt. " You're leavin' tomorrow to go be a Marine. You got a girl. Did I ever tell you you were my best friend?" Then, out of nowhere, he screamed again. Crying, he held his sorrowful face in his thick hands and allowed the grief to pass through him for only a few seconds. Then he arose with another scream and made his way full-steam—or as full-steam as he could in his condition—toward another gravestone. " Goddam Jap!!!" he yelled as he made contact and the stone wavered then toppled, broken at its base. He lay there on top of the stone for a moment, imitating death, his arms sprawled out beside him, his head thrown back. Then he arose and kicked a couple of smaller stones in the next row, representing Mississippi, one of them identifying the number of dead from that state: 424.

" No … that one was the Jap!" he hollered. " The short one was the Jap. The two big pale ones was Germans. Goddam krauts."

As if it were spreading like a communicable disease, Ronnie Langford took aim and ran toward a taller, thinner stone. Made contact with it with his shoulder like he was hitting a dummy in football practice. Over it toppled, its base cracking like a muted fourth of July firecracker. Fred Burkitt knocked two or three smaller ones over with his foot, making like he was kicking a ball. Ronnie followed suit on a few more in that same row. Burkitt slammed a taller, cylindrical-shaped one with his shoulder, break- ing two-thirds of it off the top. Ronnie hit another with his foot, one representing the army of Tennessee, 230 dead, pulling its base out of the ground. Burkitt, with a running leap, hit with both his feet near its top, pulling it the rest of the way out of the earth. Spat on it for good measure after he was finished.

Van and I did not speak. Just stood and watched. One of humanity's worst qualities, I have since concluded. With each thing that happens, every new event that transpires, believing that it will get no worse. No one reacting because no one else seems to be. Waiting for someone else.

One by one, they took running shots at the horizontal stones, using their bodies to bring out of the earth that which had been there eighty years. And one by one, the gravestones toppled like bowling pins ... until the last strike caused a scream to come forth from the darkness. Then another. And another. And the laughter to stop. Yes, Van and I had started laughing, too, as the markers of history became tattered remains of sacrifice and someone's hard work. Then there were no sounds. No crumpling tomb- stones. No laughing. No screaming. Just silence.

LUCKY CAME BACK to the table and sat down. Shook his head and rested his face in his hands, his elbows on the table. He had been in princess Jean's room when the only telephone in the house rang. Had had to pry himself out of her company so he could take the call.

"I needed to get ready for church anyway," Jean called tauntingly as she shut her door.

"Go ahead and get ready all you want. It won't make you any easier to look at," I mumbled under my breath. As the door shut, I realized for the first time how a night with little or no sleep makes you feel the next day. I'd been so tired that I'd gone back to bed after the paper route.

Van had already concocted his story on the way home: he'd play sick in the morning. And nobody besides me and Fred and Ronnie would ever know he'd been out. And they sure weren't gonna rat us out because we had so much more on them. He'd crawl back in his window and Scoot and Evelyn would never be the wiser.

Lucky breathed in deep, rubbed his face and his forehead with his palms. Let the air come out as he shook his head. "Somebody tore up the goddam graveyard," he said.

"What?" said my mother, passing through the edge of the kitchen behind him.

"Somebody tore up the Confederate graveyard last night. I got to go over there and see how bad the damage is. Miss Helen said Percy come down to her house and told her that the pig did it. That the pig knocked down a bunch of the stones and the pig was tryin' to get him but didn't. She said he looked about as bad as somebody can. You know, I hate to say it … but when I saw him this mornin', I knew how bad he looked. But some things is just easier to overlook them. She says she's got him down there at her house … and he won't come out … that she just give him a glass of ice tea and let him sit there."

"So that was her on the telephone?" my mother asked.

"No … that was Mr. Oscar. He wants me to go get Percy and then come over to the cemetery. You wanna go with me?" he asked me.

Although church seldom sounded particularly appealing, it did on this day. At the same time, though, I suspected Lucky would more likely think something strange if I all the sudden had an urge to go. "Yessir," I told him.

"Will you drop Jean and me off at church on the way?" my mother asked.

Lucky moved his head up and down, his hands still covering his face.

MISS HELEN RILEY'S HOUSE was a little brick on Fair Street, a block south of West Main, two blocks north of Franklin Memorial Chapel. As

Lucky sat in the driveway, finishing his cigarette and fishing for then hiding again his fifth under the seat, I could see Percy through the bay window, his hand nervously rising and falling from his mouth just like Lucky's. Sipping his iced tea like it was a Sunday afternoon social, passing the time of day with Miss Helen, who must have just passed the mile marker of forty. Never married, she aspired to be a librarian if she ever finished her correspondence college degree in Nashville. As he gestured with his hands and Lucky stared at the floorboard, I wondered what the hell he was telling her. I wondered why Lucky had left him to wander the town.

At the door, Miss Helen welcomed us into her living room. In the couple of weeks I hadn't seen him, the blue saucers under Percy's eyes had grown and darkened as he must have dropped ten pounds he didn't really have. As Miss Helen asked us to sit and for our drink preference, I tried to remember the last time I had laid eyes on him. I only knew I'd seen him once or twice since he'd claimed the men in the work truck were "one of them," that the television was a plot so "they" could take over our minds. He had remained scarce, he'd told me, so as to boycott Lucky's acquisition of a television. It had been easier to avoid than embrace this thing that seemed to be growing like weeds taking over a summer garden.

And perhaps Lucky wanted most to deny it. Maybe rightly so, he knew that the crux of the responsibility of my uncle would fall directly and squarely on his shoulders. Wanda Jean and Nellie were in the country, where his behavior, for everything else it was, was rendered fairly benign. Lucky's journey from the mill, to policeman, to the assistant chief had secured him staying in town, by car just ten minutes away; but lifetimes away, too. Lucky knew, as did everyone else, that what Percy did while he was in town would ultimately come home to roost at his home, no one else's.

"Hey, Miss Helen," Lucky said cordially after she had finished trying to make us comfortable.

"Hey yourself," she said. She pushed on her hair with her hand, back and front. "I know I probably look awful."

"You look fine," said Lucky. "Don't she look fine, Henry?"

I nodded. "Yessir."

Percy's attention was in the far corner of the room, next to a potted plant. Finally, he shifted his eyes toward Lucky with a passing glance, then smiled at me without opening his mouth.

"Thank ya for callin'," said Lucky.

"I didn't know what else to do," said Miss Helen. "I'd seen him go up and down Fair Street several times, makin' his way from one tree to another, watchin' cars as they passed."

"I was tryin' to keep them from seein' me," he said. "I already told you that. I assumed you were too smart to be in cahoots with the rest of them. But if you keep sayin' things like that, then I'm going to believe my assumption's wrong."

As Lucky's silence was prone to indicate, I was afraid anger was brewing in his system, frustration regarding something he couldn't control or alter. He forced a smile onto his face. "Miss Helen was just nice enough to call us and tell us where you were."

Miss Helen sat on the couch, squeezed her hands flat between her knees. Smiled and raised her eye brows. Told Lucky he could smoke in her house if he wanted to. Lucky dug one out of his shirt pocket and lit it.

"I was afraid she would let them know."

"Let who know?" said Miss Helen.

Percy motioned toward Lucky. Like the motion had been scripted for years, Lucky knocked another cigarette out of the pack, stepped across the room, gave it to him and lit it for him.

Percy drew deep on the cigarette, tried to keep his hands from shaking by laying one on top of the other on his knees. "If you don't know who, I don't believe it's worth tellin' ya."

Lucky laughed a little. Shook his head.

I wondered how many times he'd been hearing things like this in the last week or two.

"Lucky told me you hadn't been feelin' well, hunny," Miss Helen said.

"It's got nothin' to do with me except the fact that I know what they're set to do." Percy arose from the chair, paced to the bay window and stared out, everyone's eyes on his back.

"You told me he'd been sick, Lucky, but…"

Lucky nodded.

"But he didn't tell ya about the goddam pig, did he?" Percy said without turning.

"No, hunny, he didn't," she said. "Have you got you a pig now?"

"I've got ten tons of heartache now. That's what I've got."

Lucky pulled on the cigarette. Knocked the ashes off in an ashtray Miss Helen had handed him. "You've had that your whole life. And most of it you've brought on your damn self."

"Tell me about your pig?" said Miss Helen.

"I can tell you," said Lucky. "I've heard enough about him that I can tell ya' exactly what he looks like. He's big … great big, with fiery eyes and long yellow teeth. And he breathes hard through his goddam nose. Runs low to the ground and fast. So fast that can't nobody get away from him if he don't want 'em to."

"You have seen him," said Percy, motioning to Lucky for another cigarette as soon as he finished the one in his hand. "Last time I talked to you about it, you told me you'd 'never heard of such a godforsaken thing.' Those were your exact words."

Lucky handed me a cigarette to take to him, then with a deep breath and a sigh, rendered the room as quiet as waiting on a prayer at church. After I'd stepped across the way with the cigarette and a book of matches, Percy lit it and made a face. "I'm a Chesterfield man myself," he said.

"If we get you a job, then maybe you can buy the kinda cigarettes you want."

"You gonna keep my money like you're keepin' Henry's?"

"No … but I'm gonna put my foot in your ass if you don't straighten up!"

Percy turned his attention to Miss Helen, who with her robe still on, didn't appear she was going to make church on time. Much less Sunday School.

"Do you see the way he talks to me? The real Dillard Hall comes out! It's the way he's been my whole life. He thinks Mama and Daddy were too old to raise me right. So he always thought it was his job."

"Somebody's gotta help ya," said Lucky. "And it sure ain't gonna be anybody out there at Thompson's Station."

Percy returned to his chair and Lucky took his watch at the window. What we were waiting on, I was unsure.

"You sure I can't get you boys somethin'? Some coffee? Ice Tea? Some pound cake? I just made a fresh one yesterday."

"I'll eat a piece of pound cake," said Percy. "I've been so busy tryin' to stay in front of Walter, I bet I haven't eaten in a coupl'a days."

"You want some, hunny?" she asked me.

I looked at Lucky. He nodded, then shook his head when she asked him if he wanted any.

"Yes ma'am," I told her. "If you're gonna fix some for Uncle Percy."

Miss Helen made herself busy, disappeared into the kitchen. I imagined her drawing the cake out of one of those cake plates with a lid on it, slicing it with a big, long knife, and then placing the slices on small plates ... just like my mother would have done. Sure enough, she brought two small, white plates through the doorway in a matter of seconds, handed one to me, one to Percy. Asked Lucky again if he was sure he didn't want any.

"No thank ya,' he said, standing. "We're gonna have to be goin'. When'd you say Mr. Oscar was gonna meet us over at the cemetery?"

"When I talked to him, he said he was goin' back over there in a half hour or so. He said he hated to leave it for very long. But he didn't figure anybody'd bother it on Sunday mornin'. Anyway ... he said he'd be over there when you got there. I'm figurin' he's there now."

"I don't figure he thought anybody'd bother it on Saturday night either," said Lucky. "We better get on over there. Boys, y'all about ready to go?"

I nodded. Percy scowled.

"Can you guarantee me that they won't see me? That you can keep Walter away from me?"

"When did you get on a first name basis with him?" asked Lucky.

Percy finished his last bite of cake like he hadn't eaten in days and held the plate out for Miss Helen to take. "Like Jacob spending all night wrestling the angel, a night like that changes a lot of things. With FDR dyin'. With Truman takin' over. Missouri Mule. Okinawa. Vienna. Nuremberg. You tell me why I wouldn't know his name!"

"Can I speak with you outside for a minute, Miss Helen?" Lucky asked. "Henry, stay in here with Percy and finish your cake."

"Can I have another piece, Miss Helen?" Percy asked. "I'm awful hungry."

"Sure, sweety," said Miss Helen.

Across from me, Percy ate his pound cake like it was the last bit of food he'd ever put in his mouth. He chewed and smacked so loud I figured Lucky and Miss Helen could hear him outside. Between bites, he pushed the hair out his face that would fall every time he'd lean forward to meet the fork his hand held.

Out the same bay window through which I had watched Percy when we sat in the driveway, I now watched Lucky and Miss Helen discuss only God knew what. The call from Mr. Oscar Garrett, I imagined, and what had happened to the cemetery.

CHAPTER NINETEEN

RUFUS CORNELIUS was the only black man buried in the Confederate Cemetery, Percy told me. He pulled the pack of cigarettes out of his sock. Assured me that this is the way it had to be; that otherwise somebody would take them from him. Cigarettes were a difficult enough commodity to get anyway, with the war and everything, but try your hand at it in a mental hospital. Or "the goddam asylum," as Lucky would come to call it.

"They're tellin' me that there isn't any such thing as Walter," he informed me. "I find that absolutely ridiculous. That's like tellin' somebody that there's no such thing as World War II. When you see the evidence all around you, then it's hard to deny."

I had noticed Lucky's breathing deepening, his face turning a little flushed when Percy began speaking to us in the corner of the ward, then in his own room.

"I know you've been talkin' to them," he told Lucky. "I saw you the day you all brought me down here. Talkin' to them. Explainin' to them how best to take me out of the picture. With Walter, it's like a double-edged sword; he haunts me like a goddam ghost, but you put one of us out of commission and then there's no telling what can happen!"

"Percy, there's people dyin' all around you, and you're goin' on with shit like this?"

"That's precisely why I'm goin' on with 'shit like this,'" he mocked Lucky.

"You're just lucky that your ass ain't overseas, like them boys that left a coupl'a weeks ago. Langford—hell of a football player—and that Burkitt boy. Both a' them signed up before they could even draft 'em. Now … there's some heroes for ya."

Percy grimaced, almost like somebody had pressed on some of the wounds they had treated when he first came into the place. Cracked ribs, a concussion, deep lacerations on his neck and shoulder. He pinched his lip with his thumb and forefinger, cigarette smoke billowing in front of his face from the Chesterfield poised between his next two fingers.

"The attendant told us all you do is sit in the corner and smoke cigarettes. He said you don't talk to nobody else or really even have anything to do with the other fellahs."

Percy looked around him like he was observing where he was for the first time. Laughed a little. "Walter, the son of a bitch, tells me everything I need to know."

"I'm gettin' tired a' hearin' about goddam Walter," Lucky told him.

"Maybe if you'd tell him that … and not me … he'd leave me alone," Percy said.

"He's not there!" Lucky said. "I can't tell somebody somethin'—even if that somebody is a pig—that ain't there! Do you not fuckin' understand that!?"

"I understand more than you'll ever think I'll do. I understand where this world's headin'. To hell in a hand basket! I understand that you got that goddam lighted box so you could keep up with everything that I do! I know that's why you started keepin' your winda's open—so you could see what I was doin'!"

"No … I got that 'lighted box,' as you call it, because somebody was nice and wanted me to have it. The same way I got those goddam Chesterfield cigarettes I brought you today. It's nice to have friends. But you gotta talk to the people around you before you can make one."

"I wouldn't trust anybody that gave me anything," said Percy. "There's somethin' connected to everything."

"What's connected to the cigarettes and the brownies I brought you? You think Mary is out to get you, too? Is that why she made the brownies for ya?"

As if he just remembered they were at the base of the chair he sat in, he reached and got the pan. Took the aluminum foil off and held the pan out to Lucky and me. Asked where Mama and Jean were.

"They stayed at home today … tryin' to do some spring cleanin'," Lucky lied.

The truth was that they'd been so upset the only time they'd come to see him, two Saturdays before, that they'd said then they wouldn't come back. Couldn't come back. Truth be told, I think Lucky was afraid to come by himself after that. Had dragged me with him. Said it was good for me to see the results of refusing to work. Said if you can't live in the real world, then you make one up. Exactly what Percy had done.

Percy and I both took a brownie out of the pan, started chewing.

"I bet a lot a' these fellahs have come back from the war, haven't they?" said Lucky.

"'Ey ca-it sh-sho-d," said Percy, still chewing.

"What?"

"Shell-shocked," he said after he swallowed. "But you wouldn't know anything about it. It's for people who've fought in a war."

"Like you have?" said Lucky, drawing on his own Lucky now.

"I tried to sign up," said Percy. "They wouldn't let me. Said I couldn't go fight the Japs and Hitler. You … you told 'em that you needed to stay here and keep the peace. Had Mr. Oscar Garrett tell 'em that he couldn't do without ya."

Both things Percy said were true. He had tried to sign up. Mr. Oscar Garrett had asked Lucky to stay, told Uncle Sam he needed him worse right where he was.

"I'm gonna act like I didn't hear that," said Lucky.

"How's that different from what you normally do?" shot Percy.

Lucky looked at him, at me. At the cigarette in his hand. Shook his head. Hacked a couple of times as he was walking to the window.

"Deceit is a terrible thing," Percy said to his back.

"They think we're about to finish things off in Europe," Lucky said.

"I wouldn't know," said Percy. "I haven't seen a newspaper in weeks."

"You want me to go by the library the next time we come and bring you some books?"

"Suit yourself," Percy said. "I don't know if I could even read one. That medicine they're givin' me makes me sleepy most of the time. What's it called? See, that's not like me ... not being able to remember what something's called."

Lucky hadn't remembered what it was called either when we had been on our way there. He had just said that the doctor had told him that they'd give it another few days and then they'd try "other means." They were just beginning to think that electricity might help work the kinks out of some people's heads. And Percy sure had his share of goddam kinks.

Watching the oaks and elms and maples pass the car, just beginning to show their color for the year, I wanted to ask Lucky why he had done what he had. If he knew. If he'd sacrificed him. Maybe both things were true.

"I think he was with Hood, too," Percy said.

"Who?" Lucky said, sitting again. He lit his own cigarette then stretched for Percy's.

"You said you didn't want me to talk about him anymore."

"No—what I said was ... Shit, forget it. I just wanna be able to talk about somethin' real every once in awhile."

"I'd say Hood doin' what he did was about as real as it gets."

"Here he goes," Lucky said to me, "retreatin' into make-believe again. Just like the doctor said he would. Schiza-somethin' or another."

"If you think Hood was make-believe, you haven't lived in the same town that I have all these years."

"You're probably right," said Lucky as he arose and stepped toward the door. "I haven't."

"You ain't goin', are ya?" said Percy, lowering the half-eaten brownie in his hand to his lap.

"Yeah, I reckon we better be headin' out," said Lucky. "Mary and Jean'll be lookin' for us."

Fatass. Home in bed, probably. As sometimes happened, I felt bad when this thought passed through my head. Looked at Percy as he passed across the tile floor that had once been new, now dull and yellow with age and wear.

"Can Henry stay a few minutes and talk to me?" he said.

Lucky nodded, pulled the door the rest of the way open and said he'd be in the car.

"He's doin' that rather than get mad," said Percy. "My brother's always had a bad temper."

 I nodded. Felt like I needed to run too.

"When people think they're not enough, it causes them to do bad things," he said. "I think they call it an inferiority complex. Or something like that."

I wished Lucky hadn't left me. I wished I couldn't smell the odor of the place, somewhere between piss and body stink. I wished I hadn't had to see these people around Percy, the ones he refused to talk to because they, too, were in on the plot. The ones with missing limbs and a strange, faraway look in their eyes.

"He's always been that way. Thought that Daddy and Mama loved me better than him. Always knew I was smarter than he was, too," he snickered. "Your daddy blends good. That's his strength. He's one of 'the people.' People trust him even though they know he's got his hands in a lot of things he shouldn't. Craps. Stolen television sets. Bootleg whiskey. And that just scratches the surface. But they know, too, that they can trust him to do the right thing when it comes down to a tough situation. He's like Mr. Oscar in that way. That's probably why he handpicked him. I think he thought that he'd finally get Mama and Daddy to pay more attention to him when he got the job as a policeman. In a little town like Franklin, that's real prestige. But they just kept worryin' about their 'frail' son. I was the youngest, the one with somethin' wrong with him. You know what? I bet I saw daddy, when he was young and strong, beat the hell out'a your daddy fifty times. The crops weren't growin' well—whip Dillard's ass. The rains weren't comin' like they should—whip Dillard's ass. The corn and tobacco didn't bring enough at the market—whip Dillard's ass."

I sat watching him dig a pack of cigarettes out of his sock, amazed at how clear-headed he sounded now. How for just a moment, his brain must have pushed Walter and 'the plot' away. Cleared like a cloudless sky.

"YEP, HE'S BURIED right there," he told me a second time, after he'd already said it once. "You know that shoe-shine man. Jackson...umhh, Mosby. It's his great-grandfather. He died when they were tryin' to get all the bodies there. You know that they dug up everybody they could find and moved them there? The McGavock family gave the land … moved the bodies. Buried them again. Rufus Cornelius was a free man by then. He stayed and helped them. And died of heat stroke while they were movin' 'em. Didn't your daddy have a run-in with one 'a them Mosby people not long ago?"

"He watched while Sammy Samuels had a run-in with Jackson's boy, that little nigger, Arliss," I said.

"One of these days, that word's gonna be thought of as one a' the worst cuss words we can say," Percy told me. He pushed himself back on the bed and pulled his knees up to his chest. "You're gonna see a lot a' things change in the next ten or fifteen years. I bet the colored people and the white people'll be goin' to school together."

I laughed, unable to imagine it.

"That's whose tombstone Walter pinned me under," he said. "I knew it was in there. But I'd never been able to find it. It figures when I was just passin' through that Walter would pick that one to pin me under. I guess it knocked me right out. All I felt was the impact and then when I woke up in the daylight and started to try to pry myself out from under it … I saw it. There it was! You know, I guess I can see how it appears that I did it, since I have all the marks on me. But people just don't understand what he can do if he puts his pig mind to it."

"Walter didn't pin you under that stone," I told him.

"He most certainly did," he argued, finally lighting the cigarette perched on his lips.

"It was Fred Burkitt," I told him.

"Who?"

"That boy that went off to the service when Ronnie Langford did," I said.

"Pfff," he responded, wagging his head.

"I saw it Percy. I know."

"So did I," he said. "The son of a bitch chased me into the woods earlier. Then I hid there for a long time. But I kept hearin' all this commotion, so I finally came back down to the cemetery. I mean, I had just walked up and was tryin' to see from behind that stone when I heard him runnin' and snortin' again ... and then the goddam stone just collapsed on top of me. I know nobody believes me ... that they think it was impossible for a pig only I see to tear up most of a cemetery. All I know is that I didn't do it. And that even my own brother don't believe me."

I knew what the doctor had told us the week before, that no amount of "rationality or facts" would lead Percy to embrace reality. That we would not, probably could not, convince him that there was no pig named Walter and that everybody wasn't out to get him. At the time it didn't matter. I needed him to know what I had seen and participated in.

"You can't tell anybody this," I said.

"That's all right," he answered. "I know a lot of secrets. That's the reason he follows me." He shook his finger toward the corner of the room, dingy with dust and shadows. "Don't you bear your tusks at me ... you bastard. I mean it. My brother's a policeman!"

"I mean it," I said. "You can't tell nobody this. This'd be worse than Lucky and Mama knowin' that you give me cigarettes."

"Your wish is my command, my fair nephew. Godammit, Walter, quit snarlin' at me!"

"I mean it, Percy! Listen to me! They said they'd cut our dicks off if we told. If they cut my dick off, it'd be so much worse than what happened to you."

He somehow tuned his demeanor to my need and screwed the craziness out of his face for a sober moment. The last words I had spoken—so much worse than what happened to you—banged over and over in my head like a snare drum in the silence. He looked around himself at the interior of the room where he'd spent the last three weeks. At the eroding concrete of the window ledge just feet from where he sat. The decaying plaster of the ceiling and walls of a building erected before the turn of the century and poorly cared for ever since—yet still an improvement over what they had done with "crazy" people fifty years before. A lady banged on the door, stuck her head in.

"Hunny, if you don't come out and eat your lunch with the other patients today, then you ain't gonna get anything."

"It's all right," he told her. "I'm not hungry anyway."

"Dillard's probably right," he said, after she closed the door. "He's always told me if I found a woman, it'd probably make a world'a difference in my life."

"It wasn't Walter," I told him. "It was Fred Burkitt." I could feel my heart thumping in my chest like it was trying to break free from my rib cage. Run far faraway.

"He's gettin' mad," Percy told me. "Please don't make him mad. You'll leave and he'll torment me long after you're gone. Shut up, Walter!" he spoke into the corner. "If you don't shut up, I'll be fryin' up some bacon even if I don't like it."

I tried to figure some way back to that sober face I'd seen a flash of a little bit before.

"Just stop for a minute," I reasoned with him. "Just stop and listen to me. Can you do that for just a minute? Without telllin' me anythin' else about Walter. Please!"

His eyes filled again with sobriety. Fear. "Okay."

"It was Fred Burkitt who chased you up the railroad track," I told him. "It was him who tore down all the tombstones. Him and Ronnie Langford.

It was him that hit that stone that you was behind. I saw him do it."

As the words rolled out of me like the river flows after a hard rain, I felt like I was beginning to secrete poison. Sweat it out. I knew, though, that nothing short of vomiting blood would purge me of the guilt. As the words flowed, even at nine, I knew I did not speak them for him. But for myself.

"And then we heard you scream." I wiped the tears away from my face with the back of my hand. "We heard you scream a couple of times."

"'Holler' would be a better word," he said. "I don't think I 'screamed.'"

"Whatever you did, we heard it," I told him. "And then we all went and looked under the stone and found you there. Fred Burkitt said, 'Shit, boys, he's still breathin'. I saw him hidin' over here, but I thought he'd run before I knocked it over on him. I wasn't tryin' to hurt the son of a bitch, I swear.' Ronnie Langford even got down there on top of you and checked your pulse somehow that he knew to. He said he thought you was gonna be all right … was probably just knocked out."

Percy turned to the corner of the room. He made some gesture, but caught himself.

"Van even said that he thought it was you. He got down there with Ronnie Langford and looked real close. He said it three or four times and...."

I kicked him in the ass until he raised back up. It wasn't that I was ashamed of you, Percy. It was just that I thought they might do something else crazy if they knew that I was kin to you … and how much I loved you. That Burkitt man was drunk out of his head … crazy as a lunatic. No … bad word. They were both out of their heads. Ronnie had always been nice to me before. Hell, we wouldn't have even been there if it hadn't been for Van. He was brown-nosin' Ronnie that day, like he does everybody.

I picked the next words quickly, afraid I would again lose him to the pig.

" … it was so dark and I couldn't tell if it was you or not. Maybe by then they had started to sober up a little. And they started sayin' that they could leave whoever it was there and he'd either die or they'd find him there in the mornin' and figure that his last bit of tearin'-up had gone wrong. They even said they was gonna call the police and tell them that they'd seen somebody over there. They said that'd cover their ass if anybody had seen us. That's when they told us they'd cut our dicks off."

"Last chance for lunch," a different woman told him, her broad face barely visible through the crack in the door.

"No thank ya. I'm fine." He studied my face like he might believe me.

"Do you want me to tell Lucky?" I asked him.

"No … he said he didn't want to hear anything else about Walter. This medicine they got me on takes away a lot of my memory. But I remember him sayin' that."

"Are you sure?"

"Lucky wouldn't be any more likely to believe you than Walter. They both know the truth and never waiver. See … I said somethin' good about you," he said into the corner.

"It might get you out'a here," I told him.

"This had been in the makings a long time," he responded. "It's bigger than you and me both. Leave it alone. Grace. Grace is the most important thing in the world. It means lovin' somebody when they don't deserve it. Hell, none of us deserve it. We're all bastards. The bastards of God!"

On the way there, Lucky had observed, both this week and the last, that Percy was "fixated" on religious things. Seeming impressed he knew the word when he told me, he said that's what Dr. Guppy had told him shortly after they had Percy admitted against his will. Threatened him with going to jail for destruction of state property, or even Federal charges, being a military cemetery.

"Love, in its own way," said Percy, "means suffering. The two are inseparable. Grace means forgiving somebody even before they ask you. It means we live in a state of perpetual forgiveness."

"You sound like Brother Myron Brown," I told him.

"I don't mean to," he said. "But I've been thinking on that a lot. Walter, when he's in a good mood, talks to me about that kinda stuff a lot. He says if I learn things like this, then he won't ever have to use his big, nasty teeth on me."

I drew in enough air to push the choking out of my chest. I nodded and stood, afraid that Lucky had begun to get drunk or mad waiting on me. Or both.

Percy stared into the corner for a few moments, wagged his finger at the nothingness. Did his best to make a mean face.

Randomness. A Planned Nature of Things. Basic Human Frailty.

I HOPED THE RIDE DOWN Hillsboro Road would clear my head. From the moonshine. From my round with Lucky earlier in the day. From having to see Percy like this again. I'd hoped against hope, I guess, that he would never return to the state of eight years before. I felt the grief that comes with the early recognition of something you have dreaded. My heart sank in a different way when thoughts of him passed out of my head and her presence came in.

My senses felt as alive with memory as they had when what I was remembering occurred. Her smell remained instead of the scent of the trees lining the road. Her taste remained with me, even though I should have been tasting the sore in my mouth. My crotch throbbed, even though the throbbing should have been in my back and ass from Lucky earlier. The sun just starting to lose its color to a sky greying around its edges, I remembered from the night before—which surprised me—that she had said she was working from ten o'clock to six o'clock in the evening.

Castner Knott, so-named, I had been told, after the two men that founded the department store, was on the west-central edge of Nashville, bordering a neighborhood called Green Hills, that had sprung up after World War II and the prosperity that came in its wake.

As I sat at the stop light, gunning the throttle over and over, I listened to the engine combust then fire, combust then fire, so quickly that one movement couldn't be separated from another. As the light changed, I took the straight shot of Franklin Road leaving town.

All the usual voices made themselves present in the silence of the toiling engine. Percy telling me how Hood followed Schofield to Nashville down Franklin Road. The insanity of it all. Lucky having a belly laugh after Percy called somebody insane. This was the long fucking way around, Lucky would tell me. Going through Brentwood to get to Green Hills. Why in the hell would you do that? That's four or five miles out of the way. Maybe six. Because, Franklin Road clears my head. Like a soothing voice or calming music, it turns the voices quiet in my head. You sound like Percy, he would tell me. What voices in your head? Am I gonna need to take you for a few a' them treatments, too? He laughed because he couldn't let himself cry about it. Then he'd be back on my ass about the extra few miles. You kids that didn't live through the Depression just don't understand it like we do. The money that you'd spend on the extra gas you burn meant somethin' then. There wasn't no extra anything. Hell, then right on its heels came the war. Rations out the ass. People tryin' to make do on as little as they could. Then everybody come home—or at least them that come home—and built them a little house on their GI Loan and people act like we're gonna have everything forever. You take Ronnie Langford, if he had come home, he'd just be glad to have anything. Then there's that Burkitt boy. Life just ain't fair, Henry.

Just thinking about the diatribe made me madder than it had that morning when he kicked me in the ass … when he held my head close enough to the dried vomit I could see the fine details of any food that had been left in my stomach. Maybe we all get what we deserve. Maybe I did this morning. Maybe Ronnie and Fred did. Or maybe it's just dumb luck.

I never did quite get over that Langford boy, Lucky would tell me. Boy gave up everything when they were startin' to wind down the draft. You know how he got killed, don't ya? I'd nod, but he'd never notice. On that goddam island. Okinawa. They were shuttin' it down. Almost had it completely captured. He went in less than a week before they finished it off. He got there on the June the 14th, died on the 19th. He was just one of twelve thousand killed.

And then you take that Burkitt boy....

As the horn blared, I jerked the handlebars so hard that I nearly veered off the road. I caught myself with my right foot, kept from spinning out in the gravel and going down. I gave him the finger, after I made sure it wasn't Lucky. Lucky might have sat on the horn but he wouldn't have swerved.

Giving me the finger back, I watched Van make his way down Hillsboro Road. Son of a bitch could've killed me. Sitting behind three cars at a stop light, I tried to force my hands to stop shaking. Told myself that I'm the halfback, Van the tight end who wanted to be the halfback but was too slow. That's what Mr. Nedler's told us in Spring practice anyway. Van's taller, has more reach, longer limbs to throw blocks. I'm smaller, faster … tougher. He actually said that, in front of Van, but he acted like he didn't even hear it. Big Shit Van.

I NEVER FELT AS SMALL-TOWN as I did when I went to Nashville. To me, it seemed like every eye was fixed on me, the people behind them knowing that I was from somewhere else … didn't come someplace like this often. Women's Dresses, she had told me. Sometimes Men's Sports-wear. Sometimes, behind one of the makeup counters.

Why won't the goddam door open? I asked myself. I continued to shove on it until I realized it said PULL. Saw a couple of people laughing at me. The building air felt cool. Smelled like inside air, like it had been turned over and over until mostly everything but perfume had been filtered out of it. A loudspeaker called out people's names … specials every once in awhile. Women and men were both dressed like they were going to church. I tried to look like I had been there before. Squinted my eyes a little, scanned as far as I could see as I made my way a few feet inside.

"Why've you got a leather jacket on in May?" Her hand touched my shoulder as I turned.

"I rode my bike," I told her, still squinting like I might be looking for something else. Somebody else.

"You rode your bicycle?" she said.

"My motorcycle," I told her. I felt a twinge in my gut.

"Oh," she laughed. "Sorry. I forgot you said that. Are you okay?"

"Yeah, I'm fine. Why?"

She was digging in her purse for something. Her time card, she said. She took out a piece of gum, folded it and put it in her mouth. Offered me one. I took it.

"Well, I was just wondering. You seemed a little funny." She waved at somebody that walked close to us. "She works in Men's Sportswear. She's a sweet lady. Walk this way with me," she told me. "I've got to clock out. You stay right here. I've got to go in this little room, punch my card in this machine. Chink-chink, it goes. The chink-chink machine, I call it. So they know what time I left. Did you know what time I was leaving? Is that why you came now?"

"No ... actually I—" But she was gone. In the door where the chink-chink machine was. So they'd know what time she left.

I leaned on the wall outside the door, trying to make myself look like I'd been there a thousand times. Trying to convince anybody that looked at me that I was waiting on my girlfriend. Telling myself that I was desperate and rough in my leather jacket, the one out of the Sears and Rare-back catalogue, as Lucky liked to call it. I was relieved that I wouldn't have to run into Percy again. The son of a bitch couldn't walk this far. Not in a day anyway. He'd been holed up upstairs at our house that afternoon, smoking one cigarette after another, his fingers as yellow as a daisy. He'd offered me one just before he'd tried to explain to me what he had been doing.

I took it, drew long and deep on it. Felt the first hit that convinces you the shit is somehow good for you. Nodded emptily at him.

"I could have done somethin' else this mornin' besides get up on that car. I could'a gone down to Frank's and carried on a bunch of bullshit like most other men in this town, George Preston and a few others not included. I could'a gone over to Sammy Samuels' auction barn and seen what he had. I could've just come here and talked to you. But we all have a drive inside us that we can only turn a deaf ear to so long. I'm not sayin' it's good."

"Lucky's gonna have your ass," I told him. "Or at least I'm imaginin' he wants to."

"Lucky-Schmucky," he said. He laughed.

"It's like all good preachin'," he told me. "I'm talkin' to myself. Tellin' myself what I need to hear. I'm just not sure how it all comes together ... I mean, how it's related, one thing to another."

"Are you okay?" she asked me.

"Yeah, I'm okay," I told her.

"What were you thinking about?"

"My uncle," I told her as she shut the door to the time-card room.

"The one we saw that night?"

"I've only got one."

She took my hand in hers and led me through the plate glass door to the sidewalk that surrounded the building. The air felt stiller than when I had entered. Fuller of heat. Two weeks would bring the beginning of the weather that felt like summer.

"What're you going to do?" she asked.

"I don't know," I said. "I guess I thought we might go to get something to eat or somethin'."

"Can we ride your motorcycle?" she said.

I nodded as we began to walk toward it. "Here," I said, handing her my leather jacket, "You probably ought to wear this. It's easy to get cold even when it's really warm."

She nodded then slipped the jacket on before she raised her leg over the seat of my bike, a little more carefully than I had, because of her skirt. "We'll probably get arrested," she said. "Indecent exposure."

"Nobody's gonna say anything," I told her.

"It's not very lady-like, though."

I nodded. Laughed. Fired the throttle as I kicked the Indian started.

"Van's your cousin, right?" she said into my ear as she wrapped her arms around my rib cage.

I nodded. "Why?"

"Oh, no reason really. I just saw him today when he was in the store. He came over to my department and said 'Hi.' Said his parents had given him some money to come buy himself some summer clothes. I saw him a little later, walkin' out with a big bag. Well, actually I didn't see him. He came over and told me 'Bye.' He seems like a nice guy."

I nodded and gunned the throttle a couple of times. Let the clutch out and felt the Indian's power under me. Felt her squeeze hard at my rib cage as we started down the hill and out of the parking lot.

"Where you wanna go?" I asked her over my shoulder.

She nuzzled her head in next to mine. "I don't care. Wherever you do."

I nodded. Knowing that neither did I care … as long as I was with her. Could feel her touch on my skin. Know that she was close to me.

CHAPTER TWENTY

"WHEN POLICE CHIEF DILLARD HALL was asked why he had taken the negroes into custody, he responded by answering, 'The whole town thinks they did it.' And then he would answer no more questions, disappearing into the Franklin Memorial Chapel. It seems as though the Franklin Jail is being used for a holding place, so that some of its citizens will not harm others. It was always this reporter's impression that the jail was to protect the ones on the outside, not its interior."

That's how the smartass Garrison ended his commentary on my father. Earlier, he had addressed his question to Lucky on the drinking.

"'Lucky' as he is called, the Police Chief in Franklin for the past four years, stated it was none of the reporters' business if he had been drinking when an inquiry was made into the matter. Mr. Hall refused to answer any questions excepting to divulge some information that had been in the deceased young woman's pocket."

I had been trying to appear inconspicuous reading the article as I folded papers, one lying flat at my knees. Eventually my eyes would let me go no further, the choking feeling in my throat betraying my ability to read.

I was folding my papers beside Chester Mott, and he, as usual, kept his eyes and his words to himself. In his own way, he reminded me of Percy, minus the crazy. That I knew of, he had no friends; only his morning and evening route. He had lived with his mother and had thrown papers as long as I could remember; never done anything else.

On my other side was Ralph Thompson. He was not minus the crazy. He wasn't crazy like Percy; didn't think that a pig followed him around everywhere. He was simply a few bricks shy of a full load, as I had heard it said.

"So, your daddy was drunk again, huh?" spouted Collins from across the office.

I checked over my shoulder. Mr. Charles was watching us close this morning, listening to what was said so he could squelch something before it got started. Ignored the asshole.

"Does he know anything else?" Mott asked me, one of the few people in the world he'd address first. Eight years, I guess, had proved I wouldn't hurt him, wouldn't take anything that his mother had left.

I glanced at him and shook my head, the knot still lodged in my throat, already dreading *The Banner* coming out around three. Mott and his *Banner* cohorts would see it a little after noon.

"It's scary," he said. "Really scary."

I nodded. Realized he had spoken more words to me the last few seconds than he had in the last few months.

"Yeah," said Ralph Thompson. "You should'a seen her. I seen her. She was awful ugly with that huge, old cut in her throat." He sniffed and pushed up on his nose with his palm, like he was trying to tilt the thing back. Keep it from running perpetually, like it did. "Yep. I seen her."

"Glad I didn't," said Chester.

As they went on back and forth, each trying to comfort the other in his own strange way, Raymond Collins only mumbled for the most part inaudible phrases from the opposite corner of the room. That morning, Lucky had only briefly mentioned that Jack Charles had told him in passing about Collins and me the day before. Smiled when he talked about it. The first time I'd seen his separated teeth in days, maybe months for that matter, except for a sarcastic or melancholic laugh. Lucky liked to think about me like himself: small, but able to take care of myself. A scrapper. A fighter. That's why I always figured he was so concerned with my football playing. As a tailback and kick returner, I was the smallest guy on the field. Liked to think about myself as the one who gave the most. Maybe that's why it ended the way it did. I don't know. Van had said of me and Lucky: "Little Man's Syndrome. That's what they call it. Where you make up for your size with the way you act … the size of your dick, that is!" That night, I'd been too focused on everything else to worry about his smartass mouth.

"We got some big fuckers tonight," he told us after everybody had quieted their laughing. "Boys from Hohenwald. Close descendants of a bunch of damn Germans. It's gonna be World War II all over again."

It was plain that most people thought my short and skinny were more entertaining than what it had taken most of us and our families eight years to begin to forget.

"They're farm boys, too. Big ole meaty boys. Tackle hard, I've heard!"

It was the first time I'd looked at him in months without wanting to kill him. The feeling would arise again every once in awhile, but leave as unpredictably as it had come. He was the cheerleader on the team. Even though a tight end, he saw it as his job to get us worked up before a game. He had taken on this role in the absence of charisma of our present quarterback, Jerry Nance, a farmboy himself, who looked more anemic than anything else. Jerry shook his fist in the corner, which was usually all he was able to muster.

"We can beat those big boys' asses!" Van hollered. He slammed his helmet into the cement ledge below the lockers, as he had seen Mr. Nedler do, in the absence of his presence. Nedler and his wife were with Lucky, I knew. Discussing what to do … what had happened.

Van hit me and knocked me off balance. Slapped my shoulder pads hard enough that the sound hurt my ears. "Now go get that kick off," he'd said. "If we get the coin toss—and I can guarantee you that I'll call it right—you take that kickoff all the way back!" Which I did.

As I had moved, it was like there was no one who could touch me. Homecoming. Sharon up there somewhere, taking off from work so she could come. The crowd roared their approval at every cut I made, at every tackle I pulled myself through with a quick move or a stiff arm. The end zone grew bigger and closer with every five-yard section of field I covered. It hadn't occurred to me yet how big these boys were; I hadn't been hit by one of them hard. Had just seen them as they melted into the picture I was leaving behind, as my teammates, including Van, threw blocks that sent them flying two, three, four yards away. As I had grown to love, I could hear the cracks of helmets and shoulder pads around me and behind me, almost like gun shots. Could hear the grunts and groans that leave players' mouths when they're exerting everything they have, leaving it all on the field where they run and fall. The end zone was as good as anything I could imagine, if for no more than a moment, I basked in the feeling that convinces you that you've transcended the world.

I handed the ball to the referee in the end zone like it was nothing. Just another day at the office. Nothing to get excited about. My heart must have been beating three hundred times a minute as I handed the referee the ball. I bent and put my hands on my knees, my lungs grabbing for all the air they could. Reminded myself of Lucky for a minute. Thought of the scuttle-butt that had swirled around me at least a couple of times this year—that I might actually get to play college ball. The article in the *Review Appeal* comparing me to Ronnie Langford. The one that said I didn't have as much "raw talent," but seemed to have as much heart as a boy could have. Went into all that shit about how I had carried papers since I was eight. How I had played baseball and football, but that football had been my passion.

As everybody threw their arms around me, I was as sure as the fact that I drew in breath that these were the kind of moments we live for. The kind that make you forget the other ones, like what we had been going through the last few days. The referee even slapped me on the back, told me that he had seen my daddy arrive just before I took it back. Walking off the field, I had looked for Lucky in the stands … seen his face beaming from his normal spot. Mama must have been at home, I thought, waiting. Probably what Lucky had asked her to do. Somebody had to wait. As for Lucky though, he had gotten there just in time. He stood there cheering and coughing, clasping his hands together and pumping them over his head.

"DILLARD 'LUCKY' HALL, former Assistant Police Chief in Franklin, stated last evening that he remains unsure of who the woman found in front of the high school last Monday morning might be. In a somewhat strange twist of events, she was laid out at the Franklin Memorial Chapel, while hundreds of people filed by to look at her in an attempt at identification. The four deep gashes that were ruled to be the cause of death by Franklin Coroner Dr. Frank Guppy were covered as well as could have been possible, by thick makeup and a high-necked garment. 'We tried to do the best we could with what we had to work with,' said George Preston, Franklin Memorial Chapel Owner and Director. 'I do so wish, though, that we could have come up with a more respectful alternative, due to the fact that this one seems a bit demeaning. My God, it's not a sideshow!' he chastised later in the evening."

"Later in the goddam evening after the son of a bitch had broke out his second bottle!" Lucky said, then continued reading.

"Mr. Preston states that he contributed his services to the City of Franklin far below the normal price of such a procedure. 'There really wasn't much else we could do,' he told this reporter, 'besides just do the best we could. It's kind of like life, you know? You just do the best you can with what you have to work with at the time.' Mr. Preston, a man in his early forties who has made the funeral business his own for the last fifteen years, stated that so many people filed through his establishment to view the body that he thinks irreparable damage was done to his carpet."

"Do you see this shit?! Irrep—Queer motherf–" Lucky stopped himself as Jean with her pristine ears walked into the room. Began to read it again.

"Mr. Preston stated, 'I did this as a personal favor to Dillard. He's been so kind to me over the years. Franklin is indeed safer in his hands. I think that's especially good to remember now.'"

"You see, Daddy, that's nice. He said something nice about you."

I knew Lucky wanted to spew obscenities all over the kitchen. But the

Queen of Sheba was there, towel piled on her wet head, accenting her fat cheeks.

Lucky grunted and shook his head. "The story wasn't George Preston's goddam carpet—"

"Daddy!"

"The story's the dead woman still laying in the morgue because we can't decide when to bury her because we don't know who she is or what evidence we'll need."

As usual, Lucky had been out on his morning patrol—minus meeting with Sammy and the other 'boys'—and then back for breakfast. Staring at his plate, he said, "The real story is that somebody in this town slit a woman's throat four times and it wasn't the two colored men in jail."

"How can you be sure, Daddy?" Jean whined.

"There ain't no way to be sure about such things. All you can do is take what you got and work backwards. Come up with logical conclusions along the way. And the logical conclusions is that I don't think that they had a reason to do it … or really even a way. You know as well as me that it would'a took both of them to carry her body up there and dump it."

"But they could've, right?" Jean asked.

"Yeah, I guess it's possible. But what sense would that make? Why in the hell would they carry a woman they had killed to the high school where Jackson Mosby worked?"

"Maybe they were goin' to put her in the incinerator," Jean said, a theory that by now common knowledge. Somebody told me yesterday that there were a couple of kids there … early. Maybe he saw one of them."

"Well, if there were a coupl'a kids there, I'd sure like to know who they were," Lucky said.

As I swallowed down the lump in my throat, I tried to look as innocent as I could. I told myself for the thousandth time there was nothing I could do for Jackson or Arliss Mosby. There was no proof that they hadn't dropped the body before I saw Jackson that morning.

Lucky folded the paper and laid it beside his half-eaten plate of eggs and bacon. Looked at it like he could pull some of the information out through osmosis. Placed it under his arm.

"What else does it say, Daddy?" Jean chirped.

"The same old stuff," said Lucky.

"I want a copy of it," she said. "It's not every day that you're in the Nashville paper."

I stood, took my plate and dumped what was left in the trash. Jean did the same with hers. My mother emerged from the back porch, where she'd been folding clothes. Looked the table over.

"Dillard, not hungry?" she asked.

"I'm all right," he told her, which translated into their speak for her not to ask more questions. The truth was too hard to bear.

As Jean disappeared into her room—I stood on the back porch, staring through the screen that Lucky had had the time and the stamina to put up a few years earlier, when he was "the goddam assistant." My eyes dropped to the washer and dryer: another deal Lucky had gotten somewhere, if I remembered correctly, McFadden Electric, a few years before the television. First the washer, then the dryer. I remembered a time when Percy had tried to help my mother wash clothes, had run his arm up in the ringer on the machine. Stood there hollering until my mother came running to the back porch to help him, actually rolled his arm out. How Frank Guppy had told him nothing was broken when Lucky took him later in the day.

"I don't know how the hell I ended up my brother's keeper," Lucky had said. "You'd think the trouble wouldn't have followed me here ... that somebody out there could take care of him."

Lucky visited his family usually a half-dozen times a year, besides the times he'd go get Percy or take him home, even though they were ten miles away. Lera and Horace always seemed innocuous enough to me. Just old people who smiled and nodded when you spoke to them, always opened the door quick at your knock.

"Ma'am?" I said to my mother after she had spoken to me.

"I asked if you were okay."

As I turned and looked at her, I could tell that she had been a pretty woman in her day ... was still pretty for that matter. It was obvious, though, that some of her luster had been worn off. I suspected the residue was still on Lucky's hands. She smiled, then turned to the washer and started to run clothes through the ringer. I could still hear Percy screaming her name over and over and over. "Mary–Mary–Mary–Mary–Mary!"

"How do you feel about going back to school today?"

"Oh, it's all right," I told her. "I'm surprised they didn't make us go back yesterday." I scuffed at the planks on the floor with my boot. "And I guess if I thought somebody was gonna get me, it'd be my idea that they'd do it when I'm out throwing papers."

"Don't say that," she said. She shook out a couple of Lucky's tee shirts, wrung them, then threw them in the dryer. "I don't think anything's going to happen to anybody else."

"You always do look on the bright side of things," I told her.

"It's not the bright side," she said. "Just an idea of things you can live with."

Lucky passed through the back porch, paper still neatly tucked under his arm. Dotted my mother's cheek with a kiss and slapped me on the back. "It ought to be a hell of a day," he said.

"I hope it's not as bad as you expect," my mother offered.

"You and me both," he said. "You know, besides the couple of scuffles in beer joints that turned into somebody gettin' killed, I don't guess I've seen Franklin like this since the goddam cemetery incident. Well … maybe '49." He turned his eyes to what I was scuffing at on the floor, then pulled his own pant leg out of his boot top and swatted at the crease a couple of times. "At least everything's been all right down at the jail. I went by there earlier this morning."

Probably the shot fired into the grill—something like that'll do it every time, I thought as Jean stepped onto the back porch.

"You ready, hunny?" Lucky asked.

"Yessir," she told him.

She looked just like him. Broad head. Low set, thick jaw. Perpetual scowl. School was only two blocks from our house.

"Why you goin' so early?" I asked her.

"I'm going to catch up on some of my homework," she said.

Yeah, 'cause you've spent all your time over the last few days flappin' your gums about what happened like you might really know somethin' about it, I thought. But I didn't say it. Since sometime in September—just around the time my life went to hell in a hand basket—I'd held my tongue. She had just asked me, come straight out with it.

"Are you meetin' somebody in the mornin's?"

"Yeah," I'd told her, usually unable to lie to her.

"Who?"

"Nonya—that's who!"

"It's that girl, isn't it? That Bishop girl!"

"I told you, nonyabus'ness."

"She's pretty, Henry. Didn't Van go out with her, too?"

I hadn't answered her. Just stared at the floor, made like I hadn't heard her.

"How's your shoulder?" she'd asked, trying to change the subject.

"It's all right," I said. "Guppy said the ligaments would probably heal on their own. Said there really wasn't anything he could do till we knew if the ligaments were just stretched or torn. Rotator cuff was hurt some, too. You already know this. Why're you askin' about it now?"

"Just wanted to make sure you're okay," she said.

I nodded and didn't say anything else. Keep to yourself what doesn't need to be known. My mother would say nothing, I knew. Jean would lecture me on moral grounds. Lucky would attack from several fronts, asking if I knew what could happen doing what we're doing. Then he'd attack on social grounds. The have's and the have-not's, he'd explain, baiting me to disagree with him so he could get madder than hell. People need to mix with others of their own kind.

"You all start at ten today, don't ya?"

Jean nodded.

"Yeah, we do too."

"That's what you told them, wasn't it, Dillard?" said Mary.

"Dillard" I was certain was worlds away. The times he had seemed in his own body, in the moment, during the last three or four months were greatly few and far between. His hazel eyes were set hard out the window, on the backyard that Percy left through. It ran flat and straight for seventy-five or so feet and then down a slope and lost itself in a grove of Oak. Lucky had said that was why he'd picked this lot: the view was as close to heaven as anything he could imagine.

"Isn't that what you told them to do?" she asked him again.

He nodded and drew in a deep breath. Coughed it out. "Yeah, I figured that way it'd be good and daylight before people had to leave'."

"Did Mayor Everett have any other ideas?" asked Jean.

"You know he does whatever I say," Lucky laughed and coughed again. "I gotta get at it," he said, which was what he said when he'd had enough of whoever he was standing around.

"I'm ready, Daddy," chirped his princess.

My mother put her lips to our cheeks one at a time, told us she loved us and to be careful.

Lucky pressed the paper under his arm tighter. He would throw it away. We'd never see it, he knew. Or, I take that back. They'd never see it and I'd never show it to them. Another unspoken agreement. Lucky would let me slide … and I'd offer the same to him. Just like I had in September.

FOR THE MOST PART, the graves had been restored to the way they'd been before that night. In broad daylight and if you knew what you were looking for, you could see the cement that had been used to adhere what had been torn apart. I often wondered if Fred Burkitt came here, if he ever sat in his car and thought back to what happened here, knowing that no one else had ever discovered the truth. Probably not, I usually concluded. He likely thought he had sacrificed enough. Going after Muscle Eddy in Oklahoma.

Besides Percy, neither Van nor I had ever told another living soul about that night. When Ronnie's body had come home—or really, only the top half of his body—Lucky had packed us all in the car and told us we needed to see what a hero looked like.

"When will that other boy come home?" I remember asking him, after we left the funeral home, George Preston still flashing through my mind. How odd he was.

"That other boy that left when Ronnie did?" Lucky asked from the front seat.

"Yessir."

"As soon as he gets well enough to," Lucky had said. "We'll have to visit him then, too."

Yeah, anything to avoid visiting Percy, I remember thinking, who was still being held in Central State Mental Hospital. The shock treatments now down to every other day, no one ever much said anything about him except when we visited him occasionally.

"When do you think he'll come home, Daddy?" Jean said in a voice that made me cringe.

"Well, they said he'd be in the hospital in the Philippines for a little while. Said he'd be awhile learning how to use that contraption they're teachin' him to use."

No one, including Brown-nose, wanted to hear about the contraption.

"But he is … surely still alive?" Jean posed.

"That's what it said in the paper. Goddam *Review Appeal*, if you can trust that."

The only paper Lucky trusted less than the *Review Appeal* was the *Nashville Banner*, the evening Nashville paper. Lucky, himself, was a *Tennessean* man.

"Get news faster on the television anyway. Just think about it, that's where we heard about Hitler and ole Eva Braun's suicide, about our soldiers finally taking Okinawa, about Germany."

I knew what he was talking about. I'd heard it everywhere. The liberation, the concentration camps. The ultimate surrender.

"The Japs are gettin' ready to go that way, too," said Lucky.

After we had arrived home and Jean had stepped into her private chambers and I ascended the stairs into the attic and lay on my bed, next to the empty one Percy had slept in, I could not go to sleep. Ronnie Langford's face would not leave my sight. Besides the fact that it was the face of a dead man—perhaps the first one I'd ever seen—it was the face of someone I scarcely knew. But should have. It was the face of the boy … young man … somebody, that taught me to throw papers. The face I'd seen at the graveyard less than three months before. One that now not only looked scared, but strangely unlike itself, like it had been changed not only by death, but by life as well.

"HEY, BABY," I told her after she'd knocked and banged to a stop. I swear, I was sure that car was ready to give up the ghost any minute. "You really ought to get that thing fixed. It's gonna break down on you one night comin' home from Nashville."

"Maybe I won't have to go by myself much longer," she said.

"Maybe not," I said.

I scooted across the seat by her, grumbling as I did.

"Yesterday, the seat. Today, the engine. You're always complaining about my car."

"I know it," I told her. "Jean says I complain about almost everything. How does she put it? She says I'm the 'sourest person' ever. You know, she's the presence of goodness and light."

"She seems sweet enough to me," said Sharon. "She always speaks to me at school … and smiles. I think she knows about us. Do you?"

"I'm sure she does," I told her. I put my hand on her leg and felt my blood start to pump. Tried to push the thoughts out of my head about never telling my family about her. The reasons.

"And you're not sour," she told me.

"Just give me awhile," I told her. "Or ask pretty much anybody I know."

"I don't think I'd want to be with somebody the rest of my life who's sour," she said.

"Okay … I'll try to overcome it," I said.

As we settled into each other, our bodies melting together until every crevice felt filled by the other, I looked out upon the cemetery. The graves going on and on and on, the slope rose only slightly until they faded out of sight in the distance and the faint daylight. The light of the morning was cast on the ground and the tombstones, making the distance seem longer and the markers themselves, more distinct. The river, we had tried that. The old empty house next to the Bishop house, the Samuels' place; we had tried that. Too many memories. Van and Sharon. Now here. I wished there was some way to cut out parts of our brain, the parts that hold the memories that we don't like. Life, then, it seems, would be much more pleasant.

"THAT'S WHAT IT'S LIKE." Percy's words echoed through my head. "Both the first time and the second time. It's almost like it makes you forget who you are. Takes away the recollection we carry with us that we take for granted. You just feel like there's this empty space where something used to be … but you don't know what it was. And you know, that's all we really have. I've certainly not got anything but my ideas. I certainly haven't achieved riches or fame."

The exact opposite, Lucky would say. "He's infamous now. It's kinda embarrassin', you know? I'm not one who sits around and thinks about what other people think about me … but I've got to tell you that it's at least a little shamin'. Schizz–a'somethinoranother. Early on, I guess it was easier to ignore most of it, act like it wasn't happening. Take the road of least resistance."

Don't most of us, Lucky? I wanted to ask. It seems like we all like to sit back and wait for cold, hard reality to remind us of what we've been moving toward for quite some time. It's the human condition, a big part of *Human Frailty*, Percy would tell me a few days after the sermon when Mrs. Nedler had been standing there, waiting on her car in all her glory. We like to deny the truth to ourselves until we can't deny it any longer. That's part of the way we fool ourselves by employing human will. Like the will is our god … can make us one thing or another. I tell you that it can't. The spirit of the true god, the Source of Being, is what makes us one thing or another. You might use your will to go along with where it's carrying you … or fight against it … but will is useless when it comes to trying to make ourselves into other than what we are. It's like swimming against the current of a river. Eventually you just stop and melt into its current. Let it swallow you.

"Did I ever tell you about the time Lucky threw me in the river when we were boys?" he asked me the Monday after the Saturday sermon.

"Umh-uh," I shook my head.

"It's like that," he told me. "Since we were boys, I've always told Dillard that I couldn't swim..." As usual, he was in his underwear, smoking a cigarette. His hair flopped down over his forehead, covering one eyebrow. "And he's always told me I could. He swears that Wanda Jean and Nellie taught us when we were little. So when Dillard was sixteen and I was eleven or twelve, he took me down there one day. At first, he just talked me into going with him. Him bein' my older brother, I wanted to believe him when he told me I could swim."

He walked to the window and peered out. Nodded like he was acknowledging someone. Tipped his cigarette toward the general direction and smiled and snickered. He gave me a cigarette. Lit it off the end of his.

"The funny part is that I think he really thought I could swim. He was sure he was doing something good for me."

He paced back to the window and nodded. With the trouble he found himself having in '53, Walter had come and gone: present sometimes, absent others.

I drew on the cigarette, enjoying the first jolt that nicotine gives, perhaps its only gift. I blew the smoke out toward the ceiling like I'd seen Lucky and Percy do a million times before. Stared into his eyes, bloodshot and wide-open.

"He was just absolutely sure I could swim even when I told him over and over that I couldn't. Finally, he just grabbed me by the shirt and seat of the britches and threw me in."

"And what did you do?" I asked as much to get him to finish the damn story as anything else.

"I sucked in two lungs-full of water, that's what I did. Sucked in so much water that I sank like a rock. Sank to the bottom of the Harpeth like an anchor ... the anchor of the family ... pullin' everybody to the bottom. Funny thing then, the best I remember I stood there on the bottom lookin' up like I was watchin' a picture show down on Main Street. Everything else passed away. There wasn't a damn thing I could do about it. I didn't even try to swim. I knew as sure as I was at the bottom there that I couldn't. I was the anchor."

Later, Lucky would recount the situation by telling me he simply re-membered Percy jumping in, telling him he was "going in the river" and then just disappearing from the bank. Both accounts, though, held that Lucky had gone in after him, found him on the bottom. According to Percy, as peaceful and serene as a cool fall afternoon. According to Lucky, flailing and fighting for air, trying to draw it from the water, thus the two lungs-full of the river. Both said though, that Lucky fought Percy loose from the branches and mud, returned him to the surface and laid him on the bank where he spat up the lungs-full of water.

CHAPTER TWENTY-ONE

"YOU SEEM A MILLION MILES AWAY," she said. "Maybe in Alabama ... or Mississippi."

I laughed. It'd been an inside joke between us: where we'd run off to when the time came, when she got fed up with her mother and I got fed up with Lucky.

"Mississippi," I said. I knocked a cigarette from the pack in my pocket. Put in my mouth in a way I thought looked like Montgomery Clift in *From Here to Eternity.*

"Personally, I like Alabama," she said. "After all, it's where my people are from."

"Lucky says that not one good thing has ever come out of Alabama."

"Hank Williams," she said. She leaned and kissed me, leaving her lips pressed to mine only long enough to leave me wanting more. Took some tissue paper from her purse and blotted her lips. "There, now it won't get all over you."

"I kind of like Hank Williams ... and having it all over me," I told her. "Even after I wipe it off, I can smell you most of the day."

"Like to smell me, do you?"

"Yeah, I guess the only bad thing about our mornings together is that they're too short."

I felt her breath near my face again, her lips on my neck. And then I could think no more. Only feel. Only desire.

It was the first morning, I guess, that things had felt anything near to normal, whatever that is. As the clouds hinted at rain that might come again later in the day, they also held the morning light in some kind of stasis, neither letting it darken nor brighten. She stopped, sending me lurching to a stop with her.

"Godammit, hunny!"

"Do you still think about her?" she said. "I mean, still see her face in your mind? I'm not sure I'll ever get that out of my memory."

I could feel myself deflating, like an overinflated tire jammed with a knife. I could almost hear the air hissing its good-bye. I ground my teeth together, tried to stay "nice." Took a couple of deep breaths and reminded myself that I'd always heard men and women were different.

My eyes cut to the cemetery. I was pretty good, I thought, at wiping memories from my head as long as some place didn't bring them around to kick me in the ass. Again, I wanted to ask her about her crying fit at school but didn't, knowing that some things are better unsaid.

"Yeah, I still think about her," I said. "I guess, though, I've turned it off some. Seein' how it's all anybody's talked about for two days. You know, I don't believe I've heard anybody say anything about almost anything else. Christmas'll be here in two weeks."

I could feel her body tensing, trembling slightly, then releasing. "It's not every day that a woman that nobody knows ends up dead at the high school we go to ... I mean, that I attend."

It was like she was trying to convince me it was tragic ... how bad it was. I knew how fucking bad it was. I'd sat with the goddam body the night before as the population of Franklin filed by over and over again, to look at her. I knew all too well that the last couple of days hadn't been run of the mill.

"Does your daddy know anything else?" she said.

The throbbing in my crotch was beginning to subside, give me my breath and my brain back. But I still didn't feel like going into it...reliving anything, even the day before. I just wanted to go from here forward from here. Leave it dead where it lay, like the woman in the parking lot. Most of the time it just goes away. You don't have to stare it in the face again when it's been made to look better.

"I don't know."

She'd read it in the goddam paper soon enough. About my 'Daddy.' Or if she didn't read it, somebody'd tell her. I was sure the front page article would be fodder for most of Franklin and part of Nashville the rest of the day. And Lucky'd go right on. Either showing that he had a heart of stone or acting like he had one. Or pretending to himself that he did.

"WHAT IN THE WORLD are you thinking about now?" she asked.

I looked at her and shook my head, said "nothing," the way we do when we don't want to say what we've been thinking about because it doesn't make any fucking sense or you're sure nobody else in the world would understand.

"You were too thinking about something," she said.

If her smell didn't get me, then it was the way she parted her lips and smiled when she asked questions. Made me mush.

"Goddam Lucky," I said. Close enough to the truth, I thought. Not a hundred percent a lie.

"What about him?" she asked.

My memory flashed to the images that had tauntingly made their way through my head a little bit before. How that was the only time I could remember the son of a bitch ever excited about anything...or glad to have me for his son. When I broke the plane on the end zone returning kicks. Other touchdowns were little more than fodder for him to ask other questions, insinuate things could have been done better. It had been the way he was in baseball; probably the reason I had learned to hate the sport so steadily. Why'd you miss that grounder? You popped up, didn't ya? You know, I can see your swing as clear as if it was a mile an hour. You're swingin' under everything today. You're takin' your eyes off the ball. Watch the ball! Both catchin' and hittin.

Fuck you, Lucky. Then *you* play!

"What about him, baby?"

"Oh, nothin'."

I could feel that goddam feeling I had been able to push away since I was eight: the rising of something in my chest besides anger. An emptiness that felt like it might swallow itself ... might swallow me and everything else.

"Nothin's what you tell me when there's really something you need to talk about."

Sometimes with her I felt like I somehow had made my way back to five. Needed and got something that I couldn't speak. Some connection, after I had it the first couple of times, I was sure I couldn't live without. The bristled hairs on the back of neck poked at me as I rested my head, stared at the ceiling in the still-coming light.

"They said some really bad things about Lucky in the paper," I told her, still surprised that it bothered me. How could you slander someone like him?

"What?" she said. She laid her head into my shoulder, put one of her hands in the middle of my chest. "Your heart's even beating hard."

"Derived from the frustration of the last few mornings," I said, trying to sound like the chemistry teacher at the Academy, Mr. Gilbert. One of the few guys I still liked at the place.

She laughed then set in on me again.

"What'd they say about Lucky?"

"For one, they basically implied that he was a drunk."

"Well, you've said that before," she said. "That's nothing that you haven't told me."

"But it's different," I whined. "It's like when you tell me stuff about your mother. You wouldn't want anybody else to say it."

"The truth's the truth," Sharon said.

She sounded like Percy. But I wasn't going to tell her that. I didn't want one of his impromptu visits. Lucky was enough for the moment.

"You know, since what happened to Daddy and Sheila, I've gotten an idea not a lot of things really matter that much. Most things are just little things we need to let pass over us… around us."

Exactly what my people have done with Percy, I thought. But, again, didn't speak it. I, too, was a part of the conspiracy of silence.

"I don't mean acting like they didn't happen," she said, like she could read my mind. "I mean, somehow keeping your heart close to them but knowing that your heart also is above what happened. That it has to be. That we're left among the living for a reason. I'm not saying that I know what that reason is. But that there is one."

"Sounds like Brother Myron Brown to me," I said.

"I've never heard Brother Myron Brown," she said. "But I know what I'm trying to say is different from what I've heard in church when I've gone. It's like what I'm talking about goes all the way to the bottom of us. It's like it's not just something you believe … or even something you live. But something that lives inside of you. Enough about that, though. Tell me what else the newspaper said about your daddy."

I pulled the section of the paper out of my back pocket, where I had crammed it and left the paper office when I didn't think I could take anymore.

"Where do I start?" I said. "I guess everybody's like those assholes down at the paper office—they expect Lucky to get it solved in a day or so. Find out who the killer is … put him behind bars."

"Well, I guess he's kind of done that. I mean...."

"Don't say it," I told her. "I've heard enough about those two niggers. Lucky knows they didn't do shit."

She was silent for a moment. The kind that grabs the other person there, pulls at their insides.

"I'm sorry," I said.

"Thank you," she said. "Even though I don't know exactly what it's like to be a negro, I know what it's like to have people look down on you for no reason."

Godammit, Percy, go on! I wanted to scream.

"He really is tryin'," I said. "I know he ain't perfect. But he's really tryin'."

"What did it say?" she said.

I fought off the feeling in my chest one more time. She reached and took the paper out of my hand and looked until she got to the third page, where the story was.

"As was reported yesterday, a woman's body was found behind Franklin High School on Monday morning, between the school building and the gymnasium, splayed on the ground where someone had, it seems, left her in a hurry. Although it is only speculation at this time, hearsay around the small town, best known for its Civil War history and battlefield, is that the body was left in the position it was found as a result of the woman's killer failing to get her all the way into the incinerator.

"Thus far, the unofficial report is that nothing is known of the woman's identity or the place from which she came, excepting that it is highly likely she was a 'transient' and that she is not from Franklin, Tennessee.

"Dillard 'Lucky' Hall, former Assistant Police Chief in Franklin, stated last evening that he remains unsure of who the woman might be," it read, in the crisp, black ink I had grown so accustomed to over the years. "In a somewhat strange twist of events, she was laid out at the Franklin Memorial Chapel last evening, while hundreds of people filed by to look at her in an attempt at identification. The four deep gashes that were ruled to be the cause of death by Franklin Coroner Dr. Frank Guppy were covered as well as could have been possible, by thick makeup and a high-necked garment. 'We tried to do the best we could with what we had to work with,' said George Preston, Franklin Memorial Chapel Owner and Director. 'I do so wish, though, that we could have come up with a more respectful alternative, due to the fact that this one seems a bit demeaning. My God, it's not a sideshow!' he chastised later in the evening."

"I've already read this part," I told her.

"Well, I haven't," she countered. "To understand what you're talking about, I need to read the whole thing."

"Mr. Preston states that he contributed his services to the City of Franklin far below the normal price of such a procedure. 'There really wasn't much else we could do,' he told this reporter, 'besides just do the best we could. It's kind of like life, you know? You just do the best you can with what you have to work with at the time.' Mr. Preston, a man in his early forties who has made the funeral business his own for the last fifteen years, stated that so many people filed through his establishment to view the body that he thinks irreparable damage was done to his carpet."

I let my eyes drift off the newspaper to the light beginning to flood the sky with its grayness. Spring, what we had promised each other, seemed as far away as the "other side" Percy promised me was there. I squinted into the cloud-covered sunlight, to take my eyes off the paper once more, off her.

"Mr. Preston stated, 'I did this as a personal favor to Dillard. He's been so kind to me over the years. Franklin is indeed safer in his hands. I think that's especially good to remember right now.'"

"See—they said something nice about him."

"That's sounds just like Jean. How 'George Preston had somethin' nice' to say about him,'" I tried to imitate her voice, whining.

"Hush while I finish this," she said.

I nodded, like a good boy.

"At eight-thirty, Police Chief Hall arrived at the funeral home, and was witnessed crawling over the side railing by this reporter. An odd entrance for a town official, he made it over the railing nonetheless, with a plate of food believed to be for his son, who had been at the funeral home since the inception of this strange search for identification. Almost making it in the door, he was questioned only after a slight collision with a towns-lady and subsequently dropping the plate of food in his hands. It was clear that Mr. Hall wanted to answer neither questions about the murder that for the last few days has paralyzed Franklin—the identity of the body, nor about his personal life.

"'Lucky' as he is called, the Police Chief in Franklin for the past four years, stated it was none of the reporter's business if he had been drinking earlier in the evening, when a reporter from the *Nashville Banner* inquired into the matter. He refused to answer any questions excepting to divulge some information that had been in the deceased young woman's pocket.

"As he made his way into the door of Franklin Memorial Chapel, with some of the food he had spilled on his shirt and hat and still somewhat out of breath from his climb onto the side of the porch, he did disclose the content of a note that had been found on or near the woman's body. On a note, he says, is written, "Ike Beatty—219 Russell Street," a lead that this reporter assumes he and his officers haven't had time to follow. Nevertheless, it does seem that Police Chief Hall, the assistant until Oscar Garrett passed away four years ago of a sudden heart attack, has had time to tend to other matters.

"Upon the discovery of the body between the Franklin High School Building and the gymnasium last Monday morning, Jackson Mosby, a janitor at Franklin High School was soon arrested and taken into custody. The following day, yesterday, his son, Arliss, was also arrested. They both await charges in the Franklin Jailhouse. When Police Chief Hall was asked why he had taken the negroes into custody, he responded by answering, 'The whole town thinks they did it.' And then he would answer no more questions, disappearing into the Franklin Memorial Chapel. It seems as though the Franklin Jail is being used for a holding place, so that some of its citizens will not harm others, an opinion of one of its citizens, who states he speaks for more than himself.

"Sammy Samuels, who owns and runs Samuels' Auction House, located next door to the jailhouse, said when questioned about the situation outside his business establishment, 'It was always my impression that the jail was to protect the ones on the outside, not its interior.'"

"I bet it took that son of a bitch twenty minutes and a good dictionary to come up with that sentence," I could imagine Lucky saying when he read it.

"Why are you laughing?" she asked.

"Nothing. Just go ahead," I told her.

"Mr. Samuels continued, 'Lucky has always took care of the [negroes] in this town, almost before he took care of the white people. Hell, it was that way years ago. He threatened to beat me one time after that little [negro] he has in jail now tried to attack me and I defended myself.'" " Is that true?" she stopped to ask me.

"No idea," I told her. "All I knew about was the 'attack.'"

As she searched for the place to continue the article, I could feel the warmth of the two thin paths of tears rolling down my cheeks. I turned my eyes out the passenger side window. It was almost like the sky went on forever. Like it was impenetrable.

"Arliss attacked Sammy Samuels?"

"The way I remember it, it was the other way around," I told her. "He was pissed off because Arliss hadn't give him a good enough shine down at Frank's."

"It's just awful how we treat the colored people," she said.

I shrugged. "I guess."

Her eyes were back to the paper. For just a moment, she had focused on the gray morning, how the sky now looked like it might open itself and dump its contents all over us.

"'I guess, really, the town's gone a little bit crazy. Maybe it's the whole country, I don't know,' Mr. Samuels continued. 'It's two different things, I guess. The whole town seems to have lost its g__d__ marbles over this woman ... kinda the same way the whole country is losing its marbles over [negroes] in general. I just don't know what to make of it. But I do know this....'"

I assumed they had had to find somebody to talk because Lucky wouldn't. Sammy Samuels, obviously, had been glad to.

"'I know that Lucky shot at me and a couple of other boys the other night for nothing. But I guess that ain't that unusual, seeing what happened a few months ago. We wasn't doing nothing but driving down the street and the s__ of a b____ fired a shot into the grill of my Ford. I couldn't believe it ... a pretty new car. I barely made it home before it quit.'

"In the end, it seems, Mr. Samuels shares a couple of emotions with the rest of Franklin: disbelief over what has happened the last few days ... and joy to make it back to their own houses.

"'As for me,' said Mr. Samuels as he made his way back toward the car missing a piece of its grill from the alleged bullet hole, 'I just couldn't bring myself to go see that woman. I got all the way to the front door, but then I just turned around and left. It just didn't seem right.'"

As her voice trailed off into the silence that surrounded us at the Confederate Cemetery at this time of the morning, she laid her head into my chest again, rested her weight there.

"You smell like cigarettes," she said. "Your jacket."

"My whole family smells like cigarettes," I told her. "Well, not Mama and goody-goody Jean. But Lucky and Percy."

"Do you miss him?" she asked me.

"Humh?" I said.

"You hardly ever say anything about him. But it's funny, when you do, you talk about him in the present ... like he's still here."

"He told me he was," I said.

"When?" she said.

I tapped a cigarette from my pack, trying to look like Montgomery Clift again. "All the time."

"See—you did it again. You said he told you, like it's now."

I nodded. Drew in as deep a breath as I could and blew it out. I put my hand in her hair and pulled her face so close that I could feel the warmth of her cheek as it rested on my own.

"Take me away," she said.

"Alabama, Georgia or Mississippi?"

"Alabama," she said. "They say even there, Mama has to go with us ... to sign."

I lit the cigarette that had been perched on my lips. Ran my hand over my hair cut at Frank's the Friday of the week before, before everything in Franklin had gone to hell in a hand basket.

"You think she will?" I asked her.

"She'll go," she said. "She said she would. We'll just have to live somewhere close ... so I can work and help take care of her and my little sister. What about your father?"

"Fuck him," I told her. "Let him stay here and deal with what he's created. That's his biggest idea, that we all have to, eventually."

We were silent now, smoke from the cigarette rising between us and the windshield that opened itself to the gray daylight completely overtaking the cemetery.

CHAPTER TWENTY-TWO

THE ONLY THING that makes in any way right what the son of a bitch did is that we don't go out of existence. That still doesn't make it right! But at least it doesn't end there. With some things that happen, that's our only hope! It's really grace, I guess, that there's more than ... that things don't end with *Randomness* or *Human Frailty*. No matter the tragedy, what has been invested in that person, who that person is, is not lost.

To say we don't go out of existence is a perfunctory way to put it. It's more that we are always in existence ... as is God. Time is a human construct, by which we try to exert some kind of measure and control over our domain. So it is that faith is some kind of letting go. Allowing ourselves to fall into the invisible arms that support this universe. Resting in them until we know no time and become unacquainted with the space we have inhabited.

It is my belief that death does not tear us apart but draws us closer together. It is only that you cannot realize it. We often mistake our perception of reality for reality itself. The things that seem as though travesties or tragedies here, are but a mere drop of rain in heaven...or whatever you want to call the place our energy remains. I would prefer to call it here ... just not now. Or now ... just not here. There are so many limitations our mind cannot overcome, through which we cannot see for the dense cloud cover of our high opinion of ourselves. Although you will not know it ... or perhaps will only know it in your most alive moments, I am here ... will be here with you. Simply on another plain ... one far removed from human understanding. Perhaps it is more complicated than I ever let on. *Human Frailty, Randomness* and *A Planned Nature of Things* do embrace almost every event. But there's more. More than that. More than grace. More than all the things I spoke of when I spoke. It's easy to believe that what we think has somehow encompassed most things. But eventually we know our own thoughts are as incomplete as our persons ... our selves. And it is then that we realize reality is much simpler and much more complicated than we ever conceived. Simpler only in its function, which cannot be described justly by words and ideas; more complicated by our attempts to explain it, to control it, to fold down the lid of the box in which we've placed it and fasten the top shut.

How do I know these things? I am not sure, Henry Boy. I am only certain that I do. Some people call it faith ... some, other things like intuition. I only know that I know ... and do not know how I know. Confusing to you? Imagine being in my brain. It is one thing I have always asked to be relieved of. To be able to shut my head off like a car engine.

In my clearer moments I know there is a God as certain as I know that Walter was a projection of my diseased brain. Then there are times that I believe maybe my brain, with all its afflictions, had an extra eye so to speak, or better vision in some way. Perhaps at my best, I could see the Walters in the world, both our friends and our enemies, more clearly. Not everything is to be fixed ... some things are simply to be experienced, ridden out like a blizzard. Like the time Jean was struck in the head with the snow shovel and Dr. Guppy sat with her all night to see if she lived or died. Your father, I believe, almost never recovered from that. As with most things, I am certain he perceived that as his own responsibility. He is often a man who believes he has to control most everything around himself ... at his worst, even what others think.

IF YOU DON'T BELIEVE Walter was there at the Battle of Franklin, then just examine the evidence, my friend. He was there as sure as they fried my goddam brain four out of the last five days. Do you know what starts tomorrow? Two-a-days, they call it.

Walter convinces people that their ideas are more important than anybody else's. That theirs and theirs alone are worth people dyin' for. Walter convinces people that the way they see the world is more accurate than the way anybody else sees it. That their way and their way alone is right. Once he's convinced you of that, he's got you in his grasp. Right between those ugly, yellow, discolored tusks, if you will.

You know, one day I might surprise a lot of people. I might just wake up and do something different besides the craziness that's been goin' on for years. I might just straighten up, get me a steady payin' job … somethin'. Take a wife. Yeah, find me a woman. Do things like that.

Anyway, he was there. He was with them in Spring Hill when the federal troops went by. He was with them when they bedded down right outside of Franklin, Hood in the Harrison House, as comfortable as he could be … and his troops outside on the cold ground. We create hierarchy to hold away *Randomness* as much as we can. Makes us feel like we're part of the plan. But it's a world of difference from the plan. Hierarchy really grows out of *Human Frailty*.

The son of a bitch was there, though. As sure as I'm sitting here talking to you. He was there when Hood ordered the first charge at three-thirty in the afternoon. Stewart's corps had moved north along Columbia Pike to Henpeck Lane, just below the Harrison House. Cheatham's men were deployed to the left of Columbia Pike. Part of Chalmer's cavalry division and Stonewall Jackson's Cavalry division dismounted and got ready for what they knew was to come. The remainder of the cavalry crossed the river to the right of Stewart and got ready to take on Wilson's men, head-on. As for the Federals, Cox and Ruger and Kimball's division provided defense. Wood's division was guarding the river crossing north of town.

In the Harrision House, as I've told you a million times, Hood held his last conference. It was there that he issued his order of attack to his chief subordinates. And it was there that General Nathan Bedford Forrest looked him square in the eye and told him he lacked good sense.

The first charge came a little before four o'clock in the afternoon. Eighteen damned brigades moving forward in the line of battle across the broad rolling plain that leads north into town, toward the five Union brigades dug in behind their works just into town. As the boys moved through the field, many of them, I imagine, knowing that this was in fact their last charge, rabbits came out of their burrows in front of them, quail scurried where flushed from their coverts in coveys. Federal soldiers, mostly behind cover and cocked guns, even would say later that they were impressed by the grand array of the charge, battle flags waving in the late afternoon sun.

The brigades of Colonel Joseph Conrad and John Q. Lane were hit first. The day before, this division—Wagner's—had held off half the confederate army at Spring Hill, and its commander almost instantaneously decided they could do it again. Wagner, ordered to retreat before engagement, did not follow the orders, and his two brigades remained in line to fire into the charging divisions, Cleburne and Brown. But before they arrived, they checked up for a few moments, just enough time to allow Stewart and Bate to reach the main federal defense line. *Randomness. Human Frailty.*

Now Cleburne and Brown came on harder. At their flanks, Wagner's men could see long lines of Confederates hurrying by. Then, without orders—and I might add, too late—the Federals turned and ran. Now it was simply a foot race to the main line of the Federals. The old soldiers in Wagner's brigade got away, but the new recruits were captured because they were afraid to run under enemy fire. The veterans, though, ran straight down Columbia Pike, through the main line at the Carter house, and on into Franklin, where they finally stopped at the river bank. I tell you this— at some point or another, life makes cowards of us all!

Concerning this behavior, Wagner was furious! As mad as your father can get sometimes. He tried hard to rally them, but he was swept backward by a mass of men as they fled the Rebel gunfire.

The supporting Federal troops had been unable to fire at the charging Confederates without hitting Wagner's fleeing men. The same was true of Reilly's and Strickland's brigades toward Columbia Pike. Because of all this, the Federals held their fire until the pursuing troops were almost on top of them. "It seemed to me," a charging confederate wrote after the battle, "that hell itself exploded in our faces."

To make matters worse, some of the men in Reilly's and Strickland's brigades became caught up in the confusion that had befallen Wagner's men. Misunderstanding the orders that were shouted in the heat of the Rebel charge, they, too, joined the rush to the rear and Cleburne's and Brown's men poured through the gap near the Carter House. They were able to take the guns just to the left of the road, but as luck would have it, could find no primers. The guns stayed silent.

It was at this point that the crucial point of the battle was at hand. The Confederates were fifty yards inside the Federal works. For a brief few minutes, it appeared that they were on the brink of victory.

But the break in the line didn't spread. Instead, it was plugged by the third brigade of Wagner's division, the men commanded by Colonel Emerson Updike. They had been held in reserve some two hundred yards behind the main line, north of the Carter House. Needing no orders, they charged into the break and fought hand-to-hand with the beleaguered Confederates. In just a few minutes, the Confederates inside the lines had been killed or captured, the Federal lines had been restored., but the foundation for the rest of the battle had been sadly laid.

EACH TIME I GOT ANYWHERE near the place, I could remember it as clearly as if I'd been there that day. Could smell it. The piss and the shit and the vomit, the men who hadn't had a bath in a few days. "They've just give up," Lucky would describe them as they lay in the hall or sat together quietly in the meeting room, playing cards.

Before there were interstates that would carry you around it, there was really only one way through Nashville. Right through its heart and then out its other side, Central State loomed like a grotesque monument of what was done with people like Percy on a hill on its south side.

I tried to imagine if Lucky thought things like I did. Still heard his words; still remembered the two stints he had spent there. Remembered the second set of days he had been there, the ones in which he had spoken the words that had been flooding their way through my memory. Another deal cut, by the Police Chief this time, Lucky Dillard Hall himself. I wondered if he was as numb to it as he seemed, or if this was just his way of retreating from Franklin, getting the hell out of there after the spectacle he had displayed earlier in the day.

"Them goddam people are all alike," Lucky had proclaimed to me. "They're just out to prove everybody's stupid but them. I told the bastards that I was workin' on it. It ain't like we haven't had other things to do. That was the worst decision I ever made, puttin' that body out. Smartass son of a bitch."

By the time Ike Beatty had called Miss Helen and she had located Lucky, the front screen of the television was gone. Shattered into a hundred pieces, Lucky claimed, by his hand coming down on the top of it. Shattered into a thousand pieces, I theorized, by his boot after he read the *Banner*, which I never saw and didn't want to see. The *Banner* had made its way into the driveway, courtesy of Chester Mott, at around 4 o'clock, and Beatty had called at around 4:30, after a conversation he'd had with Larry Beaman.

"You ever been to Portland?" he asked me.

I shook my head, still half-scared of him. His rages had rarely ever ended with just an object. Sure, there had been plenty: a couple of doors, a few windows, a chair that had somehow made its way into twenty pieces in the backyard. There had even been a dent in the door of his previous car that had miraculously appeared after he and my mother had been somewhere one night.

"Some son of a bitch must have backed into it when they was leavin' one of the bars downtown!" he had said when I asked him about it. It was coincidental, I guess, that my mother also came home with an injured arm. I, though, hadn't taken a picture of her to preserve the way she looked for the sake of posterity.

It was the reason he had been hired as a policeman to begin with. Somebody rough as a corn cob to protect the good people of Franklin. Somebody who lacked enough class and civility to keep himself from getting mad and beating or jerking the shit out of you.

I wanted to ask him what the *Banner* had said, but it was simply not the way we operated. As I laid under the carport, changing the oil on the Indian, he had pulled in, made his statement about the day and its results, then disappeared into the house to find my mother and Jean gone to the store. They accepted his explanation about what happened to the television like it was the gospel when they returned. My mother even took the broom and the dustpan out of his hand and tried to help him finish cleaning it.

"It ain't that much farther," he said, seeming to accept the fact I didn't know where we were going. Neither did I know why I was going, excepting my idea he didn't want to go alone.

IKE BEATTY WAS an average-sized man with little hair and a large gap between his front teeth. His wife flitted to and from the room where Lucky, he, and I sat, bringing tea and coffee as fast as she anticipated a need. She appeared nervous, the initiation of sounds bringing jumps from her like coins in a ride outside a grocery store. Her hair was pinned on top of her head; her dress a little too small. Mr. Beatty and Lucky sat across a small, well-scarred coffee table from each other, silence proving to make everyone a little uncomfortable. Lucky held out a cigarette to Mr. Beatty, whose own pack remained hidden in his shirt pocket. He nodded silently, took it and waited for Lucky to offer a light, which he did.

The Beattys had appeared nervous from the moment they invited us into their two-bedroom house to the northwest of Nashville. "I do believe I know her," Ike had told Lucky on the phone, when he had described her.

After Ms. Beatty had gotten everyone's tea and coffee fixed, she perched herself on the corner of the couch where Ike sat. She studied the badge on Lucky's shirt glimmering in the sixty watt light.

"You think we're gonna get this bad weather they're talkin' about?" Ms.

Beatty offered. Sipped her coffee, diverted her eyes from Lucky's badge to his for a moment.

"I don't know," said Lucky. "Me and the boy were listenin' to the radio on the way down here. They said there wasn't no way we were gonna avoid it. But you know how that is."

"Yeah, it's like that blizzard we had in '45. You remember that one?"

"I do," said Lucky. "Recall it like it was yesterday."

Never forget it, I thought, but didn't speak. I hadn't spoken yet, except to nod my head, mumble my name and tell Mrs. Beatty what I wanted to drink when she asked.

"You remember, they didn't have one idea under heaven or hell that the thing was comin', and then it just hit us and covered us up."

"I do," said Lucky, inhaling the fumes from his Lucky. He let them rest a few seconds then hacked them out. He offered me a cigarette and a light. I took both. "It took us a week to dig out from under it. That's the thing about this part a' the country. We don't get much weather like that … but when we do, we don't have what it takes to get ourselves out from under it."

"I guess it shouldn't surprise me that didn't nobody know it was comin'," said Ike, rubbing his fuzzy head, a few stray hairs standing up straight from the static created. "They didn't know nothin' about the weather back then. Didn't know nothin' about the weather and didn't have much of a way to let people know what they did know. We just got us a television," he said, pointing to the cabinet sitting in the corner. "Hadn't even quite figured out how to work it yet."

"They're nice," said Lucky. "We've had us one for awhile. Ours just went on the blink today."

Mr. Beatty nodded his head like he could both understand and not imagine. He deposited a long growth of ashes into the tray on the coffee table, which Mrs. Beatty immediately collected. She set one new ashtray in front of Ike, one in front of Lucky.

Lucky felt his pants pocket to see if the two or three Polaroid pictures were still there.

"How long y'all lived in Portland?" Lucky asked.

"Pretty much all our life," said Ms. Beatty, a strange, slow smile coming to her face as the words exited her thin lips. "We lived in Watertown for a few months years ago … in Mt. Juliet another time. But we been here for a long time."

Mr. Beatty nodded and knocked the end off his cigarette again. Snuffed it out.

I watched the smoke rise aimlessly toward the ceiling. Lucky bobbed his head up and down.

"Used to come up here to go to Lebanon sometime myself," said Lucky. "Used to have a friend who came."

Mr. Oscar Garret, I thought. To play poker and shoot craps, is what Percy had told me.

"You said the name right," said Mr. Beatty as he searched for another cigarette, then seemed to remember Lucky had given him one. He waited for Lucky to offer, which he did. "Most people don't say it right. They say it like the name a' that country overseas. You said it good, though."

"Thank ya," said Lucky. He leaned and lit Ike's cigarette.

"Our daughter ought to be home in a little bit," he said. "What time is it?" he asked his wife.

She spun and stretched to see a clock on the kitchen wall. "Almost five," she said.

Ike nodded and turned his gaze back in Lucky's general direction. "It's gettin' pretty close to bein' the shortest day of the year. It's hard to believe it's almost dark already."

"Yeah," said Lucky. "It always fools me when it's like this. Seems like the whole day's gone."

"You gonna want us to come tonight, ain't ya?" said Ike, whose real name was Isaac, Lucky had informed me.

"Probably so," said Lucky. "If the pictures look familiar. You're gonna have to come see her." He picked up his tea, shook the ice cubes loose from the bottom of the glass, sipped it.

"I don't want Eugene to see them pictures," said Mrs. Beatty.

"I know what ya mean," he said. "Got a daughter a' my own, about his

age. Wouldn't want her to see them either."

Goddam princess. Let Henry sit with the body for hours. Run all over the world with you. But Eugene, some boy you don't even know … you protect.

"But," said Lucky, "it'd be good if he'd look at one. How'd you say he knew her?"

Mr. Beatty started to speak, but Mrs. Beatty cut him off. "Eugene's my sister's boy. He come to live with us a few years ago … how long ago, Ike?"

Ike took a break from his cigarette, from some concoction I assumed was stronger than tea. "'Bout three years ago, maybe four. Naw, I think it was really closer to three."

"Anyway," said Mrs. Beatty, "he's my sister's boy and she couldn't do nothin' with him. She said he was just like his daddy, who was already in the penitentiary and that if she kept on raisin' him, that's where he was gonna end up." She checked everybody's glass, must have concluded they were fine. "The last time he got in trouble in Illinois … somewhere close to Chicago, that's where she lives … the judge told her if he got in trouble one more time he was goin' to the reformatory." She held out her hand for Ike to pass her a cigarette, which he did out of his own pack this time. She clicked his lighter, shot a flame before she kept on. "I guess they're more easy up there. In towns around here, they go to the reformatory for almost anything."

"Yeah," Lucky nodded. His eyes moved around the room then back to her face. I could hear his breath going and coming from his chest. He produced a pad and pencil. "How'd you say he met her? What'd you say her name was on the phone?"

"What did Eugene tell us her name was, Ike?" asked Mrs. Beatty.

"Rose Mary," he said. "Rose Mary … Dean, I think." He shook his glass, rattled his ice cubes.

She come with Eugene, but I think he's better now, don't you, Ike?"

"Why'd he bring her here?" Lucky asked, before Ike could answer Mrs. Beatty.

Ike snuffed the mostly smoked cigarette out and pushed back the tuft of hair on his forehead. "If I 'member right, she said she didn't have anywhere else to go."

"She wasn't no big woman," said Mrs. Beatty. "Maybe a little shorter than normal. We felt sorry for her ... let her stay here. How long would you say? Maybe a week or two back then?"

"How long was 'back then?'" said Lucky. "Can you give me a year?"

Ike and Mrs. Beatty looked at each other, seemed to be counting back the years. Ike produced a hand, wandered through a few fingers. "Three ... four years," I believe. When was it, hon?"

Hon answered, "I believe it was more like four. Around 1949. I guess I could call Helen and see. I ain't talked to her in a few months, though. Might have hard time tracking her down."

"Yeah, that's prob'ly somethin' I need you to do if you can."

"Are we gon' have to come to the police station?" Mrs. Beatty asked.

"Yes ma'am, most likely," said Lucky. "I think we can have Eugene—that's what you said his name was, right?—identify her from her picture. But I gotta have somebody come there and see her. Lucky we found you today. We're gonna have to bury her tomorra'."

"Well, let's us have a look at them pictures now," said Mrs. Beatty. "I hate puttin' off things and dreadin 'em. I'd rather just go ahead and do 'em right now and get 'em over with. Specially before the kids come home."

"Yes ma'am," I understand," said Lucky. He felt for the pictures in his pocket once more. Produced them.

CHAPTER TWENTY-THREE

M Y ENCOUNTERS WITH Dr. Johnny Guppy had been fairly few and far between. As other things that would come to pass from our existence, he still did house calls in 1953. Doubling as the town doctor and the town's coroner, I am certain he was often at the same place with George Preston; yet I recall that only with Percy and during the last night of the Blizzard of '45, if Tennessee can in fact have blizzards. The ice sealed the snow beneath itself until both melted after five days. On this evening, though, George Preston and Dr. Johnny Guppy were sitting, waiting on the arrival of the people who would identify Rosa Mary Dean.

I could not recall being inside the police station more than a handful of times. Now, after all these years I was aware of how the place had taken on Lucky's aura. Smelled like him: a little whiskey, the stale smell of smoked cigarettes, some cologne that my mother gave him every Christmas.

Dr. Johnny Guppy seemed as though he was a perpetually peaceful man, one of the Franklin citizens in the social class that families like ours could never transcend into. And he was comfortable being so. His stature was grand as he sat in Lucky's office, waiting, as we all did for Ike and Carolyn Beatty to arrive to identify the real woman they'd seen in pictures.

"It's her," Eugene had said, turning shimmering blue eyes away from the picture Lucky protruded across the coffee table.

"Look at it good," Lucky had told him, the Lucky Strike bobbing on his lip as he spoke. "Since you knew her better than your moth—better than Mr. and Mrs. Beatty, I gotta know that you think this is her. She's gonna be buried tomorra'. Once that happens, it's hard to take back an identity."

Tears coming to his eyes, Eugene took the picture in his soiled hand and stared at it. He ran his hand over his hair, wiped his face with his palm. Ike rattled his glass as Mrs. Beatty checked everybody's again.

"Boy was in trouble," Lucky would boast to me on the way back to Franklin, beginning to sip at his bottle. "That's the reason that woman didn't want him to come to the police station. Some people think about such places like a deep, dark hole. Fall in … never come out."

His bottle was bringing the levity that it did the first half-hour or so, relieving him of the weight pressed perpetually on his shoulders. "I didn't give a shit if he came or not. I just wanted an ID on the picture."

Central State loomed on a nearby hill, like a shadowy beacon barely showing its face through the night, reminding of how fragile, how short things are … can be. Lucky didn't look at it.

"I just wish we hadn't had to wait so long on him. I know George Preston and Guppy are already there. Waitin'."

"Eugene," Lucky had said to him after we waited what seemed like five minutes, "I ain't tryin' to push ya, but you're gonna have to tell me if this is a woman you think you know … and what you know about her."

Eugene stared stone-faced at the other pictures Lucky produced from his pocket and laid out on the coffee table. The Beattys let their eyes float back and forth between the pictures, the lacerations barely visible but death very apparent.

"She come here from somewhere up north." His voice was higher, almost choked down in his chest. His hand shook as he drew the cigarette Lucky had given him. "Rose Mary," he said. "Or Rosa Mary Dean. She come down here from somewhere up in Indiana. She got on the train I was on when Mama shipped me off down here. Sat down right by me. There wasn't no other seat available." He glanced at the Beattys. "Nothin' against y'all. You know how much I've 'preciated livin' here."

"It's kep' you out'a all kinds a' trouble," Mrs. Beatty reminded him.

"I know," said Eugene.

"And when was that? When did you come down here from Chicago?"

"It was 1949," he said. "When I was thirteen years ole. Wadn't that when it was?"

"Your aunt and I was just discussin' that while ago," said Ike.

"'49 sounds right," Carolyn Beatty said.

"Did she come to this house?" Lucky asked. "I'm assumin' you were livin' here then."

"We was," said Mr. Beatty. He stood and took the couple of steps to join his wife, who had moved to Eugene's side.

Lucky's pencil was poised above the small pad in his hand, smoke rising from the cigarette two fingers away.

"She come here 'cause I reckon she didn't have anywhere else to go," said Eugene. "Don't you think that's why she come here the first time, Mama?"

His aunt nodded her head.

"Did she stay here with y'all?" Lucky inquired. Drew from his cigarette, coughed a little in rebellion as I had grown accustom to his doing.

"Yep, she did," Eugene answered.

"Yessir," Carolyn reminded him.

"Yessir," he echoed.

"How long?" said Lucky.

"How long ago was it?" asked Ike.

"Umh-umh," said Lucky. "How long did she stay?"

"I reckon she probably stayed goin' on a week," said Mrs. Beatty. "We let her stay here 'cause she said she didn't have nowhere else to go. After she got off the train, she just took a seat over at the far place in the station. We was waitin' on Eugene to come out of the restroom and she jus' went over to the other side and sat down by herself. I remember sayin' to Ike at the time how sad it was that somebody didn't have nobody there waitin' on them. When Eugene come out of the restroom he told us that he'd been talkin' to her since she got on at Indianapolis. I jus' couldn't stand to see no child with no place to go...."

"She really wadn't no child," Ike interrupted.

"She wadn't full-growed neither."

"Awright, awright, that's true," Ike said.

"I'd say she was in her late teens ... maybe twenty," Eugene stated. "The fact was, though, that she was gonna sleep right there in the bus station."

"She'd already laid her head on her little bag and settled into the chair," Carolyn Beatty said. I couldn't a' stood it if Patty Ann was like that ... and nobody didn't help her."

"Who's Patty Ann?" asked Lucky.

"Our daughter," said Ike. "She's at work at the dairy dip. She's a senior in high school."

"I jus' couldn't stand to see somebody with no place to go. I've always been that way," Mrs. Beatty said. "My sister and me ... when we was little, we was adopted out. Bounced from place to place, until one nice lady finally kep' us. It's amazin' we still know each other. If I hadn't still knowed her, then Eugene wouldn't have had no place to go. Funny how things work out like that, ain't it?"

Lucky nodded his head more out of politeness than anything else, I figured. Snuffed his dying cigarette out and lit another one. "So ... how long did she stay with y'all?"

"Jus' a few days," said Mrs. Beatty. "Maybe a week at the most."

"Mama, I think it was longer than a week," said Eugene, staring at the posthumous pictures of Rosa Mary Dean. "I tell you why I think that. 'Member, she went down to Franklin then. Said she was goin' down there, lookin' for a job or somethin'. She was a waitress where she come from. 'Member that? She was tellin' us how good'a money she made doin' that."

"I do 'member that," said Mrs. Beatty. "I 'member that 'cause she told us that she growed up in a' orphanage. I 'member that really tugged on my ole heart strings."

Lucky again nodded. "Do you know any other reason she went to Franklin, I mean, besides lookin' for a job?"

"I ain't sure," said Mrs. Beatty. Ike concurred. They both turned their eyes to Eugene.

"I don't know neither."

"I bet y'all don't know where she stayed either, do ya?"

"Can't say I 'member that either," said Ike. "It's been a long time, Mr. Hall."

Lucky smiled at his politeness, looked at the notes he'd recorded. Would tell me on the way back to Franklin that he thought they told him all they knew. That he didn't think Eugene had a thing to do with anything that had happened.

"I think y'all for your time," he told the Beattys and Eugene Johnson as he stood in the doorway. "Y'all are comin' on down there in jus'a few minutes, right?" he asked them.

They nodded and offered their hands. "You sure it's awright if Eugene don't come? I want him to be able to get on his homework."

"Yes ma'am, that's fine," Lucky told her. "As long as y'all are kind enough to come."

"We plan to," said Mr. Beatty.

"Can your daughter come with ya?" Lucky asked as we were halfway to the car. "I know she might be tired, but the more people we can get to say it was her, the better off we'll be. Once you give somebody a' identity, you can't take it back."

"ONCE YOU'VE GOT A' IDENTITY, you can't take it back," Lucky said an hour and a half later, like he hadn't already said two or three times.

She just got the goddam identity a little while ago, I thought, his comment sticking in my own throat like a piece of food choking me. Almost muttered it under my breath, but realized Dr. Guppy would hear me. His presence was one of the few that somehow silently called you to be ashamed of your worst self, like he didn't have one. He looked at his watch and smiled.

"They did say they were coming, right?" asked George Preston, holding the cigarette the way that identified him as "queer" to the rest of the town, at least those who admitted we had one.

"Mrs. Beatty said she was gonna fix the boy supper and then they was gonna be right down."

"They might be waitin' on their daughter," I said. The sound of my own voice almost scared me. Seemed hollow and shaky.

"Are you sure they had good directions?" George Preston asked.

Lucky smirked, cut his eyes to Johnny Guppy like maybe George Preston didn't think straight or right. I could feel the emptiness of my own stomach. Since we hadn't eaten supper, Lucky had promised we'd go to Datsons after we were done.

At seven o'clock in the evening, Lucky met the Beattys along with Patty Ann at the front door after the sound of their car alerted him they were there. He brought them in and made the introductions, then had them follow us in the squad car as we made our way toward the clinic Dr. Guppy had opened in the early fifties, simply named the Franklin City Clinic. Somewhere between a doctor's office and a hospital, Lucky had described it to me, and also doubling as the city morgue. In the darkness of the alley behind the building one block south of Main Street, Dr. Guppy opened the door with the click of a key and we all entered. Mrs. Beatty took Lucky's arm with one hand, her husband's with the other.

Down a corridor Dr. Guppy led us, until we were at a doorway that opened onto a room not much bigger than a closet. On a gurney, wrapped and zipped in a bag, was Rosa Mary Dean. The woman who now had a name. Lucky let Mr. and Mrs. Beatty and their daughter stand in the front just behind Dr. Guppy. He shook his head at George Preston; George Preston frowned.

"Before we go any farther," I heard Mrs. Beatty tell Lucky, "Ike and I got to tell you somethin' that we didn't know till Patty Ann come home. I know it's hard to believe, but somehow she'd missed the whole thing. I know Portland's not but thirty or forty miles away from here, but for a sixteen-year-old girl, I guess it's like a different world. Miss Dean come by there whilst we was gone and talked to Patty Ann for a little bit. Ain't that what you told us when we tole you where we was comin' tonight, baby?"

"Yes ma'am," said Patty Ann. She flashed a crooked-toothed, pretty smile and turned her eyes to the floor. "She come by last Saturday night, I believe. Wadn't that when you and Daddy had gone to the bar?"

Carolyn Beatty nodded her head, cast her gaze to the floor as well.

"That's when she come then. Y'all hadn't been gone long. I remember when she knocked on the door, I thought it was Bubba, done locked hisself out again."

"She calls her cousin Eugene Bubba," Mrs. Beatty explained.

"Yeah, I thought it was him," she said. "But when I opened the door, it was Mary Rose, and—"

"I thought you said her name was Rosa Mary," said Lucky.

"Sometimes she called herself one … sometimes another. Ain't that right, Mama?"

"I don't rightly remember, hunny. But go ahead, finish what you're sayin'."

"Anyway—Mary Rose, or whatever her name was, said she was lookin' for you and Daddy. Well, when I tole her you wasn't there, she looked kinda sad and said that she hoped she could catch y'all. I tole her y'all was gonna be back in a little while, and she said she'd probably come back. Then she knocked on the door again and handed me a note."

"She left you a note?" Mrs. Beatty inquired.

"Yes ma'am … the best that I recollect."

"And where is that note, sweety?"

"Prob'ly still in my pocket book," she said. "I was fixin' to go with Juanita to the picture show, so I didn't think no more about it. I guess that's why I didn't think to say she come by."

"Have you got your pocket book with ya, Patty Ann?" Lucky asked.

"Yessir," she nodded. She dug through the contents of her purse until she produced it.

Lucky took the note from Mrs. Beattys shaking hand after Patty Ann had handed it to her. He put it in his shirt pocket along with the Polaroids.

Dr. Guppy took the few steps between them and the bag and began to unzip it. "We're going to bury her tomorra', right George?" he asked.

"As long as the city's going to cooperate," answered George Preston.

"We already got the plot lined up," said Lucky.

"No disrespect intended at all," said George Preston, "But I really need to get home. I'm expecting a call. Would you believe I ran into Michael today? Well, I really didn't run into him. I'd called him about the carpet. And he said he'd be happy to help me. He said he'd call me tonight and let me know when he could come down. If I don't get home, one of my nosey neighbors'll pick up the party line."

"I just appreciate your help, George," said Dr. Guppy. "Tell Michael hello if you talk to him. Haven't seen him in awhile. He's that boy that used to help you with your work, isn't he?"

George Preston nodded his head, shook my father's hand and disappeared out the door.

"You know your way out, don't you, George?" Dr. Guppy called behind him.

From the darkness outside the room in which he stood, he answered that he did.

As a matter of course, I guess, at least two people had to identify the body. Patty Ann had been an extra. Yet, the only one who had actually seen her that night. It just made sense, I assume, that Lucky asked her to do first what it was obvious nobody wanted to do.

She stammered as she tried to speak her protests. "I-I-I-don't-wan–"

"Can't we look at her first?" Mrs. Beatty asked. "I mean...."

"I know, ma'am," Lucky said. "Like I told you back there at your house, I got a daughter right about your girl's age. I wouldn't want her to have to see her first ... or really to have to see her at all. But I need to do it by the book as much as possible ... and the way it's s'posed be done is that the last person to see 'em should be the one to do the identifyin' first."

As Lucky's words rolled off his tongue a little easier and quicker, I thought the cause must surely be the bottle he'd been nursing on the way to the police station from Portland.

"I don't want to!" Patty Ann shrieked. "I'll be damned if I'll look at her."

Mr. Beatty looked at her like he was perhaps used to this kind of behavior. "Baby, Mr. Hall says you got to. I don't see that you have a real choice."

Patty Ann burrowed her head into Mrs. Beatty's shoulder, muffling the sounds of her cries.

Lucky stepped forward to the bag and pushed at the space Dr. Guppy had opened earlier. "Just a look, hunny." He placed his hand on her quivering back. "You don't have to look long. Matter a' fact, if you can even just look at her face. John, can you cover everythin' but her face? Do you think you could look at her face and tell me if it's the girl who come to your house Saturday?"

"Yes," she was able to speak between the sobs from her mother's armpit.

As Lucky pulled the bag open and her face was exposed one last time, I prayed I would not have to look upon it again later. That the death that had taken her would be allowed to be done.

In the silence that followed, I was back to the last time we had been in the room, doing the same. Remembered that precious Jean had gotten out of it, that I had gotten the shit duty that time, too. Lucky began to cough, so hard the third or fourth time he had to remove himself. I wondered if he, like I, was remembering. I could hear him gagging in the hall. Dr. Guppy moved his eyes to mine only briefly, shook his head, then turned his attention back to the Beattys.

"Is it her?" he asked. "Is that the woman you remember? That came to your house?"

"Yes," she said, having turned her face to Rosa Mary's long enough to tell. "That's her."

As Lucky made his way back into the room, Mr. and Mrs. Beatty made their way to the gurney. Dr. Guppy finished unzipping the bag and they stepped close as Patty Ann surrendered the space she had taken. She stepped by me and smiled coyly, blank-eyed as she sniffed and dried her tears. Lucky placed his hand on my shoulder and stood in the doorway for a moment, watching as Mr. and Mrs. Beatty nodded. Quietly, he pulled the note from his pocket and held it far enough away from him that he could read it. I would do the same after he removed himself from Datsons an hour later, so that he would not disturb the few other people in there as he coughed once more until he gagged himself, unable to finish his dinner of fried chicken, mashed potatoes and green beans, his favorite.

Dear Ike and Aunt Care,

I was so hoping that I'd be able to find you. It had been so long since I've talked to you that I thought I would come to see you in person. A lot has happened since the last time I was here. It seems that my luck has kept on the way it has been most of my life. When I left here the last time, I thought the best thing to do was go back to Indianapolis, but after the way everything turned out, I guess I was wrong. I probably didn't tell you when I was here the last time that my parents had died. Or maybe I did tell you that. Anyway, I went back to Indiana because I thought I should be able to help raise my sisters, and I got married to a man named Andy Dean, who said that he would help me raise my sisters because my parents was dead. He got him a good job with a trucking outfit and was learning how to drive one of them big rigs. Just as he was learning how to drive it, though, he got in a wreck and it kilt him. Worse than that, though, was that he had got me pregnant the year before, right after we got married and I give birth to twins. One of them didn't make it out and was born what they call still, and the other one only lived a few days. So, then all we had was my sisters again. Then when Andy died—sorry, got to go, the train is stopping and I'm going to get off and use the bathroom and walk around.

Okay, I'm back. Let's see, where was I? When Andy died, I thought that I could raise my two sisters by myself, Ella and Mira, but they didn't seem to cotton to me trying to raise them. They just give me trouble all the time. They wouldn't do what I said. I told them that they was going to end up in reform school just like I had been if they didn't straighten up and fly right but they didn't seem to care and they just kept on going down the wrong road. They was like I had been—nothing but trouble since Mama and Daddy passed away. I told them though that they at least had me and that I could help them be a different way. And I tried. I mean I tried, tried like you all had with Eugene. Maybe you all was my inspiration, the way you had been so nice to him and took him in like he was one of your own like Patty Ann. In the long run, I bet you all have helped him. At least last time I talked to you it seemed like you had. How long has it been? I ain't sure accept to say its been longer than it should be. I guess I haven't talked to you all but once or twice since I left there in 1949, it was 49 wasn't it? Anyway, I been writing off and on since I come back from the bathroom as thoughts come to me that seemed like something you should know. I hope that I find you home and I don't have to leave this note, but if you do get this note then it means that I didn't get you and I'll see you in a couple of days. If you're not home I may go on down to Franklin, but I'll be back, probably the next day.

Lucky spoke from behind me. Scared me so bad I almost pissed in my pants.

"Sir?"

He was wobbling now, the initial levity from his drinking having passed into its own shackles and chains. He made his way up behind me and sat at the table. "I said that that goddam note is somethin' else, ain't it?" he wheezed as much as spoke.

"Yeah, I have to say that it is," I told him.

There were dark circles under his eyes as he covered the lower part of his face with one of his hands, supported the weight of his head with it. He shook his head and sighed. Wheezed. "You think we're gonna get the weather they been talkin' about?"

"I don't know," I told him. "I hope we don't. I tell ya, it makes it hard to throw papers."

"If we get it tonight, you can take the car in the mornin'."

I could feel the sting of his boots on my ass. The warmth of the blood from my lip making its way down my face. The embarrassment of the source of the physical pain. Wondering who if anybody had seen it. Swore at the same time that I didn't give a shit.

"I'm bettin' that it just turns off to rain," he said. He rubbed his face with both of his hands, placed his chin in them and rested his elbows on the table.

CHAPTER TWENTY-FOUR

IT HAD BEGUN TO SNOW on a Thursday morning and continued past noon and through the day. For a little while, it let up as darkness hinted at coming, then came again as the light failed. The flakes were the biggest things I'd ever seen, each somehow like the last but at the same time brilliant in its individual nature. Under the porch light, they drifted onto the concrete to remain intact for only a moment then to blend or dissipate, never to be seen again. On this night, the iridescent glow of the television had been absent from the window, ours and the Pitts'. All up and down the street, people gathered in their windows, families of three and four and five and six, to watch the half-dollar sized flakes make their way from the heavens in swirling paths to the ground or a tree or some other final resting place where they became part of the mass beginning to accumulate.

Through the night and into the next morning it snowed, well over a foot finding its way to the ground. Pristine in its envelope of the country-side, there was not one place disturbed as far the eye could see. Not one footprint, not one car track. The only movement was as the flakes continue to waft from the sky.

I had been awake what I guess was an hour, lying on the bed that had been empty the balance of the night, listening to the silence that only a snowfall can bring. Wondering if he was ever coming home. "Home," I thought. His home, the real one, I guess, had been with Horace and Lena, on the Hall Farm, where they grew corn and tobacco and beans and raised cows and pigs. Perhaps, though, he had no home now. Or maybe his home was on that goddam ward he'd been stuck in for going on seven months. "At least the treatments have become more infrequent," he'd tell me. "Only one a week now as long as I tow the line. Act good."

But towing the line and acting good had been difficult for him. As the country settled into the last few months of the war and began to accept that not only its landscape but the landscape of the entire world had somehow been irretrievably altered, he had read the paper religiously. Digested every piece of information that he could arrest with his hands.

"I know they say it's necessary, what they've done, but I tell you that it has probably opened the door to the devil. I know that most religion thinks the devil tries to get them to do what is against that religion, like drink or smoke or be in general a bad person, but...."

Sometimes now he seemed unable to articulate his own ideas as he had even a few months before. As the treatments had increased and then pla-teaued at three a week, his faculties had seemed to consistently diminish until they finally came to resting place of stillness like the falling snow.

"I mean, this is power to destroy the world. Once that's been used, you can't ever go back from it. We'll never know how many people were killed. Maimed. Their and their families' lives altered in some way that can't be changed. People can't be unbombed."

Lucky had told him, "Well, goddam, what would he think we could do? Just keep sending our boys one after another for them to come home in a box? I think enough a' that had been done. Too many come home like Ronnie Langford or Fred Burkitt ... or didn't even come home."

In Franklin, Tennessee, these names had become almost synonymous with World War II by the time the man from Independence, Missouri decided to put an end to it fairly succinctly. The mere mention of their names explained what can happen to men who go to war, their families.

A few months before, I am certain Percy would have been absolutely convinced it had something to do with him, somehow had missed its intended target. Now though, the medicine, the electricity, something, had leveled his suspicion, returned him to just a mild level of contempt of the way things were handled.

"Your daddy has always been a man who believed in violence," he told me. "That's primarily why men have run the world. Force others do what they want them to do. Force them like he's forced me to stay in this place. It could have been worse, I guess. They could have kept up with the three-a-week shockings, but now they're down to one. The food's not bad … but they just don't have much of a library. I think they want to limit our ideas. At least I do get a newspaper."

He picked his newspaper up off the scarred nightstand and rifled through the pages until he found what he wanted to show me. "You know they dropped those two bombs last week, don't you? The last one was dropped a few days ago. Looks like the Japs are about ready to surrender."

The first one, on August 6th, had been mentioned on the television set and then again when Lucky had said at dinner that he thought it would be likely to end the war. That men make hard decisions sometimes, that's what makes them men. The second had come some three days later, the less deadly, killing only thirty-nine thousand, maiming and injuring twenty-five thousand.

"I'm just not sure what else could be done," he said sadly, I imagined paralleling this situation with his own. "I'm not saying that there's not a place for force, I just think that it has to be used with the utmost discretion. It's the easiest, quickest solution always, with the worst eventual consequences. As I was sayin' earlier, though, we're fooled into believing we can solve problems with it. It just makes them disappear temporarily, not go away. It's just further proof of Walter's presence in the world. I haven't mentioned him much lately, but he's here. Always here."

Except for comments like that, Percy appeared almost as sane as the next person. Of course, I really had nothing to compare him to except the way he had been most of my life, with each month progressively worsening, it seemed. Precisely the reason, Lucky had told me, that I should talk to him no more than I had to. Usually, his trips had been clandestine enough that I did not ask to go, that is, until Percy starting ringing through consistently on the party line, asking for Lucky to get him released and bring me. Finally, he had consented to one to keep from having to consider the other.

As the snow continued to cover the earth along Cleburne Street, I guessed we hadn't been there in two or three weeks. When he had first come up missing, it had been easier to remember. This was the first night in a long while his empty bed had reminded me of his absence. Of course, I had also been reminded by a strange little boy across and down the street called Tully, who had come to live with his grandfather due to what Lucky described as his mother's "bad habits."

Earlier in the evening, just before the catastrophe, he and Mr. Shafer and Van and Scoot had come to our driveway to help us shovel in case Lucky had to get out. "Hey," he said as we took a break from shoveling, "you know they're just lettin' us shovel to think we're doin' somethin'."

"Lucky says if you never let it pile up, then it's not so easy for the other to freeze on top of it."

"Who?" he said.

"Lucky. My Daddy."

"Oh," he responded, seeming to understand.

"He might have to get out or somethin', too," I said. "He's a police-man."

"Didn't another man live here for awhile?" Tully had asked, innocently.

"My uncle," I told him.

"He wasn't right, was he?" he asked.

"What'd you mean?"

"Well, I guess I mean he was umh … crazy."

"He'd say we all are in some way or another."

"Okay, boys, your turn again," said Scoot as Tully and Mr. Shafer began the short walk home.

Van had done more leaning on his shovel than working. He gladly handed it to me. "Raymond Collins said he was gonna come help us after while. I saw him when we were sleddin' earlier."

A strange custom though it was, it was one none the less. People came to help shovel. To share the bottle while they did so.

"Can I have some, Daddy?" Van asked Scoot as he took a slug.

"No," he answered. "And don't tell your mother that I did either."

Evelyn was the less easy-going of the two sisters, my mother and she. Van nodded.

"And why don't you shovel some more? Lucky and I are old, tired men."

"I'm tired, too," he said. "I've been sleddin' all evenin'."

"You don't know what tired is, boy," Lucky said as he rested beside us, leaned on a porch pillar. Still breathing normal.

Van laughed. Wouldn't argue with Lucky.

"Now you come right back in a little while," I heard my mother's voice call from behind me. "I don't want you out more than a few minutes."

So appeared the princess. I could catch the death of pneumonia and nobody would give a shit. But not her. Don't stay out too long. She had on what looked to be four coats and two hats, as she stood smiling behind us. I turned and glanced at her and huffed.

"Daddy, do you want me to shovel?" she asked.

"No, sweetheart," he answered. "We're fine … getting it done fine. Why don't you go back in and help your mother. I'm sure she could use your help inside."

"But I wanna stay," she said like she was five, not ten.

Lucky nodded and turned away as he squinted at Scoot. A woman's presence, much less a girl, in this group would put an end to the conversation and the drinking. Both of which, I had grown to assume, were the real purpose behind a lot of things men do.

"Henry," he said, "why don't y'all go to the end of the drive? Work from there back toward here. You and Jean. We'll work toward you."

I nodded at Lucky's crazy solution that sacrificed me, not him. Then motioned for Van to come with me, which he gladly did so he could be away from the adults. I heard them begin to laugh, figured the bottle had come out again.

"Here," Van told her, "let me show you how to use this thing." He took the shovel and began shoveling to show her how it was done correctly. He flung snow twenty feet down the street, then at Raymond Collins and Paul Chester, Jr. when they were within sight. They gathered the deepening snow in their hands and threw it back at Van, missing him and hitting me and Jean.

"Watch out," I told them, my words mostly focused at Raymond Collins.

"Oh, he's tough," Raymond said. "Watch him, Paul."

"I'm tough as I need to be," I said, "'specially with this shovel in my hands."

Jean hit me in the arm, told me to hush.

"Here, I'm showin' 'em how it's done," said Van. He scooped a couple of more shovelfuls of snow, tossed it at Collins' and Chester's feet.

"Watch out," said Paul Chester. "I don't wanna have to go home and change clothes again. I already had to once. I got so wet and cold sleddin' that I thought I was gonna freeze."

Van threatened to throw another scoop at him. He scowled and they both laughed.

"I still wanna try to shovel," whined Jean. "Daddy said I could shovel. That's what he said."

"I don't remember him sayin' anything like that," I argued. "Do you, Van?"

"Let her shovel if she wants to. She'll be tired after one or two swings," he said as he wielded the shovel wildly. It looked like he was just scattering more snow than he was actually moving.

"Here," said Ray Collins, "let me show you how it's done." He snatched the shovel I had been leaning on out of my hand. "Look here, Jeannie, this is how it's done. Right here." He thrust the shovel into the snow, the pavement underneath screaming, then threw the snow toward the middle of the street.

"Y'all throw the snow in the ditch," Lucky yelled. "Not in the street."

"Yessir," Van responded, then made a face barely visible under the streetlight.

He and Ray Collins returned to their shoveling, seeing how much they could move with each attempt. Van, almost as scrawny, or maybe lanky, as he'd still be at seventeen. And Raymond Collins just as surly as he'd be later. Throw the snow. Throw the snow. Throw the goddam snow.

By the time they were seven or eight feet up the driveway, they were both breathing like switch engines, their breath making great clouds of moisture as they blew out.

"Here," said Ray Collins. "It's y'all's turn." They threw the shovels at Paul Chester and me, mine rattling at my feet in a space I'd begun clearing away with my boot. Paul Chester picked his up and began to shovel where they'd stopped. Van and Ray Collins sat down by the side porch on the house, leaned against the bottom step. Paul Chester and I began to shovel.

"Your daddy got the store open?" Lucky hollered to Paul.

"No sir," he answered. "He tried to open it this mornin', but then it just kept gettin' worse."

Lucky nodded. Offered Scoot a cigarette and a slug on the bottle. He took only the latter. Jean made her way from the end of the driveway, where she'd been standing, watching some of the many Pitts children attempting to sled. Paul Chester and I shoveled until we were out of breath.

"I think we'll just stand back and let y'all finish," said Scoot. "You're not gonna leave anything for anybody else when they come."

"Who else is comin', Daddy?" Jean whined.

"I don't know, hunny. Whoever wants to, I guess."

"I want to shovel something before we get finished," said Jean. "I already told you that."

"You already had a chance and didn't take it," I told her.

"You're just afraid she'll out-shovel you," said Raymond Collins.

"Is that what you're afraid of?" Van asked.

I shoveled harder, breathed hard enough that my chest burned. Threw my shovel at Collins' feet when I thought myself done. Chester threw his to Van.

"I ain't ready yet," said Ray Collins.

"I'll go," said Van, watching Scoot watch him. "Give me the damn shovel," he muttered under his breath.

"Here," said Collins, moving off the step. "I'll go."

As it is in many such moments, I'll always be uncertain what exactly happened next. It was my recollection then that Van took the few steps between us and grabbed at the shovel in my hand. Perhaps took it from me. Or perhaps it was Raymond Collins who took the shovel from my hand and Paul Chester had given his to Van. Or maybe it was even that Jean tried to take one of them or actually took one of them out of one of our hands. No matter. It would be Ray Collins and myself who ended up with the shovels in our hands. And Ray Collins and myself who began to attempt to shovel the same four or five square-foot area, our shovels actually throwing sparks a few times as they collided. And it would be Van and Paul Chester who sat on the step of the side porch that they had cleared off with their hands, hollering as we attempted to out-dig one another.

And it would be Jean who stood between us and them, watching, to see if her brother could outdo the boy who lived up the street who had always been an asshole, the same one I had fought when he had pushed her into the mud one time, "accidentally." Got my ass whipped by. Lucky and Scoot hollered with Van and Paul, their bottle having rendered them painless and louder.

As I am not sure how the shovels arrived at their own destination in our hands, neither can I say that I know how the swing came. It did not then, nor does it now make sense to me how a shovel being moved in the manner it was can somehow rise above the half-circular motion to make a downward descent. Perhaps that was how hard we were shoveling. Or perhaps none of this happened the way I remember. I only know for certain that when Jean lay bloody in the snow, a gash somewhere between the temple and the crown of her head, Ray Collins and I stood there, shovels in our hands, certain that the blow had come from the other's hands.

As Lucky fell twice in the unshoveled portion of the driveway and Scoot paused uncertain whether to help him or continue to make his way toward Jean, I was of all things aware of how quiet the night had grown so rapidly: strangely stiller than I had ever known after she had grown quiet with a grunt and collapsed.

Although I am sure Lucky had seen things much worse in the years he had put in on the police force, it seemed as though this had captured his breath, stolen his sense. He began to scream my mother's name over and over and over. I half-expected Jean to come out with my mother when the door on the side porch opened and panic descended over her face. But Jean lay in front of and under me now, as I had dropped my shovel and ascended the three steps to the porch where I watched over the shoulders of those who attended to her. The one river of blood began to break and form tiny streams, disappearing into the snow beginning to cover the areas cleared a few moments before.

I COULD HEAR EXACTLY what he'd say after he had some whiskey in him: that arrogance gives way to mistakes, makes us believe that we're somehow invincible and that how our actions affect the things around us is just a consequence of what was done. In other words, some people believe how what they do affects other people is just because the other people were in the way. Wrong place at the wrong time. I would wonder later if he still believed that, if things were still that simple.

What he'd say, I thought of Raymond Collins. The thoughts gathered themselves in my head like Lucky and Scoot and Van had gathered Jean and taken her in the house and laid her in that bedroom that would become hers forever now. And I knew this: what I thought of Raymond Collins, Lucky was likely to think of me. I would sit on the bottom step of the attic stairs and listen the majority of the rest of night as Lucky and my mother made their way in and out of the room where Dr. Guppy now sat with Jean.

"How bad is it, John?" had been the first words I remember anyone speaking after he arrived.

"She's still bleedin' pretty good," he said. "But I'm not as worried about the bleedin' as I am the actual injury to her head. She went right out, right? Lost consciousness almost immediately."

As I tried to formulate my own answer to his question, I realized that the few moments of the actual event had now become like the moments preceding it: a mass of tangled movements, one running into the next so that none could be identified alone.

"Yes," said my mother. "That's what you told me when I came outside. She was already out by then … just laying there. You said that she just went straight down."

"I couldn't tell," he said. "All I know is by the time we got to her she was completely out."

From the stairs where I listened, my father's voice sounded like it might crack and break as I had seen ice do when it hung off the side of the house. Neither he nor my mother had left the room where Jean lay since they had brought her in. In turn, I had not entered it. That I could recall, neither of them had spoken a word to me since the event transpired.

"Head injuries are strange things," Dr. Guppy said. "They're just hard to predict. The ones you think will be utterly serious can turn out to be very minor … and ones you think aren't going to be bad can turn out to be extremely serious."

"Do you think we ought to try to take her to Nashville? Would she be better off th—ere?" my mother asked, her voice cracking.

"No, Mary, I think she's just as well off here … really. To be completely honest with you, there's not a lot more we can do except wait and see how she responds to what's been done."

When he had first arrived, as Lucky and my mother still hovered over her bed and Scoot watched the foot, Dr. Guppy had given her two shots. Lucky and my mother had agreed to them, seemed as though they would have agreed to anything at the time.

"We ought to know something by the time the sun rises," said Johnny Guppy.

"What can happen?" Lucky asked him, after my mother had walked by me as if I weren't there. "We've known each other a long time. Went to school together … what school I went to. I'm dependin' on ya to give it to me honest. I'd rather you lay it out."

There was stillness where Lucky's words had been, silence that swallowed them. I heard my mother moving around in their bedroom. Wondered if she could hear what they were saying … if Scoot and Van were still in our house. If they weren't, when they'd be back, bringing Evelyn with them. Van hadn't spoken to me after the incident either, just looked at me standing up there on the porch and mouthed "Oh shit" like he knew as well as I what I had done. Raymond Collins had only said, "I knew somebody was gonna get hurt the way you were swingin' that shovel. You should'a just let me do it."

I heard my mother weeping from her bedroom, on the party line with Evelyn, I figured. Or perhaps just allowing the tears of fear and desire of a few moments back to overtake her alone.

"There are, I imagine, three things that could happen," Dr. Guppy spoke finally. "The first, that she comes to in a little while and has had nothing worse than a concussion." He cleared his throat, once then twice. "The second is, God forbid, she stays unconscious for an undetermined amount of time. That's called a coma. Research aside, they still don't know what causes them or brings people out of them." Throat cleared again. "Third, she could come to and have some kind of damage, either from the blow itself or the blood loss. Was her pulse and her breathin' steady?"

"I never checked," said Lucky. "I like to not got to her. Fell down in the damn snow t...."

At the end of his words, it sounded like he was choking. The times I had seen or heard him employ this method of crying had been few and far between, but I knew the sound. Choking the pain down into his throat and chest, where the smoke swirled when he drew in his Luckys.

Through the back door and across the porch came Evelyn, my mother's sister. She frowned a smile at me and headed through the hall to my mother. Lucky nodded at her, as did Dr. Guppy. I allowed my eyes to fix on the doorway, the one through which Percy had walked on the morning that Lucky "talked him into" going to the place where he'd been ever since, at Dr. Guppy's suggestion. As the night passed, my mother and Evelyn came and went from the room to which they had retreated into the room from where Jean lay and Lucky and Johnny Guppy held vigil. I sat at the bottom of the steps, knowing that the next morning I would still have to carry my papers, throw them to the people who bought and paid for them. Do it on foot in galoshes, that neither Jack Charles nor Lucky would have it any other way. As Lucky and my mother passed me sitting at the bottom of the stairs, they would reach out and touch my head now, as if to say that it was still all right … that it did not have a three-inch gash in it. As if they felt sorry for me for killing my sister.

CHAPTER TWENTY-FIVE

EAN'S FUNERAL, in its own way, was similar to the "viewing" they did for Rosa Mary: people filing by and viewing the body, trying to discern where the original gash was. In Jean's case, trying to figure out how a place so small could produce not only death, but so much blood. They'd been driving by for a week as the snow melted, looking for what was left of the evidence of the act. Then the whole town had come to look at her after George Preston had done his job. Lucky and Evelyn were there in the front, holding my mother up as everyone in Franklin told her how sorry they were, not only about her daughter, but her son. Was it true that he had even gone and thrown his paper route the following morning? Wasn't that when the spirit that she was left her body?

Even Percy made his way there, sitting with me in the back because he knew what was like to feel outcast. Wanda Jean and Nelly, Lucky's sisters were there, and all Mama's brothers and sisters, so many that I hardly knew all their names. Lucky's friends, too, Sammy Samuels, Jimmy Langford, John Harvey, Paul Chester, Sr. With Jimmy was his son Ronnie, and with Ronnie was Fred Burkitt, big, lumbering Fred Burkitt, who still had both his arms and was minus the contraption he normally wore on the one that was gone just below the mostly withered bicep.

"Wasn't her name Inez?" I heard Dr. Guppy ask Lucky.

For a long moment, Lucky didn't respond. He had that characteristic smirk on his face, I knew that. Was holding himself in such a way he appeared taller, his chest poked out. I knew the posture and the facial expression, because I, even at nine, used them often, too.

"How long's that been?"

"Longer than I'd care to admit," Lucky answered. "So long that it seems like another lifetime ... but you know, in another way, it seems like yesterday. I can still see her layin' there, plain as day. Spread out on the ground where they'd put her. I can still remember thinkin', how does somethin' like this happen so quick? It never will make sense to me. Even with Jean, if she don't make it, God for–bid," his voice broke, "it took a few hours for it to happen." For the only time that I could ever recall, Lucky cried, tears that did not dam in his chest, but ones that found their way up through his throat and out his eyes and down his cheeks. I could hear the looseness, the release, in his voice. "With Inez, though, there wasn't no warning or nothin'."

"Refresh my memory," said Dr. Guppy. "How did it happen?"

He could ask questions that, if from someone else, would seem at least callous, at most monstrous.

For a long time Lucky was silent, so much so that the house cracked with it, filled itself with its presence. He cleared his throat or coughed a couple of times, I couldn't tell which from the bottom step, the place to which I had returned after the dream about Jean had awakened me. I was surprised that my hollering when everyone in the funeral home had begun to accuse me of killing her just before I had awakened hadn't brought anyone to check on me. But the sounds had merely echoed off the sloped ceiling and paper-covered walls and fallen into the silence surrounding me.

"You know, we never was sure," Lucky finally said. "We just found her down by the river." He laughed sadly. "Percy and me accused each other of it for a long time. Said that she'd been down there watchin' us swim. We never was sure. She wasn't but ten. We never did know why she went in. The only thing I could ever figure is Percy and me had been down there the week before and gone in the water. Matter a' fact, it was the only time I can ever remember him goin' in the water. He like to drowned himself. I had to go in and get him out."

I heard Lucky try three or four times to produce a flame to light a cigarette. Dr. Guppy cleared his throat twice.

"They always thought that Inez must'a been behind us that week that me and Percy went down there. Must'a seen us go in. The rains come in the next week and the river swelled, especially down there in its bottom, and she must'a decided that she was gonna go in like us. I've always wondered if that's the reason Percy talks about that goddam river all the time."

Dr. Guppy laughed sad, like Lucky had earlier. "Might be. When've you seen him?"

Briefly, I heard my mother and Evelyn's voices in the room. Coming to check to see if anything had changed, I assumed. Dr. Guppy told them that nothing had, in the last hour. I stretched to look at the clock on the kitchen wall. I'd have to leave in an hour or so.

"You know, that 'bout killed Mother and Daddy," said Lucky. "Like I said 'while ago, I can still see her body layin' there on the ground after they'd pulled her out. She had that look that people do after they drown. You know, they don't look like theirself. Like their body ain't theirs anymore. I remember, when they found her and come to get Daddy, he took his Bible and read a verse out of it as he sat down by her. You know, Johnny, I can't remember the words he read ... couldn't tell you the verse, but I can still see him sittin' there, chokin' back the tears with every breath and then Mother comin' and gettin' on her knees and huggin' him as he read."

Personally, I'd heard of Inez only a couple of times. Until this moment, I'd not known how she died, just that she had while they were children.

"When was the last time you said you saw Percy?"

"I don't know, maybe a month."

"You know, when we talked about him goin' somewhere, I didn't intend for him to be there this long," said John Guppy. "I, like you, didn't want him to take the brunt of the town's wrath for tearin' up that cemetery. You and I both know that he wasn't strong enough to have done that; nor would he have done it. But ... I guess I saw it as an opportunity to get him in somewhere that could help him. He'd needed it for awhile. You know that. Your mother and father knew that."

"Yeah, I reckon it's easier to ignore somethin'," said Lucky. "At least till you can't ignore it anymore."

"Yeah, I guess we're all guilty of that sometimes," said Johnny Guppy.

"I just don't know what the hell else I could'a done. When everybody else believes somethin', and you know it ain't true, it's the hardest thing in the world sometimes to stand your ground."

"I think you did the right thing by Percy," said Dr. Guppy. "I'm afraid he's on a bad course. By what we've done we might slow it or even give him a chance to be better. Even though they don't know a lot about what's wrong with him, they do know kinda what to do to help."

"You mean shockin' the hell out of him?"

"Those treatments are a part of his overall treatment there. I've talked with the doctor that's treating him. He thinks they've helped him enough that he's stable now...."

I heard my mother and Evelyn at the door once more, talking so quietly I couldn't make out what they were saying. Poised in sadness, reaching for hope. They seemed unable to enter the room where she lay, where in some strange way our whole existence seemed to rest in the balance.

"In all honesty, it's not a cure-all, but as far as they can tell it seems to create an arresting affect of the most significant symptoms. I'm sorry, I'm falling into speaking like a doctor—what I mean is that most of what's wrong with him can be counteracted by treatment. The shock seems to make the symptoms go away for a prolonged period of time, maybe years."

"So ... he is crazy?" said Lucky. "I mean, sometimes, I know that. Like the last time I went to see him he was so normal it almost scared me. He was talkin' about the news different. He talked about us finishin' off the Krauts and the Japs and it not havin' a thing to do with him ... Roosevelt dyin' and Truman takin' over and it not havin' a thing to do with him. When I see him like that, even though it's been years since the last time I did, I know that he's been crazy as hell for a long time and I've just grown as used to it as the change in the seasons. Come to expect it without even knowin' it."

I heard Dr. Guppy rustling around, rifling through his bag, I imagined. Maybe taking Jean's pulse and blood pressure and temperature as I'd seen him do several times when I'd peeked around the corner from my hiding place. "She's still stable," he said. "That's a good sign, Lucky. A damn good one. It's been going on eight hours since it happened now. If she's been stable this long, it means that she's likely to stay stable."

"So what does it look like from here?" Lucky asked.

"I'm hopeful," said Johnny Guppy. "Hopeful for Jean … and for Percy."

"You still tellin' me that it'll take the same thing?" Lucky asked. "Somebody being willin' to vouch that they'll take care of him?"

"We'd have to have a hearing, but that would go a long way … somebody saying something that they'd watch out for and take care of him. It'd be somethin' like the hearin' we told Percy we could have if he didn't consent to go into Central State. It'd just be reversed … and it wouldn't necessarily have to be in a court. We'd just have to have a group a' the professionals that have worked with him say that he's fit to return to the general population."

"Do you think he is?" Lucky asked.

"Realistically, I don't think that Percy's a danger to anybody or anything. Maybe himself … but that's probably it. And I can't imagine what's worse: him havin' to live in the place where he is the rest of his life … or the slight possibility that he might hurt himself."

"Then maybe it was the wrong thing to leave him in there," said Lucky.

As I sat on the stairs, the door still cracked as it had been most of the night, I wanted to scream through the opening that Lucky damn well knew it had been wrong. If he had ever at any point stepped forward and requested he come out, if he had not gotten him sent up the river for something he didn't do in the first place… if he had ever acted as if it were even happening, instead of just ignoring the fact that Percy had basically disappeared for six months. I wanted to tell him from my place there in the stairwell that he was only talking about it now to avoid the fact Jean was lying on her possible deathbed. But I simply sat still and quiet, knowing as the months had grown, Lucky seemed to be able to stand his presence less and less. His tolerance for him had dimmed like the lights in Central State at eight o'clock in the evening.

"Do you have to leave so soon?" Percy had asked him the last time we'd been there.

"Yeah. Mary's waitin' dinner on us. Better be goin' so that we don't keep her and Jean waitin'. You know that Mary, she can get pretty mean if you ain't there to eat her supper on time."

This is what Lucky had told me in the parking lot that he'd say when we needed to leave, which had occurred after just ten minutes. After he spoke he paced the room, his eyes set on the floor, waiting for me, I guess, to arise from the seat I'd taken in the corner.

"Can Henry stay awhile?" Percy asked. "It gets pretty lonesome in here."

"That's just ,cause you don't have nothin' to do with other people here. They're prob'ly good people. Prob'ly just got problems … just like you."

"How would you know?" spat Percy. "You're never here long enough to even see any of them."

Lucky stopped at the corner nearest the door and stared across the room at Percy, where he had sat in the chair next to me.

"Why don't you stay in here a few days and see how much you'd feel like socializin' with the other patients? It's not the most enjoyable place in the world."

"We all have to do things we don't want to do," said Lucky. "That's just a part of life, Percy. Sometimes, I don't think you've ever learned that. Do you think anybody here wants to be?"

"I don't know about anybody else … I can't speak for them. Only for myself. Most of them are casualties of war … not of their damned brother."

I could see the rage in Lucky brewing as he stopped his movement toward the door, cut angry eyes back across the room at Percy. He shook his head and cleared his throat like he did when he was nervous, or didn't like what someone had said.

"Henry, come on in a few minutes," he said as he drew the door open and passed through.

Each time Lucky would leave, Percy would appear all over again as he had the first time we had left him: like somehow he'd lost his best friend.

"Some of these people," Percy said after Lucky had exited, "they won't even let them have a table in their room." He made a face I assume he thought looked crazy. "They might use it as a weapon against themselves … or someone else. I know you all thought I was crazy … but I couldn't hold a candle to some of the people in this place. Going through what a lot of these men did, it makes people lose their bearings.

"You wouldn't believe what that war has done to some of these men. They act as if it hasn't bothered them … but then they just sit and stare into corners for hours at a time. Talk to themselves. Don't say anything to anybody else." He fished a cigarette out of the pack in his sock and a book of matches out of his pocket. "I guess your daddy would say that that's just like me."

I nodded, trying to be polite. Watched out the crack of the door for the kinds of men he spoke about. Pictured in my head the one's I'd seen sitting in the main room when we came in.

"I guess I'm lucky," he told me. "At least they let me smoke … have a way to light my cigarettes. Some of those men, they don't even let them have their cigarettes. They have to go to the desk and ask the nurse for one … ask them to light it. It makes me feel sorry for them. But I know at the same time that they're heroes. It makes me wonder what takes more courage: to stand against killing or to go kill and become numb to it. That's what made these men go crazy. They haven't always been that way like me. They've gone that way because of what they had to do, what they saw."

Now he talked about himself and his craziness matter-of-factly, like he was reporting the news as they did in the evening on our new television set. It was just that way.

"Maybe all our craziness is the same. I'm not sure. I just know there seems to be a kind where people don't do anything but hurt themselves. And another kind, where people seem to draw other people into it. Destroy them, too."

Now when he talked it often seemed someone else was speaking. His face had a bleakness to it, like the person who was once behind it might have left when the electricity hit his system.

"You know, being in here has reminded me that there's just some things in this life that we have little or no control over. You'd think I would … I mean, it's me who's in here. And I guess I could try an escape attempt or something. But it just seems as if all the powers that be, both seen and unseen, have landed me here. It's almost like it's where I'm supposed to be. Not just because I'm crazy, mind you, but in that everything that seems to have any influence at all has seemed to move me in this direction. That's one of the hardest parts of our existence, Henry … going from believing something is random to believing it is planned. Or that it's part of some plan, some...." Quietly at first, then more loudly, came a knock at the door. Sure it was Lucky, irritated because I had sat and listened to his brother too long, I was already up from the chair. The knock came more loudly a third time, scaring me so that I apologized all the way to the door, reminding myself of my mother. What I found when I opened it was a short, somewhat strange-looking man with thinning salt and pepper hair, his hand raised to knock a fourth time.

"Hello, Efim," said Percy, half-smiling. "Don't tell your father I have a friend in here," he told me, "the more miserable he thinks I am… Anyway, I tell them to wait ,til he leaves to come by."

"Allo," Efim said to me as he took the only other chair in the room.

"Efim's from the down the hall," he said. "He's kind of an outsider, too. He's a Russian-Polish Jew—Dillard would certainly say that's two if not three strikes against him—a weightlifting coach, who made it out with his family and somehow made it here. Came through Ellis Island, met someone there who told him there might be work down here. After he got to Nashville, he somehow began to believe that everyone on his street was out to get him, coming to take him away. He held his wife and his kids at gunpoint for a week, believing he was fending off his neighbors. Now, that's more my kind of crazy. Not crazy like a hero, but more self-centered and deluded like me. Anyway, he doesn't speak very good English. Does calisthenics in front of his window in the nude every morning. They've had to take to shutting his shade and taping it shut with electrical tape so that he won't raise it in the morning. Or at least it makes it harder."

Obviously understanding English well enough to know what Percy was saying, Efim started to demonstrate his routine for me. He threw his arms out in front of himself, shook his hands and fingers, then lowered himself in a partial squat before he arose once more. His exhibition made me glad Lucky had gone. Even if he was in the car cussing me at that very moment.

"They're having some kind of meeting about him this week. Called a Denova or something. Never heard of it. But it's where they'll try to force him to take his medicine because he's refused it for so long." Around here, they think medicine will cure anything. I've a feeling that's where the country's going. Like what I was telling you about black and white living together, going to school together."

I laughed like I had the first time he had told me that. Efim chuckled while he was still raising and lowering himself in the doorway. For a moment, I tried to imagine what this would look like if he were naked. I couldn't. So I turned back to Percy.

"I guess—" Percy began, but didn't finish.

"Papsi," said Efim. He smiled as big as he could at my uncle. "Papsi," he repeated.

I looked at Percy for interpretation.

"Pepsi Cola," said Percy. "He wants a Pepsi Cola. He and his family don't have much. His wife brings him a quarter a week. Nothing's free here but the horrible food they serve three times a day and whatever drink concoction they give you with that. Toilet water, I'm pretty sure. Anyway, he loves Hershey bars and Pepsi Cola. Dillard, out of guilt, brings me money. If you'll look now, there's some in that sack he left over there. I bet it's brownies your mother made and a few dollars. It makes him feel better for a little while, like he's doing something to help me."

I studied Percy's face as he talked. Its gaunt paleness made the circles under his eyes more definite. He drew on the cigarette he'd lit and pointed to Efim, who was now becoming out of breath and puffing like a locomotive, and laughed. Efim stopped and smiled.

Percy made his way to his nightstand and fished in the back of the drawer until he came out with some change and handed it to Efim. He told him he wanted one, too, a Pepsi, that was, not a Hershey bar. Asked him to hurry back so he could tell him the last of what he'd been telling him earlier in the day. He hoped he could remember it, he told him, because they had come and got him that morning and... .

I'd looked at the clock, I know, fifty times, all the time hoping that Lucky was drinking, enjoying a few minutes of peace and quiet that he usually didn't get. When Efim pushed the door open once more, he handed me a Pepsi and a Hershey bar, signaled to Percy by touching his pocket that he'd bought mine with his money. I thanked him and told Percy I'd better be going.

"No–stay–story," said Efim. "Stay–story."

"What?" I asked Percy.

"He wants you to stay while I finish telling him a story I was telling him earlier in the day."

Efim walked to an empty chair, patted its seat.

"I better go," I told Percy. "You know Lucky's goin' to be here lookin' for me."

"Go ahead ... go ahead," he said. "You know as well as I do that you don't want Dillard on your bad side. You might end up some place like this."

"No-no-no ... stay," said Efim, smiling.

I couldn't help smiling back at him.

"He's right," said Percy. "Stay. It serves him right ... to come and bring you and just stay a few minutes. He's expected me to stay months in this hellhole and all he can produce the will to do is stay long enough to drop off Mary's brownies."

Efim patted the empty chair again and smiled. I tried to imagine him holding his wife and children hostage, afraid that his neighbors were coming to get him. I could not.

CHAPTER TWENTY-SIX

F ROM THE COTTON GIN to the Carter House, the fighting was desperate. Men charged into the rifles firing as if they were running into a strong wind, their heads down, their caps the only shield from the lead death approaching them from the end of the enemy's rifles.

A Federal officer wrote, "I saw a confederate soldier, close to me, thrust one of our men through with a bayonet, and before he could draw his weapon from the ghastly wound his brains were scattered on all of us who stood near, by the butt of a musket swung with terrible force by some big fellow whom I could not recognize in the grim dirt and smoke that enveloped us."

A member of the 100th Ohio Infantry said, "I saw three confederates standing within our lines, as if they had dropped down unseen from the sky. They stood there for an instant, guns in hand, neither offering to shoot nor surrender—dazed as in a dream. I raised my gun, but instinctively I felt as if about to commit murder—they were hopeless, and I turned my face to the foe trying to chamber our abatis. When I looked again the three were down—apparently dead; whether shot by their own men or ours, who could tell?"

The battle wasn't confined to the center of the Federal troops, though. On the left and the right, things had gone worse than they had in the center. Forrest's two divisions on Stewart's right had pushed back the Federal cavalry early in the fighting and had crossed the Harpeth River. Upstream, the dismounted cavalries from both armies fought a hell of a fight. On the right side of the attack, Stewart's divisions were crowded to the left by the curve in the river and the higher ground near the railroad. They were even more hindered by the fact that they ran into Osage Orange trees, or hedge apples, and their formation was broken. In the confusion, a Federal battery opened fire on them from almost point blank range. Across the river, from an earthen fort called Fort Granger, shells poured into their lines. The ditches of the works were already filled three and four deep with the dead.

Long after dark, Hood sent Johnson's division of Lee's corps stumbling and falling through the locust grove west of Columbia Pike: a last-gasp assault upon the works west of the Carter House. But the battle was over. Over! And the last charge was no more than the other charges had been— a waste of men. Until nine o'clock that night, November 30, 1864, the fighting would continue. Attackers and defenders firing at no more than the mere flashing of guns. And then, at last, the night was as quiet as death. The Rebels drew back. And the front was quiet as the night previous.

At eleven o'clock, while most of Hood's remaining men slept, Schofield started his withdrawal. At the crack of dawn, Hood's artillery began to blaze away once more and the confederate officers, at least those left, began to prepare for a new assault. Soon, though, it was discovered that the Yankees had stolen away in the night.

There had been enough tragedy the day before to last a lifetime. Generals Adams, Granbury, Gist, Strahl, and Cleburne were all lost, laid out on the porch of the Carnton mansion. Tod Carter had been mortally wounded and taken to his own house to die. Overall, comparing the losses with another battle, Pickett's loss at Gettysburg was 2,882, while at Franklin the Confederate Army suffered over 6,000 casualties! The Army of Tennessee had penetrated the breastworks and then had renewed its charge time after time. Though they had not prevailed against Schofield or stopped his movement toward Nashville and further north, they had shown their commander they could fight without the aid of breastworks. If I were to quote the bastard, I would say something of the nature, "Never have troops fought more gallantly." They, the men who had charged again and again into the Federal lines, now belonged to the school of Lee and Jackson, an aristocracy of valor, atop the hierarchy of fighting men.

General Strahl, who would soon lose his life, said just before the charge began, "Boys, this will be short but desperate."

And so it would be.

WHEN PERCY GOT TO THIS POINT, he always sighed, shook his head, and turned his eyes to the floor. Depending on how sane he was at the moment, he might throw in a couple of comments about Walter if he was on the far side of his mental health. The second time around, when he had become so enraptured with religious ideas (which, he would assure me, these weren't; matters of faith and religion have very little if anything to do with each other, he would say), he would tell me that this was a fine example of God's grace: that even someone like John Bell Hood could be loved eternally by God. To which Lucky responded that he just got nuttier with the years. Not to him of course, but behind his back, when he stepped out of the room to smoke a cigarette.

Years before, almost eight years and ten months to be exact, he seemed to use these stories to connect with people, in a strange but almost desperate attempt to allow someone to see into him, to identify some vestige of his tortured soul. But now, it seemed, he used them more to hold people away, like armor to keep himself from being exposed, to keep from revealing what the second half of his life had done to him.

Overall, it was hard to believe that eight years had passed since the last time he was in the "crazy house," as he would call it after his first release, which he referred to as his "escape," and credited to the fact that Jean survived the blow that I inflicted upon her. Percy, of all people, was probably the one family member who actually believed me when I regained my voice and tried to explain exactly what had happened, that is, as best I could remember and recount it. Nonetheless, in his better, lighter moments, when he wasn't worried about the grace of God or the three components of every human event, he would often refer to the happening as "when you hit Jean in the head with a shovel to try to regain the upper hand on the bedroom situation." He would then go on to remind me that he knew relationships with siblings could be hell.

Nevertheless, after Lucky sprung him from the crazy house, he was eternally grateful to him. Over and over and over he'd ask me what was said between Lucky and Dr. Guppy that night, what they talked about that had somehow changed Lucky's mind. What had made him come down to the crazy house the next day and begin working with the doctor to let him out. Or perhaps it was just almost losing Jean, he surmised; something like that could penetrate the hardest of hearts. I never mentioned to him in any of our conversations that Lucky and Dr. Guppy had discussed Inez. I concluded that what had been silent and unspoken for a quarter century was likely better off left that way.

FOR THE TWO WEEKS he'd stay in Central State in 1953, the breadth of his ideas had seemed to increase to encompass almost everything he had talked about in the past: *Randomness, A Planned Nature of Things, Human Frailty* and God's never-ending grace. He continued to attempt to explain the Battle of Franklin to me, and in his opinion, how it affected the Battle of Nashville, and, thus the Civil War and how the war affected what America was to become, and in general, what we were to become living as Americans.

On his bad days, he was still convinced that Walter roamed the earth, was eternal and omnipresent, from everywhere from the Battle of Franklin, Hood's confidant and advisor, to the Cemetery that night to Christine Smithson's house, in the shrubs, watching and tattling on him like a jealous schoolboy.

"Better than the way he was last time, I guess," Lucky said the day he was taking him back to Central State. After the standoff at our house. "The last time he was convinced that the goddam pig was on trial at Nuremberg. You remember when he kept saying that they had the number wrong in the news? That they'd said they were trying twenty-one of those Krauts, and that they'd missed the most important one. Hell, I thought he was talkin' about Hitler, but who was he talkin' about? He was talkin' about Walter the pig!"

When Lucky said this, on our way back from leaving him there, literally having to pry his fingers loose from the doorjamb of the car, he laughed, a sad sound nonetheless.

"And then do you remember? When the verdicts came back, he decided that Walter had escaped and would be back to get him. You remember? He screamed, 'How the hell could they prosecute and convict every one of the others, yet let him go! How could that have happened? Walter is a professional at slipping through the cracks!'"

Lucky shook his head, glad, I am sure, like I was, that the night had finally ended and we had successfully deposited his brother once more at the asylum. That we had been able, with minimal injury, to get him across the parking lot and through the front door. The two large guards who had helped us the last half of the way had been indispensable at getting him through the door. It was the first time I had seen Percy act the way he did. I guess, the only time.

"Goddam everyone of you!" he had screamed as we all pulled on him, trying to get him into the lobby where they could wrest him to the floor. "Every fucking one of you! Goddam you, Henry! I thought better of you than this! Do I not deserve some semblance of a life? What have I done to deserve this? It's that goddam pig, isn't it? I should have known. Walter, you son of a bitch, get off me!"

"You shouldn't have done what you did," Lucky said from his position on top of him.

I struggled to get his feet still, which is what they'd told me to do. Remembered that I had feared that it was going to come to this on the back porch when Lucky confronted him after he had come in the back door.

"Old Man Smithson," he said, "says he's gonna turn your ass in. He says that he'd tried to talk to you about it and that you'd just denied it."

Percy wouldn't answer Lucky. Just stood there staring at his shoes and shaking his head.

"Have you been doin' it?" He took him by the shoulders and tried to make him look into his eyes, which he wouldn't. "Is what Old Man Smithson told me true?" He shook Percy until he glanced into his eyes. "I'm talkin' to you, Percy! Did Old Man Smithson tell me the truth?"

I thought how it was odd that Lucky called Mr. Smithson, Old Man, seeing how he was only maybe half a dozen years older than Lucky himself. They had never particularly liked or disliked each other, but simply lived next door. Speaking when spoken to, nodding when the other did. Passing the time of day if necessary. Helping each other if the other needed it. Lucky had explained it saying that he had always resented us because we had a television. I thought the cool feelings were due to Jean snubbing Christine at school. I knew she thought she was odd; she had said that to me a hundred times. Talked about her hair, her glasses, her clothes, and her shoes. The things the angel said only when Mama and Lucky weren't around. Todd, their son a couple of years younger than me, and I had always gotten along. Sometimes I gave him rides on my Indian.

"What if I did?!" Percy screamed. "Don't I deserve to have somethin' that's normal?!"

"If you did then you ought to go to jail!" Lucky retorted.

As the two men screamed back and forth at each other, I turned to look at my mother and found in her eyes the look I had grown accustomed to over the years. It was the look I assume we all emitted when Lucky's rage began to overtake him: praying it would not finish claiming his senses and that if it did, someone else would be his target.

"I've lived by this man peaceably for going on ten years. Never had one problem!"

"What about the time that Mrs. Smithson got mad at Mary for what she thought was stealing her laundry?"

Lucky paused for a moment, like he was having a hard time remembering. Their sheets had blown into our yard off the clothes line, gotten mixed up with ours.

"What about their dog stealing your papers?"

Lucky shook his head back and forth, stared through his brother insolently.

"You can't go to jail for either of them things," Lucky told him. His hands were bound in fists at his sides, both of them and his voice beginning to shake.

"There could be no worse jail than where you left me for months eight years ago."

"You might be findin' out if the old man swears out a warrant on your ass. I can't control that," said Lucky. "Goddam you, Percy!" Lucky's foot made contact with the electric dryer, knocked a dent in it the size a bowling ball would have produced. When he knocked out one of the windows on the back porch with the flat of his hand, his forearm almost immediately bled through his rolled up shirt sleeve. My mother, used to such things, motioned for Jean to go get him a wet towel. He wrapped it around his arm when she handed it to him.

"I can't get you out of this. Don't you understand that?"

"Do you mean that you can't make up something else I did so they can ship me off to the crazy house again? Shock the hell out of me for months. I'm sure you can come up with somethin'."

For the entirety of the exchange between them, Lucky had been positioned between Percy and the door. His job had taught him to do such things, I imagined. My suspicion was that Percy wasn't leaving the house of his own will. He made a few slow steps toward the door.

"This'll kill Mother and Daddy," Lucky said. "Don't you know that?"

"I don't ever recall doing anything like this before," said Percy. "Never has my life, for one minute, seemed normal … seemed like I could have what everybody else does."

"No, you'd have to have a goddam job first," Lucky said. He lifted the towel and daubed at the blood still flowing. "And you couldn't even hold the simplest of those … at Earl's Fruit Stand."

"Some of us aren't meant to work jobs like that! You've never understood that … or you've forgotten it if you ever did!"

As I watched them trade their views of the world, of life, back and forth, it seemed to me that both of them had forgotten, even though the name of the malady wasn't readily spoken, Percy wasn't like the rest of us. Couldn't be. It wasn't a question of laziness … but craziness.

Lucky leaned backward and looked out the side window at the Smithson's yard and house. He grimaced and shook his head when he saw lights were on, as springtime darkness descended.

"He said we had tonight to do somethin'. He was takin' her to the hospital to get examined in the mornin'. He says there ain't ever been anybody else. Hell, the way he keeps her and Todd in that house he ought to know. So you got till mornin' to come up with some kinda explanation or I guess the only explainin' that's gonna be done is why I had to arrest my own brother."

Percy turned just enough to look at the door behind him, glanced away when he saw my mother and Jean still standing there. "Would you want me to say I did somethin' I didn't do?"

Lucky pulled out a cigarette and lit it. Handed one to Percy and lit it. Leaned against the deep freeze door. "You know, the idea of you goin' back don't… But it's the only thing I know to do."

For the moment, Percy would agree to go. Eventually sitting down with Lucky on the step leading from the back porch to the backyard, they smoked several cigarettes together as they discussed what my mother, Jean and I could not hear after Lucky told us to stay inside. He would only ask me to come outside when the time finally came for Percy to leave.

"I think he's been seein' Christine Smithson," Jean said when we had settled at the kitchen table, still half-fearing we'd hear a scuffle. "I think that's what he's been doin'!"

"You mean you think he's been fuckin' her?" I said low enough that my mother, at the sink, couldn't hear.

Jean gasped, like I'd slapped her. I smiled.

"Do you know anything about it?" my mother asked me, sitting with us. I shook my head. "No ma'am."

It was true, he'd never mentioned anything like that to me. I remembered the few times I'd seen them looking back and forth, him making gestures and nodding out the window. I remembered Lucky telling me that Mr. Smithson had called, said that we needed to pull the shade. But nothing else. In the last month, I'd had my own problems. Been so immersed in them I could seldom see out from the dirty glass I stood behind.

"I bet I'm right," said Jean. "I never thought about it ... but one afternoon, when I came home from school early because I wasn't feelin' well, I saw him comin' out from behind the brush and the fence back there behind our yards ... back there where they burn the trash sometimes."

A feeling came over me to slap the smugness off my sister's face. But I really had no idea. All I knew was that going on a couple of months before, he'd seemed stranger than usual, preached from the top of a car without most of his clothes. Taken and lost a job at Earl's fruit stand. I couldn't have told you what the hell he'd been doing while I'd been gone. And I'd been gone a lot. "Chasing skirts," as Tully called it. Really, just one skirt. Then I'd been sitting on my ass for about a month, feeling sorry for myself, trying to figure out what in the hell I'd done wrong.

CHAPTER TWENTY-SEVEN

I F I'D KNOWN THE HOLE I'd fall into when we left on that goddam motorcycle that day, I'd have never stopped, but left Nashville and driven west off one of those bluffs near the hillbillies down in Ashland City. I guess I should have known from the first couple of times I'd talked to her. By the second time I saw her, it didn't seem to make any difference anymore. The night, even the poison moonshine hadn't washed it away. Lucky's asskicking the next morning—the split lip, the torn knee—had not. Even seeing Percy almost naked on top of Mrs. Nedler's car had not removed her memory.

Perhaps "memory" isn't the right word; it seemed to go so much deeper than that. Everything did. Talking wasn't really talking, but something more. Her smell, her sound, they were hers, but more than that, too. The words she spoke carried both the meaning that they did, and the meaning that she was in fact saying them to me. This girl, beautiful enough to be saying these words to anyone in the world she wanted to, was saying them to me. Had for some reason chosen to hold my hand across the seat, had chosen to stop on the street and talk to me, ask me to her prom. She not only didn't want Van, she wanted me.

That Saturday afternoon, her arms wrapped around me as we rode west through Green Hills and then to the rich people's section of Nashville, Belle Meade, I was invincible in a way I'd never been. I'd somehow been given the antidote for a malady I'd suffered from my whole life. I needed to be nowhere else with no one else. Time could have stood still or stopped all together, never taken another step and I would have been satisfied.

"I want a house like that one day," she whispered in my ear as we made our way down the boulevard that ran through this part of town.

I nodded, looked at it. Thought of her house. Of how her family made us, as solid as concrete in the middle class, appear rich. "Yeah," I said over the rumbling of the Indian.

It was the perfect spring evening, the way it is in Tennessee in May, before the heat takes over, before the air becomes sticky and clings to you in the form of sweat. The smell of everything beginning to bloom. As the daylight began to lose itself to darkness, the air was like silk rubbing against my bare arms as were her hands on my waist.

As the ride had begun, she had barely laid her hands on my sides, almost like she was afraid to touch me, like her memory from the night before was as shaky as I'd been. But as the speed increased, so did her grip on me, perhaps a natural reaction. Even through the wind that whipped around us, I could feel her breath on my neck.

"It's gorgeous out here," she told me. "It reminds me of where my daddy comes from."

"What?" I said. Told her I couldn't hear her.

She said the same more loudly.

I nodded. Didn't tell her that Lucky would laugh till he pissed on himself at the idea that any part of Alabama would remind anybody of Tennessee. "Yeah, it is nice," I told her. I down-shifted for a curve then hit the accelerator again; felt the power in my hands. "Lucky says it's like it's a million miles from Franklin. Says that Franklin and Nashville are like him and my Uncle Percy." For a moment, I felt a great sense of relief that she hadn't seen him that morning, like I assumed about half the town had. A streak of anxiety fired through me like May lightning that maybe she had, was just too nice to say anything. Then I remembered she'd been at work. I then began to wonder whether she'd seen Lucky kick my ass down Lewisburg Pike. Knock me down, bloody my lip, rub my face in my own puke. I assumed that had been too early for most people to see. "He says that one does what it has to do: Franklin. And the other is more of a spectacle. Draws attention to itself all the time in one way or another: Nashville. But, nonetheless, Lucky likes his Hank Williams."

"Wasn't it sad when he died?" she said. New Year's Eve, or really New Year's Day, I guess, in a car, in the backseat by himself."

I nodded. Turned onto a road I knew led into the park. Which one I wasn't sure. On the far west side of Nashville, there had been several hundred acres reserved and named after brothers with the last name of Warner, Edwin, and Percy, oddly enough. Roads ran through them like mazes, cutting from one tree-dense lane to another. Everything was getting close to full bloom. I watched the trees pass, trying to identify them by sight: elms, oaks, hackberries, ash, cedar, birch.

"Didn't you think that was sad?" she asked again, nudging me in the ribs with an open hand.

I jumped then glanced at her and smiled and nodded.

I wound through as many roads as I could, riding hard enough as to impress her but not hard enough to scare her. I remembered that one time last year I had brought Jean out here then got the wild hair to try to scare the shit out of her, like Van had bragged he did with Scoot. Taking some of the curves fast enough that I almost had to lay the bike down, she beat me in the shoulders so that I had bruises for a couple of weeks. I laughed so hard my ribs hurt almost as long. She swore she'd never ride with me again and had only when she was too lazy to walk to the store.

"Where are we going?" she asked.

The truth was I didn't have any more idea than I had when I just showed up at her work. "I thought we'd just ride till we saw a pretty spot then we'd just sit for awhile,"

"I'm kind of hungry," she said.

"All right," I said. Started trying to run through places in my head I could afford.

"I can wait awhile, though. Let's find a nice spot and park for awhile first. It'd be a shame to waste such a pretty evening."

I nodded. Told her I agreed with her.

On the far side of one of the parks, by where they had recently put in a golf course, we stopped. I laid down the coat I'd had bundled and tied on the back of the bike so she would have a place to sit. She sat down and pulled her skirt over her knees. I sat on the ground by her.

"So I hear you're a pretty good football player," she said.

I laughed. Partly because I was nervous and partly because I never believed it of myself.

"They said that you might get to go to college and play," she said.

"I guess I got an outside chance. Some people say I'm too little, though. Who's 'they'?"

"Van," she said.

"Right—" What I was going to say if I had finished was, "Right after he got off my ass about my shoes." But I stopped. "That surprises me."

"That's what he said," she said, the dying sun over my shoulder making her eyes sparkle with green, like pictures of the ocean I'd seen. "He said that he was a pretty good football player … but that you were probably the best player on the team."

I laughed again. "I doubt it. When did he tell you that?"

"Well, first, when he was trying to get me to fix you up with Sheila. He was singing your praises. Telling me everything that was good about you. He even said you were cute."

"I better watch out for him," I said.

She laughed … averted her eyes to a tree near us, its spring growth trembling in a slight breeze.

"He thinks a lot of you," she told me. "He even said that today. I told you he came in the store today. Said his parents had given him the money to buy a bunch of clothes."

"You must have been workin' in the department he bought 'em in," I said.

"Umh, no. You know, they call me a ‚floater‘, so I go from department to department, wherever they need me. I have worked there before. But he came up to where I was working just to say ‚Hi‘ I guess. He said he thought that he remembered that I worked there."

"Let's talk about somethin' besides Van, all right?" I said.

"If I remember right, we were talking about you. I was asking you about football."

"Somethin' besides Van or football."

She looked around her at the hundred trees as still as stone now. I wished that I could pull back in the words that had leaked out my mouth.

"Where you wanna eat?" I asked her.

She shrugged and set her eyes on a stray, late golfer making his way down the fairway in sight.

"I don't know," she said. "I'm over my hunger for the moment. I'm enjoying just sitting here. I feel like I never get to sit anywhere very long; I'm always so busy with everything." She smiled a smile at me that I would eventually grow accustomed to, one that somehow touched a part of my heart no one had reached before. She reached and took my arm and pulled me toward her, patted the space behind her on the jacket then leaned back on me once I had repositioned myself. She took my hands in hers, and lay her head on my chest.

PERHAPS WHEN ANYTHING HAPPENS, or at least anything bad, we always find ourselves secretly posing questions in our silent, aching hearts. What if this had happened differently? Or, wonder if I'd done that rather than what I did do? What if I had just paid more attention to what was happening? Done nothing. Just noticed more. Not have been so focused on my own interests? Would that have made a difference?

Percy assured me that things, no matter how they are or seem, work out as they're supposed to. He once told me that believing that something happened that was not supposed to was the most soul-corrosive thing we could do. Yes, there are things that happen randomly but that does not in and of itself mean that an event is not included in the *Planned Nature of*

Things. Each soul has a destination, he assured me, and that, in the end is what cannot be thwarted. The twists and turns as we get there, these things might well be random, but the end event, the destination, is part of the plan. And believing this is, in the end, what faith really is.

It is the easiest thing in the world to stand back and scream that every bad thing that happens to us might in fact be of some other power than that we call God. Makes things simpler. And simplicity has its place. But utter simplicity and serenity lies most completely in knowing that all things come from God and all things go to God. As humans, we are constrained by time, bound with it as if someone with rope. Perhaps years after an event occurs we will attribute meaning to that event because we believe we understand the other events brought about by it. As *Randomness* occurs, as time unfolds and we understand more of the reality of the situation in which we find ourselves, then we allow the effects of what has occurred to be included into *The Planned Nature of Things.* Beyond all intellectual pursuits and problems, belief, in fact, seems to be the thing that most enables *Randomness* and our *Basic Human Frailty* and their effects to be assimilated into what is supposed to happen, or *The Planned Nature of Things.*

These things had been his latest ideas, he told me. Given to him, he believed, directly from the hand of God. These had been the things that he had attempted to say the day he stood on the apple and pear table at Earl's Fruit Stand after Lucky had, at Dr. Guppy's suggestion, gotten him a job there. The job he lost when he was forced from the table directly across from where Lucky shot craps and drank bootleg whiskey, and threatened with dire consequences, such as being put back in the crazy house. What he did not include, that Lucky would only tell me later, after Percy had in fact been sent there again, was that he had once again stripped down to his underwear to do his talking, something that he had obviously learned would bring people's attention quickly. The next time it had occurred after the Saturday on top of Mrs. Nedler's car, Lucky was going to have no more of it. In between his more formal speaking engagements, he had taken to smaller ones, the specifics of which I cannot name, during which people had begun to call Lucky and identify his actions. Lucky would pull out of the driveway in the Ford, not wanting to embarrass himself in the squad car.

"It's the same shit as always," Lucky told me when I tried to explain to him what Percy had told me. "What else can he say? You think he's gonna say that he's crazy?"

I didn't bother to tell Lucky that he well knew that.

"In '45 at least it was just one or two things," Lucky went on to say, staring out the front door, I was sure, wondering if he had done the right thing. "But now, not only is he talkin' all that crazy stuff about God all the time but he's runnin' around town naked. Do you know what he told me when I pulled his ass off that table that day? He said that he didn't enjoy bein' naked out in public any more than anybody else ... but that he felt like it was his mission. His suffering so that life could be better for other people. Ain't that somethin'? I wonder if he thought the same thing when he was fuckin' her? Was that makin' his life or her life, or everybody's life better?"

Of course, he did not say these things in front of Jean or my mother. Besides his cussing fits in the kitchen as he passed through headed toward the carport to get the Ford, he told them very little of what was occurring with Percy. Only that he was certain that it was going to come to no good end.

I, of course, could not answer the question he had asked. It was still hard for me to believe that he actually did what they said he did ... that Christine had admitted once her father pressed her hard enough. Nevertheless, as Lucky had not given me a chance to speak my piece as he began talking once more, I was certain that neither had I given one to Percy. I couldn't have told you what he had said in the last two and half months. I had been much too occupied with my own interests, with the seeming tragic ups and downs of my own existence. The only things I could in good conscience affirm were that he had started and lost a job at Earl's Fruit Stand, had been seen around town almost naked several times and had slept upstairs with me, as far as I could recall, every night. No more.

"That was the end for me," he told me after his two-week stint of a job had ended. "I know that Guppy told your father to get me a job there. I don't doubt that; I don't doubt that he did it with good intentions."

When Percy spoke these words to me, the days had almost reached the zenith of their length. Through the eastern window in front of which he often sat or stood when we talked, I could see only the orangeness that the sun produced at this time of day over his shoulder. He scratched his head and pushed his hair away from his eyes.

"I even went to almost a year of college. I bet your father never told you that, did he? As a matter of fact, he was mad as hell about it at the time. Do you know why? He was mad, I think, that Mother and Daddy were going to pay for it. The farm had done better and the hard times of the Depression were about over. I had even graduated high school. Your daddy didn't graduate high school, did you know that? So, naturally, when it was obvious that I had a chance to do better, he didn't like it. He was workin' at the mill then. Sellin' feed. Before Mr. Oscar Garrett came along. And here his brother was going into Peabody in Nashville to learn to be a teacher. He knew I might be able to do something that in its own small way might change the world a little … and it would be in a way that wasn't violent. But you know, it wasn't even a year into those classes that the goddam pig started comin' around. I'll have you know I'm not even saying his name these days. And then there was Hitler and Pearl Harbor and it was somehow like Dillard had filled them all in on what I intended to do. It's hard to believe when one of your own family members sells you out."

For a few moments, Percy stopped his rambling and sat on the end of the bed. Scoured his face with his hands once more and pushed his hair back again. Seemed in some odd way to be attempting to allow his words to catch up with him, so maybe he could begin to understand what he had said. He got up and made his way to the window, peered into the failing daylight. Smiled.

"He shouldn't have jerked me down off that table. I even told me as he came toward me that it was the last time I was goin' to speak. He said he knew it was. You know who comes down there a lot?" he asked me.

As I had been much of the time during the last couple of months, I had been only half-listening. Pretending to listen more than actually taking part in the activity itself.

"Huh?"

"Do you know who comes down there a lot?"

"Umh-uh," I shook my head.

He took one last look out the window and then produced two cigarettes from the pack in his sock. A book of matches. He handed me a cigarette then stretched to light it. Took a drag off his own.

"That Smithson girl," he said. "I guess her mother or her father must send her down there almost every day to get some fresh produce or something."

"Really?" I said.

"Yeah," he said. "It's funny how I've been livin' here off and on for nine years and I've never really talked to her. Her or her brother." "Yeah, they're kinda funny people," I said, beginning to return to my previous state of stray attention. Then it came to me what he had said, the span of time he had identified. As many things are when you're embroiled in and living them, they just pass like a river does in the night. Silent and seemingly without motion. Just cut through the space that is cleared, through the ground that has been moved by forces and power unseen to the eye and unknown to the soul. He had been living with us off and on for nine years. Each time he had made his way home, the powers that were, namely Lucky and his sisters, would decide that his parents needed to be protected from this, their crazed son. In turn, they longed for and missed him; that was just as plain. Each time we had been there over this span, unless it had been a time when he had once again tried to live with them, they asked about him, his welfare, and it seemed that Lucky hid from them what Percy had become. Crazy. The more Lucky misrepresented, the more questions they asked, until the game, I think, had became the way they related. From the front room of their farmhouse, as they sat on a couch, gray and dusty, as I remember it, they seemed content to play the game, and just as content with their knowledge it was being played. It seemed in some way to comfort them. Lucky, though, had not seemed to fare so well. The worse Percy had gotten, the more estranged Lucky became from the place from which he had come, until he seemed almost a stranger there, but a welcome stranger, to be told by their smiles. During the first stint Percy had done in Central State, the much longer of the two, they had not known he was there until almost three months into it when Lucky could misrepresent it no more. I am unsure of when they learned of the things that happened in 1953.

CHAPTER TWENTY-EIGHT

"WAKE UP! Wake up. You're dreamin'."
   I felt myself lowering into the down mattress from the force he exerted on my chest every time he spoke my name. The hands moved from my chest to my shoulders, in an attempt, I assume, to slow my rise as I sat up. The full moon lit the white-washed walls and thus the night as gray.

"You were dreamin'," he told me again.

"How the hell do you know what I was doin'?" I asked him.

His hair and face were wild, like somehow he might have been a stranger to who he was two weeks ago, when Lucky had pulled him off the fruit stand at Earl's. For a few seconds, I was scared that I had overslept, missed my route time. But rarely did 3 a.m. ever pass without me waking. It seemed as much a part of me now as breathing.

"'Cause I've been listenin' to ya. You were sayin' all kinds of wild things. You were talkin' about the wreck you and Tully had. You were beggin' your daddy not to hit you."

"I've never, ever begged him not to hit me," I proclaimed, like it was a badge of honor. Still more asleep than awake.

"Well, you were in the dream," he said. "That's all I can tell ya. You were goin' on about Sharon and Van. You said his name several times, then after you said it you'd say son of a bitch every time. I knew you and Van had some trouble this summer, but I hope it wasn't near that bad."

As I sat and stared at him, that feeling came over me that often does after just awaking from a dream: a sense of peace that the dream wasn't in fact reality. The sense that leaves you when you realize you may not have the problems you had in your dream, but that you still have the ones you had when you went to sleep the night before.

"It hasn't been great," I told him. "But what ever is?"

He nodded and smiled half-ass. Offered me a cigarette.

I took it and drew deep from the thing, hoping the first jolt of nicotine would knock me back into place. I switched on the light and took a look at the Mickey Mouse on the night stand.

"It's one-thirty," I told him. "Where've you been?"

"Sittin' here for quite a while," he said. He drew on the cigarette again and blew a bank of smoke toward the ceiling that dissipated as it exited the ring of light the lamp cast. "Watchin' you. This Sharon person must be somethin' else. Every time you'd talk about her, your voice would ease and this real peaceful smile came to your face, like you'd figured out you were in heaven or somethin'."

In the weeks that preceded his going to the crazy house again and what would come after that, there were moments when he seemed crazy as hell. And then there were other moments, when whatever took hold of him had relinquished itself, when his sanity had rolled in, like clouds that quiet the land before a storm.

"Yeah, maybe I was," I told him. I laughed.

"Is that the girl you been seein'?" he asked.

"Huh?" I said.

"Look," he said, "I might be crazy, but I ain't stupid. The stupidity was distributed among other members of my family." He rolled his eyes toward the downstairs.

"Yeah," I said finally. "It is. She's gorgeous. And sweet … as sweet as sugar."

He nodded. Smiled.

"How long you been seein' her?" he asked.

I'd marked the days in my head as clear as charcoal marks on the wall.

"Twelve days."

"Twelve days? I thought you went to a dance with her. Do you know how much I'd like to have gone to a dance with a girl? Everybody in high school, though, thought I was too odd to pal around with. Your daddy didn't finish high school, did you know that?"

"Yeah, that's what you said," I told him. I drew on the cigarette for a moment, anger flashing through my chest. Assuming everybody should know as much about it as I did, even though I hadn't breathed a word to anyone. "And I did go to a dance with her. She asked me … or at least asked me to ask her to her prom. That was after she had been out with Van. But he just didn't measure up. His dick was too small," I said, immediately reminding myself of him.

Percy laughed but didn't look at me. Crushed his cigarette out with yellow fingers in the ashtray my mother kept upstairs for him.

"Her father and sister died two weeks ago," I told him. "Didn't make a curve down south just before you get to the Alabama line. Lost the car. It threw her daddy from the damn thing and then rolled up a fuckin' hill and came down on her sister. Pretty much cut her head off. Goddam Lucky made me go tell her that it had happened. He was prob'ly too chicken shit to do so."

"You know, in my better moments … or worse ones, I'm not sure which … I like to be as hard on your father as possible. But I believe that happened the same day he ran me off the fruit stand. Wasn't that a Saturday?"

I thought back, tried to remember two weeks ago that now seemed like two months, two years … something. "Yeah, as a matter of fact, I think it was a Saturday. It was the first time that Van and I had spoke in a month. Tully had tricked us, got us together over at the Gilco. Then Lucky comes pullin' up and asks me to go see her Mama."

"Yeah, I think he'd just finished with me at Earl's. I think he had such hope for me at that job. Thought I'd own the fruit stand one day or somethin'."

"Yeah, he's like that," I said. "He thinks everybody'll rise to the place he did. I'll be the sheriff!" I proclaimed. The nicotine and the sudden awakening had gone to my head like booze did some time, made me errant and giddy.

"Police Chief," Percy corrected me. "Never get that wrong."

"Don't I know it," I told him. I turned the cigarette up and drew on it like a bottle. "Anyway, that's pretty much the day we got together." I stopped, hesitant to tell him the rest.

"That's too bad about her father," he said. "And her sister. Yeah, I'd heard about that. As a matter of fact, when I think back about it, one of the first things your father said to me was that he'd just gotten the call that two Franklin people had been killed just inside the state line. 'See what happens to some people's family,' he told me. 'Some people got life and death incidents goin' on, not crazy bullshit like losin' a job for givin' a speech from the top of a table.' I tried to tell him that they hadn't fired me yet. But in typical Dillard fashion, he wouldn't listen to anything but the sounds coming out of his own mouth."

He finished his cigarette and crushed it out in the ashtray, dug for his pack in his sock then remembered he had laid it on the nightstand. Handed me another, took another for himself.

"Lucky said you were naked," I said.

"I most certainly wasn't," he assured me. "I had on my skivvies. My shoes. And my socks. Completely naked would surely offend my listeners to such a degree that they would hear none of my message. No, the goal of any orator is to draw to and hold attention by surprising enough to do so but not offending enough to turn away. The one time I've done otherwise was in that lot over off Strahl Street. In the yard of that house Sammy Samuels owns. That was a day they called Dillard right away."

"Yeah, I remember hearin' about that one: that you were hollerin' about how some people thought that it was better to not rent a house than rent one to black people."

"Dillard told you all that?"

"No ... Van told Tully and he told me."

"Yeah, now that you say that, I can remember Van there, goadin' me on. That doesn't seem like somewhere you'd catch Van ... with the poor and black people."

"Do you remember the night we saw you when I was takin' Sharon home?" I asked.

He nodded.

"We were in front of her house. That's where she lives. And that's why Van was over there."

"But he was comin' out of the empty house that afternoon."

"Yeah, that house is right next to the Edwards' house."

"Is her brother the one who sells the whiskey … brings it up from Alabama?"

"The one and only," I told him.

"Van over there buyin' whiskey from him? Van's crazy enough. He doesn't need to drink."

Downstairs, I heard the backdoor shut and Lucky start the barrage of coughing that seemed to accompany his presence every morning and most nights now. I followed its sound to what I guessed was his final destination, the chair in the living room. I said, "And no, he wasn't there buyin' whiskey from Bobby Edwards." I could feel the truth choking up in my throat, threatening to loose itself to another human being. I had breathed it to no one. "No, he wasn't buyin' whiskey from Bobby Edwards," I said. I could feel my hands shaking. I tried to steady the one I brought to my mouth to draw on the cigarette he'd given me.

"He prob'ly had a woman in there," he said. "Or I guess a girl's what they're called at your age. It's hard to discern between the two sometimes. I bet that's who he had."

I wanted to bust Percy right in the mouth, like I'd done with Van that day in June, the first and only time we'd actually come to blows. And I guess it really hadn't been "we." The first time I'd seen him with Sharon, her sitting right by him in Scoot's car as they tooled down Columbia Pike and then through town on Main Street. I'd passed them going the other way then wheeled the Indian around, flagged them down and then just knocked the shit out of him when he stepped out of the car. Bloodied his nose. After he'd pulled himself up off one knee and Sharon was wailing and yelling at me, he simply pulled his handkerchief out and covered his nose with it and shook his head. Like I had been the fucking villain.

"He had Sharon in there," I said. "Aren't you listenin' to me?"

Percy nodded. "I'm tryin'," he told me.

"He had Sharon in there because I had no more than gotten to where I thought I couldn't live without her and the son of a bitch took her from me." I could feel the tears pushing at the back of my eyes. "I made the mistake of tellin' him how I felt about her. I mean, I can't tell you, Percy, how just bein' around her took me over. Worse than moonshine. When I was away from her, all I wanted to do was be with her again. And he knew that. The bastard knew that."

Even though my brain sent the order to stop, my mouth was an unruly subject. It felt so good, like a good washing when too long dirty, for anyone to hear the words, even Percy. Crazy Percy.

"He knew that and he started workin' on takin' her from me from the night he saw us together at the dance. He couldn't stand it that she liked me better than him!"

"I thought you said he went out with her first," said Percy, who for that moment looked crazier than he ever had to me. And stupider.

"I did say that. But he only went out with her once … he didn't even know her. "

"Maybe he didn't know how much you liked her."

"Didn't you hear me awhile ago? I told you that I had talked to him about it! He's just a goddam asshole. And you know, when you've tried to talk to me about things that matter to you, I've tried to listen. When you've gone over and over and over the same shit, I've tried my best to listen to what you were sayin' even if it didn't interest me one damn bit."

"You've slept through a lot of it, too."

"And I've never tried to tell you what a good guy Lucky was when you were complainin' to me about him. And believe me, you've complained a hell of a lot over the last nine or so years. I can't tell you how many nights I've listened to you complain about him!"

Percy put his finger to his mouth, reminding me that I was likely to draw someone upstairs and that someone would likely be Lucky and Lucky would likely be pretty damned unhappy.

"All I'm sayin,'" he said after another trip to the window, "is that Van's not all bad and I'm not sure that he'd do something so it would hurt you. Maybe inadvertently he might do something that did hurt you but I think that was probably a side-effect of another goal, not his identified goal, so to speak."

"I wish you'd speak English sometime." I scowled at him, reminding myself of Lucky.

"All I'm saying is that people are much more likely to do things out of their own weakness or *Basic Human Frailty* than they are just to hurt you. I can even say that I think that's true of Lucky, as you call him. None of us have pure motives, purely good or purely bad. We all, though, have self-interest and go about trying to carry that out in all kind of strange ways, which hurts other people sometimes."

As he took a seat on the corner of the bed again and I stared at him insolently, I weighed his words for only a moment. I quickly decided that this was in no way true about Van … and that he was a son of a bitch, like I'd been calling him in the dream I couldn't remember. What I would say next would prove it to be true and release from my gut what had been burning there all summer. Like most of the best and worst things in life, it could not be altered, but only spoken of.

My voice shook and tears fell from the corners of my eyes, in anger not grief I wanted to believe. "He was fuckin' her. That's what he was doing in that goddam house you were talkin' your shit outside of. He was in there fuckin' the daylights out of her. And do you know why he was fuckin' her? He was fuckin' her for four reasons … and I've thought about this. Because she and her sister wouldn't do anything but barely kiss us when we'd gone out with them before…because she was a virgin. And because I'd told him that I thought she and I were gonna do it soon. But most of all, for the first time in our lives it was something I had that he didn't."

"Besides football," said Percy. "Or at least bein' as good as you are."

"Yeah, I guess so. Besides that."

As he sat listening to me, as I had so often been when he shared his words late at night, he seemed only half-listening and perhaps as we often are, lost in his own world. His eyes moved around the room several times, to the window; he even removed himself again and peered outside once more. Of course, this was before I knew the power had overtaken him, too. The power of finding solace in another human being, who at least for awhile, makes everything, the victories and defeats, the tragedies and good fortune, disappear as if they had never been in the first place. Renders them powerless.

"All I know," he said, "is you seemed awful mad at him."

"I was," I told him. "But the son of a bitch still lives across the street. I still have to see his cocky ass when I come back from my paper route in the morning, stretching in his pajamas, looking out the window at me. I still have to see him at school … or I will when it starts back up. And this week, I'll see him at football practice."

"Does that start this week?"

"Yep," I told him. "First week in August. The games don't start till September, but Lucky won't be able to wait and he'll be there watchin' the practices from his squad car, chain' smokin' and catching swigs from the bottle when he thinks nobody's lookin'."

"He does love your football."

"Yeah, a lot more than I do."

"It's your senior year in high school. You're supposed to enjoy it. You've got everything in front of you. Life by the tail. You might as well enjoy it."

"Since when did you become so optimistic?"

"I told you recently, I'm plannin' on livin' my life now."

"I am lookin' forward to gettin' through this year," I told him. "I think that Sharon and I might get married. At least that's what we're talkin' about. She says that she had known what she wanted even before the wreck happened. Known it from the end of June when she and Van went their separate ways … when the bastard had gotten what he wanted and decided to move on to get it from somebody else."

As I talked on, Percy said nothing. Only lit cigarettes and drew on them and nodded his head up and down, listening to me now like I had listened to him for all the years. Giving me his undivided attention except when he looked out the window till I had to get ready to go on my route and he disappeared in front of me out the back door and into the darkness of the still morning.

"So what if I did do it?" he scowled at me across the room. "Lucky—I think I will start calling him that out of disrespect—thinks he knows everything about the law. He acted like it was a crime if I had a relationship with the girl next door. There's a reason they say, 'the girl next door.' It's synonymous with something good ... not something bad. It's not even against the law, that is, if it's consensual. She's sixteen. He says it's eighteen, but that makes no sense. He married your mother when she was seventeen. Made her parents madder than hell. Did you know that? Married into what money they had ... and kissed Mr. Oscar Garrett's ass. That's what he's been good at doing. That and talking about work and how far it gets you and then drinking and playing craps on the job. He's never wanted in his whole life for me to be happy. This is just another symptom of that. Ever since Inez drowned in the goddamned Harpeth River, he's always tried to make it look like things were more my fault than they were. If he cared about my happiness, he certainly wouldn't send me to a place like this!"

This time he would stay a little more than a week, not forced to take up residence like the last time. Medical technology was better now, Lucky had assured me. There might be another way besides electricity, Guppy had told him.

As to whether it was a crime or not, Percy had believed it the night Lucky had enlisted me to help him force him into the car, and so had I. The belief, true or false, had served as the leverage it took for it to happen. The rest, in the parking lot and the lobby of Central State, came off because of the weight bestowed upon the matter by Lucky's badge. What the law was, I still could not tell you.

"I think she's goddam fifteen," Lucky told me on the way home. "The man's in his thirties." Even in the darkness of the car, I could tell his eyes were bloodshot from the whiskey he had ingested earlier that evening to carry out what he thought he had to. "Doyouknow—howoldheis?" His words pushed together from the slur that had developed. Rarely did I see Lucky's tolerance allow his body to show its drunkenness.

"Isn't he thirty-six or seven?" I said. I couldn't remember him ever having a birthday … or at least him celebrating one.

"Idontknow."

During the two times I visited Percy during his second stint in Central State, I did not remember to ask him. The visits, I am ashamed to say, were short because Sharon could not be with me.

As for his girlfriend, she had been an outcast, too. They were just different kinds of outcasts, he explained. Where Lucky had been afraid he might hurt or disturb his mother and father and thus removed him, Christine Smithson had been held a prisoner in her own house. Her brother Todd had not been treated so badly because he was a boy. She, though, had been allowed only to go to school and back. Her family really kept everything among themselves. Hadn't I ever noticed? he asked.

"No, I've always been too busy tryin' to keep Lucky from beatin' my ass," I had answered.

"For eight years?"

"Yes, for eight years." That and the fact that my own life captivated me enough that I believed that it was the worst life you can have. Crazy uncle. Mean as hell father. Shitty sister. A mother who turned her back on almost everything. Van trying to fuck me all the time. Having to work since I was eight turning nine. Hell, no, I haven't noticed. I didn't say these things; neither did I speak the fact that I was certain anger and self-pity had taken much of my attention also. Either then or years later when I came to know it as truly as anything that ever happened to me.

It had started innocently enough, he explained to me. He was there a lot. So was she. I had my own life, was out and gone most of the time. Had had all the mess with Van and Sharon … and ever since that day Lucky had kicked me in the ass going up Adams Street when he found out about the

night before, I'd been like a different kid. And Lucky, whether you've noticed it or not, hasn't been himself. You notice, I'm still calling him Lucky.
But he hasn't been right either.

I had to remind him across the dimly lit room of where he had begun.
Sharon, her piece of ass, was waiting. I cringed, reminding myself of Van.

"Anyway, you and Lucky, not Dillard but Lucky, have your lives. And
your mother, Sweet Mary, sweeter than any woman in the world to put up
with my brother, has her work and seems utterly involved in it most of the
time. She would listen to me, but her heart seemed as burdened as my own
most of the time. Then ... then there was Jean. Well, whatever she does,
she was doing it. And the streets and the cemeteries and the river eventually
get as lonesome as I imagine hell is. And it gets lonesome, people thinking
you're crazy. So, sometimes I'd just go out in the backyard and sit under
that big elm out there and smoke a few cigarettes and stare at the sky and
try to remind myself that life wasn't that lonely. And then I'd come back in
and lie on the bed and Lucky's voice would echo through my head and I'd
think that I should go get a job and I wouldn't be so lonely. Then I'd go
back out in the yard and more ways than one, be right back where I started.
Lonesome and alone.

"I swear, the first time I ever talked to her, she told me that she was a
junior in high school, and then later a sophomore. Then she told me she
was a freshman. I swear, I didn't know she was fourteen going on fifteen.
You can't ever tell your father ... Lucky this, but if I'd known that she was
that age I'd have never gotten near her. I'm still not sure we have the truth.
Anyway, she'd wave at me and smile when she was coming in from school.
And it would do my heart good. Make me not feel so bad for a little while.
She smiled and waved like she was lonesome, too.

"You know, it's funny how you can live by somebody that long and
never really even take a close look at them. Never really look in their eyes.
Years ago, so long ago that I can't tell you how long ago it's been, I'd see her
looking out the window like she was trapped in that house, longing to get
out. She wears her mother's old dresses but she's not a pound overweight.
Did you know that?"

I assured him that I'd never thought about it. Also reminded him that maybe she was trapped in the house because she was so young.

He immediately identified that neither Jean nor I had ever been treated that way.

True, I said, but we had just suffered different maladies.

"Well, she wasn't … isn't … she's not dead … have you seen her? She isn't overweight at all. I really thought she would have called by now … or come see me. I wanted to know how that would happen since she wasn't old enough to drive a car." He said he thought maybe her brother, Todd, would drive her down. Todd liked him too, he assured me. He had come out and sat behind the shed with them a few days, smoked cigarettes he'd given him. And, he added, he didn't feel one bit bad giving Christine cigarettes, because she could buy them, as well as beer, at Chester's Grocery. But he and Christy, that's what she wanted him to call her, had sat out there every day for going on six weeks. Sometimes he thought he might die from Friday evening to Monday morning when he couldn't see her, that was, if her parents didn't go somewhere and she couldn't sneak out behind the shed.

"And we were fine till one day Old Man Smithson came out looking for something. I could hear somebody rustling around in the shed, and kept trying to tell her I heard somebody and she kept telling me that she didn't hear anything. She was smiling when she said it. You know, when she'd smile it was like her blue eyes picked up the glimmer of whatever light was around and danced. Anyway, she just kept sayin' over and over that she didn't hear anybody. And then the noise just stopped. She said it was probably just the cat.

"Well, the cat didn't come back for another few days and she started tellin' me that nobody was gonna find us and that it was like our own private little place. And I guess I kind of believed her. Or at least I wanted to. You know how it is back there: the back of that old shed just pretty much runs up against the back of Lucky's carport and then there's that great mangled growth of bushes and trees between them. On the other side, you know there's that thicket of blackberry and dogwood bushes. It felt like nobody in the world could see us. That somehow we'd fallen off into a world that was all our own.

"All I can tell you is that was the best two weeks of my life. Man, did we live in it. For those days I began to realize what it was that normal people, if there is such a thing, do with their lives. I'd never thought I'd have that opportunity. Even Walter couldn't take it away from me. When he was there, he'd just sit over there in the shadows and act like he couldn't speak. In here, they're tellin' me that he's a delusion or a hallucination. But I think they need to check their dictionaries, because I don't think either of those terms encompass the power the heartless—no, I shouldn't call him that— the plain bastard has. At least, for the first time, he cut me some slack. For the first time, it seemed more important to live things than think about them. For the time I had with her, I let myself settle into nothing but being. Pure Being."

"Pure Fucking," Lucky told me when I was at home that night, trying to explain to him for the last time what Percy had tried to tell me.

"So, you think he was just fuckin' her to fuck her, then?" I said.

"'Fuckin' her to fuck her?'" he said. "What the hell's that s'posed to mean?"

I wasn't sure if it was Lucky or the bottle talking. Most likely the latter, I concluded, since he had been on it heavier than usual ever since we'd had to drag Percy through the yard and lock him in the back of the squad car and then drag him across the parking lot at Central State.

"It means," I said, "that I think maybe he just wanted somebody to love him. Just like all the rest of us." It had sounded just like something Percy would say. Possibly had said. And I found myself wanting to argue with Lucky.

He was probably too drunk to get up, I knew, like many times before, but he was also different. Something had given, a leak had sprung inside him. He wasn't so sure he was right anymore. He simply stared at me for a long moment and then fumbled with his cigarettes until he finally lit one. He inhaled and held the breath a long time, then watched as it rose to the ceiling and disappeared into the darkened stain made by years of doing the same.

CHAPTER TWENTY-NINE

THE AIR WAS COLD ENOUGH to bite by the time Lucky and I came home from our meeting with the Beattys, Dr. Guppy, and George Preston. And, as it is prone every once in awhile to do, the snow had made its way directly through middle Tennessee, covering us in a three-inch blanket. Against Lucky's suggestion, I had taken the Indian anyway, knowing the car was much more likely to be seen when I went to meet Sharon. By the time I left home for the paper office, the snow itself had stopped and the world had become its quietest. Down Cleburne and Adams, there was only a single line of tire tracks, where one car had been out after the street had been covered. Much the same as Rosa Mary Dean's murder had shut down Franklin, the snow always did the same. As Lucky had said the night before, from Nashville to Franklin to any other town nearby, no one really had the implements or resources to fight it. I imagined that Lucky would be cursing upon his arising from bed, knowing that along with the information he had come by the night before, he would also have the dozen wrecks around town as people tried to make it through the mess.

When I left the paper office, without a word between me and Raymond Collins, I might add, it had begun again: huge, white, soft flakes that flew rather than fell, skidded to a stop rather than landed. Throwing my first papers down South Margin, I recognized what I did every time it snowed: if you hit a sidewalk just right, the paper would slide on top of the snow with hardly any evidence of having crossed there. The first real marks it would actually make would be when it came in contact with the first step and became airborne. Then, and only then, it would sail into the air three or four feet, then onto the porch and leave a final mark through the dusting of snow that blew in under the front porch roof. I always wondered if anyone noticed the paper's path or the fact that there were almost no marks along the sidewalk. It often reminded me of skipping a rock, which Lucky had taught me to do when I was a small boy.

As many memories tend to do, this one had announced its presence there for the first time in years. For just a moment, it's like your mind is a movie screen and across it comes a part of your life only vaguely seen before. Like some of the images that had passed in front of Van and Tully and me as we sat in the dark, cool theater on Main Street.

An hour into my route, the snow had begun to let up and masquerade as freezing rain, throwing itself from the heavens almost sideways and pelting me in the back and face. I cursed myself as I drove, for not having taken Lucky up on his offer. Hollered loud enough that I was sure that some of the families to whom I threw papers would hear me, like a mad, frothing dog howling at the hint of a moon that had left itself showing behind the rolling silver clouds. I cursed Lucky. I cursed myself for having left the house that morning in my leather jacket, afraid for anybody to see me in the rain suit and galoshes I should have been wearing. By the time I knocked on her window, I was shaking so hard I couldn't clench my teeth hard enough to keep them from chattering.

"Get in, silly," she said as she pushed the door open.

I laughed in the face of my pain, knowing that anything she said to me would be like salve on some chronic wound. I sat down, peeled my coat off and slung it in the back seat.

"Too cool to wear your poncho?" she said, a word I'd heard only when she called it that.

"Style over comfort," I said.

She laughed where she'd barely part her lips, showing her white teeth between the lipstick, tilted her head back. Sighed at the end, like for some reason I imagined her father had.

I pulled the rearview mirror toward me and checked myself, sure I looked like a drowned rat. Ran my fingers through my hair after I pulled my cap off.

"You're as cute as ever," she said.

"I figured," I told her. Laughed like she had, amazed at how quick we pick things up.

Thankfully, under the leather coat, most of the weather hadn't penetrated. I touched my shirt, only damp from the moisture that filled the air everywhere. But there was no rescuing my pants. Their rolled cuffs, ever-popular in the day, had even wilted like a dying flower and gathered themselves around the ankles of my boots.

"You can put them on the floorboard and let the heat dry them out," she said.

"There isn't any heat in this car," I told her.

"Bobby fixed it yesterday. He'd stopped by for a little bit after I'd come in from school to see how everybody was. I told him that I'd been cold in the mornin' ... not you."

"Good," I told her. "Because I'm tough enough I could make it."

"Yeah ... you look tough enough ... shakin' there like a leaf." She pulled the mirror back her way, checked herself. Smiled, at her own beauty, I imagined. "Did your cigarettes keep dry? I hope you didn't let them get soaked."

"They're somewhere inside my jacket," I told her, still contemplating whether or not to take off my pants. I did so before I searched my jacket for the half pack of cigarettes I had left. I tried to remember the last time she had smoked with me, had asked for a cigarette. To the best of my recollection, it had been when we found that goddam woman ... no, now she had a name ... Rosa Mary Dean. Maybe the next day. I knocked one out of the pack, damp enough I feared it might not light. Snapped a flame out of a match, lit it for her. Did the same to one for me. I handed her my pants, which she laid on the heater vent that had eluded me all the early winter.

"You remember when you always used to tell me that the reason that you hung on through high school was because of football?" she said.

"Yeah, I remember sayin' somethin' like that," I told her. "I guess that and so I won't have to end up throwin' papers the rest of my life."

She nodded. I watched the rain slog down outside, begin to wash away the snow that had collected overnight. Knock the whiteness off the hood of her car. I could feel the heat making its way to my bare legs. Wished they were not as white and skinny … that I could get them to quit shaking.

"You think you all'll have to go to school today?" she asked.

"Yes, the goddam Academy always goes," I told her. "I'm surprised they let us out the day Rosa Dean was killed."

"Who?" she said.

I realized that I hadn't told her about our night previous. That note that I couldn't get out of my head, that had haunted me almost as much as seeing her body had.

"That woman," I told her. "That's her name. We met with these people—"

"The woman we saw?"

"Yeah, her. Lucky and me met with these people last night that ID'd her. It was that man that they'd found his name on her … in the paper. You remember."

"Lucky and I," she told me. "And I do remember."

"You think you'll be out today?"

"Who knows," she said. "I guess we ought to turn on the radio."

The station she switched on was WAGG, Franklin's oldest and now only radio station. There had been another one make a run at it a few years before, but now had faded so far from memory that its call letters were no longer present to me. For the most part, WAGG played the same kind of music that WSM did out of Nashville. The popular country music of the day. Had local and national news, the former every fifteen minutes, the latter on the hour. Since Hank Williams had died, it seemed like every other song was one of his. It was hard for me to hear his voice without imagining Lucky singing along with him, the only time I'd ever heard him sing.

"Good ole WAGG." I tried to pull cool on the cigarette, look as little like George Preston as possible.

She broke her wrist back and drew on hers the way girls and he did. I watched her eyes as she stared at the dashboard dial for the radio, a home-made job I was sure, one of Bobby's creations. Probably hot. The brown flecks danced against the green background of her irises as the rain broke the daylight just coming.

"Good old WAGG," she repeated. She drew in a sigh long and hard, then blew it out with the smoke she had harbored.

"What's wrong?" I asked her.

She laughed a little. Showed her teeth between her painted lips again. "Turning the radio on WAGG made me think of the other day … on that show. You've heard that show, Trade Time?"

"Yeah, I've heard it. Percy thought they were sendin' out signals to get him right around the end of World War II," I laughed. It was the first time I could remember speaking of him spontaneously, without weighing out whether or not to say it … whether the memory was worth the feeling connected to it. "Well, what I heard on there the other day … when I was listening … was that someone … I can't even remember who … was trying to sell a trailer. You know, a small house trailer that you could actually pull behind a car."

"You mean a pile a' tin on wheels," I said.

"Some of them are pretty nice. Anyway, that's not my point." She crushed her cigarette out in the ashtray. "My point is that the man who was selling it must not have needed the money right away, because he was willing to do what they called 'owner financing.' He said somebody could get it for twenty-five dollars a month."

"Probably for ten years," I told her. "Then you'd end up with a three thousand dollar pile a' tin on wheels." I remembered how Lucky had always bragged that he paid eighteen hundred dollars for the house we lived in; had watched the builders so close he'd driven one set of them off before the place was finished. I also remembered that he was sure no one worth continuing to live lived in a goddam house trailer, or a "mobile home" as I had heard them called. "If he needed the money right away, as you say, then wouldn't he be not so likely to finance it? Wouldn't he want all of his money up front?"

My questions brought a silence to her that I couldn't stand. Tore at my guts like her physical body might leave next, go wherever her soul was visiting.

"Wouldn't that make sense to you?"

She shrugged. By this point, I was learning rapidly what I perceived as facts no longer made a difference. The crux of the situation had become the way the facts were presented. I reached to kiss her. She pulled her face away, turned her eyes out the driver's side window, water flowing so heavily down it the view took on a milky blur.

"Wouldn't it? I didn't mean to hurt your feelin's."

Her eyes cut through me, holding grief and joy together. "I just thought it sounded good. If a person had something like that, they could go any-where … live anywhere."

"That's true," I told her. I knocked out another cigarette and tried to act like I'd forgotten I thought it was a stupid idea.

"I know it is," she said. She nuzzled her head into my shoulder, careful not to mess up her hair.

"Have you got to work today?" I asked her. In the background, WAGG had started going through a list of the closed schools in the area, hers being one of them.

"I guess," she said. "I knew we wouldn't go to school though."

"You're dressed for work, though. If you thought you wouldn't go to school, then why'd you already get dressed for work?"

"I can always go in and get more hours at work. We can always use the money and they usually find something for me to do."

That goddam Mr. Smith, I thought, but didn't say it.

As had often been the case, silence and simply allowing our bodies to blend into one another took us. Me, in the passenger seat, without a car except the one my father would loan me and then kick my ass for using, and her, with one, because her father had met his death in her uncle's and no longer had use for the jalopy he drove when he was alive. It arose in me again, that I was certain that Mr. Smith wanted to fuck her … like Van had....

"We're doin' it twice a day," I heard him say, that smirk written across his face like a fancy signature. "I think she might be the best piece of ass I've ever had. I'll let you have her back after I get through. Now, you know I wouldn't have fooled with her a bit if I'd thought you had wanted to keep goin' with her. I just thought you went to the dance because she wanted you to go."

I could feel my body stiffen then soften as the surges of anger flowed through me like lightning across a darkening sky. As it usually was, a part of me simply wanted to melt into her arms, move so deeply and so closely to her that there was no more me and no more her, only us.

She moved her hands through my close-cropped hair and sighed again. "Wouldn't it be nice to leave everything here behind? I mean, can you even imagine for a minute doing that?"

For a few moments I tried to imagine no more Lucky, no more Jean, no more Mama. What it'd be like to call them once a week, filling them in on what was happening.

"It just seems like to me that you can leave things that surround you. I mean, I've always heard that you can't really leave your troubles behind, that they follow you. But I'm just not so sure of that. Sometimes … I know I've said this before … after what happened with Daddy and Sheila … I just feel like if I could get somewhere else, it might help me forget it. And even if that went with me, I don't believe that Mama or Bobby would. I guess I worry about what would happen with Suzy … but then I think that maybe if I wasn't around it might make Mama where she might take care of Suzy and maybe she'd know that she had to go on. I think right now I almost make it where she doesn't have to."

I watched as the rain continued to throw itself without reservation at the windshield and then collapse and roll down and away. In the time that it had fallen, it had washed away completely the snow that had found a temporary home overnight. Even from the distance we sat from the river, I could tell that it was beginning to rise, swell out of its usual containments. Just over the bank's first good fall, I could see hints of the water starting to gather itself together. The last time I could remember being here was that weekend. I could recall sitting near the same place with Sharon, talking about how everything had happened that night, unable to even lift my goddam arm, shielded by the lack of knowledge of what had occurred. Time had yet to bear it out.

"Why Van?" I asked out of nowhere. Surprised myself.

Her, too, by her reaction. She jumped almost like I had pinched her. "What?"

I decided fairly quickly that it would be too hard to steer away from what I'd said. I could be stubborn and obstinate and even vengeful as hell, but I wasn't worth a damn as a liar. I knew that.

"Why'd you fuck Van?" I said. I had given her hell for it for months. I would ride her about it as long as I could, until she would get mad and quit taking my shit.

Now she watched the rain as it fell softer on the windshield. Her eyes didn't leave the drops as they flattened and then rolled their way to the drain at the base of the hood, the metal unpainted and rusted at its edges. She withdrew her head from my shoulder and rubbed her face and eyes hard enough to smear her mascara. She took in the breath for another sigh, shorter and more shallow this time. The first few times I'd brought it up, she'd sworn she didn't, but then admitted it to me later. He'd told me, or told Tully who'd told me, that he'd fucked her almost everywhere in Franklin. At the Willow Plunge, in the dressing room, at the picture show in the balcony when there was nobody else around. In that old, abandoned house, in the car in the driveway of her house, because her mother was so out of it and her daddy so old they'd never notice. In the parking lot of her work after she got off. There had been more than one night I had lain awake in bed, especially when Percy was absent at Central State, thinking of how I might go about doing him in. Poison. Tampering with the brakes on Scoot's car. Stealing Lucky's gun one night after he fell asleep and sneaking in the upstairs window and shooting him right between the eyes. But I knew I'd never get away with it … and that I hated myself enough already.

"Why does anybody do anything?" she said.

I didn't think the response deserved an answer. I didn't give her one.

"Because he wanted to, I guess. I made him use something … you know, so we—"

"That makes it a hell of a lot better. Didn't you realize he was my best friend?" I asked. I laid my hands on the dash so they'd steady. My legs had finally warmed enough that they'd stopped shaking.

"I thought he loved me. He said he did."

I turned my eyes to her. She looked somehow loosened, her head hanging from her neck almost resting on her small breasts. It seemed in this moment that everything had flattened about her. Her hair, her smile, her posture. She slumped like I'd seen Tully do when he got drunk enough to forget he was a badass.

"And you believed him?"

"Yeah," she sighed.

I laughed, a sound I partly hoped would be like a knife in her belly. "Wrong guy to believe," I said, making out in my own mind that I was miles above him. Years later, I would realize our sins were just a different brand. Same product.

"He seemed sweet enough in the beginning. No, as a matter of fact, he seemed really sweet."

"Fuckin' asshole," I said. "He's sweet to himself. That's really all."

"You know," she said, "you can say about him what you want. He really does love you."

"He's got a hell of a way to show it," I retorted. The impulse came to tell her that she was no better, like I'd done many times before. Each time, she endured the tongue lashing, the dragging through events past, because she hoped, probably against hope, that I would indulge myself in it so fully that I would have no desire for it ever again. The impulse also passed through me to place the back of my hand across her nose and mouth for defending his stupid, arrogant ass. I'd been close one of the former times we talked about it, had my hand wrapped up in a sweater she'd had on, the other drawn back. And she'd told me to go ahead, do it. That she deserved it. I'd let her go and dropped my other hand, then sworn I'd give her the money to have the buttons I'd torn off fixed. I never did. She told me I did enough for her when I tried.

Once again, it seemed as if we'd run out of words. Her head resting at least partially at the top of her seat and myself, still sitting half naked in the middle of the goddam front-seat bench, we stared out the windshield together. The rain fell in opaque sheets now, covering the windshield with its thick invisibility.

"Didn't you see he preys on people like you … girls like you?"

"Like who? Girls like who?"

I never knew the right word … or words. Girls who never had. Virgins. I always hated that word, for some reason. Possibly because it would have been what I was called if I hadn't always lied good enough to cover it up.

I turned to my right, peered out the window in the direction south of the rising daylight, where the river was closest to us. Close to the spot I always imagined. Close to the road. Oh yeah, as a matter of fact, there it is. I think I'll go in. I wondered if that's what he'd said, or even thought. Back over my left shoulder, she was drawing some design on the windshield with her fingertip. She took the moisture from its end and put it on my neck, cold and wet.

"Like who?" she said again.

I could feel my body starting to change. Soften, harden. Made me mad all over again.

"Girls that hadn't ever been fucked," I blurted out, truly crude.

She didn't take the hand away from my neck that she'd placed there. She nodded her head up and down, gave a kind of wry smile I saw out of the corner of my eye. I'd always found it impossible to look at her when we talked about something like this.

"Is that what he told you?" she said. Then she laughed. Not a fake laugh, but neither one from the belly. Somewhere from in between, perhaps where irony takes its rise, has its power.

"Yeah," I said. "That's what the son of a bitch told me ... oh ... probably two or three weeks after I came down there to see you and we went out to the park on the motorcycle. He said that he'd ... well ... I don't know any better word for it ... I'm sorry ... that he'd fucked you the night before in your driveway. I remember it plain because he said that your father had come to the window and looked out and then turned off the light and that he had inched Scoot's car close up behind your daddy's ... I guess, this one ... and that you all had ... in the front seat. Isn't that the truth? I mean, I guess if that wasn't true, maybe he was lyin' about all the other times, too."

I couldn't believe of all the times we'd gone over and over this information like directions for a bad trip, we had never discussed the specifics. Perhaps I'd never been able to push the emotions aside long enough to talk about the facts underlying them.

"No," she said, "he's telling the truth."

"About the first time ... or the rest?" I asked.

"Probably all of them," she said. "I mean, I didn't keep a log or anything. But we ... you know."

"Yeah, I know," I told her, still a bit confused.

"I don't know whether to tell you this or not," she said. "But I guess I will. If somebody doesn't know the truth about you ... I guess ... then what good is it for them to know anything about you?" She began once again to draw whatever design she had on the condensation on the inside of the windshield. She traced the same lines she had outlined a few moments before.

I waited, not having much if any idea about the information getting ready to come my way. Whether it would comfort me or kick me in the ass. Give me a reason to get up tomorrow, or stay in bed and pull the fucking cover over my head. I felt like I'd had enough of the latter.

"I don't know if I'm followin' ya," I finally told her.

She didn't comment on my admission. Only stared through the rain at the same rising water I was, drawing whatever the hell the shape was on the windshield, over and over and over. "Van is a liar," she said, matter of factly.

As she withdrew her hand from the windshield, I noticed that the shape she'd been tracing resembled a crude heart. I couldn't say for sure, though.

"Or maybe I lied to him. I really couldn't tell you. I don't think I told him he was the first. I think he just wanted to believe it. All I can tell you is that he's not the first. I wonder if it's as much a lie if you don't tell somebody different when they assume something...."

The smile that I tried to hold back soon turned itself to laughter. She looked at me, startled, I think, that I, like the dozen times before, wasn't mad. At first I tried to keep the laughter from breaking into sound. But then I allowed it to take on a life of its own, making my chest rise and fall, my stomach belch the sounds out my mouth involuntarily.

"What?" she said.

I didn't answer her quickly when I quit laughing. First it went through my head just how damn strange life is. How every situation as it changes is both better and worse than it was previously, time seeming to flush out the opposite of what's initially apparent.

"What?" she said again.

"I don't mean this to sound bad," I told her, letting my eyes drift to her finger-painting on the windshield again, now mostly distorted by new condensation, "but it's just not very often ... never has been very often that I get one up on him. A' course, I wouldn't ever tell him ... or maybe I might if you didn't care—"

"It's not something that I want floating around," she said. "I think most people would think badly of me."

"I'm not sure they would," I tried to convince her.

She reached and searched my pocket for another cigarette. This time, her hands were shaking like my legs had been a few minutes before. I reached and felt for my pants in the floor. Almost dry. She knocked the cigarette from my pack and then got me one. She handed me the book of matches and waited for me to light hers, which I did. She looked ten years older than she had few moments before. Her face. Its hardness. Something.

"I know … they would. It's not something you know much of anything about. I know you don't think you've got it made," she said, drawing on the cigarette, for the first time reminding me of someone who might be a waitress, a barmaid, "but you don't have to always worry about the way somebody looks at you. I know you may have problems with Lucky, as you call him, and you think a lot of people in this town might not like him, but everybody still looks at you as his son … the Police Chief's son … and him as the Police Chief."

I wanted to tell her to put this new person away. Run her off back where she came from. The Sharon I knew was young and innocent, full of smiles and strangely correct English. She was soft and open and believing. Not this narrow-eyed person who had now gotten in the car without my knowledge and spoke in a voice like she smoked constantly as a cigarette danced on her lips. Nevertheless, as soon as this look had come and overtaken her countenance, another replaced it: her eyes draped with the weight of sadness pulling at their corners.

"He was really just like most every boy I've ever been out with," she said. "He wanted what he wanted and he was willing to tell you what you wanted to hear to get it." She tried to draw the tears back into the corners of her eyes, to keep them from further damaging the mascara, its running remnants. She caught them with the end of her index finger, wiped them on her skirt. "I'm sorry. Just thinking back through it makes me sad. There's been so many … all of them in their own way like him. Knowing that they've got somethin' on you. Knowin' that they've seen where you live. I live in the "Mixed Section," did you know that?"

Of course I did.

"I live in the section of town where the darkies live … the coons … the niggers. The only white people who live there are the people who can't live anywhere else. You know if this goddam town had its way, they'd get rid of all of us, the poor white people and the colored. I'll guarantee you when they figure out who killed that woman, it'll be somebody from our section of town. It might not be one of the Mosbys, but it'll be somebody that lived over there. You saw the article that came out after they found her—not the one about your father—the one that said how they need to get rid of the element that caused this whole thing. Well, I'll tell ya this, they don't have to try to very hard to get rid of me. I'm ready to leave them … Mama … Bobby … Daddy and Sheila's ghosts all behind. You know, I will say one thing for Van, at least he didn't fuck me after Sheila died. At least he didn't use that so he could have gotten more of what he wanted!"

In the moments following her raw exultation, I found myself assuring her that whatever she experienced she would not experience the same in kind with me. I wasn't like all the others, I explained to her, but somehow different, I believed. There would be no fucking and leaving with me … only fucking. And what the hell if Lucky didn't like trailers? He didn't like a lot of things. And about the other boys, it really didn't make a difference. What was the difference between ten, twelve, etc.? I wasn't going to ask. The whole thing had calmed me for some reason. Somehow made me her salvation rather than just another stop along the way. Just another fuck. If I had anything, had ever had anything besides the football career that had left me on that previous September night, it had always been perseverance. I could stay the course better than anybody I knew.

CHAPTER THIRTY

L UCKY STOOD AT THE KITCHEN WINDOW, his hands propped on the edge of the sink and his back slightly hunched, watching the rain continue to wash away every memory of the fallen snow. He sipped at a cup of coffee, never breaking his gaze on the Smithson's house and backyard. My own eyes wandered from his image to the edge of the carport where the bushes at the back of their yard started. I thought about how Christine Smithson had been sent away to live with her aunt shortly after she had admitted to her misdeeds with Percy. How it had afforded her the opportunity to miss that last weekend in September, those strangest of days. I wondered if she even knew, and if she did, what she knew. If she even had contact with her family. The times I had seen Old Man Smithson, he had simply been wandering the backyard, like he was perhaps still looking for evidence of what they had done or someone else who had taken their place, doing it. From the look he wore under his low-slung hat, he may have believed what she had done was somehow his fault, his doing. I finally concluded that I did not know, and as with many things, would probably never know. I only knew that there are moments in which it seems that strangeness brings clarity, or a completely unique thought or vantage point serves as the springboard into an idea that somehow seems as if it is guiding the synthesis of the moments that have come before it. I also knew that this morning would be another that would perhaps later be, as had other days come and passed, that way.

From my clothes still damp, I searched for a cigarette and lit it and watched Lucky as he stood at the kitchen window and did the same. From where I was under the carport, it appeared that he was intermittently speaking one or two word answers to my mother or Jean when they passed through the room behind him. Then he would take to his staring once more. Perhaps at nothing. Perhaps at everything.

The weather had warmed so much that I hardly noticed I was wet again from my ride back from the river and Sharon's and my meeting place. I wondered if Lucky would even question why I had come back home, guessed that he would assume that I had returned home because I was wet, to change clothes before my Thursday morning, two-block journey to the Academy. I wondered if he even knew what time I normally came home from my paper route, if he had noticed that I hadn't been doing so the last few months. I wondered if he knew this day would be different from all before it. I wanted him to know that because I knew it.

"Maybe something new will help and things will change. If not, maybe something new will just make the pain from the old go away for a while … just a little while," she had told me after she'd returned to what seemed to be herself in the car. The smeared mascara had turned itself into streaks down her cheeks, tiny black rivers flowing over her high cheek bones and toward the corners of her mouth. It was one of the only times in our long tenure as lovers and friends that she would overtly grieve the death of her father and sister, although it seemed to me that it almost always affected most things she did. The ice, to her, was always thin, ready to give when any weight was placed on it.

"You really think it'd be good?" I asked her, the way someone might when they have at some level already agreed with what was said.

"I do," she chirped. She was back to the side of herself that wore a perpetual smile, laughed off tragedies like they were simply bad days. "I just don't see any reason to live in the past. Do you? What's happened has happened. There's really nothing you can do about it. I don't know one thing that can be done to change anything that's happened."

"Yeah, but I don't think you can ignore it either," I told her, slipping back on my pants, surprisingly dry.

I wondered how much time we'd spent, her telling me how horrible it had been to hear the words she had heard from me last July. How it had cemented in her mind how good a man … a boy … whatever I was, I was. How her mother was crazy as hell now, her words.

"Yeah, but you like to live back there," she'd told me, which had made me madder than hell. "You kind of ruminate over everything. I know you don't often say it … or maybe don't say it all the time, but you have it in your head, I can tell."

I wanted to ask her how the hell she had any idea of what was in my head, but didn't. I wanted to tell her that at least I hadn't fucked ten guys. But the truth kicked me in the ass: that I was a virgin. As bad for a guy as what she had done was for a girl, which didn't make much sense to me. But I simply said I thought she was right, agreed with her. Then asked her where in the hell we might get the money to carry out the fool thing she was talking about.

"I've got some money saved," she told me. "I've been saving money since I was fourteen. Maybe if I was from another part of Franklin … maybe then I could stay here. But we'll never be anything here but poor white trash people … after all we live in the 'mixed' section of town. I bet even if I marry you, that's how people would always think about me. But I'm going to show them. What about you? Do you have any money saved?"

I started to tell her that I had but that Lucky the bastard and the Academy had taken it from me. At least for all practical purposes. But I'd never even mentioned it to her. That's how much I rume—what the hell was that word? I couldn't even remember. Further proof that I didn't sit around and think about all the muddy water that had passed under the goddam bridge.

"Maybe a hundred dollars," I admitted to her, watched the rain slack for a few seconds, then start again, its rhythm dividing the silence into tiny segments. "How much have you got?"

"More than that. Enough that we could get a tin box on wheels. Wouldn't you like to do that?"

I didn't answer her because I was reliving for the thousandth time the conversation in Dr. Bugg's office. Of all the things that had come down the pike and hit me head-on since the summer, it was the hardest for me to believe.

"We're going to ask you to pay half of the tuition this year," he had told me, staring at me the way he did at people when he was trying to intimi-date them.

My nervous eyes fluttered over his shoulders to his degrees on the wall. I tried to remember what Ph.D. stood for and then remembered he wasn't one. An Ed.D., he had.

"As a matter of fact, you're really fortunate to finish … after what happened. You know with an honor offense like this we hold the right to the discretion of dismissing you."

Lucky had told me not to say a word, do nothing to incriminate myself. Reassured me that they couldn't prove a goddam thing, his words. Little had I suspected they wouldn't try to, just take a parting shot with what they had left to swing.

"Yessir," I told him, feeling like I needed to remove my lips from his ass.

"Does that seem fair to you? I mean, you won't be able to play baseball in the spring. You still had at least two-thirds of the football season left."

"Six games," I'd told him before I caught myself. Did catch myself before I asked him if he ever played football.

"And then there's what happened after that."

"Yessir," I agreed, biting my lip on the inside where he couldn't see it.

Lucky and I had talked about it the evening before, after I had been notified of the meeting the next day. "Just agree with whatever he says," he'd told me. "The word is he's gonna give you a break. At least that's what I heard through Paul Chester down at the store."

Really, I imagined, when he had been shooting craps with him the night before. It seemed like he hadn't been home since September. Nevertheless, Paul Chester had talked to Dr. Bugg's secretary and she had some-how known of the "deal" he was going to offer.

Lucky had tried to explain his vantage point to me the night before the meeting, under the same carport where I now stood watching him. He'd assured me neither Mama nor Jean needed to know a damn thing about any of this. They didn't understand that sometimes you won by knowing where you stood. He knew where he stood, he slurred to me; he knew what he came from. A farmer's son, a crazy man's brother. He'd banked it all on me, too much on me. Then he'd just hushed. Not said anything else except for me to do what they asked.

Like I was hearing them again, Sharon's words right before we left the river still echoed in the valley of my memory. "I know I just brought this up to you today, so I'm not saying that I want to do it today ... or really even this week ... or even this month. I just want you to think about it."

"Don't we have to be eighteen?" I asked her. Somehow, my leather jacket, my motorcycle, the fact that I'd been the best football player in Franklin since Ronnie Langford, these things no longer covered my naiveté.

"Eighteen or somebody sign for you. Or make them believe you're eighteen. I believe Mama would sign for me. I know she wants me to stay around to take care of Suzy. But I know she knows, too, that I have to be able to live my own life. I mean, that's what everybody's supposed to do, aren't they? And I know if I leave, Mama'll just let Bobby come back and live there again. Sometimes I think maybe it'll get better. That Mama'll get better ... will find somebody else to marry. That Suzy'll be fine. I guess wherever we ended up, she could come live with us ... at least for awhile, if that was all right with you. And ... then I think that Bobby'll get better and not be in and out trouble the rest of his life. And then other times I know that with every change, there has to be something new ... something we've never experienced before. And even if there's not a change, maybe some-thing different would just help the pain from the old go away for awhile. I'm tired, Henry. I'm just tired. Just for a little while, I don't want to be tired anymore. Just a little while. Sometimes ... no, most of the time, I feel forty at seventeen."

ATTEMPTING TO REMEMBER Sharon's words had so engulfed me that I didn't notice him or his coughing until he laid his nicotine-stained hand on my shoulder. He looked short to me, maybe even shorter than he'd been before, like the last few days, the last few months, had stolen something from him, his stature. Had placed some invisible weight on his back that had hunched his shoulders and seemed as if it might buckle his knees.

"Did you get wet?" he laughed, sputtered once more.

"Yeah, I guess." I pinched my pants at the pocket, wondered if they were as wet as they would have been had I not dried them on the heater Bobby Bishop fixed.

He leaned against his Ford, looked into the squad car. "Why didn't you take the Ford?"

"I thought it'd be easier on the Indian. I figured it'd be easier to get around, too, with the snow and all. But then it quit snowin'...."

"Yeah, I been out in it already," he said. He lit a cigarette and offered me one, which I refused.

Fear shot through me that he'd been by the river, seen her car or spotted my motorcycle in the bushes. It quieted when I let the part of me that believed he knew about us speak louder in my head, snuff out the other voices. I laughed to myself in the silence between our words, thought about one of the last things Percy had said to me: that he was no longer sure he was crazy because he had never heard voices. The few people he'd talked to while he was there at the end of August, while they were fryin' his brain again, cookin' the life out of him, most all of them said they heard voices that weren't their own. "They can only take so much of your soul," Percy had told me. "But they've quieted Walter," he told me. "I guess that's the important thing. He's not talking to me anymore. But, you know, he never did really talk to me. It makes me wonder if I'm really what they call 'crazy,' because so many men I'm in here with have imaginary figures talkin' to them. First of all, Walter's not imaginary ... and second, he doesn't talk. I'd say the way he communicates with me is more 'telepathic' in nature. Do you know what that word means, Henry?"

I shook my head. Efim, on the other side of the room, nodded. He was back for his tenth or so stint at the nuthouse, a new term Percy used for it. They had become fast friends after these eight years, not having seen each other.

"I bet Efim knows," said Percy, the nuthouse's own college professor.

"It mean when toughts toe stong zat zey do not af to be spokken," Efim said, obviously having come by better English in the last few years. "I af ad a few of dem myself."

Percy cut his eyes at me from across the room, suggesting that he believed that Efim might be able to define the word but possibly had no real-life experience of such phenomena. The story had gone that Efim had submitted to the will of the state back when he was there in '45, and then had been able to keep under control his impulse to hold his wife hostage. Five years later, though, he had begun to believe Dwight D. Eisenhower was personally going to send him back to Russia and that he was somehow secretly in cahoots with Hitler, not really dead like they said he was. That, along with his bent toward doing calisthenics naked in front of the window of his small brick house, had landed him back at least once a year since then. He said he'd spent his other time learning the English language. "Vich I must zay I fell I have become quiet—how you zay?—profizient at. Vouldn't you zay?"

I nodded my head at the short, strangely complected man with a round and placid face, bulging eyes.

"Why is your father not coming?" Percy asked, changing the subject on a dime.

I stared at the floor, watched my feet as they crossed and uncrossed. I wanted to give him a good answer, one that at least made sense. But there was none that I knew of: as long as he says he's tried for years and years … let you live with us … been embarrassed around town … took you in when I guess he could have left you in the country with your parents … as long as these things don't suffice for an answer. Perhaps, he would've kept trying forever … but then you went and fucked Christine Smithson and left him no choice except that you disappear or go to the penitentiary … or Old Man Smithson come out of the house with his rifle and do you in. Some people handled things like this, Lucky had assured me.

The fact was that I didn't know. What I did know was that Lucky asked me about him when I got home. Inquired as to whether or not they were "electrocuting" him again, like they had done all those years ago, a question to which I had to respond in the affirmative.

"Do you think it was the right thing to do?" he'd asked me the other time I'd come home from visiting him, ridden down there while Sharon was at work. I wondered why in the hell he was asking me. "I just didn't know what else to do." Then he turned to my mother, who had made her way temporarily through, out, and back into the room. She looked at him there in his chair, like I could remember myself doing a few times of late, like she wasn't sure what had come over him. "What d' you think, Mary? Was it the right thing to do?"

In the way it seemed only my mother could do, she answered and avoided doing so all at the same time. Most concrete answers, she had a way of allowing other people to take responsibility for. I agreed with her, nodding my head, like I'd seen her do to things he said ten thousand times.

"I just ain't sure," he told us, Jean now having surfaced from her suite. She nodded, of course, patted him on the arm, pretended he didn't smell like cigarettes and whiskey, hadn't just made his way in, his knees still dirty from shooting craps down at the filling station. He laughed, sad and resolute, and patted her hand.

I tried my best to hide my glare, scuffed my feet on the hardwood and watched my weathered boot tops. "He seems all right to me," I said. Of course, everything in the world, at the moment, was all right to me. I was almost eighteen, Sharon and I had been enjoying the broad front seat of her car for going on a couple of weeks now. The world truly seemed a brighter place.

Two days later, Lucky would go without telling any of us, and recount it to me late at night after my mother and Jean were asleep. I pictured Jean standing next to her mostly shut door, her hand cupped around her ear, saddened that he was talking to me about anything he wouldn't speak about to her, a tear making its way down her fat cheek. It did my heart good.

"I went to see him today," was how he began. In his chair, he offered no name, no introduction more than that. I took my place on the couch.

"You did?" I immediately tried to picture my father and Efim trying to carry on a conversation.

"Yeah, he had some strange little man in there with him. Couldn't understand a goddam word he said."

Efim was Lucky's height, I thought, and it didn't surprise me he couldn't understand him. Efim probably couldn't understand him either, his drawl more defined than mine or Percy's, a sign he was at least on the outskirts of the good ole boy club in Franklin.

"I finally just acted like he wasn't in the room and said what I had to say to Percy. He wouldn't leave."

I nodded, picturing him like he'd been the last time I was there, perched in a chair, staring, smiling, because he understood slowly.

"He said they's givin' him those goddam shock treatments again. I wish they'd do somethin' else besides that." He took a cigarette, out of his pocket, a match, stared at them both." I guess if he'd take anything else they wouldn't have to. He even said they made him more clear-headed. Told me maybe this was the right thing to do. Did you ever think you'd hear him talkin' like that? I know I didn't think I would."

I shook my head, cursorily.

He finally lit the cigarette and dropped the match in the ashtray. Drew deep and hard on it. Sputtered quietly, so as, I thought, not to wake Mama and Jean.

"Maybe I did do the wrong thing. I just didn't know what else to do. He really didn't leave me no choice. You know, people do that sometimes … paint themselves in such a corner that there doesn't seem to be but one or two ways out … and neither of them ain't too good. He told me that he didn't care no more. That we could go on and do whatever the hell we wanted to do. And he didn't say it mean, he said it more like he just meant it. Like he was … re—what's that word?"

"Resolved," I told him. "I think that's it."

"Okay. Anyway, I got to thinkin' after I left that maybe it wasn't the right thing to do. That even if it was one of a couple of bad choices, maybe that still didn't make it the right thing to do. I mean, I believe he's crazy. Both times we've took him down there, they believe it too … keep him after the three-day period they can watch somebody. But I ain't sure that it makes it right what I did to him. He's my brother." Lucky choked a little, coughed, stared at his cigarette. "Goddam things."

I nodded, again cursorily.

"I mean, I just ain't sure what freedom's worth? And I don't mean the kind that the Japs and the Germans would take from us if they could. I'm talkin' about the freedom to make your own choices … even if they are wrong. Maybe they are the same kind, I don't know. All's I'm really sure of is if we don't have the freedom to choose what we need to do, then I don't know how much anything is really worth."

For a short moment, I heard rustling sounds coming from the far side of the house, figured it was Jean, trying to listen. Lucky never missed a beat, never took his eyes off the darkened window pane.

"If you're forced to do the right thing, is it still the right thing? Or even if you do it because you're scared of what will happen if you don't, is it right? I ain't sure."

"WHERE'VE YOU BEEN?" I asked him.

"Down at the courthouse," he told me, "in the basement. Place always seems like it's about a hundred below." He grasped himself in his own arms and made a shuddering expression. Then he looked back toward the house, like he might expect Mama or Jean to come out, or that they were watching us. "Lookin' through the archives. You gonna go in and change? What're you doin' just standin' out here anyway? You know … it's still not fifty degrees or anythin'. You might get sick just standin' out here."

In all the times that he and I had found each other standing out here, I couldn't recall an instance we'd asked each other what we were doing, what we were thinking. Neither of us, I think, really wanted to know, had any desire to merge the hells.

"I'm goin'. I'm gonna go in and change clothes … and then off to the Academy I'll be."

"It's pretty early yet. You not goin' early to socialize with Bugg, are ya?"

"I was thinkin' about it. Thought I might just go right in and prop my feet up on his desk, tell him I was there to visit with him."

He laughed, the way I had become accustomed to him doing, with gravel that shook and rattled in his chest and throat. He dropped his cigarette to the pavement and snuffed the life out of it with his boot. Took his hat off and wiped his forehead, glistening with sweat under the pale daylight and the overhead bulb he'd pulled on. He ran his hand over the hair left on his head, the bumps and marks left from Jimmy Langford's pistol.

"I need to let Arliss and Jackson out. I ain't gonna be able to keep them in there forever. You know, in another town, one a little bigger and that probably worked a little better, I couldn't have ever held either one of them. I ain't sure whether that's good or bad."

I nodded, watching his eyes as they turned to the backdoor and the sound of its opening. He listened as my mother told him that Miss Helen Riley had called and was waiting to speak with him. She was already at the jail and he could either come there or call her on the phone or the radio. Lucky raised his hand and acknowledged what my mother had told him with a closed-mouth smile. He shook his head and patted me on the back and then began to make his way back into the house through the door that had swung shut when my mother had said her piece and disappeared.

CHAPTER THIRTY-ONE

THE REASON HE GAVE for wanting me to go with him was that Lucas Reasonover and Don Walton and Johnny Forrest were already doing other things. The same kind of reason he gave for wanting me to sit with her body that night. The shit work. I wanted to ask him what they could all be doing. But I didn't. Any excuse to skip a day at the Academy was good enough for me.

"I'll let Bugg know I need your help," he had said when he told me to go in and get ready. "What're they gonna say? You can't do it?"

I had just nodded, watched him as he sat in the driver's seat of the squad car and lit a cigarette.

"Reasonover's gone to Nashville to pick up a sample we had sent to a lab down there. I've got Johnny down at the jail. Forrest's a good man like that. He's been down there every night with Arliss and Jackson Mosby. I gotta let him go home. His wife and kids have been scared every night this week, 'cause he's been gone. I had to call Walton to go down to the archives to have him take up where I left off."

As I walked away, I cut my eyes back to him. He'd draped his hands over the steering wheel, his back was hunched slightly, as it seemed now most of the time, his hat's brim rested on his hands, one on top of the other on the steering wheel. His foot was propped against the lowest part of the door, where it had no upholstery but only metal, keeping it open.

"I need somebody to go with me so I got a witness to what I do. It's you or the mayor," he laughed, "but he doesn't get his ass out'a bed till seven o'clock … and he's grouchy as hell."

Really, I imagined, he just didn't want to go alone. Even though he lived in a world unbeknownst to most of us around him, at least in our family, it was a world that had not seemed infused with loneliness until lately. Had not seemed filled with a desire to avoid it until recent days.

ALTHOUGH I NEVER SAW THEM, I imagined Jackson and Arliss to be in the same cell together, one of the two in the jail, no more than a seven by seven space with a cot on each side. The last time I had been to the jail, I had avoided going through the door past the offices, for the same reason I did on this morning: I was afraid that Jackson Mosby had gotten a good enough look at me from time to time that he might be able to proclaim confidently I was the one he'd seen outside Franklin High School this fall.

I took a seat in Lucky's chair while he laid his hat on his desk and disappeared into the relative darkness of the back of the jail. My eyes floated from thing to thing, catching only the objects surrounding me that were familiar. A picture of all of us at church, the only such of its kind: Fourth Avenue Church of Christ having begun taking them for the church directory the year that this one was taken, my estimate three or four years ago. Neither Lucky nor Mama had since made the decision to have it retaken. Just use the same old one. The one with the princess with a scowl painted across her ugly mug. With me looking like I had something up my ass sideways.

As my view moved to a newspaper article on the wall my mother had framed for Lucky, I tried to recall the situation and could only remember that Fred Creason had written it. As I crossed my feet and propped them on his desk just for the hell of it, I remembered that it had been a story of Lucky shutting down stills down in Little Texas, because according to Lucky off the record, the mayor had gotten a "wild hair in his ass" and decided that too much of the moonshine was making its way into Franklin. The picture beside the article was one of Lucky and Lucas Reasonover posed with the axes they supposedly destroyed the stills with. I remembered Lucky telling me that he had let them take the picture, write the article, because it would satisfy the powers that were. He had told the Bennings that they could keep making it, he later reported to me after, I think, he'd had some himself, but they would have to move their equipment deeper into the woods. Years later, after Jean had married a man from down in Little Texas and Lucky had left, too, we came across what I suspected to be the same stills in the woods while we were hunting on his family's property. Jack, Jean's husband, simply waved at them on the property that met theirs in the woods; they stared for a long moment and then threw up their hands, returning the gesture.

On the credenza by the far wall, both of which needed a coat of varnish or paint, sat a picture of Lucky's other family in front of the farmhouse where he was raised. As with most pictures of that day, it appeared that perhaps the subjects had been asked to pretend they were statues as the picture was snapped and the likeness registered. It was my assumption that the picture was probably taken before World War II, maybe even in the late twenties, before the Great Depression that I'd only heard about. Lucky appeared to be perhaps as young as eighteen, with a look on his face as stoic as any I'd ever seen. Beside him was Wanda Jean, a big, hard-looking woman, still closer to a smile than anyone in the picture frame. Beside her was Nellie, shorter than Wanda Jean, built more like Lucky, looking more like my grandmother than grandfather. On the far side of her, Percy. Behind them, my grandmother and grandfather, Lera and Horace. They were good people, Lucky had always told me, just people who would remain forever where they were and like they were, out there on that farm in Thompson's Station, Tennessee. People who wanted to know no more ... seemed could do no more.

Lastly, there was a picture of my mother. Sweet Mary, as quiet as any mouse, whose life had revolved hopelessly around ours, around who's ever made its way into her path. The woman who let Percy live upstairs for time upon end, the same woman who put up with Lucky, the woman whom I could never remember speaking one word of guile about anyone. So unlike the son she would bear and raise. In the picture, she was young, innocence still her ally, a smile not yet more difficult to come by. Her blue eyes pierced the paper the picture was printed on, even in black and white made their way iridescently through the glass that shielded it from the light, the years, even from behind the thick, round glasses that covered them. Years later, for some reason, I would be reminded of it when my son found in a drawer a picture of myself and Sharon at my senior prom, taken five or so months after those few days in December of 1953, innocence, too, still our ally, love its close friend. Me, still thin as a rail besides any weight football had put on me over the years, hair so short it made my ears look twice as big as they really were, not small to begin with. Sharon nearly as big as I was, maybe just a couple of inches shorter, taken away with her hairstyle that night. Living on love, the truth it conveys, the lies it tells. I never told him it had been in my office for years, but simply put it back in the drawer where he found it without explanation.

In the silence of the distant droning voices of my father and the Mosbys, I tried to imagine where Percy had been that night, or really, tried not to think about it as soon as the image entered my head. And knowing that I would never ask because there was at least a part of me that did not want to know, assumed he would have had to be in one of the two cells there, as Lucky was probably trying to teach him a lesson. That's how I could have imagined it. Make sure he wouldn't do any of it again. I also imagined it as the synthesis of events their combination rendered stranger than they would have been if isolated from one another. How one thing, each thing fairly innocuous, happened after another, until their combination produced something totally separate from themselves. How, if she had not been home, or if that had not been the exact time Lucky had made the decision he did. Or if he'd made the decision from the start to send him back to Thompson's Station, I wondered if it would have changed anything. It seemed I had wondered these things, their kind, a thousand times since that last week in September that now seemed as if it might have been years before. A part of me knew there was no use in wondering such things, but then another part could not stop, as if the questions would only be rendered void by thinking about them over and over, not by answers themselves. I knew they—answers to the questions, that is—would never be produced.

Two days after his first, and at the time, only visit to see Percy in Central State, Lucky would again return to the facility for the crazyasses, Percy's last characterization of it, and visit him one more time, the second and last visit he would make to his brother in this stint in 1953. Again, it was, to my knowledge, just a clandestine appointment with his brother, the officials there, and I guess, destiny. He would return with the questions he had before, or really the next set. The ones that seem to come after questions like, Is the right thing really right if it's not freely decided? The questions that no longer contain hypothetical or philosophical elements as their main content, but questions that facts weight more tangibly.

"I talked to the head man down there … a Guy Tomley … and I talked to Dr. Peterson, Percy's doctor. He was the same man that treated him back in '45. I explained to 'em what had happened and why he had ended up back there this time … and asked them what they thought."

From the looks of him, the smell of his breath, he had obviously made a stop at the filling station to shoot craps and pull on the bottle with his buddies rather than alone, a bit more comfort, I assumed. It was the first night I could recall his waking me up, the first in a series to come over the next couple of months. He looked at me as if he expected me to at the level of consciousness he was, instantly. The light from the kitchen bleeding up the stairwell and into my room was the only illumination.

"They said they thought he could—" He stopped abruptly, listening for my mother, I imagined, whom I also imagined had told him to get Percy out under no circumstances. "They think he could do just as good here. Said he's not respondin' as well to the treatment this time. That's what that Peterson man said … the doctor. He said he'd given it some consideration after we brought him in there this time … he said Percy was probably lonely … that's why he did what he did with that Smithson girl. Reminded me that he'd never been a danger to anybody … really even hisself. Asked me if this—that's what he said, 'this'—was the way I wanted my brother to live. He even moved his hand all around, like he was showin' me the place like a used car. 'This,' he said. Is 'this' what you want for your brother? I guess they was all questions I'd been askin' myself. You know, most questions are like that. Other people just help us realize we been askin' ourselves. Your mama does that with me all the time."

I peered back at him, my head and neck the only parts of me showing from under the cover, sweating underneath the blanket, producing the smell of salt and worry like I usually did at night. I was not only unsure of what to say, I thought anything I could say would not serve to comfort him, but most likely anger him. If I had spoken, I would have reminded him that he'd been trying this for years.

"I'm likely gonna go get him in a coupl'a days." He lit a cigarette and stared at the beam of light cutting a thin, angular line in the darkness on the floor at the top of the stairs. "That is, if they still think it's the right thing when I go back. You wanna go with me?"

"Maybe so," I said, knowing that it was about as likely that I would as Percy would come home and act normal. Neither Sharon nor I had started back to school; I was seeing her in the afternoons and the evenings when she didn't work. The two times I'd been to see him myself had been when I couldn't see her.

He rubbed his face with his hands, then nodded, then shook his head, as if his gestures made some sense. He appeared to be listening again like he thought my mother might be stirring downstairs once more.

Two days later, he'd pull into the driveway with Percy, sitting proud in the front seat once more. Waltzed in with him, down the same path he'd been coerced that night less than three weeks before. First, though, leaving Percy in the car, he'd made his way in to find my mother, speak with her about what he'd done, because he, it was fairly obvious, previously had not. It was one of the few times I could remember hearing my mother's voice raised. Her questions, I believed he'd say later or at least try to convince himself, were the same ones he'd asked.

"Why do you think it'll work this time if it hadn't before?"

"It's not like it hasn't before. There were long periods a' time when it seemed like nothing bad was goin' on at all. Before that little girl next door, he was pretty much just doin' crazy things like that preachin'. And you know Ole Man Smithson sent her off. We ain't got that to worry about now."

"That's not how you looked at it then," she said. "You used to say it was somethin' all the time. Don't you remember that?"

"All's I know," said Lucky, "is that I can't just leave him there. It ain't right. I been thinkin' a lot about this … and he should have the right to choose his course like all the rest of us. Even if it's wrong, Mary. That's what he should have."

Although I could not see the conversation between Lucky and my mother, I could imagine her seated in the chair at the end of their bed, where she had parked herself when he'd told her he'd brought Percy home, Lucky, standing by the door, so that he might escape his rage when it decided to come, which I was certain it would if the situation was discussed long enough. A conclusion to which my mother would come quickly, too, I imagined.

"What do you want me to do?" Lucky half-huffed.

"I'm not sure what can be done now," she said. "Maybe he can go live with one of your sisters."

"They got enough with Mother and Daddy and their boys," he told her. An edge had started to grow in his voice. "A-goddam-nough."

"I'm not sure what else you can do," said my mother as she evidently conceded, or at least made a comment ambiguous enough that protest could be interpreted as concession.

The princess passed through the hall and added her two cents worth, worth less than that. "I'm thinkin' it'd be okay with the Smithson girl gone now."

"'The Smithson Girl,'" I mocked under my breath. "She had a goddam name. Christine."

Lucky came out of the bedroom and turned a sad, loathsome look my way, which I chose to believe he meant toward the princess but wouldn't show her. Truth be known, I thought in that moment Lucky was probably proud of me and ashamed of her, her dumbness, if that's a word. She'd be lucky to graduate from Franklin High School and marry some bum. I was a star fucking football player. Nevertheless, I wasn't able to think about myself this way very often. Most times, I was son of Lucky, corrupt "sheriff," nephew of Crazy Percy, brother of the dumb, snobby princess. Son of Mary Hall, the one most of the town believed suffered in one or more ways at the hand of Dillard "Lucky" Hall behind closed doors.

"THERE GONNA BE FUCKIN' SCOUTS at this game," he'd told me, acting like nothing had happened. He'd been able to somehow forget, or at least transcend my busting him in the mouth, bloodying his nose on Main Street. What's fair is fair, I guess, was the way he'd looked at it. I'd beat him at his own game. Stole the girl ... that I guess he really didn't want anymore. Taken her away when I delivered the news that her old man and her sister had gotten killed.

I tried to act nonchalant, like it didn't matter. I was glad he couldn't see my insides shaking, my knees trembling under my pads. "You think so?" I choked out.

"Fuckin'-A!" He slapped me on the back hard enough it made me jump, smacked my shoulder pads together so loud they almost sounded like a gunshot.

"I doubt they're comin' to see anybody in particular," Collins said from across the locker room.

"We know they're not comin' to see your ass," said Van. "That's as plain as the ugly nose on your face."

"Lay off the nose, Manor," said Raymond Collins. He'd caught grief about it as long as I could remember, probably since grammar school.

"It's hard to miss," said Paul Chester, Jr.

Collins gave him some unmistakable sign language from across the room, then turned and dropped his pants, his hairy ass shining for all to see.

"I'd put that thing up if you're not gonna use it," said Coach Nedler as he stuck his head around the corner, shook it along with his hand at Collins' display. "That means now. My foot would just about fit right in there."

Mr. Nedler wasn't afraid to use his foot, that way especially. He'd let it go on several people that I'd seen. Van, Chester, Collins, they'd all gotten his wrath at one time or another. A foot in the ass, an open hand to the back of the head. He'd especially always had it in for Van, who, rumor had it, had paid a few clandestine visits to his wife. As for me, I'd always suspected I'd been able to avoid his wrath because I was good at sensing when to avoid him, when to say the right things, as I had learned from my life with Lucky. I was also his boy, I knew that, too. His only chance to win a state championship that year, an award that had eluded him for the half-dozen years he'd been the coach.

We'd been getting ready to play Columbia that night, a town twenty miles to Franklin's south. I had heard that there were college scouts there, unidentified in the stands, right along with Lucky, who I knew was in the stands thirty minutes before the game started. It was hard for me to imagine anybody was there to see me.

"They're here to see you, buddy," Van said, slapping me on the back again, taking the image of Lucky and the imaginary scouts out of my mind, especially the one wearing University of Tennessee orange like the ones who came to see Ronnie Langford. "You ... you ... you!"

I tried to laugh it off.

"They're hear to see you!" he said, checking the door as Nedler stood still as the statue.

"I'm not sure who the hell's doin' what," said Coach Nedler, "but, Manor, I'm sure if it's bad you got somethin' to do with it."

Van just smiled at him in a knowing way, waved at him before he cast his eyes to the floor. He took me by the shoulder pads and stared into my eyes. "You got a chance here, buddy. A big chance. You go tonight, they'll be back to look at you again. You're the first one since Ronnie Langford. You know that, don't ya?"

I have to say that Van seemed on my side that night, throwing a block every chance he could, especially a couple that freed me to score on a long drive right before halftime, the third touchdown of the half, two of them mine. He'd gotten up and come to the end zone as I tossed the referee the ball and asked me, "Who's takin' care of you? Huh? Who's lookin' out for your ass?" I'd score once more in the second half on our way to a 28-14 win over the Columbia Mules, so named for the animal their county was famous for. I don't believe I ever saw Lucky as proud as he was after the game, then when the next issue of *The Tennessean* came out.

"'Hall may be the best since Ronnie Langford,'" he read while we were sitting at the kitchen table. The princess sat there, trapped in the middle of chewing her eggs, unable to escape Lucky's reading. "'It's taken eight long years, perhaps, for the town to heal from the loss of its golden son, at least as far as football is concerned. But the spotlight seems to have re-emerged. His name is Henry Hall, son of our own 'Lucky' Dillard Hall, former Assistant Police Chief, now Police Chief.' They could have left part of that out," he interrupted himself reading. "'In the opening game of the season last Friday night, he rushed for a hundred and forty-two yards for the Battle Ground Academy Wildcats and single-handedly outscored the Columbia Mules. He had a strong season last year, but 1953 seems to promise even more. Next week, we'll see how he fares against the Spring Hill Cougars, who posted a 7-3 record last year and made a trip to the annual Butter Bowl. It promises to be an interesting season as scouts descend upon Franklin from across the state to observe Hall, assess his playing, and gather the information that will determine whether or not he's offered a scholarship. We can only be glad that the conflict in Korea is over, so that Hall might be able to go the way of football and not the way of war.'"

The next week would bring the Spring Hill Cougars to the Academy and even a better week for me, except for the fact that I felt distracted most of the time. One moment I'd be in the game, carrying the ball or fielding and returning a kickoff, and the next I'd be in the car with Sharon or at the hospital with Percy. Halftime brought Nedler giving us a speech in the locker room. His blues eyes flashed and popped as he spat his words. "You're playin' like a' bunch a' sissy girls. A bunch of g—f—d—" He couldn't decide on his expletive, so he didn't use one, the moment passed.

"My wife could outplay you." Spit formed on his lower lip as his emotions hovered at the edge of his control. He took his fist and shook it at the heavens … at the locker room ceiling … at something. He slapped the closest locker behind him with the flat of his hand.

Van elbowed me, which drew a look from Nedler." His wife can do a lot things."

"What'd you say, Manor?"

"I said that I was sure we'd play better in the second half … because we'll change a lot of things … like you said," he said, smiling that smile of his. "I think we need to tighten up the line, protect our boy here."

"Good advice, Manor," he said. "But maybe you ought to let me be the coach, huh?"

Coach Langley, or Fester out of his presence, walked up behind him and exhibited the fact he liked to repeat what Nedler said. "Yeah, maybe you ought to let him be the coach, huh?"

"Just trying to be a blessing," said Van.

"Yeah, you always are," said Nedler.

"He's been talkin' to his wife," Van whispered to me.

As for me, I was trying to imagine what the scouts had thought about the dismal first half I'd had. I'd run for only twenty-seven yards, if I'd kept up with it right in my head, which I'd never done before this year and all this talk had started. I thought about the punt I'd dropped after calling for a fair catch. I thought about the two kickoff returns I'd had that had been under twenty yards. Pretty much, a botched attempt at any real effort is what it had been, which had landed us down 14-3 to a team we should have already put away.

"We gotta block better," said Nedler. "We gotta execute, all fire off the line at the same time. Some of you d—darn guys look like you've been glued down in your stances. If we can get off to 2-0, we can start on a march toward the goldang state championship."

"I bet these boys don't wanna win a state championship," said Fester, the veins bulging in his head and neck as they did.

"Yessir, we do!" shouted Raymond Collins.

"Well, you boys sure ain't playin' like it! Are they?" Nedler directed toward Fester.

He shook his head. Breathed heavy enough I could hear it all the way across the locker room.

"You boys get off your asses and play like you know you can play," Nedler finally let go. "And I mean in this second half, not next goddam week!"

"Yessir," most everybody shouted.

What Nedler described to us, we were able to execute in the second half. The line tightened and began to open holes, at first just big enough to get through for four and five yards, then for ten, then finally large enough to drive Sharon's car through. Van pulled us ahead halfway through the third quarter when he caught a twenty-seven yard pass from Johnny Nance. From there, we looked only forward as we scored once more in the third quarter, then again to begin the fourth. As the tide turned, I was able to push the images of Percy and Sharon out of my head and focus on the ten-foot wide holes the line was opening. At the end of the game, even Raymond Collins and I were friendly toward each other, patting each other on the back for a job well done. Van laughed at the sight, and told everybody who would listen, "See, I should be the coach. Nedler's wife told me I was better than him anyway."

"You're crazy as hell," Tully told him, after he'd made his way into our locker room after the game. "I thought you boys were gonna get your asses whipped after the first half. I was kinda thinkin' that I ought to have gone to the Franklin game."

"Any asshole can go to the Franklin game," Van told him. "You're lucky you've got friends at the Academy, so you have somebody else to come watch."

"I hear you talkin', Manor," said Tully. "I sat up there by Lucky Hall. I don't know if I've ever heard a man holler or cough so much. He was lookin' all around him every play, tryin' to figure out who might have been the scouts."

"I thought y'all quit talkin' about that shit last week. There probably wasn't one scout in those stands," I said, hoping I was wrong.

"You're probably right," said Raymond Collins as he finished putting his things in his bag and slung it over his shoulder and let the locker room door swing shut behind him.

"He's just jealous," said Van. "You see that don't ya? Come on, let's go down to Willow Plunge. Tully, you got some beer, right? And some good shine."

"The best," Tully told him, drawing on a cigarette, daring our coaches to tell him to put it out. "Right out'a Little Texas. Straight from the Bennings."

"I think I'll pass on Willow Plunge," I told them, throwing my own bag over my shoulder. "I got other things to do."

"Yeah, we know what you got to do," said Tully. "I didn't see her in the stands tonight. Where was she?"

"She had to work," I answered, as the door shut behind me and the cold night air touched my face. "See y'all."

Before I got to the spot where I was going to meet Sharon at the river, I pulled over myself and let the silence of the night take me into its own arms. Just starting to become sore from the hits I'd taken during the game, I thought about how such punishment was a relatively small price to pay to have a chance like I did, how I might have a ticket that few others had been lucky or fortunate enough to receive. How, like most things, I'd never asked for it, but it had just been given me, mine to do with what I would, after I had started playing football and baseball in the eighth grade. How I'd been given the speed to outrun people and the eyes to see where the next step should go. Up the hill half a mile or so, I could hear what I thought were probably the initial whoops and hollers of Van and Tully and whoever had joined them at Willow Plunge, then they, too, became quiet. In the silence, I sat and listened to the almost silent voice of the river and the soft language it spoke under the distant, star-scattered sky.

CHAPTER THIRTY-TWO

I T TOOK LUCKY A LONG TIME to finish his conversation with my usually pliable mother, Mary. Out the same window in which I would watch Lucky that December morning, I had looked out on Percy in mid-September, clutching to his chest the bag I had packed for him, at Lucky's request the first time I had visited him. In the fading light, he appeared thinner than when he had left, even thinner than the last time I'd seen him, perhaps a week before. In Lucky's absence, Percy appeared to be watching something on the floorboard in the mostly darkened car. Every so often, he'd shake himself, look into the mirror and speak as if he were talking to someone else in the car with him. He scoured his face several times with his hands and pushed his hair out of his eyes and off his forehead for it only to fall once more.

Finally, after his conversation with my mother, Lucky had made his way back through the kitchen and out into the evening that had grown completely darkened except for the yellowish glow of the light on the driveway-side of the house. He made his way to the car and opened the door, sitting in the driver's seat beside his brother. After several moments of what appeared to be silence, they began to talk, I figured, about what happened from here.

Just before I climbed the stairs with a cold glass of milk, I had seen them exit their respective sides of the car. In the half-light of the driveway, Percy stood still, his bag clutched to his chest, waiting for Lucky to lead him inside. In a few moments, he would make his way in the back door, across the porch and ascend the steps like he was home, which, in fact, I guess he was.

WHEN LUCKY EMERGED from the back, he stared at then fiddled with some notes and papers on his desk, arranging them one way then another. In his absence I had heard Miss Helen make her way in the door and then seen her briefly as she passed his office and took a seat at her desk near the front of the station. Just after she had gotten settled, Johnny Forrest had come from the back, mumbling something to himself about Lucas Reasonover. Never seeming to notice me, he had then disappeared into the room in which I assumed he had been staying these last four days. I wondered if perhaps Lucky had put Percy in that room and not in a cell at all. But then I figured what had probably happened couldn't have if Percy had not been locked down somewhere. Or perhaps they had been in that room and he found what was taking place so unbelievable that he could not bring himself to flee. Or perhaps, he thought he deserved it. Dr. Guppy had told us when we went for the formalities that Monday afternoon, that he believed the bruises and lacerations on his face, hands, and neck were very unlikely to have been from the same cause as his death. That was all that was said. He suggested that there be no autopsy unless we, the family, had questions that were unanswered. Otherwise, he would identify the cause of death as that which was obvious.

When Lucky finished sorting through his papers and put an armful in a briefcase he carried only when he had to, he motioned me to come behind him. We made our way to the police car in silence, only broken by the sounds of the doors opening and closing and their echo off the back of the police station.

The Burgess house was on a short, thin street named Evans Alley, just off Strahl Street, which ran parallel with Columbia Pike, and was probably a half mile from where we lived. It had been there as long as I could remember and had been home to many different people over the years, and was, in general, viewed as a place of all kinds of debauchery. It was the kind of place Lucky normally stayed well clear of, except, I assume, on this day and perhaps on Tuesday, when he had visited the boarding household and talked to its inhabitants to make sure that one of them, Miss Mary Ivy, imaginary horse rider and purported prostitute, was still alive. As Franklin had settled into the fact that it had a body and possibly its blood on its hands, there had been, according to Lucky, several reports of Miss Ivy seen walking down the road the night before, so identified by her riding britches. The two black men seen following her, had supposedly been the reason the Mosbys were still in Lucky's jail.

"You remember me tellin' you that the Ivy woman was still alive, don't ya? That I talked to her when I was over there?"

"Yessir," I told him." You said you talked to most a' the boarders there. Bobby Bishop and Fred Burkitt, too."

"That Fred Burkitt's a sad sight," Lucky said, something akin to what he always did when he was mentioned. He turned the squad car on Strahl Street then held his hand over the top of the car for a right turn into Evans Alley. "I guess it's just about quit rainin'. I bet with the snow that come first though, and as hard as long as it rained, the river'll be out."

I nodded as he slowed the car in front of the Burgess house.

Lucky, as he most usually did, parked the car and sat silent in it for a few minutes before going in on a call like this. Perhaps he was thinking through what he was to say or do, I imagined, the situation itself, the ways it could go. He looked at some of the papers he had collected in his office and nodded, like a conversation was playing out in the privacy of his head. He tilted back the brim of his hat and looked at himself in the mirror then snuffed out the cigarette that had almost burned down to his fingertips.

When we entered the Burgess house, we did so without a knock, because most people came and went that way, I had always been told. Having rooms for six people besides herself and her family members, which now only consisted of one son named Sherman, most of the people who lived in the place were people who could find no where else to live. White people who had been driven a peg below just the "mixed" part of town, to the boarding house in the "mixed" part of town. The derelicts, the bootleg runners, people like Miss Ivy, who either sold or gave her body away on a regular basis, people whose drink ruled their life, whose history rendered them powerless and some almost lifeless.

Upon first entering the room, I began to look for Bobby Bishop, who I imagined would be here if he had not in fact moved home with Sharon's mother in the last couple of days. Nevertheless, he was nowhere to be seen, but probably down in Alabama picking up shine. According to Sharon, he was experiencing having a growing rift with the Bennings down in Little Texas about running shine up from Alabama and losing them business. The Burgess woman, who ran this house, was a direct descendant of theirs, having taken the name Burgess with marriage.

In the room, though, was Miss Ivy, wearing her characteristic riding pants and a blouse cut low enough to show half her bosom. Next to her, getting a light off her cigarette, was Robert Woodson, long time resident of the house and somebody Lucky had always referred to as a "derelict," different from "drunk," which was what he often called Louis Smith. He was the finest house painter in Franklin at one time, Lucky had told me, until the bottle completely took him over and made him shake so bad that he couldn't paint when he wasn't drinking. When he was drinking, he couldn't keep the amount of intoxicant to a level with which he could remain functional, so demonstrated by a call Lucky had to go to when he had fallen off a ladder and broken an arm and a leg. The other current inhabitant of the house wasn't in the main room, one Fred Burkitt.

It took Mrs. Burgess a few moments to come out of her and her son's part of the house, once we had entered the main lobby-like room. She was a silver-haired woman who appeared in her mid- fifties. The only times I had ever laid eyes on her before was in the grocery store in town. She nodded at Lucky and motioned for him to take a seat in the only empty chair. Ignored me.

"No thank ya," said Lucky, "we ain't gonna be stayin' but a few minutes."

"Suit yourself," she told him.

"Howdy, Louis … howdy, Robert," Lucky said. "Hey, Miss Ivy."

They all nodded back; Louis Smith tried to raise himself to shake Lucky's hand, but lost a handle on his balance about half way up and sat back down in the chair.

"It's all right," Lucky said. "Just keep your seat, Louis. Looks like you've already had a few."

"Sober as a judge," said Louis, half-smiling, offering his hand from his seat.

Robert Woodson, a smaller and stockier man, drew a couple of hostile puffs off his cigarette and nodded at Lucky, then removed himself to the far side of the room by the door. Mrs. Burgess stepped to the couch but did not sit.

"The other boys not here?" Lucky asked.

"I can't keep up with everybody that lives here," said Mrs. Burgess.

"Yeah," Lucky said, nodding, looking at the floor. "Yeah, I understand that."

"So what brings the pleasure of your visit?" said Bette Burgess.

"I think I will sit down," said Lucky. He sat on the slick, green sofa and pulled out his cigarettes. He knocked one out and lit it, offered anybody else one who would have it. Hacked a couple of times.

"That cough sounds bad," said Louis. "Real bad."

"Yeah, it's been a hard winter so far," said Lucky. "Y'all know my boy, Henry, here, don't ya? With all that's goin' on, I been pretty short-handed. He's helpin' me out for a few days."

Louis Smith again tried to raise himself from his seat, but stopped quicker this time and returned his weight to the chair in which he sat. Robert Woodson spoke my name and gave a slight wave. Mary Ivy asked me if I knew Van. I nodded, as it took a moment to sink in why he might know her. Later he would tell me he'd "given her a couple of rides."

"Well," Lucky finally said, "Mrs. Burgess … or is it all right if I call you Bette?"

She nodded.

"You remember when I was here the other day, right? Came because some people thought that woman ... you know, the one they found up by the high school, might be Miss Ivy here. And I'm sure you remember I asked you about a window, then I had some boys come in here and take a few samples from around it. Fingerprints and some places that looked like blood. If I remember right, they did it in that room, correct?" Lucky pointed toward the next room of the house, the part that was private to Bette and her son Sherman.

Bette nodded again. "Yeah, and you remember what I told you, too, don't ya?"

Lucky nodded himself, drew on his cigarette and blew the smoke out quick. "Yes ma'am, I do. You said that your boy, Sherman, works at the slaughterhouse out Carters Creek Pike, which I knew. And if I remember right, you said that they had give him a runt hog to bring home if he wanted to and that he had done the hog in out back and then y'all cleaned part of it in here ... the head if I remember right. You said you was mad at him, too, because he wore his clothes in and got more blood inside. And you said, too, that you had had a bloody nose sometime in the last coupl'a weeks and that could'a got in them places we pulled out'a the kitchen. But, you know, Bette, I still got a coupl'a other questions for ya."

Mary Ivy shifted her weight from her butt to her legs and then stood. She walked across the room and feigned looking out the window. Bette stared at Lucky with squinted eyes.

"I'm still wonderin' about that window on the far side of your room in there. You know, it was the one that was so clean ... the one that was missin' the curtains."

"And you know it's still just like I told ya when you talked to me and Sherman that mornin'. My grandkids was over here and they pulled it down. Tore it up so bad that there wasn't no way to fix it. When I took them curtains down, I tried to wash 'em first ... not seein' how bad they was tore up. But then I ended up throwin' 'em away and that really didn't leave me no choice but to clean the rest of the space around the winda' pretty good, with it bein' bare and all. You can understand that, can't ya?"

"Yes ma'am … that seems to make sense to me," he said. "My wife said that made sense to her." Lucky scuffed at the floor with his boot.

"And did you, Mrs. Burgess … or Bette … ever know the woman that was killed and found at the high school?"

"You mean the one them niggers kilt?"

"I mean the one found behind the high school," said Lucky.

"I hadn't never seen her before," said Louis Smith. "I hadn't never laid eyes on her before I seen her at the funeral home."

"I told your ass not to go," came a voice from behind me.

"I know you did, but I was afraid I might know her. Wasn't her name Rose Mary or somethin' like that?" At the end of his question, Louis withdrew his bottle from its place under the chair in which he sat and took a quick drink. Offered Lucky one, which he refused.

"Rosa," said Fred Burkitt after he pushed the door completely shut. "Rosa Mary Dean, I think. Wasn't that her name, Police Chief Hall?"

Lucky turned to look at Fred Burkitt, which always seemed to pain him. I was never certain if it was the absence of Ronnie Langford he saw when he looked at him, Percy or what had happened to Fred himself.

"Yessir, Fred, that was it … is it. They're buryin' her tommora'. Hi ya doin'?"

Fred offered his only hand, his left one, and Lucky shook it. It had been years since he'd worn consistently the contraption that simulated a right arm. He'd told Lucky once that he'd stopped wearing it because he didn't have enough of a shoulder muscle left to control it. He'd lost the arm so deeply into the socket that he'd have to just learn to live without one. But he was lucky, he'd said, seeing what had happened to Ronnie. He even considered himself lucky that it had been the opposite leg that he'd lost above the knee, so it made it easier to walk with the crutch he carried with him everywhere. With his good hand, he patted the empty space on the couch then took a seat and propped his crutch on the arm. He took the bottle Louis Smith offered him and drained a good drink, then handed it back to him.

"And Bette … gettin' back to you. Did you know this woman at all?"

Lucky asked after Fred, too, had offered him the bottle and he'd declined once more.

"You know, Mr. Hall, it's like I told ya the other day, I didn't know who in the hell she was because I'd never seen her before. That's the god's honest truth. I didn't have no idea who she was or where she come from."

"Well, she was from Indianapolis, we believe," said Lucky. "We know that much. Believe she had been from Pennsylvania before that. We believe she'd been here one time before. Maybe three or four years ago. We're still tryin' to figure out why she was here." Lucky pulled his cigarette to his mouth, ashes now longer than cigarette, then searched for an ashtray in which to place it. Finally, he stepped over by Robert Woodson and snuffed it out in the ashtray there.

"I tol' ya before you sent them other fella's in here to take them samples that I didn't know nothin' about her then … and I'm tellin' ya the same thing now. I don't know why y'all got in your head to pick on me. You come to look and see if Miss Ivy here was okay. You found that out."

"Your boy at work?" asked Lucky.

"Sherman?" she said.

"Yes ma'am. Sherman."

"Yeah, he goes every day."

"Out on Carters Creek Pike, right?' said Lucky.

"Yessir."

Lucky paused, lit another cigarette and looked over everyone in the room. Louis Smith had taken another draw from his bottle before passing it to Fred. Robert Woodson scowled at Lucky's profile until I turned my attention to him, when he pretended to be looking out the window. Fred Burkitt now propped himself and his crutch up on the arm of the couch. Mary Ivy arose from her seat, adjusted her pants and blouse and made her way toward the stairs, but stopped at their base.

"How 'bout any of the rest of ya?" Lucky said. "Any of you ever seen her before the other night … I mean the night she was … put out?"

"That's the only time I ever saw her," said Louis Smith.

"I'm with him," said Robert Woodson.

"Miss Ivy?" Lucky asked.

Miss Ivy lit a cigarette with shaking hands, then raised it to her mouth and drew from it. "I've never seen her."

"Me neither," said Fred Burkitt.

Mary Ivy dropped her cigarette and scurried to pick it up before it burned the wood floor. Lucky's eyes followed her hands as she retrieved the cigarette then placed it in her mouth.

"Hi' you been doin' since what happened to your brother?" Fred Burkitt asked.

"Yeah, that was bad," said Robert Woodson. "We sure was sorry to hear that."

"I'd forgot that," said Bette Burgess. "That was just a coupl'a months ago, wasn't it?"

Lucky only nodded. "Thank ya for your time," he said. "I'll get back with y'all if I know more and it's important."

"You do that," said Mrs. Burgess.

"Sheriff, good to see ya," said Louis Smith as I followed Lucky out the doorway onto the front porch. Before the door closed, Lucky looked once more into the lobby of the rooming house where we'd been and shook his head. As we made our way down the three steps onto the flat of the yard, its grass dry and brown, Lucky dropped the cigarette he'd lit and crushed it out with his foot.

CHAPTER THIRTY-THREE

LUCKY STOOD AS CLOSE as he could get to the bank of the river, his hands in his pocket, watching the water move. As the river tended to do from time to time at this bend, it had poured over its natural banks and started making its way toward the road. There was nothing else it could impede or destroy in this area, at least at this time of the year. The nearest house was a mile away; the Confederate Cemetery and the Carnton Mansion, a mile and a half. Lucky's main concern, I knew, was that the road would become impassable. Still just within the city limits, he had complained for years that this spot was covered by the city.

As he motioned me from the car where he'd initially asked me to stay, I craned my neck to see if I could see the spot where Tully and I had made our way into the bushes, his grandfather's car on its roof. I did the same to see if I could spot the place where Sharon and I had been meeting. And as always, wondered where the other spot was. The day Lucky had had to go to claim him, to drag his own brother from the bank and the weeds and brush in which his body was tangled, he had not told any of us where he was going. As he usually did, he took the call and told us in passing that he was going on a call. "Down at the river," was how he said it, if I remember right. That was all.

Probably all of us that day, my mother as she worked busily around the kitchen—her way of not thinking about things—and Jean and I as we sat and played cards to pass the time, knew that the call had to do with Percy. Even Lucky, as he arose from his chair and made his way into the kitchen where my mother handed him the phone and told him it was Don Walton, seemed to know. As I have heard people say before—which I must admit had always sounded preposterous to me—the way the phone rang seemed to signal all of us. I guess it would be the truth to say we had all been waiting on the call since late Friday evening, since Lucky had called his sister Nellie and told her that Percy should be coming back to Thompson's Station, although he did not go into full detail of what had happened. We had all been waiting since more and more time passed and we did not get a call signaling his arrival. Lucky had then called Wanda Jean and Horace and Lera, to see if Percy had in fact shown up there. But he had not.

And I must say that I would be dishonest if I said it was all I thought about that evening and the following day as we waited. I, too, thought about my shoulder that had seemingly been ripped from the socket the night before. Had for all practical purposes, although it was still without official diagnosis by Dr. Guppy, ended my football career.

As I waded through the bushes and the brush, I remembered when I had met Lucky at the station no more than six weeks before and he had brought me in the squad car to almost the same place he stood now. Even though I now felt big enough most of the time, and he appeared sick enough most of the time that I could defend myself from him, I would have laid good odds on an ass-kicking that day. One that I deserved. I had ridden my motorcycle away from school, just left, after Nedler had taken up a paper I had copied a whole test onto after I had finished taking it. I had told him I was writing the test down so I could look over it when I got home, but he was a little too bright to believe me, angrily telling me, "Don't give me that bull—" and then checking himself. Knowing that I would probably go before the honor council, the normal punishment for such an alleged crime, and knowing that I was as poor a liar as I was a lover, I had called Lucky and told him I was coming to talk to him about something. As for Van and Chester, for this day, they would have to fend for themselves.

Lucky did not say a word to me that day when I told him; less than a month after that Friday night and with my arm just getting again to the point I could write with it, he simply motioned me out of his office and to the squad car. As we rode down Main Street and then Lewisburg Pike, I thought how it had kind of felt good to be caught by that bastard Nedler, how it had kind of been my final "fuck you," to him, when I could offer him no other. "That'll show the bastard," I had even mumbled under my breath as Lucky and I made our way through the brush that day. I did not realize at the time that the good old Academy would indeed have the last word, as they always seemed to, revoking my scholarship and making me pay for the whole goddam thing. For the cheating, the honor council would place me on probation and make me work a month of Saturdays on the grounds of the school, which I had done during November, freezing my ass off picking up trash and trimming back hedges and shrubs, white-washing fences and bricko-block and scrubbing bleachers.

Lucky, though, had just sat there long and hard, letting one cigarette burn out between his fingers before he lit another one, taking an occasional slug out of his bottle. Thinking he would eventually speak to me about the evil of my ways, I sat in silence with him, but he did not speak. For a strange eternity we sat there together in the silence created from the absence of our words and I began to think he might tell me what he believed happened to Percy, perhaps what even happened the last night at the jail. But he did not. He did not speak about that Thursday and Friday night in September, nor did he speak about what I had told him that day.

As moments devoid of obvious visceral content tend to do, sitting there with him put me in mind of when I was a child and he would take me to the river with him. Young and healthy, he was in his early thirties at the time. He stood by the river with me, our having finished the first round of fishing, I remember. His day off from the mill, he liked to go to he river and find a good spot and rest on the bank with a six pack and his Luckys. His hand on my shoulder, we stood together, looking into the river, at a spot almost level with the flow of the water. Sporadically as we stood there, he picked up rocks he pulled from the soft ground and hummed them across the water. They almost looked as if they were flying, coming only close enough to the water to contemplate their own landing but then rising again upon their decision not to descend until their journey was further toward complete. As the rocks took on their energy, sailed and then came to their watery graves, he'd comment on fishing or working at the mill or me and Jean or something else just as unmemorable. For the most part if I said that I really remembered one word that was actually spoken, I'd be speaking something other than the truth myself. I recall only that he seemed happy then, or at least to have some kind of levity that would later be lost, stolen or at least come up missing along the way. And what he said after he had unsuccessfully attempted to teach me to skip the rocks as he was doing, saving the smallest and flattest ones for last.

When he'd accepted it would take more time practicing the art before it would take hold, he sat on the bank and began to tell me about his family: Granddaddy and Grandmama Hall, as we called them. And Wanda Jean and Nellie. And Percy, whom I'd only seen a handful of times by then. And he began to tell me how they farmed … and that the land he came from was much like the land behind us, the land that actually lay between us and the Confederate cemetery, that Lewisburg Pike pierced down its middle.

"That farm that your grandparents still live on," he told me, "that land was always good for farming. You don't realize how rich the river makes the soil, or at least how good things'll grow in it, when it's that close to the river. That's the best farmland." Feeling the beer, he put his arm around me and pulled me over next to him. Squeezed my shoulder like he was seeing how close he could pull me into his own ribcage.

"It's called Bottomland," he told me. "I've never even known if that's just what it's called around this part of the country or if that's a word a lot of people use for it. Funny thing about it is that it ain't no good for anything in the world but plantin'. And there's a chance that what you plant might just get wiped away in the blink of an eye if the river does something out of season, like floods in the summer or early fall. That's the reason that all this property down here is empty. Probably never be anything here … but empty land. I'm guessin' that's the way God intended it, that is, if God intended anything."

"WHAT D' YOU THINK?" he asked me as I walked up behind him.

I turned my eyes on the margin of the river, now lapping at flat ground twenty or so feet over the bank. "I dunno," I told him.

"It has quit rainin'," he said, holding his hand up to check for moisture in the air.

"Yessir," I agreed.

"Won't be long till it comes out over the road," he said. "You know, we'll have to shut Lewisburg Pike down, right up there just past the railroad tracks and the Gilco. I remember the last time I didn't get it shut down quick enough. Old man Tywater drove off in it and then blamed me because he wasn't watchin' where he was goin'."

I was beside him now, my shoulders perhaps an inch above his. If he'd not had on his hat, I'd have been looking down into his eyes, rather than at its brim. He tilted his head back and glanced at me, then shook his head. He took his hat off and rubbed his head, the marks from Tuesday morning still visible.

"You remember a few years ago … maybe four or so … when an old man knocked his wife in the head with a cane and threw her in the river? Or at least that's the way it came out in his trial. Old Man Golding, was his name."

Right off hand, I didn't recall it. I shook my head.

He spit on the ground, reached for his cigarettes and knocked one out of the pack. Offered me one, which I took. "About a mile down river here … or really maybe not even a mile … between here and the jail, a woman went into the river and drowned, or at least that's what they thought at the time. When we found her, she had marks all over like she'd been beat. Especially one mark on her head. Right in the temple, where it was almost caved in."

As he spoke of it, the details began to sound vaguely familiar, like a book read long ago and mostly forgotten.

"When they did the autopsy on her, they figured that she'd been killed from the blow to her head rather than the water … and that somebody had thrown her body into the river. I guess the mistake the old man made was let people see him with her before it happened. We had maybe four or five people that either saw 'em in the car together goin' that way or people who even saw 'em together after they got out of the car. Funny thing was that after we found the body and Dr. Guppy said what he did, me and Oscar Garrett went out lookin' for the place she was likely to have gone in. He said he had a' idea that it couldn't been that far from where we found the body. The river was down at the time and he didn't think that she could'a gone that far before gettin' caught in somethin'. When we found her she was caught in a bunch'a brush and bushes."

He paused and lit the cigarette that had been pinched between his lips as he talked. He cupped his free hand around mine and lit it. Gave his customary cough and hack then spat on the ground.

"It wasn't fifty feet up the river that you could tell that somebody had gone through the bushes on the bank and it wasn't fifty feet away from that that you could tell that there'd been a struggle. When Chief Garrett and I questioned Old Man Golding about the way she died, he said that he didn't know what happened. He said that she just set out one day walkin' and didn't never come back. I remember that Chief Garrett went through that scene with a fine-tooth comb. And when he was goin' through it, he found three sets a' footprints there, still in the mud. He had some boys from the state come in and make some casts a' them things."

I stared into the river and drew on my cigarette like he was doing.

"One set a' footprints was Old Man Golding's, one was Sallie Goldings, his dead wife's, and do you know who the third was?"

I shook my head, blew out a mouthful of smoke.

"Bette Burgess's. That woman that we saw a while ago. That's whose. I remember that Oscar Garrett even tried to prove she was involved at the time. It was a well-known fact that she and Old Man Golding had been seein' each other for years … ever since Bette's husband died. But he took the fall … wouldn't have nothin' to do with the fact that she helped him. In the end, he even confessed that he had hit his wife with a cane and drug her to the river. I remember that Mr. Oscar even offered to work with the prosecutor to get him a lesser sentence if he'd tell us the truth … but he never would. He just went on to prison when they convicted him. He'll be there whatever time he has left."

Without provocation, Lucky dropped his cigarette in the wet brush and stepped on it and then turned toward the car and began walking. In the car he sat still, seeming to attempt to gather himself or the energy to go on to what came next. He took in a long breath and rattled out a sigh then turned the key that set the engine to rumbling.

"I think we've got time to go see Sherman Burgess before we go home to eat lunch with your Mama. If I pull up in the driveway, will you run in and tell her we'll be back in an hour or so? We need to eat a good lunch … 'cause it's prob'ly gonna be a long day."

I nodded, and did like he said once he braked the car to a stop in our drive. As I made my way back out of the house, I saw that Christine Smithson had come home for her monthly visit. She waved at me, and I waved back.

"Thank ya for goin' with me," he told me.

I nodded, told him he was welcome. Passing the Academy as we turned on the end of Cleburne Street, it went unspoken that I was glad I wasn't there. And they wanted me gone, too, I believed, so that the memories of their hopes of a state championship would disappear when I did. The only part, I was certain, that they regretted was that the conflict in Korea had ended earlier in the year and they couldn't orchestrate my journey there. In one of the last conversations I had had with Bugg, he'd told me that they'd be sure to let the draft board know if I did not go to college, knowing good and well I had little no other way other than what I watched disappear on that Friday in September.

"It was human blood," he said after we'd moved another few blocks down Columbia Pike.

"Sir?" I said.

"At that house this mornin', the samples them boys took from the state, it was human blood on the floor. We're waitin' on 'em to tell us what kinda blood it was, what type. This man that we're goin' to see, they found blood on his overalls and under his fingernails, too. Human blood. I guess we'll know more once we get the type … to see if it matches."

THE SLAUGHTERHOUSE that Sherman Burgess worked in was on Carter's Creek Pike, around three miles out of town. Lucky asked a redheaded lady at the desk if she could get him to the front. As we waited in the only two chairs in the room, I wondered at why Lucky had really had me go with him. Although I guessed that the reason he'd stated—to verify and witness what he did—might technically fit the bill, I knew Lucky had never before been one to go by the book and did not believe he would start on this day. As we sat there, and I cast my eyes on his as they were set on the floor, I believed in some way, for some reason, he needed me. Although I could not identify the reason and we never in his lifetime discussed it, it seemed as though he was tired and could no longer carry alone the load asked of him. His eyes broke from the floor when Sherman Burgess, six foot two if an inch and two hundred and twenty-five pounds, made his way into the crude lobby area with us.

"Police Chief Hall," he acknowledged, extended a blood-stained hand in Lucky's direction.

"Sherman," my father said.

Sherman Burgess wiped his hand back and forth on his pants leg before he took Lucky's hand. "Hi ya doin'?"

"I'm all right, Sherman. How 'bout you?"

"Been better … been worse," he said. "Mr. Crosby's been closin' us down some. Business just hadn't been that good lately. He's even took to runnin' ads in the *Review Appeal*, tryin' to talk housewives out'a the dirty job of killin' their hogs … tellin' 'em we'll do it for 'em."

Lucky scuffed at the floor with his boot, reached for his cigarettes and offered Sherman one, which he took. "Sherman, I did want to ask ya somethin'…and I want you to think real good before you answer me, okay?"

Sherman looked into Lucky's eyes for only a short moment as Lucky extended his hand and lit his cigarette.

"Now … I'm goin' on what you told me on Tuesday. You said that you hadn't ever seen that woman, right? The one that we found up at the high school. That's what you told me, right?"

"Yessir, it is," said Sherman, who seemed to notice for the first time I was in the room with them. "Hadn't never seen her. I didn't even go to the fun'ral home to see her. I see 'nough blood and guts 'round her every day."

"Yeah, I always thought this'd be a hard job," said Lucky. "It was a job I hated when I was a boy on our farm."

Sherman walked to the only window in the room, three by three and situated so close to the floor he had to stoop to look out, and stared at the half dozen trees and two trucks he could see before the flat ground turned up a Tennessee hill.

"Sometimes," he said, "I think it might just be the wors' job in the world. And then sometimes I think it might be alright … maybe like a preacher or somethin'. I'm there at the end … the last one that they see. But then I think that maybe I'm the one that caused it and the last one that they see is the one that caused it and they know it. And then sometimes I think that I ain't the one that caused it … but that if I wasn't doin' it, then somebody else would be. A man's got to make a livin', Sheriff Hall."

"I know they do, Sherman," said Lucky. "I know they do." Again, he scuffed at the floor with his boot, removing some invisible something, some filth I couldn't see at the time.

Sherman ran his free hand down the sparse hair at the center of his head and smiled at my father without looking at him. He paced back to the window and had another look.

"Sherman," said Lucky, "that sample that we got the other day … or that the boys from the state got, it was human blood. It was human blood on your overalls and it was human blood under your fingernails. And I know what you told me the other day … and I know I believe ya. So there's got to be some explanation. That's what I'm figurin'."

Sherman continued to stare out the window.

"When did them boys come an' take the sample? It was the same day you was there, wasn't it?"

"Yeah, Sherman, if my memory serves me correct. I gotta admit that it is one a' the worst parts a' me now. What day was that? Henry, do you remember?"

I answered. "Tuesday, I believe. 'Cause I remember you tellin' me that you hadn't had time to check on Miss Ivy on Monday evenin'."

"Yeah … he's right. It was Tuesday. The day we put the body out. That's when I come."

Sherman watched a car make its way slowly down Carter's Creek Pike, tap its brakes a few times in the curve in front of the slaughterhouse then disappear around the bend. He drew long and slow on the cigarette Lucky had given him before he dropped it on the concrete floor and smothered it.

"You know, I bet I can tell ya how I got that blood on there. I can't rightly remember the day … but Ward Wells, a ole boy down here at the slaughterhouse … the one I ride back and forth with sometimes … he got him a bad cut on his arm one mornin' last week, right after we got here. I he'ped him with it. Got it on my overalls … I remember I even got it on my hands."

"Is that right?" said Lucky. You think Ward'd remember that?"

"I bet he would," said Sherman. "You know why? 'Cause we couldn't get it to stop and Ward was gonna leave … and Mr. Crosby said to go on an' go wif him 'cause he was my ride an' we was slow that day anyway, like I been tellin' ya."

"That's interestin'," said Lucky. "Is he here today?"

Sherman stared intensely at Lucky for a few moments, then broke his gaze to peer out the window again. "Yessir, I lef' him jus' awhile ago to come up here and talk wif you."

"Alright," said Lucky, nodding his head. "Alright."

Sherman paced quickly halfway across the room toward the door then stopped, as if he had realized that Lucky hadn't said they were through. He cast his eyes on Lucky again, his face twitching just below his left eye.

"Sherman, any idea how blood got in your livin' room area back at you and your mama's house?"

"Yessir," he said. He watched the redheaded woman make her way briefly to her desk and then leave again. "I reckon it was a hog head that Mama was cleanin'. They give me a runt pig from here and I took it home wif me. Mama was mad at me that we got all that blood all over the house. An' she had her a bloody nose real recent, too. I can't remember the day a' that neither."

For a long moment, Lucky and Sherman Burgess locked in eye contact, the kind that normally would have brought something to bear after it. But it did not, only silence and the other sounds that came from behind the closed doors. The redheaded woman returned and Sherman asked Lucky if they were through, if he could go.

"Yeah, Sherman, we're done. Thank ya for your time. I tell ya what you can do if you would. You can have Mr. Wells come out here and talk to me if you want to."

Sherman wiped his hand on his britches leg again and offered it to Lucky and then disappeared through the flapping double doors, from which Ward Wells appeared momentarily.

"I don't rightly remember," had been Mr. Wells' answer when Lucky asked him when he had cut his arm. "Some time las' week or this week."

"What about on Monday mornin'? Was Sherman ready for work when you got there to pick him up?"

"Yessir," answered Mr. Wells, a short man with a clean uniform and a bandage on his arm. "He was out there where he always is. Right out there in front of the house on Evans Alley … waitin' on me. I remember … daylight was just fixin' to break and he was there like he always is … with his lunch in one hand an' a thermos a' coffee in the other. The first thing he done when he got in was offer me a pour a' coffee out'a his thermos bottle, 'cause I've normally drunk mine all up by the time I get to his house."

"An' you're sure that was Monday, right? When he was ready. I wish you could remember what day it was that you cut your arm. He said that Mr. Crosby told him to go, too, since you were goin' home."

"You know," Mr. Wells said, picking at his fingers on one hand, "I believe that was Monday, 'cause when I got home, my wife tol' me about that young girl they'd foun'. Wasn't that Monday, Chief Hall?"

Lucky stared out the same window through which Sherman Burgess had been peering a few minutes before. "It was, Mr. Wells. It surely was."

CHAPTER THIRTY-FOUR

"I THINK I HAVE AN IDEA how all my ideas work together," Percy had told me in one of his last few days there. As had grown to be normal over the years, except for the time he was in the asylum, he was sitting on the edge of his single bed across the upstairs from mine, smoking a cigarette. He pushed the hair out of his eyes, which again had grown long with his last institutionalization.

"I've been trying for years to figure out how all this mess worked together. Randomness, A Planned Nature of Things, and Basic Human Frailty. This godforsaken battle in Franklin, the war in general where so many suffered for such a strange and pathetic idea. I think it's what I was tryin' to get at this last summer when I talked about faith from the top of that car and from the tomato table."

I didn't bother to tell him that it was technically still summer, for about another week. That those days only seemed like they had been a season ago.

"Do you remember that day when I was talking about being what we really are, not what we want to be or what other people expect us to be, to shine through like sunlight? And how that was faith? Not so much believing some dogma ... or whatever they call it ... but believing that there is some direction in this blind river of life?"

387

Again, I didn't remember the words … but recalled the overall concept, which meant little to me at the time, seventeen, going on eighteen. Downstairs, I could hear someone rustling and assumed it was Lucky, home early from a crap shoot, stumbling around with his whiskey bottle, forlorn because he again had lost five dollars and had to come home to us. I heard the princess's whiney voice, like fingernails on a chalkboard. Imagined my mother scurrying around, trying to do anything for them that she could to garner their favor. For the moment, I was glad I was upstairs with my crazyass uncle.

His eyes saddened for a brief moment, lost the tension at their edges. "I think I understand it after Christine … after our time together."

Images of the last time I was with Sharon ran through my head, my groin. I told myself that I understood love. Knew exactly what he meant.

He craned his neck and checked as far down the stairwell as he could see. I had agreed with him the day before when he'd mentioned that Lucky had seemed "hyper-vigilant" in watching him, making sure he stayed in the house, in his own yard.

"Things happen," he said. "That's just the way it is. I guess some are meant to and some aren't … Randomness and The Planned Nature of Things. But now I know it's hard to tell one from the other most of the time. And I've begun to believe that maybe it's not that important to tell one from the other. Some at the time, like the Battle of Franklin, seem as though they might be the most horrific tragedy ever besetting humanity, and others, like me meeting her, seem as though they might be salvation. And yet the time that has come after them has proven them both very different. Something abhorrent proved to be a major factor in the salvation of thousands and thousands of people and something that seemed so good became somehow malformed."

I was nodding with the rhythm of his words, not their content. His question caught me off guard, made me review in my mind what he had said.

"Have you seen her?" he asked.

"Sharon?"

"No. Christine?"

"No," I lied, omitting the times I'd seen her in the yard, waved to her.

"And then," he said, "what you have to consider after that is: What will become from what has happened, from the results produced? There just isn't a clear answer until time makes it clear … and then the next segment of the same thing, time, might serve only to muddy the waters once more."

"Take the battle of Nashville, for instance," he said. "Efim … do you remember him?"

It was hard to forget the short, heavyset Russian man who did nude calisthenics in front of the window in his room. I nodded.

"One day he came back to the hospital after he'd had a pass. You know, you could get a pass if anyone from your family would come get you and take you anywhere. Anyway, he came back from his pass one day and his wife had taken him down Franklin Pike and he saw one of the signs and that strange statue that commemorate the Battle of Nashville off Franklin Pike. At suppertime that night, he came to my room and asked me what I knew about it. He said ever since he'd been liberated at the end of World War II, he was interested in how one thing related to another … how one small piece combined with another to make the greater whole. I know you may think that those sound like my words … but they were his. Really, I think, he just wanted anybody to talk to, to pass the time of day. It gets pretty damn lonesome in there. Have I ever told you about the Battle of Nashville?" he asked.

I wanted to lie, to tell him, yes, he had. But I wanted another one of his cigarettes, too. He handed me one when he took his out of the pack. Lit both of them with the match he struck then he rose and opened the window a little more, stretching to see into the darkness of the cool September night. Unsated, he sat on his bed again.

"Hood was going to try to take Nashville by a counter-charge. He was going to try to make Thomas attack him … had dug himself in halfway back to Brentwood. Like in Franklin on November 30th, Hood knew that the attack was coming. At 2 a.m. on December 15th, he sent a message to General Chalmers, warning that the attack was likely to fall on him in a few hours. Ever since Hood's arrival south of Nashville after the Battle of Franklin, Lincoln and Grant had been urging Thomas to attack him immediately, thinking they should have been more offensive in Franklin. Every horse in Nashville and the surrounding areas was gathered: carriage horses, work horses, plow horses ... even the performing horses of a circus that had gotten stranded in Nashville. Telegrams were sent back and forth between Thomas and Grant. On December 6th, Grant sent Thomas a straightforward command that he must attack. Thomas replied that he would ... but then on the 8th, sent another telegram, apologizing that he had not been able to concentrate his troops or get their transportation in order. That very evening, a freezing rain covered the countryside, making attack nearly impossible.

"On the 11th, Grant telegraphed Thomas directly, saying, "If you delay attack longer, the mortifying spectacle will be witnessed of a Rebel army moving for the Ohio, and you will be forced to act, accepting such weather as you find ... Delay no longer.' Thomas replied, 'The whole country is covered with a perfect sheet of ice and sleet ... As soon as we have a thaw, I will attack Hood.' On the morning of the 14th, two weeks after the travesty at Franklin, there was a rise in temperature, the ground began to thaw ... and Thomas wired Grant: 'The ice having melted away today, the enemy will be attacked tomorrow morning.' But Grant had already started for Nashville that day."

"At 4 a.m. on December 15th, the blare of reveille bugles was heard all along the Federal lines under a heavy blanket of fog that hung over the city. The first movements were on the left, by General J. B. Steedman's men. Shortly thereafter, Schofield's men took their battle positions. Soon after, General Cruft's men were put in their positions. And so on and so on. The way the troops were placed, they almost had provided a continuing defensive line around the city, at the same time relieving the fifty-five thousand men who were moving to attack."

For the moment, he smiled at me like he was aware he had spared me many generals' names, many details my face obviously reflected I had no interest in hearing. He cleared his throat and snuffed out his cigarette, listened for Lucky again and then continued.

"One of the many thousands of Nashvillians who watched the battle from a hilltop described the initial movement of the troops like this: 'Far as the eye could reach, the lines and masses of blue, over which the nation's emblem flaunted so proudly that it was easy to imagine the coming victory.' Sparing you all the details, because I saw you yawnin', I'll just tell ya what Thomas telegraphed Halleck that evenin'. He said, 'I shall attack the enemy again tomorrow, if he stands to fight...and if he retreats during the night, I will pursue him. As soon as Grant heard the news, he sent a telegram saying that 'I was just on my way to Nashville, but I shall go no farther. Do not give the enemy rest until he is entirely destroyed.' The next mornin', Lincoln telegraphed 'the nation's thanks,' and added, 'You made a magnificent beginning. A grand consummation is within your easy reach. Do not let it slip.'

"The 16th brought 'one of the fiercest conflicts that ever took place in the civil war.' The contagion of defeat had taken over the Confederates and they retreated in wild disorder and confusion. Wilson's troops gave chase to them and chased them south through the falling darkness and freezing rain. Finally, the Confederates realized no retreat was going to save them, so they gathered and stood and fought as the Federals charged, thousands against hundreds. Wilson would later describe it as a scene of sheer 'pandemonium,' saying that the Rebels stood their ground bravely but were overrun at every turn and stand."

Once more, and the last time that night, Percy stopped his talking and listened for what I guessed was Lucky. He knew, I believe, as did I, that Lucky wanted no more to do with him than he did with Lucky. Percy made his way to the top of the steps and peered down the dimly lit well until the door that led into the corner of the kitchen stopped his view. He shook his head as if there were no one there, and returned to the window where he took up his watch once more while he spoke.

"Hood's official report of the battle was about like his report about Franklin," he said. "He wrote it from Tupelo on January 9th the following year. No matter, he had to know in his heart the bitter truth. His invasion of Tennessee, the last real aggressive action by the Confederate States of America, had ended a disastrous failure. His army taking the Ohio would remain only a dream. The Confederate flag wouldn't be seen in Cincinnati or Chicago. It was there, at Franklin and Nashville, that he had risked everything … and lost. One of the two great armies of the Confederacy had been overthrown … and its cause lost, too."

"The next ten days were a grave hardship for both armies. Marching and fighting, they took almost a running battle from Nashville to the Tennessee River. The temperature remained below freezing and almost every day brought freezing rain, sleet and snow. Hood's army ate parched corn and corn pone and only a few had blankets or overcoats they had picked up on the battlefield. Many didn't have hats, but it was the scarceness of shoes that presented the most severe problem, their feet leaving bloody footprints over the frozen wagon ruts."

I waited for him to finish the story, to give some ending other than he had. But he did not. He simply laid back on the bed and folded his hands behind his head. Every so often, as my eyes batted with sleep, I would stretch myself to see if he was still awake. Each time I looked, he was smoking a cigarette, staring at the ceiling, like he had done so many nights before.

CHAPTER THIRTY-FIVE

THE SECOND KICKOFF RETURN was in the late minutes of the third quarter, the lights of the stadium cutting through the mist starting to gather in the air. I knew that if I cradled the ball in my hands, I'd be able to take it the length of the field. Beyond the cheers of the crowd and the hushed silence that comes over them the split-second the ball first touches your hands then your chest, I could hear Nedler's voice. I could hear Lucky's. I could see my mother's eyes as she sat across the kitchen table, trying to follow Lucky's voice as he wove the story about what he believed had happened. Both on Tuesday and then again, on Thursday. How I was surprised at what Lucky had said, about both days, how he had divulged so much more information than usual. I wondered at what he didn't say, what was offered in the spaces between the sentences he spoke, the events he described and the deal he had once again worked with everyone involved. Percy had even been present with us at dinner the previous Monday, while Lucky read the *Review Appeal* aloud again, another article about me, not all positive this time.

"It seems like they could'a come up with a better title than that for the damn thing," said Lucky. He sneered across the table at nobody in particular and flicked the first ashes of his after-supper cigarette on his plate, the food half-eaten.

"Daddy, I wish you wouldn't talk like that," said Jean.

I made a face and mimed the words at Percy, at which he laughed silently.

"I saw that," she said.

"He's sorry," Percy said. "He should be nicer."

"We all should be nicer," I commented. "The world'd be a better place."

"They wrote a nice article about him last week," my mother said, always one to find a shred of positive if it was there. "It even talked about how nice it was he'd been working all these years."

"Goddamned Fred Creason—"

"Daddy—" Jean interjected.

"Well, if anybody is, he is," said Lucky. "He's badmouthed everybody in this town at some point."

As far as I knew, what Lucky said about Fred Creason was true. But, as far as I was concerned, it didn't seem that either article had been that different to me. The second one, I thought, had probably been more honest and somewhat of a reaction to how I had played when we played our neighbors, the Franklin Rebels.

As we had done the week before against the Spring Hill Cougars, we had started slow, falling behind in the first half only to recover closer to halftime. I would have assumed it should have been the apex of my career: the phantom, unidentified scouts in the stands at every game, Lucky and even Mama and Jean there as we played our most bitter rival. Even Sharon had taken off from work that night and sat somewhere on the Franklin side with her brother, Bobby the Bootlegger. Nevertheless, it was tied 3-3 at halftime, and even Nedler and Fester didn't eat our asses, but simply sat quiet, huddled in the corner droning to each other. Even Van and Collins were quiet; Johnny Nance, our anemic, blonde quarterback was the only one still smiling, like he almost enjoyed the fact the offense had become like his iron count.

Although we were able to squeak out a win against them as Van caught a pass early in the fourth quarter for the only touchdown in the game, overall it was a dismal performance, one in which Fester and Nedler only told us after the game that we'd played at about fifty percent capacity. And perhaps this was the primary reason I disliked football more than I cared about it: the hero quickly becomes the goat.

"More Heart than Speed," Fred Creason had described it in the title to the article he wrote about the game. "Henry Hall represents the Battle Ground Academy Wildcats in more ways than one," he had begun the article. "If you've been around at all this year, you know that he is the premiere offensive player on the team, but it's easy to miss, in the excitement of watching him play, that this team is driven more by will than raw talent. That was never more clear than this past Friday night as the Wildcats visited the Franklin Rebels' field, just down Columbia Pike.

"During this game three days ago, both of these components inherent in Hall and the team were glaringly evident as they fought the almost completely powerless Franklin High School offense to a 3-3 tie at half time. Most people attending the game, I assume, thought as I, that we would see a different Battle Ground in the second half, the one projected as having a good possibility of going to the State Championship. But the same team returned to the field in the same state as they'd left it. The coaches seemed removed, both Nedler and his defensive coordinator, Langley, and this spirit had seemed to spread across the ranks of the team, as they were able to muster only one touchdown to secure a 10-6 win over Franklin."

Fred Creason had generously and eventually woven the story back to me, revisiting some of the things he'd said the week before, but now identifying the fact that he thought I was basically folding under the pressure of becoming well known, being "scouted."

"He appeared as if his short legs just couldn't produce the speed to make a turn at the corner," he commented, "which serves to remind us that not many players who are 5'8" ever make it further than high school. If he can't turn corners with his speed and then elude players with the same gift, he certainly is not going to bowl them over with his power. And speaking of 'bowl,' I must still question if the Wildcats as a whole can combine their talent in such a way that an appearance in the Clinic Bowl for the state championship is in their future. Perhaps we'll see evidence one way or another as they square off against the Hohenwald Loghaulers next week."

Even with the weight of everything else the following week, I have to admit that it wasn't difficult to eclipse the forty-seven yards I'd gained the week before. The game against those big Germans, as Van described them, proved to be one of the few nights of my life when, at least for awhile, I existed on another plane. Even though people had told me I was good, I had been, for the most part until that night, unable to conceive it. I had been the short kid all my life, the skinny kid, the paper boy who had lived in the shadow of Ronnie Langford in more ways than I could count. But on this night, I was the star I had read about, emerging for all to see. The ball in my hand even felt as if it were almost electric. The vision with which I executed my moves felt as if it were as broad as the field. Every hole, big or small it seemed, was not only within my sight but within the reach of my legs as they moved toward it without thought, but only with the memory my muscles had gained in the dozens of games and hundreds of practices I'd been through.

As I made the cut that freed me and was able to sidestep the last player before the sideline came within view, I heard all the typical sounds: the grunts and exhalations of the kickoff team players meeting their temporary ends as my blockers laid them low with textbook hits. I heard the trampling of feet as they approached and ran with me and then the sound of people as they hit the ground and slid on the grass of the field, damp with the dew of the early evening. From the stands and sidelines, I could hear the voices yelling, could almost separate their tenor, know who was who. Lucky. Nedler. Fester. My mother, had she been there. But she was not. She was home waiting for him, above all others, past all others. Her loyalty to my father obviously stretched itself to include his crazyass brother. Perhaps Lucky had really thought he would come back there, would return with his things the same way he had the last time he had brought him home from Central State, I do not know.

In the conversation that had occurred just before I left for the locker room that day, I'd heard Lucky telling my mother what could not happen. "He can't come back here this time," he'd half-yelled.

"Where else will he go?" my mother, the saint, asked.

"How the hell would I know?" Lucky said. "I can't keep up with him, Mary. God, if there is one in heaven, knows I've tried."

I had tried to act as if I weren't hearing the words pass between them. As I passed the princess's room, she made a face like she had already grown tired of the exchange but was trying as hard as me not to hear anymore of it. I shook my head and passed on up the stairs, where unfortunately their voices followed me.

"You can't just tell him he can't come back."

"I didn't tell him what he couldn't do," Lucky had said. "I just told him what I needed him to do ... go anywhere but back here. I told him that I didn't give one shit where he went ... just away from me ... from us."

Silence enveloped the conversation for a moment as I tried to imagine where Percy would go if he weren't with us. Maybe Wanda Jean's or Nellie's for a few days, but they probably wouldn't put up with him for long ... then he'd be back. He was always back.

"I've tried," Lucky finally said. "You know that, don't ya? Everybody has to know that."

"I know you've tried," my mother told him. "I believe that."

"You know, I even tried to keep from putting him in jail. The first time, I let it go ... just told him to go home ... that that would be a better place for awhile. But he couldn't even do that. Now he just disappeared and reappeared the next day lookin' in some goddam woman's window."

"It wasn't just any woman," my mother said. "You know that."

"Maybe it wasn't ... but it wouldn't have mattered. Anybody else ... I'd have to have done the same thing."

"I know you would have," my mother said, either unaware of what he was likely to have done, or believing better of him, as she tended often to do. "But don't you think it maybe would be best if he went back to the hospital again?"

There was a long pause before my father spoke again, one in which I imagined him dragging on his cigarette and exhaling two or three times before he answered. As the words came from his mouth, my eyes settled on

Percy's empty bed, across from the one on which I sat.

"No hospital," said Lucky. "I told you that before. For him … for me … I can't do that again."

"Not even if it was the best thing for him?"

"Takin' somebody's freedom is never the best thing," he said. "Maybe sometimes it's the necessary thing … but never the best. And this far in his life, necessity hasn't worked in his favor."

I swear, if that line has run through my head once since that day, it's traipsed its way across the path of my memory at least a hundred times. I'm not sure I will understand it by the time I breathe my last.

My mother said no more, but simply resigned herself, I imagined, to the plight she usually suffered. Waiting silently for the repercussions of Lucky's decisions.

It's funny in times like those: it's the easiest to console yourself by thinking that somehow things are unlikely to work out the worst that you imagine. The worst plausible alternative seems within the realm of the most unlikely occurrences.

And funnier—or maybe stranger is a more accurate word—than those thoughts was that as I moved over the last twenty yards into the end zone, I thought of Mrs. Nedler's reputation, true or untrue, another thing I'll never verify. Van, believe him or not, had told me he'd been to see Scoot one afternoon almost evening at work and was walking home past the Academy. As he passed Mrs. Nedler's house, he had seen her standing in the bay window of the house, all dressed up and as sad as anybody he'd ever seen. He walked a half-block past the house before he turned around, he told us.

"Anyway," he went on, "she was still just standing there in this red dress that was cut so you could just see the top of her cleavage … not even enough to really get ya goin' … but enough to hint at what was down further. And her hair was all done … and her makeup was on … and her lips were shinin' pretty and red. That's what I remember about the way she looked. She had on this red dress with red lipstick … and you know she's kind of light complected. And with that off-color kinda red hair … just the sight of her when I went back made my dick stand up and take notice."

"Hey, short fellah," Tully had saluted Van's private area.

Van flipped him off as he kept talking, weaving his tale. "And when I came back by … she had made her way out to the porch and was just standin' there, actin' like she was lookin' at the street. But her look was a million miles away. You know that look, don't ya? Where somebody's just starin' out into the middle a' nowhere."

Tully nodded, drew on his cigarette and checked himself in the mirror of the car. Smiled.

"I was almost by the house when she smiled at me and spoke. I can't tell ya how strange it was. It was like she just stood in that window, dressed up … waitin' for somebody to pass by so she could get their attention. So I decided I'd just walk up and start talkin' to her. I really wasn't even sure who she was at the time. I thought maybe that was Nedler's house … but you know how all them houses look alike."

The strip of street he was talking about was a street called Everbright, located directly across from the main entrance to the Academy, where coaches and a few administrators' houses lined up one after another.

"Well go on with the damn story," Tully chided him. "Don't take all day."

"He's just jealous," Van told me as he tapped my shoulder over the seat. "He's seen her. He's just jealous."

"No, I just don't want to listen to the story all day," Tully said. "I've got other shit to do."

"Torment your grandfather?" said Van.

"Just tell us," I said.

"Anyway," he said. "So I went back and started talkin' to her after she'd smiled at me a second time. And she tells me that she's lived there goin' on two years … and that she still don't know some of her neighbors. She says that a lot of the women are older than her and they don't like her because of the way she dresses. She's out on the porch as she tells me this and motions up and down her body like she wants me to say somethin' about the way she's dressed. Or at least look at her. So I let my eyes run up and down her.

From the top of her head with that hair down past the little cleavage that's showin' … all the way down that hourglass and then to them legs and these red high heels she had on. Up close, I could tell that what had looked like a red dress had these real little, almost invisible pink polka dots on it."

"He's doin' this just to torture us," Tully told me. "We don't give a shit what she was wearin'."

"You would'a if you'd seen her. Anyway, so we start talkin' about football and she tells me how much her husband loves football. And then she tells me that she thinks her husband loves football more than her. Says it's all that he thinks about night and day and she sure does get lonesome there in that house. She says she wants a baby but he won't have anything to do with the idea. Sometimes she just stands in the door and watches for people so she'll have somebody to talk to. As she was tellin' me this stuff, I was lookin' all around, at all them big old oaks and elms that line the street and tryin' to keep from lookin' at her. ,Cause I was already gettin' a little scared that Nedler was gonna happen up any minute."

"Not too scared to go back the next time," said Tully.

"Yeah, but I was that day. I could just imagine that big, hairy son of a bitch comin' up that part of Everbright that you can see from their house and grabbin' me by the hair and draggin' my ass all the way back to Scoot. You know how he's liked to rail on my hair anyway."

At the time, we were sitting in the parking lot of the Academy, having our morning time bullshit session as we watched cars park and their occupants saunter in through the gate that led to our scheduled day of hell. Paul Chester Jr. and Raymond Collins pulled in. For the most part, they represented the two of the three particular strains of the Academy. The boys that were too poor or lacked the "class" to go to the Academy, who were included and tolerated because of their athletic ability, and the boys in Franklin who were given their place because of the money their family had, either earned or inherited. The third group were boys sent from Nashville whose families were in the latter group.

"Yeah, I went back," Van said eying Chester and Collins make their way across the parking lot. "Wouldn't you have?"

"Can't say without seein' her," said Tully.

"You would've," Van told Tully, like he knew everything. The same way he told me he knew I'd "show up against Franklin" when he slapped me on the shoulder after I returned that second kickoff for a touchdown.

As a matter of fact, everybody rolled on me in the end zone, because it was, I guess, fairly unusual for somebody to return two kickoffs for touchdowns in one game. Proved I wasn't slow. Told Nedler to go fuck himself, too. Take his wife with him. I'd tried to ignore him when I made my way to the sideline, like he had done with me when we went in at halftime. I had wanted to stand up and scream, "It wasn't me! It was my crazyass uncle and your crazyass wife! At least she wasn't like Christine Smithson!"

The sidelines brought my breath back, allowed me to take it to the bottom of my lungs again. I checked for Lucky over my shoulder, saw that he was present with the look on his face that had taken residence there in the last few days. A sad, kind of lifeless look, that suggested his face might have forgotten how to express his heart.

Perhaps it wouldn't have been so horrible a thing if Percy had not already done what he did with Christine Smithson. In a town like Franklin, even though Lucky had tried to keep it as secret as the fact that he could be mean as hell to his family or shot craps at the filling station, it did not take news long to spread. By the time that the situation had arisen with Percy and Mrs. Nedler, I would assume that at least half of Franklin's thousand or so inhabitants knew about what he had done with Christine Smithson, not only the first time but now the second. And what had resulted from it.

I have often wondered what Percy would have said had I been able to speak with him about the second set of episodes after they happened. I wondered if he would have tried initially to explain the situation away like he had done previously, or if he would have admitted his involvement right away. If he would have argued that he still did not know what age she was … or that they were both innocent of wrongdoing and guilty only of loneliness. Or perhaps he would have come up with a new theory that would have made it make sense, or resurrected Walter to blame it on.

Or would he have simply told me as he had woven through many of his last conversations that love was simply stronger than the powers that kept him in check?

I will never know.

As to the last days that he would spend at that house, I can only project my thoughts backward onto history as if it might change or control it, at the same time knowing it can do neither. In the only conversation concerning the matter, the one I heard yelled over the fence by Lucky and Mr. Smithson, they attempted to blame it on one another.

"She's been gone for months!" Lucky had hollered, my mother and I near enough to the kitchen window to look out almost immediately.

"No ... he's the one that was s'posed to be gone!" Mr. Smithson responded.

"He was gone!" Lucky hollered back, so loud that it shook the window we stood at.

"For what? A couple of days!?"

"None of your goddam business, that's what! That's how long he was gone. How's that?"

Both men were shaking, trembling like they were perhaps scared of the other ... themselves...what could happen. Lucky was in his "civvies" as he called them, a kind of khaki pants that he fished in and a white tee shirt he'd had on when he walked outside.

"Well, regardless of how long he was gone," said Mr. Smithson, "you didn't do what you said. 'Cause he's back here and he's been with her again."

"How the hell do you know he's been with her? You ever thought your daughter might jus' be tellin' stories?"

Mr. Smithson smiled as broad as he could, showing all the teeth he had at once, and rubbed his chin. "You want to see what a liar she is?"

Lucky did not answer him, but simply stared at him after he finished the question.

"Come on," said Mr. Smithson, who, it occurred to me, had been speaking quieter than Lucky. He motioned for him to cross the boundary separating our yard from theirs and Lucky followed him reluctantly.

CHAPTER THIRTY-SIX

No one has ever claimed to know where Percy went for the three days he disappeared. I can only be sure that he did not go to Thompson's Station as Lucky had requested, which I thought he might have done in front of Old Man Smithson to say, see, you can't tell me what the hell to do with my own brother. And as we never spoke of where it was that Percy might have been for those few days, neither did we, as a family, ever speak of what my father witnessed when he went with Mr. Smithson to the spot that was neither our property nor theirs. The only information I ever gathered concerning the scene came from Todd Smithson, Christine's brother, that I would later feel as if I had a strange, unspoken connection to, who said that he was sure they were just lying back there together, asleep. He told me they had been doing that for days, and although he had never asked them what else they did, he had in fact helped them find one another again and watched out for them so that they didn't get caught. That particular day, he had run an errand for his mother and came home surprised to find his father, who had gotten off early from work.

As Lucky and Mr. Smithson returned from their foray around to the back of the garage, there were no words with them, only two men walking silently, covering the hundred or so feet of space. I would assume whatever they had seen had served the purpose of providing significant enough information that both men accepted something had been occurring that shouldn't.

As they strode back across the driveway toward the porch on the side of our house, I wondered how such a thing could have happened. It occurred to me that perhaps they had both been so concerned with concealing the presence of their own family member, that neither had noticed that the other's had returned. Todd Smithson would later tell me that Christine had been home for a weekend and then had talked her mother into talking her father into a few more days, saying it was lonesome and boring in the country where she'd been sent.

"She smiled a lot after she was with him and seemed to be sufferin' somethin' awful when Daddy took her back to our relatives' house," Todd Smithson finished his description of the situation to me the week after everything happened. "I know a lot of people thought your uncle was crazy and that him bein' with my sister wasn't right ... but as far as she told me he always treated her real good. He was kinda funny ... but I'm gonna miss seein' him around here. Sorry to hear about what happened to you, too. You think you're gonna be all right?"

I nodded and told him yes. Told him thanks for asking. As he walked the short distance between our houses, I began to consider the one of the many questions that would haunt me. It is a question, I assume, I will never answer.

Often at night, I would lie awake and wonder if Percy and Christine Smithson had not somehow found each other twice, lonesome strangers living next door, would the situation with Mrs. Nedler have been as big of news? If Lucky had not experienced the situation with Mr. Smithson, surprisingly defending his brother only to be shown the evidence, its tangible nature for him there to see, would he have handled the situation with Nedler different? If all these things had not gathered themselves and spilled over on Percy in the brief period of a few days, would his response have been different? Or was this simply somewhere he'd been headed for years, the only question being when he'd actually get to his final crazy act? Lastly, had what Lucky wanted for me, and for himself, given Nedler something few people had? Power over him. And had this affected me and the way I tried ... what I did?

I only know that when Christine and Percy emerged from the back of the garage late on that early autumn day, Christine's clothes were somewhat torn and battered, a condition Todd Smithson attributed to their father in the brief bit we spoke about it later, the same condition Mr. Smithson blamed on Percy, saying he had "been at her ... had his dirty fingers all over her." Even though the place they had been holed up was no further than a hundred feet from the back of either house, it hinted at being a separate world, with the wild greenery unkempt and blurring the edges of the space and blinding anyone who entered from the places bordered by it.

Lucky did not speak to Percy as he pushed his head down and placed him in the back seat of the squad car, but only checked the door once he had pushed it shut. Outside the car, he watched as Mr. Smithson led Christine back across the yard toward the back door of their house, that for the most part looked enough like ours that an unaccustomed eye would not have noticed the differences. She, as Percy had done into the car, disappeared through the back door of their house without incident or comment.

As Lucky made his way into our house, he said to me, "Will you go upstairs and get Percy's things? He doesn't have that much, does he?"

"No sir. I mean, yessir, I will ... and he doesn't have much stuff," I said, picturing the night Lucky had brought him home the last time, his small bag clutched to his chest as he exited the car and entered the house ... like it was "his own." I remembered I had thought that.

Lucky nodded then turned his attention to my mother. "That Smithson is supposed to be a good Church of Christ man. I mean, I know ... I don't know what the hell I know anymore."

He would leave the house with a paper sack under each arm, to return an hour later saying that he had let Percy off three-quarters of the way to Thompson's Station. When my mother asked him why he had not taken him all the way, Lucky had not answered, but simply placed himself in his chair and turned his eyes to watch smoke rise over his head toward the darkened spot on the ceiling. "I guess it didn't make a damn," he told me early the next week, "he still came right back here. Or at least he did that evenin'. I don't know why he did that."

I wanted to tell Lucky that I had begun to believe that most of us didn't know why the hell we did most things, especially the most important ones. But I didn't.

Neither did I tell him that four days later after I sat on the sidelines, unable to lift my arm. The play had presented itself much the way the former ones had: the kickoff had floated down after they had once again tied the game. As the ball descended end over end through the night that had now grown clear, I could see the reflection of the stadium lights on its side.

My feet stopped temporarily as the ball first touched my hand. As I surveyed the kickoff team's defense, I saw a hole close on the right to open on the left. The wall of blockers had begun to form in front of me, Collins shifting his position and leading the charge. Almost as if I were in someone else's body, I moved laterally then began to move diagonally then south to north down the field. The defensive players and my blockers came together for the first time in front of me.

I watched as Van laid a hit on some guy that literally knocked him out of one of his shoes. Collins delivered a similar hit, on a number fifty-two that was coming within a few yards of attempting to make the tackle. Then Chester gave me a similar block. The wedge had completely formed now and the hole that I'd seen had been magnified two or three times. I must have been at the thirty-five when I made the cut that sent me through that hole ... and when I noticed the last two men that I would have to beat at the fifty.

I could smell the bacon and eggs as Lucky came back after his first round out Monday morning and we all sat down and he read the paper aloud. He'd open the paper and there would be the article that Fred Creason had written about me ... about the speed that this kid had shown by returning three kickoffs for touchdowns in one game. Wasn't that a state record? Wouldn't that finally get me out of Ronnie Langford's shadow, his legend … Ronnie the hero, which I could not eclipse because there was no current war? Not only was I a scrappy, heart-and-soul-filled halfback, but I was a dynamic kick returner. And wouldn't this put Nedler in his place? Nedler, the man who couldn't keep his own wife satisfied, the man who had arrogantly taken his lack of power and apparent impotence out on someone who simply through strange fate became available.

It was at the forty that I would make the cut to move away from their kicker and the safety. You'd think I would have known his name, but I never did. I saw only that his number was one removed from my own, number twenty-five where I was number twenty-six, and that he was really no bigger than me. Neither he nor the kicker was, but I wasn't concerned with the kicker, who I'd already outrun twice and I was certain couldn't catch me.

As I approached them, the kicker was closer to the sideline, almost hinting that he did not care to try to make the tackle again. The safety, for lack of a better term, was a half-dozen feet inside him, waiting for me to make the cut that threw the kicker off, the one he would react to in the opposite manner of the only other available tackler. I had played enough defense in my time, attempted and made enough tackles, to know that he'd play off the kicker, going the opposite way, knowing that I'd likely cut in that direction. In the split second it took to make the decision, I decided I'd cut toward the kicker, hoping both of them would collapse toward the sidelines. This would make my next cut easier, I knew, that is if I had their legs moving the opposite way. That's the art of running a football, I assume, at least it always seemed to be to me: keeping the man who is trying to corral you off-balance, kind of like life does as you're living it.

As I made my first step toward the sideline and the kicker's feet tangled around one another, my eyes cut to the lower body of number twenty-five. In my imagination, I was certain they'd put him in to do exactly this, to make sure I didn't run another one back. That was his sole job on this team. And I knew what the repercussions would likely be if he didn't. I'd played football since I was in the seventh grade, baseball since then, too. I knew what men like coaches expected from kids in these positions. Somehow this world took on more importance than it actually had, meant more than it ever should have. Distraction, perhaps, so the real world seemed less serious. The real world as it was occurring probably around this time, down near the river somewhere. That real world. Everybody's eyes were focused on me. It made them, me … us … forget.

The Little Man—that's how I've come to think of him in the years that have passed—in my memory now looks like I did at that age, innocence and self-will still in his eyes. Determined he was going to make this play or be goddamned. His feet planted for that moment, two or three feet apart, waiting for his next move that would mirror my own. His eyes green and tired, his face expectant. As I had thought, he made the opposite move from the kicker, toward the inside of the field. I had then decided I would make the opposite cut of the one he'd suspect: back toward the sidelines. I could hear Nedler's voice, Lucky's voice, the voice of every coach I'd ever had, hollering at me, telling me to switch the ball into the other hand. So I could use the free arm to fight off the tackler if need be; so the ball would be harder to reach and more likely to go out of bounds if fumbled.

The ball moving from my right to left hand, I tried to make my way into the space that was created when number twenty-five had made his move the opposite direction. The space seemed have grown from six or so feet to probably ten, and I knew I stood more of a chance trying to shoot that gap than I would attempting to make another cut back toward the inside of the field. There would be one last surge that would take place that would, I suspected, include acceleration or impact. If the acceleration was quick enough, then there would be no impact; if impact came, then the chess match that had occurred within the few split-seconds that had passed would have been for all practical purposes useless.

By his number, he was a running back himself, I guessed, and probably played in the defensive secondary if he played defense at all. As the night had progressed, I had noticed little. As I sat on the bench on the sideline— no longer playing defense because of my "potential"—I had watched nothing but my feet, the eyes of my heart turned inward. If this man, boy, whatever he was, had been in the secondary, I would not have known it because I had yet to make it by the linebackers for the second straight week, trudging out two and three yards at a time until finally Nedler had elected to let Nance and Van and Collins try to produce some kind of offense.

"If you are gonna get hit," Lucky had always told me, "use that arm first. Keep 'em at a distance so they can't wrap you in their arms. If they ever get their arms around you then they can sure as hell bring you down!"

As I tried to make it through the space between number twenty-five and the sideline and he tried to close my space, I could feel my arm rising so I could make one last attempt to keep him off me. From the look in his eyes, I think neither he nor I really wanted to make this play. All things being equal, I imagine he would have just let me go. For the brief moment when my hand touched his chin, neck and upper chest and he was able to wrap his right hand in my jersey right below my shoulder pad, we made eye contact again. Even though I cannot remember what he looked like to this day, I just recall his eyes, that they looked like mine. Green. A million questions in them. Wanting this and not wanting it. Knowing that this would make him the hero or the goat. Somehow knowing that this play made a great difference … would probably make the difference of the game. And really, in the grand scheme of things, didn't make a goddam.

The struggle began around the fifty, my arm locked in the neck of his jersey and his tied up in the underarm of mine, each of us spinning the other, attempting to fight free from the binding force that held us. The other. On the second turn, almost as if we were dancing, our feet moved in unison, more lateral and circular than forward. On the second complete twirl between us, I knew I'd be tackled by other players who'd caught up to the play, that is, if he kept his hands on me for even another few steps. With my hardest push I was able with to loosen his hand from my jersey and break free for another three or four steps, mostly up-field. Once again, though, he was able to grasp me, this time by the arm.

Such major injury, I always thought, would perhaps take more time, play itself out more slowly. Something that prominent to the body should surely make itself more known, I always imagined, not just be the period at the end of a sentence but be the sentence itself. As he and I went around a third time, in desperation to make the tackle, rather than try to pull me down, he used our spinning to propel himself and me as he slung me toward the sidelines by the grip he had on my wrist. He was down now; there would be no other attempt at tackle unless someone else had made it up from behind us in the momentary struggle. As my feet slowed and my balance steadied, I began to believe I was, in fact, going to stay in bounds. As I tried to make the last step that would have moved my body in the north to south direction once more, the pain of hot coals on naked skin tore through my free arm, and almost as if someone had let the energy out of me like air out of a punctured tire, I began to melt into the ground. The ball hit at my feet and then made its way with a bobble and roll out of bounds. Just like it should have.

CHAPTER THIRTY-SEVEN

ON THIS SATURDAY MORNING, I had been surprised when I found him sitting awake in his chair when I descended the stairs into the kitchen. Initially, I had only seen his feet, flat on the floor, a foot or so part, as I glanced into the dimly lit room. Before I could make my way out of the kitchen and across the back porch, he put his hand on my shoulder, causing me to nearly drop the glass of milk in my hand.

"You wanna meet me down at the river after you get through with your papers?" he said. "You ain't got nothin' else you need to do after that, do ya?"

In the last couple of days, I had come to believe he knew there was someone, just perhaps not her name. Sharon was at work all day this day, a Saturday, December 18th. There was nothing further that I knew to do, except sit around and wait for her to get off, shoot the shit with Van and Tully—which I knew I'd do later in the afternoon anyway—or be exposed to Jean all day, listening to her talk about this new boy she'd started going out with. She'd been going to school with him since she was six years old, but now for some reason he was big news. Jimmy Platt was all I'd heard for a week before the woman was found at the high school and for the two days after, since the situation had somewhat resolved.

"You gotta check again?" I said.

"I do," he nodded. "I think it's pretty much under control. But you know how that river can be. Damned unpredictable at best."

I nodded and he returned to his chair, where again I could only see his feet and a cloud of smoke when I passed out the back door to go the paper office. My arm moved in rote that morning as I threw my papers, my mind making its way back to September, when he had for the first time asked me to meet him there.

Then and now, it was almost as if perhaps he were looking for him to return, for someone to tell him what had happened had not. For something to indicate to him that there is an answer past the hardship and strife of this life. It was now as if the water helped him to think more clearly, its movement somehow calming him, reminding him that there are forces far beyond those we perceive of our power and accord. I have no doubt that my uncle believed that. Many people, I am certain, thought what he did as a mere extension of his craziness, but on my good days I have always preferred to think about it as if he lived with perhaps one foot in whatever it is that comes next. As if in some ways he saw more clearly than the rest of us, or at least most.

Fred Creason, though, did not think so. Although I will not affirm his journalism by repeating these years later what he wrote following my uncle's disappearance and eventual recovery, it was neither kind to nor true of him. And the same, I believe, of Mrs. Nedler, although I know little to nothing about her except what Van had told me and the fact that she and her husband would move the year following my breaking free from football and the Academy like a rusty cage.

I knew that if I had really wanted it I perhaps could have gone back … could have rehabilitated myself so I could have played once more. But, I also know, in my heart of hearts, I did not. What I wanted at the time, even though the reality would skew further away from pleasure than I could ever imagine, was her. That was all I wanted.

As we had sat at the river that day in September, my arm hung by my side in the makeshift contraption Dr. Guppy had placed on it, that in its own way reminded me of Fred Burkitt and his arm, Lucky did not ask why; he only replayed the scene over and over with words. "I thought you had that return. I thought you'd broke that tackle," he told me as he watched his own hand flick ashes from the end of his cigarette, like he had done a hundred thousand times.

"Me, too," I'd said, watching the river pass as we sat on the bank.

"How is it?" he'd asked.

"It hurts pretty bad," I'd told him. The truth was that it had hurt so bad that I pissed down my leg twice: when Van had tried to help me pull my jersey and pads off over it in the locker room after we'd won the game … and the night before this day when I was trying to take my shirt off. I was always too embarrassed to tell anybody besides Sharon, and hoped against hope that nobody had seen me in the locker room. Van, in one of those brief moments of kindness he could display, had acted like he hadn't noticed. Hadn't mentioned the huge splotch of water that covered my crotch and the upper portion of my left leg.

"You want me to give you a ride on your paper route?" Lucky asked me.

"No sir," I told him. "I've been makin' it." The truth of this was that it had been taking me twice as long because I could neither control the Indian nor sling the papers with my right arm. I'd been throwing a lot of it parking and walking. But I wanted no one's sympathy, including his. For some reason, the whole week had seemed to affect me that way: like I was in a trance almost, having the strength from somewhere to make it through the motions, yet remembering or feeling very few of them. There had been things to do; I had tried to help Lucky as much as I could, help my mother help him. Tried not to ask questions, knowing that there would be no answers. Even on this day, I had gone to the river with him at my mother's suggestion, because there had to be one last going-over of what, I guess, though never mentioned, was called a "crime scene," to see if there was anything else that suggested what was apparent. Just get through the day—that was the objective upon arising. Say as little about what had happened as possible. Only Jean and I would speak of what had occurred. Late at night, when we'd return from the visitation two nights before they buried him on a Thursday, Jean and I would retire to the upstairs and hash out what we believed … thought … knew.

"You know him well enough to know he wasn't goin' to do nothin' to that woman. Percy didn't have that in him," she said.

"You know that you and I know that. But to a lot of this town, he was just the man who roamed around, protected by his brother the Police Chief, who had done 'that' to Christine Smithson not long ago. Twice."

I turned my eyes to her, the first time I could remember in a long time looking in her eyes, blue like my mother's. For all practical purposes, they were my mother's eyes. I felt my pants pocket for my cigarettes but started not to pull one out in front of her. Then thought what the hell, that nothing seemed to matter much anymore.

"He was just lookin' in her winda'. Don't her husband think it was likely that maybe it did happen like Percy said it did … that she motioned for him to come over there like she was gonna talk to him."

"I don't know what he thinks," I told her. I lit a cigarette and watched her through the smoke rising. I had to handle the thing with my left hand, which I could barely do. I started to tell her about what Van had told me, even felt the urge to explain to her that for once I believed him but then realized, or at least believed, it futile. Tears were dammed in the corner of her eyes when I looked back at her. She pinched them with her thumbs, tried to keep from smearing the mascara she still had on. As I watched her, it came to me that it was September, burning-ass hot September in the middle of Tennessee, and I was sitting in this attic, without even a fan running in the window. The air thick and syrup-like, almost solid, like it was sticking to me and then peeling off in sheets.

"You know what Todd Smithson told me?" she said.

As I shook my head, I immediately found myself wondering what the hell he had to do with any of this and knew it was probably no more than what he had to do with Percy and his own sister. Wrong place at the wrong time. Or maybe just a certain place at a certain time would be a better way to say it. Ever since Monday I'd found myself trying to find almost any-body to blame, besides the characters that really were culpable.

"What?"

"He told me that he saw Percy there when she was at her winda' … said that he was just out walkin' 'cause he was lonesome and missed his sister and couldn't stay in the house no more with his mean ole daddy. Said he passed Percy on Everbright … well, that he had been behind him and then he walked by after she had waved at him from her winda'. He said Percy looked bad, like maybe he'd been sleepin' somewhere it was muddy for a coupl'a days. But that didn't stop that woman from wavin' at him. Said she waved and he stopped and jus' looked at her from the road a little bit like maybe he was tryin' to remember who she was. Then he acted like he did and went up to her when she said somethin' to him. Todd said that they stood there and talked awhile … and that was the last thing he saw when he got to the end of Everbright and turned on Academy."

I nodded, knowing that it mattered little how much we talked about it: what had happened, or exactly what had happened, would never be known. It would never be known if my uncle had finally gone over the edge that would transform him, in the collective eyes of Franklin, from a nuisance to a danger or whether he had been drawn into something that he did not understand. I think he had been so used to seeing people look at him with sideways glances and suspicious, incredulous eyes, that probably any positive attention from a stranger would have been interpreted kindly. Especially when he had been removed from the only family he knew a few days ago and the stranger was Mrs. Nedler.

"So … do you think he meant her any harm?" Jean asked me.

Before I could even consider her question, come up with an answer that made sense, a voice almost not my own came from inside me. Spoke itself. "Harm? What's harm? Do we ever really know?"

She looked at me like she thought I was as crazy as my uncle had been.

"So why do you think he was lookin' in her winda'?" she asked. She said the word just like our daddy, downstairs and I was certain drunk as he could be by now. He'd lived on the bottle since Monday, worn it like armor to protect himself.

"I don't fuckin' know," I said, before I got a handle on my words. "I'm sorry. I don't know."

I looked at his bed, the one he had slept in just a few days before. The one that had been Jean's before it was his, before she reached the status of princess and he reached the designation of my chronically crazy uncle. It looked as if it were ready for him. I doubted that the sheets had even been washed since he was there. Around our house for the last week, life had all but stopped, first with his absence and then with the call that would come on Monday.

The tears that had been threatening to escape finally did so down Jean's cheeks. I stood and covered the few steps to the chest of drawers and handed her a handkerchief I never used anyway. She blotted at her eyes and gave me an awkward hug, the kind that asks you not to notice tears as they fall.

"I guess there's just some things we'll never know," I told her.

All I really did know was that we had seen him that night, looking like someone whose death had been in the water. His body and especially his face, thick with the makeup George Preston had applied, appeared to have that quality that they had been saturated with the substance that naturally fills the river. Gathered as much of what had taken his life as possible, held it so closely it would not leave. His face appeared almost not his own. As I stood at the side of the casket and pressed my arm across Jean's back for the first time I could remember in years, I tried to figure whether it was the bloat or the semi-peaceful expression that made him not look like himself. Or perhaps it had been the suit that Lucky had gone to Pigg's Menswear and gotten for him that had made him look unlike himself. His legs, underneath the closed section of the coffin, I knew, were covered in britches not hemmed for time's sake. Lucky had told Mr. Pigg that would have to do, then choked back sobs with his free hand before disappearing to the bedroom.

"You could tell there was bruises under that makeup," said Jean, who either hadn't noticed I was smoking or didn't care. I thought about how death had its own way of calling quickly into question our priorities.

"Yeah, I heard George Preston tellin' Daddy that he had done the best he could. He said it was right on the line of bein' a case where they closed the casket. He said he made him look as good as possible."

"All things considered," said Jean as she walked to the window, looked out at the Smithson's house, "I guess he looked pretty good."

As I stared at her back, her wavy blonde hair, crimped and tamed so that every one was in place, I had to wonder what was to be considered. What were all things?

"Did you hear that Nedler hit him?" I said.

"No ... did you?" She sat on the bed again, stretched out her legs and stared at her feet.

"No," I said. Rethought it. "Well, yeah. I've heard everything in the last few days. From Van ... from Tully."

"If Daddy...."

"Yeah, if Daddy...." I said, but didn't finish.

The object of our statement went unspoken. Always has and always will, I assume. There are some things Jean and I have carried from the family from which we come that we do indeed continue to carry.

"I heard that Nedler hit him in the back of the head," I told her. "That's what I heard. Saw him tryin' to get in the front door and his wife yellin' and he hit him in the back of his head with his fist and then called Lucky. That's what I heard. I heard that when he appeared on the end of Everbright, headed toward his house, Mrs. Nedler started hollerin' that she wanted Percy out'a her yard. Supposedly, he fell down after Nedler hit him one time and just huddled there in a ball till Lucky got there."

How information like this passed from person to person, I did not know. I only knew that it was again a quality of language that somehow, as Percy had suggested, fell short of correctly or accurately conveying reality. I also knew that it had been passed from person to person and could have been so diluted by the time I heard it that it could no longer even be called real information. These were just words now. Possibly as empty as I felt. As empty as life seemed in this moment.

"He just hit him once?" she asked.

I nodded.

"What about all them br—?" but then she quit, not liking, I assumed, the answer she quickly concluded.

"That's what I heard. But like I said, I'm not sure we'll ever know exactly what happened." I crushed my cigarette out in the ashtray by the bed, the one that had been placed upstairs years ago for Percy, after a long battle about him smoking up there. He had finally won, convincing Lucky he was no more likely to burn the house down than Lucky himself was. He was not a drinker, Percy had finally told him, and was much less likely to fall asleep accidentally.

"You think he got all them bruises in the river? I mean, after he went in … was took … I mean, taken by the current?"

I looked into her eyes again, once more concluding they were my mother's eyes. They were open wide in their corners, the broad whites suggesting she expected an answer.

"I don't know," I told her. "Like I said, I imagine there's just some things we'll never know." I lit another cigarette and diverted my eyes out the window, staring at some tar patching on the Smithson's roof under the faint glow of a close-by street light.

"But if he didn't get them in the river and he didn't get them from Mr. Nedler, then..."

"You know better than that," I told her, and felt for the first time I was protecting her from the truth. Somehow I now felt responsible to do so.

I am unsure if she actually knew better than that. Although she did mention it twice more as we sat on the bed in the suffocating heat of that attic that night in September of 1953, after this night, she never alluded again to the possibility of anything we did not know having happened to Percy. Although his name was mentioned often between us over the years, and still is on occasion, what happened to him was never again discussed. Like so many things involved with living in this world, to the mystery we deferred and ultimately defaulted.

As we sat there for another hour that evening, knowing that the following day, as was the custom in our part of the country, we would again see his body and the morning following that, bury him, I could not tell you what else we spoke about. Perhaps, we spoke about the things that seem to matter when you're seventeen and eighteen, how the world in all its possibilities, even in the worst of times, seems to be calling you forward, whispering those secrets that only you and it know. For those brief years that childhood and the struggle of adolescence is behind you and adulthood has yet to fully come upon you, the promise of dreams and the perfect world we'd like to believe in seems just within our grasp. For the most part, we are not old enough to take seriously the potential consequences of our decisions, nor have we experienced enough sorrow to realize that as often as not life comes to its own conclusions, far outside the boundaries of wishes. Our course, it seems, is still charted, not measured.

The times in that evening when she did come back to the question she had quickly and efficiently avoided earlier, she once more focused her eyes on mine, perhaps more deeply than we had looked at each other in a long time, the same eyes searching mine for the more honest answer past the tone and content of the words I spoke.

"Wonder what happened to him?" she said suddenly, changing the direction of whatever we were speaking about at the time. "I bet them branches in the water caused them bruises on his face. I bet that was it."

I nodded in response to her statement, as if I agreed with her. I recalled hearing Lucky speaking with Dr. Guppy after they had found Percy on Monday, saying that the bruising had to have come before the drowning for some reason I didn't understand. Lucky had acted as if he didn't either, his eyes turning to the floor.

"But he did die of drownin'?" Lucky had asked.

Guppy had nodded and said nothing further.

"Maybe the current knocked him up against things as he was goin' down the river," Jean said, like my eyes had betrayed me during my last agreement.

"Maybe so," I nodded again. "Maybe so."

Again, I wanted to tell her that what I had come to believe over the last year or so of my life, and especially the last week of days, was that there are things that we neither understand nor can fathom, and of those things we must trust somehow that they do … or at least will someday make sense.

Randomness … The Planned Nature of Things … Basic Human Frailty. I wanted to tell her about these things, at least what I understood about them at seventeen, of which I know only a little more now.

Accordingly, I did not want to tell her what I believed to be true about Percy's death, partly because for the first time that I could recall, I felt the need to protect her from something, and partly because I did not want to admit to myself that I believed it.

Perhaps it was not that my father was a worse man than others I have known. And, in some ways, I would argue, and believe, that he was better. He was, I believe, loyal almost to a fault. Loyal until anger rather than removal overtook him. It wasn't that he did not care; it was almost as if he cared too deeply. I, though, am not creating an apologetic for him and his ways, and neither am I apologizing for him. Somehow that person that seems to lurk inside all of us, that person who represents the worst of us, the worst of humanity, often seemed utterly apparent in him, as if it lived a bit closer to the surface than in most people. Nevertheless, perhaps none of us wants to believe that we have that person inside us. It seems very seldom that we come into true contact; I believe many of us go a lifetime and are never faced with the cold, hard reality of what we're capable of.

"IT AIN'T COMIN' AS HIGH as I thought it might," he told me, his eyes set hard on the river, still ten or so feet out of its banks.

I had to remind myself it was not September, that that month, those happenings had been three months and a strange lifetime ago. It was now December, a Saturday in December, six days before Christmas.

"No sir," I agreed. The day and a half of rain that had come in the last two had served only to keep the river at its current level, not deepen it.

Though I had not turned, I knew it to be him by his voice, the sound of his legs and feet now moving through the brush and weeds behind me. He found a dry rock to sit on a couple of feet away. Lit a cigarette.

"There never will be nothin' here," he observed.

"No sir … bottomland," I said, showing him that I remembered what he'd said.

"The road can stay open," he told me.

I nodded.

"You know why I was up when you left this mornin', don't ya?" he asked. He studied the cigarette in his hand and flipped ashes at the wet weeds around his boot. It was unusually warm for December in Tennessee, mid-fifties.

I shook my head.

"'Cause I'd been at the jail most a' the night. We got so many people in there, I'm afraid to leave just one patrolman there. "I been thinkin' about sendin' some of 'em to county. I don't know what I'd done if I'd had to keep Jackson and Arliss Mosby there. Hell, they shouldn't never have been there in the first place. That's twice I ain't done right by that family. I should'a just shot Sammy Samuels when he done that to Arliss all them years ago."

Again, I nodded, neglecting to tell him that I too had served the Mosbys, particularly Jackson, a bad turn, protecting my own ass.

"It looks like two of 'em are gonna turn state's evidence," he said. "We found one weapon in the house. I got Don Walton and a crew a' men drainin' the outhouse right now. They say there might be another knife in there. I guess the fact that I got him doin' that job goes to show ya ever' once in a while it's good to be somebody's boss."

I laughed, hollow as it left my chest. Again, nodded.

"You know why I remembered that case?" he asked me.

"No sir."

"'Cause in September I went down there and looked through the records, wantin' to believe that somethin' like that happened to Percy. Ain't that a hell of a note? Hopin' somethin' like that might'a happened to your own brother? At the time … even now … it just seems like it might have been better than what happened."

I wanted to ask a blue million questions but did not.

"You know, he called from somewhere that mornin' and talked to Mary. Did you know that?"

I shook my head.

"Son of a bitch said he was goin' to the river. That's all he said. 'Tell

Dillard I'm goin' to the river.' That's all he said. He must'a just walked in."

This was the extent to which my father and I would ever speak about Percy's death, after the death of Rosa Mary Dean and the subsequent capture and arrest of her killers. As the years have passed, though, that is not what I most prominently remember from that day at the river, that last Saturday before Christmas in 1953.

"Where's your class ring?" he asked me, his eyes focused on my right ring finger, where it had been placed for a year before I gave it to Sharon.

I started to lie, but then thought better of it. "A girl's got it."

"I figured as much," he said. He lit another cigarette then crimped his lips around the end of his tongue and made a spitting noise. "I ain't stupid. I figure you been doin' somethin' every mornin'."

"I might marry her," I said.

"A family life's the best life you can have," he said. He offered me a cigarette from the pack he hadn't put back in his pocket yet. I took one and lit it, drew deep and felt the calm that first comes when nicotine hits your bloodstream.

For what seemed like a long time, we sat still and in silence before he spoke again. "I got somethin' wrong with my lungs," he said. "A few weeks ago, Guppy sent me down to Vanderbilt and they said I got what they call emphysema. I think I'm sayin' that right. Whatever it's called, it's where your lungs don't work right no more. They don't take in air and push it out right."

In the day it was, even though his symptoms had been fairly apparent for awhile, I believe I would have been less surprised if he had slapped me in the back of the head with his pistol.

"Do you remember that spat that you an' me got in back in May?" he asked me.

I did not remember a spat. I remembered him, as he had done many times, allowing himself to become outside his own control and kick me in the ass after he had pushed me down. I nodded anyway.

"I went to see Guppy after that. Hell, it was the first time I'd been to the doctor in ten years. He wanted me to go to Vanderbilt to see a lung doctor.

Then I put that off and put that off until I knew I had to. They told me a coupl'a weeks ago what I'm tellin' you. I ain't even told your mama. Not Jean. Nobody. I'd appreciate you not tellin' nobody."

"All right," I told him. I wondered why he'd told me. As with most things, I had no answer.

"Guppy tells me if I quit smokin' then it's likely it'll be all right or at least won't get no worse. But it's funny, I can't bear the thought. Ain't that funny, how we can love somethin' more than life itself? Not just your own … but anybody's?"

Once more, and the last time of the day, I answered silently by nodding. Then, as I'd done all those years before when Lucky had taught me to skip rocks, and probably had not done since, I laid my head on his shoulder and just sat and listened to the silent sounds of the river moving slowly by. Invisibly by.

EPILOGUE

T HE ACCUSED in the Rosa Mary Dean case would go to trial in January of 1954. The Franklin Courthouse was packed to overflow each and every day. Van and Tully skipped school one day to go, saying that they knew if they got caught there wouldn't be anything that happened to them; I declined the offer when Van came to my house and asked if I wanted to join them. And even though Lucky spoke of it little, Fred Creason wrote about it each time the *Review Appeal* was published, as he had done when Bette Burgess and Sherman Burgess and Fred Burkitt and Bobby Bishop and Miss Mary Ivy were charged. The only two arrested that were not charged, besides Jackson and Arliss Mosby, were Robert Smith and Louis Woodson, whom I've always assumed Lucky and John Hendricks, the county prosecutor, believed to have nothing further to do with the matter than they were simply living in the house where it took place.

As for the information that would come to the surface in the trial itself, it was mostly as Lucky had theorized: that this woman, Rosa Mary Opinsky Dean, had come to Franklin to extort money from Bette Burgess, knowing that she had been involved in the murder of Mrs. Sallie Golden, which John Golden was already doing life for. He had refused to implicate Bette, a woman with whom he'd been having an affair for years. Although it was never known exactly how Rosa Mary knew of the murder of Sallie Golden and its details and participants, it was an accepted fact corroborated by the Beattys that she had been there in 1949. Of course, Bette Burgess never admitted her involvement in either of these murders, as she stated to the end that she had never seen this woman who had been found at the high school early the morning of December 13th and had no reason to know her. Her son, Sherman, stated the same. The saving grace, if you can call it that, of the prosecuting case came at the hands of one Fred Burkitt, who turned state's evidence for immunity. As a result, the story that most everyone has believed to be true, including myself, came to light.

In the crowded courtroom, with Jack Noonan, the lawyer that Fred's wealthy parents who now lived in Nashville provided him, watching as he testified, Fred Burkitt told the dark tale that he said had haunted him since that Sunday evening turned Monday morning. His testimony, which Fred Creason described as "flawless but believable," told of him bringing himself downstairs in the Burgess boarding house late the evening of December 12th. His stump was hurting, he said, something he had heard called pain of a "phantom limb," and he was going to ask Bette Burgess for some aspirin. In the room that connected to the lobby of the boarding house, he could hear voices and thought that it was simply Bette and Sherman still awake talking. Upon pushing the cracked door open, he found Bette seated at the table, watching as Sherman performed the last touches of slitting Rosa Mary Dean's throat for what he guessed was the third or fourth time. The moment his eyes met Bette and Sherman's, he stated, he knew he was next, which Sherman told him in no uncertain terms. As he described Sherman Burgess's threat and referred to himself as a "wounded veteran of the war," he began to cry and stated that Ronnie Langford had been a hero, not him. If he'd been a hero, he explained, he wouldn't have gone along with such a thing as he agreed to that night. With little more prodding, he explained, he had used his one good arm to help them wrap the body of this woman, still warm, in a sheet and lay her under the window out of which they would take her a few hours later. He had also helped them clean up the mess and dispose of the towels and the weapon. Bobby Bishop's involvement, he explained, would come when it was time to dispose of the body.

Unable to help with carrying the body to the extent needed, Sherman again threatened him to find someone else to help. Going up to the rooms upstairs, he explained, he quickly decided that Robert Smith and Louis Woodson would be of little help, one crazy and one drunk. The two able-bodied people there at the time were Miss Ivy and Bobby Bishop, just having come in from a whiskey run from Alabama. When he returned downstairs with these two, Sherman immediately berated him for bringing Mary Ivy and sent her back upstairs to bed with a similar threat as to the one he'd made to Fred Burkitt. As for Bobby Bishop, he had helped Sherman and Fred Burkitt, what little help he was, carry the body to the high school, where they had planned to place her in the incinerator. Upon arriving, though, the janitor and some kids across the parking lot had appeared and Bobby Bishop had abandoned his efforts and run. Sherman Burgess had struggled for a few moments, again threatening Fred Burkitt if he didn't help him, and then given up when he seemed to realize he was again getting the woman's blood, though now mostly dry, on himself. Finally, Fred and Sherman left the body and made their way back to the Burgess house, some hundred and fifty yards away. According to Fred's story, the next thing he had heard about was later in the day when he was at the pool hall downtown, something he could successfully do with his arm contraption, when word got there that there had been a murder overnight in Franklin and the body had been found at the high school.

On cross-examination, the public defender, Jefferson Daly, questioned him dutifully about the morphine habit he had, that had been developed and maintained since the Second World War. He was asked if this habit ever affected his ability to perceive and interpret reality correctly, which he answered affirmatively. The public defender so lambasted him that in the end it seemed as though he might ask about the destruction of the cemetery, but did not. According to Lucky, who was at the trial at least a good portion of the time, Fred's parents sat on the back row of the courthouse, his mother often weeping concerning what her son had become. Even before the trial, Lucky's theory had long been that they had moved to Nashville after Fred had returned, fairly derelict, from the war, so they did not have to cast their eyes on him on a near daily basis. Right or wrong, it is easier to avoid family members sometimes, he explained to me, than face what they have become.

Bobby Bishop did not fare so well. The day of his testimony, the only day of the trial that his sister Sharon attended, he was forced to admit what he had been doing for a living for the last few years, even before he dropped out of Franklin High School and became a full-time whiskey runner. He was also drawn to testify that his mother had made him leave his own home in the last year, though I was unsure this was the truth. Nevertheless, in the end, he reported utterly the same story of the night that Fred Burkitt had, which Mary Ivy also corroborated when she testified.

According to Fred Creason in one of his kinder moments, my father's testimony and ultimate police work, although possibly "acrimonious," were in their own right fairly accurate. It was almost as if he had not previously criticized him, but now held the opinion that the case had been fairly airtight from the beginning and Lucky had simply carried through with the things laid before him.

The jury of twelve, men of course, did convict Bette and Sherman Burgess of first degree murder. According to hearsay around town, the last holdout was Sammy Samuels, still convinced that Arliss and Jackson Mosby had something to do with it. But, in the end, faced with the evidence and eleven other jurors, he, too, voted for guilty and the death penalty for both. Neither of them, though, would come to their end in the electric chair, but of cancer and a heart attack, respectively, as they awaited their state-designated fate. As for the boarding house they ran and lived in, the tenants, Robert Woodson, Louis Smith, Mary Ivy, Fred Burkitt, and Bobby Bishop, were scattered to the four winds. Robert and Louis disappeared, perhaps together, and only resurfaced occasionally to paint a house or do handy work for somebody around town. Mary Ivy rode her horse to a hotel downtown that went out of business in the early sixties when the interstates began to initiate their change to the American landscape forever, and disappeared then. I will never see a woman wearing riding pants that I don't think of her, and subsequently, Rosa Mary Dean, who was buried in Mt. Hope Cemetery on the outskirts of town at a service that included only Lucky, myself, George Preston, and George Dillon, the Methodist preacher good enough to donate his time to this woman nobody knew. There are still days that it feels to me that grave is somehow strangely calling me. Seeing how it is the place where many of my family members are now buried, including my own mother and father, I go by and stare at it for only a few moments, and as I stand there I always wonder if anyone has been there since the last time I was. I also wonder at the nature of life and its strangeness, Bette and Sherman Burgess laid in their plots under a big elm tree, little more than a hundred yards away.

As for Fred Burkitt and Bobby Bishop, they would move back in with their respective parents, Fred with his wealthy parents in Nashville, who now seemed to realize he was somehow better off taking morphine in their house than in some flophouse in Franklin, and Bobby Bishop, back in with his mother, who seemed to realize she had a need for him, especially after Sharon left. As for the Burgess house itself, it was sold at auction by Sammy Samuels early in the spring of 1954, bringing about enough for its bull-dozing. Another row house was built in its place but then itself sold and eventually torn down. The site of the crime now lies under the concrete and asphalt that constitute the road that runs between apartment buildings and the back of a grocery store that Van's mother and father opened when Scoot left his job with the city.

As for Sharon and me, we would leave the day after my graduation and ten days before hers, to travel to Mississippi so that we might be wed by a local justice of the peace. Sharon's mother accompanied us, because Sharon was yet to turn eighteen, as I had a month before. As Sharon had dreamed, we bought a used house trailer and put it, of all places, in the yard behind my mother and father's house, blocking the view that had drawn them to the property in the first place. Our escape had lasted a good weekend at cheap motel on Lookout Mountain in Chattanooga until we had returned and figured we barely made enough to pay for the trailer, much less a lot to put it on. Tully would marry the same year and father a child with his longtime sweetheart, Christine King.

In 1956, Van married Georgeanne James, a school teacher four years his senior who had moved to town to teach at the high school. His charm always remaining intact, he would become a salesman of farm equipment and supplies and move to several acres in the country where he lived until cancer claimed him just after his fiftieth birthday. Over the years, we always remained in touch, except for a brief few years after Sharon told me he had once again made a pass at her when we were in our late twenties, propositioning her to visit a nearby motel after they had lunch together one day. Of course, he denied it, and eventually, I once again forgave him. In the end, I concluded as I had before, that it was just Van. No more, no less.

IN 1958, I RECEIVED MY draft order to move to Fort Sill, Oklahoma and became a soldier for two years. Thankfully, the conflict in Korea had ended and the war in Viet Nam had not yet come to a full boil. As for the trailer, we pulled it the distance between Franklin and Fort Sill with the 1939 junk heap we'd bought after Sharon's car had pretty much played out. We had no more than made it through the Arkansas hills and across the flat dusty land of Oklahoma, than my mother called to inform me that Tully had been killed in a car wreck. His wife and daughter, riding with him at the time, were unscathed but he was propelled through a window after being struck hard in the side by a truck after running a red light. According to my mother, who'd gotten her information from Van's mother, he was going to visit his mother, who'd called him from a truckstop on her way through the outskirts of Nashville.

Three years after Lucky was told to quit smoking by Dr. Guppy, he was hospitalized for the first time after passing out in the driveway on a hot day, near the same spot that Jean had fallen after I'd hit her in the head with the shovel in the winter of 1945. The hospitalizations, at first, would come infrequently, with months of what seemed like normalcy between them. By 1960, though, it seemed as though he was spending as much time in Vanderbilt Hospital as he was out. Each time, the doctor—Guppy at first, and then his lung doctor, Dr. Clemons—would lecture him just before he was again birthed into the world a free man. And each time he would nod his head, then be smoking like a freight train again in a few days, if not the day he was released.

It was in 1959 that Sharon and I came home from Oklahoma to surprise Lucky for his birthday. Mama, age beginning to take at least some of her spryness by now, rose more slowly from the chair when we knocked at the door.

"Dillard's gone to the river," she told me. As she hugged and kissed me then Sharon, she explained he had wanted to go fishing for his birthday.

At the river, on that sunny fall afternoon, Sharon and I found the Ford and pulled in as quiet as we could behind it, then crossed through the brush and the bushes on our way down the hill to the bank. Stepping on a twig, Sharon alerted him to our presence and called him by name. "Daddy Lucky," she called him. Without further provocation he threw two packs of Lucky Strikes and a book of matches into the water, neither looking back to see who it was or offering any explanation of what he had done. When we reached him, he acted as if what he had done had been invisible. In the end, it seems, he had made the same decision concerning himself and his situation as he had his brother's. Wrong or right, the freedom to make your own decisions seems to hold as much importance as anything else in this life. Without the power to choose, the object of the choice is worth very little.

In the last years of his life, Jean having moved to the next county with her husband and two babies, he grew close not only to Sharon, who could say things to him and speak to him in ways that none of the rest of us could, but he somehow came to think highly of Bobby Bishop, her brother. Many times they traded stories about his running whiskey up from Alabama and Lucky's knowing it and subsequently monitoring who could bring whiskey in and who couldn't. Occasionally—or to be honest—almost as often as not, they'd have these conversations over a bottle of the near pure grain that Bobby still had access to and Lucky asked no questions about, because he would have had to tell the new police chief, Johnny Forrest.

In the end, or at least in the last half dozen or so hospital visits of his life, when his breath would become as escapist as the smoke that once rose from his mouth in the living room and stained the ceiling, Bobby, initially against my better judgment, would bring him cigarettes and sneak them to him when the nurse was out of the room. In the last few weeks, his introduction to a respirator and his smoking a phantom cigarette while he smiled, convinced me that Bobby's method was, I believe, the right thing to do.

What was done, was done. The days now were a gift, or a curse, I wasn't certain. Nevertheless, I knew they were the last ones he was to have. And should be lived fully, whatever that word might mean. I'm convinced it means something different with each breath. More convinced of that each day I live.

In the middle of June in 1960, he was laid out in Celestial Gardens of the Franklin Chapel, the same room where Rosa Mary Dean had been ... and Percy after they had recovered his body from the river. George Preston and Michael, who had returned by then, made Lucky look as though he had not suffered a many-year battle with the devil we all fight in some manner for his air and his life, and both stood proudly and stately at the door and greeted most of the town as they filed in to pay their respects. My mother, the constant companion and brave soul she was, stood just past them, and welcomed each one who came to pay respect to her late husband, smiling and continually expressing her appreciation of their appreciation of him. Forgetting, as they did, what was left to forget. As I began to hope that, in the end, such things are indeed forgotten. Prayed, for Lucky, for myself, that it is so.

A dozen years later, on a July afternoon, my mother would call and tell me that her intent was to marry a man she'd been seeing who lived on the next street. For the years since Lucky had left this world, she had remained single, living on his life insurance and pension, keeping herself busy working at Henry's Grocery by the Gilco five half-days a week. Initially, I gave her steady grievous hell about her decision to marry another man besides my father. But eventually accepted it, then reassessed my attitude and thinking after my own life made its way to hell in a hand basket. I came to believe that we should embrace joy when it in fact presents itself. As Sharon was, I believed, forty at seventeen, she would in turn become seventeen at forty. Two years later, I found myself alone, raising the only child we'd had, a son named Dillard Percy Hall. I never once called him lucky.

Unmarked grave of Rosa Mary Dean

CPSIA information can be obtained
at www.ICGtesting.com
Printed in the USA
LVHW092208100221
678939LV00039B/187

9 781515 005155